PRAISE FOR A

CW01391023

Ever After

ALSO BY AMANDA PROWSE

Novels

Novellas

Children's books

Non-fiction

Ever After

Amanda Prowse

LAKE UNION
PUBLISHING

Published by Lake Union Publishing, Seattle

www.apub.com

Amazon, the Amazon logo, and Lake Union Publishing are trademarks of Amazon.com, Inc., or its affiliates.

EU Product Safety contact:
Amazon Publishing, Amazon Media EU S.à r.l.
38, avenue John F. Kennedy, L-1855 Luxembourg
amazonpublishing-gpsr@amazon.com

ISBN-13: 9781662515200
eISBN: 9781662515194

Cover design by Jo Myler
Cover images: © WinWin artlab © LEV16 © Volha Kratkouskaya © Rameez Baig / Shutterstock

Printed in the United States of America

This book is dedicated to the memory of Ann Prowse, loving wife and mother, who is now at rest. Ann loved her family, books and her garden and will be missed by all who knew and loved her, ever after . . .

Chapter One

Enya Brown's phone buzzed in the middle of the night.

Throwing back the duvet, she sat up straight, skinny legs dangling from the side of the bed, widening her eyes to help clear the foggy edges of sleep. She took a moment to centre herself with a long, deep breath through her nose and out of her mouth, just like the lady she had found on YouTube had suggested.

It helped, a little, in that her flustered pulse calmed and she was able to quietly locate her glasses, which were on top of the book on her nightstand. There was something about a text or call arriving in the dark when the world was sleeping that had the power to put the fear of God into her. Her first thought was for her son, was he okay, had something happened? Her second, a prayer that he was safe and sound. Then came the devastating prediction of utter desolation, knowing that if anything should ever happen to him, her life would lose all of its meaning.

It was daft really, the idea that bad news could only be delivered after office hours, or that the Grim Reaper preferred to work the night shift, understanding that the very worst news had far more impact when delivered to someone in their pyjamas. They might have a point.

She wondered what percentage of people died at night, not underestimating the powerful addition of booze, drugs, poorly lit roads, inclement weather: *were* we more likely to die in the dark?

She wasn't sure who she could ask.

Feeling far more alert, she reached for her phone. The house was quiet. She detested the silence of the empty hours. Similarly, small noises of irritation like the creak of a door, the whistle of the wind and the chirp of birds, as they only served to remind her that she had once lived in a home with so much noise, so much life, that she would never have noticed such an inconsequential thing! What *had* she become? *Who* had she become?

'Sometimes, Jonathan, I feel that I'm no more than a trick of the light,' she whispered. 'Almost invisible.'

This she spoke as she opened the text, incredibly relieved to see it was a message from Jenny. Any contact with her friend triggered a thunderclap of joy that pulled her out of any potential panic.

GOT ANY KITKATS?

These three words from her best friend, akin to opening a window in a stifling room to welcome a breeze, or a warm hug on a cold day, were crucial reassurance when she needed it the most. Invisible people did not receive messages like this.

The text had been sent some five minutes previously, at precisely 3 a.m. She smiled.

NO, BUT IVE GOT A TWIRL, HALF A TOBLERONE AND THOSE CHOCOLATE DIPPED SHORTCAKE BISCUITS FROM MARKS THAT YOU LIKE. OH AND HALF AN EASTER EGG

ON MY WAY – the instant reply.

Throwing her kimono over her cotton PJs, she made her way down the stairs and opened her front door, taking a moment to look along the street, very much liking the pink-edged, lilac-tinged light that hovered over the terraced chimney pots, giving the place an ethereal quality. It promised warmth tomorrow and she felt it a privilege to see this little corner of suburbia in its idling time, where only the scamper of tiny creature feet foraging, the flutter of leaves disturbed by breeze, and the thump-thump of her friend's slippers as they made their way down the path of the house next door but one, cut through the quiet.

Enya smiled and waved. Jenny smiled and waved back. Their faces, devoid of make-up, crinkled in delight, shoulders raised, fingers on lips. The two more like excited kids who were sneaking out, breaking curfew, than grown women, who could, if they so desired, venture out and about whenever the fancy took them. Even at this hour.

Enya made her way into the kitchen and filled the kettle. What was a 3 a.m. snack without tea to accompany it? She heard the front door close, and the sound of her friend, babbling, as soon as she walked in, as if it were mid-afternoon, normal.

'Who in the world has *half* an Easter egg hanging around? It's nearly July!'

'I am aware.' Enya gave a slow blink as she plopped the teabags into the mugs, comforted by her friend's presence, aware of how having someone else near her halted all feelings of despair.

'I hate people who save their Easter eggs, it's not natural! They're designed to be shoved in your mouth, eaten in one go and then you have to dispose of the foil and cardboard as soon as possible, hide the evidence.' Jenny took a seat at the kitchen table.

'This actually speaks volumes about your secret chocolate habit, the fact you feel the need to hide the evidence! It must be hard being married to a police officer, does he check the recycling for dabs? And also, hate is a strong word. I don't *hate* anyone, but if I did, it wouldn't be because I disagreed with how they did or didn't eat their chocolate!'

She pulled the pretty tin with the chocolate stash in it from the shelf inside the larder and grabbed the biscuits, placing both on the table in front of Jenny.

'That's the difference between you and me.' Her friend levered the lid from the tin with her thumbs and, with something close to urgency, ripped the wrapper from the Twirl, before stuffing a whole stick of the stuff into her mouth. She continued to speak with her gob full of chocolate. 'I hate lots of people, and for the most ridiculous reasons, not that they're ridiculous to me. I have a list.'

'You have a list?' Enya was shocked.

'Yes! And don't look at me like that, Angela gets it, she has a list too.'

She poured water into the mugs, fascinated, unaware that her sister also had a list. 'Who does Angela hate?'

'Well, I wouldn't want to break any confidences,' Jenny pulled a face and carried on, 'but I know for a fact that woman who does the weather – too smiley, too keen, with undertones of smug.'

'I can't believe I'm last to know about this! So who do you hate and why?'

'I hate Poirot,' Jenny over-enunciated.

Enya whipped around to face her friend; this was a revelation that she couldn't allow to pass without comment. 'Oh you can't! I love him!' She fished out the teabags and lobbed them into the sink. 'Why do you hate him?'

'It's the moustache, it looks like liquorice, and it makes me feel sick.' Jenny shuddered. 'I imagine it going soft and then having to eat it.' The thought clearly didn't repulse her that much, as she reached for the second stick of chocolate.

Enya laughed loudly. 'You can't hate Poirot because you fear having to eat his moustache!'

'I told you it was ridiculous, and I think you'll find that, actually, I can hate whoever I want. It's my list.'

'So, who else?' It was always a delight when after two decades of friendship, they revealed new facets of each other; she loved how her friend checked in like this regularly, chocolate craving or not.

Although unspoken, it was obvious that Jenny understood how much Enya needed this companionship. She sloshed milk into the tea and took the mugs to the table, where she sat opposite her friend.

'Erm, Blake Dunlop.'

'Blake Dunlop?' She repeated the name of a gangly boy who had been in their kids' class at primary school. A name she hadn't heard for a while.

'Yes.' Jenny, straight-faced, sipped her tea. 'If he walked in right now, I'd punch him in the face!'

'You would not!' She did her best to contain her laughter.

'I bloody would!'

'You know he runs the reclamation yard up by the quarry?'

'Does he now? Hmmm . . .' Jenny stroked her chin as if making a plan.

It made her chuckle. 'Why do you hate him?'

'He made Holly cry.'

'What, recently?' Enya felt the flicker of concern. She loved Holly Hudson.

'No!' Jenny tutted. 'Of course not recently. If it was recently, Phil would have punched him in the mouth.'

'Or Aiden would,' Enya pointed out. She had known Holly since she was in nappies on account of the fact that she had grown up next door but one. Holly had been (almost) surgically attached to her son, Aiden, by the hip, for the last decade. 'Not that I can imagine Aiden, or you, punching anyone, for that matter.'

'There's always a first time.'

'Mmm.' Enya sipped her tea. 'What did he do to make her cry?'

'Karate-kicked her art project, broke it clean in two. I'm sure I told you about it at the time.'

'Probably. But a lot's happened since then.'

Enya swallowed, thinking of that time when Aiden was little, and she'd been so busy. Busy with mum jobs, her actual job, looking after the house, running around with a timer in her head that meant she leapt from chore to chore like a bee harvesting pollen. *Busy*. . . Unlike now, when lonely hours stretched ahead of her each evening and the night often felt endless.

'Ain't that the truth.' Jenny nodded. 'Holly spent hours making it, don't you remember? They were about seven and had to build a puppet theatre in a shoebox?'

'Vaguely.' She couldn't remember what she'd had for supper last night, let alone an event decades before that hadn't concerned her.

'Well, Holly walked into the playground with hers in her hands, she'd gone for a *Wind in the Willows* vibe, river background with weeping willow, Toad, Ratty and Mole stuck on to lolly sticks, it was lovely. Then Blake bloody Dunlop comes along, high kicks it right out of her hands and runs off. The little turd.'

'That was over twenty years ago!' She pointed out the obvious.

'Your point being?' Jenny sipped her tea.

'Holding a grudge for that long only damages you. I bet Blake won't even remember it!'

'I'd still like to punch him.'

Enya laughed at her diminutive best friend, a talented florist whose hands were more used to arranging stunning floral bouquets than brawling. 'I take it you couldn't sleep?'

'Nope. The usual.'

Enya understood only too well the debilitating pattern of insomnia that meant she often went to bed dreading a disturbed night ahead.

'I slept soundly from ten until three, then my cogs started turning. I'm thinking about the shop, excited for our plans!' Jenny danced her slippered feet on the wooden floor.

'Me too.' She beamed.

'Shall we redo the sign, put your name next to mine?'

It was a lovely, generous suggestion that thrilled her. 'Oh, Jen, as wonderful as that sounds, let's give it six months before we do that, just in case I'm pants and you have to fire me!' There was a subtle truth to her words, a lack of confidence that meant she tended to err towards the negative.

'You won't be pants, you'll be ace, and I can't fire you if you're my partner, can I?'

'I'm not sure, actually.' Enya sipped her tea. She was indeed excited for the venture that would see her become part of Jenny's business. An excitement tinged with the inevitable nerves; she didn't do too well with change, who did? But losing her job of over two decades was a big deal.

She loved her job at the solicitors', working for the genteel Messrs Greengate and Greengate. Mr Richard Greengate and Mr Robert Greengate whom callers, on occasion, referred to as 'Mr *R* Greengate', with great emphasis, as if this might be defining enough. To say it made for much confusion was an understatement.

The building on the pretty, curved High Street, where she spent four days a week between the hours of nine and five, was from a bygone era, and one where sunlight highlighted the rich soup of historical dust. Six decades of particles swirling right there in the room that made her wonder if she ever breathed in the tears her mother had shed when listening to the will of her father being read, or inhaled the fear and shame of her great-uncle Maurice as he dealt with the paperwork pertaining to his bankruptcy. Or maybe she had sniffed Jonathan's laughter, as she'd cradled their newborn and he'd jovially taken care of business.

'So, Mr Greengate, this is our son, Aiden Jonathan, who needs to be added as sole beneficiary and also we think it worth making a note about his guardianship, should the worst ever happen.' Jonathan had shot her a look then, with a wink. It was what he had done, protected her, soothed her worries, smoothed her path, letting her

know it was just a precaution. Nothing to worry about. '*He would be placed into the care of Mrs Angela Rudd . . .*'

It felt like weeks ago, minutes, this another reminder that the whirlpool of life seemed to spin quickly, and it was all she could do on some days to keep her head above water.

It was a jolt to think this would be her last few months in their employ, as they had decided to retire, shut up shop and spend time with their respective Mrs Greengates. The ending of her job of over twenty-five years, another change of routine that would require adjustment, another severing of rope that kept her pleasantly anchored to all that was familiar.

Her old life.

A life she missed. Not that she wasn't looking forward to joining Jenny at the florist's and being surrounded by that glorious scent each and every day, learning all about the business and honing her creative skills. Her best friend had thrown her a lifeline, and she had grabbed it with both hands. It occupied a lot of her thoughts as she chased ideas, imagining how glorious it would be at Easter, Christmas, Valentine's and all the days in between.

Jenny swallowed her biscuit and continued. 'Then I started worrying about how Holly will cope over the next three weeks, you know how she frets when Aiden is away for work.'

'It ain't easy!' Enya sighed, glancing up at the ceiling towards her bedroom, trying to remember what it had been like when she and Jonathan were of a similar age.

They'd been desperately in love, that much she knew, but the feeling like she might crumble if he were not within reach? She couldn't quite remember, preferring to think of herself as capable and grounded.

'Well?' Jenny raised her voice.

'Well, what?' Enya stared at her.

'You were miles away! I just asked you if you think I can fit this half an Easter egg in my mouth and eat it in one.'

Laughing now at her friend, Enya shook her head. 'Without a doubt. For someone so tiny, you have a very big mouth.'

'None taken.' Jenny took a deep breath, like an athlete preparing to perform, before cramming in the half an Easter egg.

She stifled a yawn as she watched Jenny's antics.

'Ta da!' Jenny opened her mouth to show that the egg had indeed disappeared.

'Magic!' Enya smiled, wishing she believed in such a thing, knowing that if it were possible, she'd wish to turn the clock back to a time when her life had felt full, and she had thought loneliness and anxiety were what happened to other people . . .

Chapter Two

Enya felt a little out of sorts, a residue no doubt of the disturbed night just spent. Not that she hadn't enjoyed Jenny's company and the unexpected laughter that had filled the kitchen. It was her best friend's superpower, the ability to make everything feel just a little bit better.

'Where *are* you?'

She now leaned against the kitchen sink and spoke firmly down the phone while rubbing her temples, feeling the beginnings of a headache. It was too hot and too early on this sweaty June day to feel this harried. Only thirty minutes out of the shower and already she wished she could pop back upstairs for another one. She pushed out her bottom lip and blew upwards, an act that was habit, and yet curiously did very little to cool her down, bar maybe lower the temperature of her rather downy top lip, another gift bestowed upon her by the menopause gods.

'Yeah, I'm just . . .'

She could hear her son on the other end of the phone, fannying around.

'Aiden, it's so unfair! I'm feeling all the anxiety of wanting to get to the airport on time. I'm worried about a queue at check-in, the hassle of having to cram my decanted liquids into one of those slightly too narrow plastic bags, which I can never quite close properly. I'm watching the minutes tick; my pulse is through the roof and it's not even me who's flying! I'm happy to drop you off, love, of course I am, but you said you'd be here by ten past and it's nearly half past and I already thought you were cutting it fine, supposing we hit traffic!'

Aware she sounded a little manic, it was, she thought, preferable than admitting to her only child that Holly wasn't the only one who was anxious about him being out of reach for three whole weeks. When had she become this needy?

'Mum, just take a minute, chill, please! Jim has only just left and I'm getting my stuff together.'

Suddenly, it all made sense! Jim, her son's rugby friend, was always big on drinking and seemed not to pay any heed to timekeeping. She liked Jim, liked him very much, but he was that friend whom, at the risk of sounding like one of *those* mothers, she'd describe as a bad influence.

Memories of her boy as a teenager calling from a field in the middle of Wiltshire filled her mind. There had apparently been a mix-up and two cars had driven off leaving Aiden in the wilderness, each car believing he was a passenger in the other. The whole jaunt planned and poorly executed by Jim. Jonathan had sleepily grabbed the car keys, ready to retrieve their boy from wherever he'd been abandoned. She had watched him shuffle out of the door with a sweatshirt over his PJs and his hair sticking up at all angles. A good dad. The kind of parent who, like her, didn't think twice, but was simply always on the end of a phone, for whatever their son might need, whenever he might need it.

'Getting your stuff together, you mean you haven't packed yet?' She felt the flare of anxiety at the thought. 'And you want me to *chill?*'

This word enough to see her teeth clamp down hard and her jaw flex. What was it about being told to calm down or chill that was almost incendiary!

'What would happen if you missed your flight?' This was how she parented, getting him to think things through, figure out the consequences that she hoped might inform his future decision-making. It mattered little that he was now twenty-seven. Old habits and all that.

'Erm, I'd probably get the next one?'

His sarcasm wasn't lost on her. She glanced across the room at Jonathan, who sat at the dining table with a smile that suggested that, like their son, he found the whole thing highly amusing. It didn't help. She gave him a slow blink of dismissal.

'Get the next one? It's not like buses! You're going on an aeroplane!'

His laughter was loud and instant, and she could hear Holly joining in. She felt outnumbered, ganged up on, and a little dismissed, *silly old Mum, getting her knickers in a twist*, and this too did not feel good.

'Actually, Mum, it's exactly like buses! In fact, I had to go up to Manchester three weeks ago and my train ticket from Bristol cost three times more than my flight to Rome today. In fact, my plane ticket cost the same as when you, me and Holly went to the cinema! So, I can just get another one.'

Really? This was certainly food for thought, even if he had missed the point.

It was another salient reminder of how the world had moved on. A fact trotted out that made her feel older than her mid-fifties, a scythe to her belief that she was smart. Was she getting dumber? Did that happen? It was as if by staying in more, avoiding all sources of news and current affairs, sometimes finding the world a little too hostile and unkind, she was getting softer, losing her sharp edge of reason. It worried her. That, and the fact that because she was unaware of trends and technological advances, she lost skills or, rather, was getting left behind. When your life was a little set and unchallenging, it made it hard to keep up. Was that the answer, to challenge herself more? Possibly. She wasn't sure. But as a proficient taker of shorthand, someone who used to be able to remember everyone's telephone number, map reader extraordinaire, the best dahlia grower this side of

Cheltenham, a dab hand at photocopying and a whizz on the Rubik's cube, this downward slide was also a scythe to her confidence.

She hoped that going into business with Jenny would be the mental shot in the arm she needed. And even if it wasn't, just being in her friend's company made her happy, like she was part of a team, protected, loved. Especially now she knew that should the need ever arise, Jenny was not averse to slugging her way out of trouble. The thought made her smile.

'I just don't want . . .' she began.

What didn't she want? To have her day disrupted, not that she was busy, and in fact had nothing else in her calendar, but she liked to know what she was doing and when. Any last-minute change of plan had the potential to throw her completely. What *did* she want? To spend as much time with her son as possible, even the thirty-minute drive to the airport was something she looked forward to. It wasn't that she missed him, not exactly, but she missed seeing him alone, and not that she didn't like Holly, she did, in fact she *loved* Holly. Her headache pulsed, maybe she was overthinking it. Maybe Aiden was right, she needed to take a minute.

'I'll see you when you get here.' She ended the call. 'What's wrong with me, Jonathan? Have I always been like this?'

Her phone buzzed. A text from Jenny.

LET ME GUESS, THEY'RE LATE AND YOU'RE PACING!

She laughed out loud and replied immediately.

AM I THAT PREDICTABLE?

Jenny fired back with:

NO BUT THEY ARE!! WHERE DID WE GO WRONG??

13

It was true, but my goodness how the two women adored this young pair, loving nothing more than to chat about the time when they would both be grannies to the same baby! Something on the horizon that filled them both with excitement at the mere prospect. She pictured her days full of trips to the park, reading stories and the feel of a little hand in hers once again, the thought alone enough to move her to tears. She couldn't wait, knowing the arrival of a little one would be the most glorious gift, a focus for her life that in recent times had felt lacking.

Pickle meowed at the back door. Enya let her out to go wandering, no doubt to catch up with other cats, chew the fat, swap stories, sit in the sunshine, a bit of mutual grooming. It was a sobering thought that the cat had a better social life than she did.

Taking her son's advice, she tried to *chill*, did her very best not to let the tick of the clock on the kitchen wall grow louder in her thoughts. She filled the time by watering the plants in the hallway, even the one that was hard to reach, meaning she had to teeter dangerously on the spindly chair that lived in the corner and on to which they piled anything that needed lugging up the stairs. A holding bay for items heading to the bedrooms, clean laundry, letters, replacement tissues, parcels. There was always something in need of ferrying up. She stood on tiptoes and eased the jug of water into the planter of the devil's ivy that she didn't particularly like. More than that, actually, she hated it, but the fact that it thrived made it hard to get rid of, as if it were daily trying to earn a place in her affections by growing well and never moaning when she neglected it.

As she stepped down from the chair she spied Holly's car pulling up, dropping Aiden off.

Finally!

Her son jumped out and retrieved his carry-on bag from the boot. Enya ditched the watering can and grabbed her handbag, car keys and water bottle. She waved, awkwardly, watching the young love birds out of the window, wondering when it might be opportune to interrupt them. Entwined was the best way to describe them, thoroughly entwined. She pulled a face. She wasn't a prude, not at all, but found watching people smash noses together and stick their tongues into each other's mouths quite revolting. Especially when one of those tongues and mouths belonged to her only child. This too, she was aware, was probably a view that was out of step with more progressive parents, quite unable to imagine carrying on in this way in front of her own mother! It occurred to her then that maybe she was *actually* invisible . . .

She stared at the back of her hands where the skin was a little crepey, the small bulge of prominent veins, a scar around the tip of her finger from a winter's night eight years ago when she'd slipped while peeling potatoes with a short, sharp knife. Hands that no one held anymore.

With one eye on the clock, she made her way outside and banged the front door shut, loudly. Giving the snogging duo the opportunity to part, should they so desire. They did not desire and so she mumbled a vague commentary on how lovely it was to see them, which was ignored, and jumped into her little Audi, taking her time, setting the sat nav to the airport.

Aiden opened the rear door and shoved his bag inside.

'Don't leave me! Don't go!' Holly spoke in a mock whine with distinct undertones of moron.

'Come with me!' Aiden laughed. 'Hop in my pocket!'

Enya resisted the temptation to mock-gag, knowing it was both unkind and ungracious. Why did she feel this way? What more could a mother ask for than a partner who looked at her child and saw only starlight?

And that partner was Holly, who right now had her head in the small of Aiden's back and her arms clamped tightly around his waist, pulling hard as if this might prevent him leaving.

Enya beeped the horn; it was all she could think of and took no pleasure in from the way they both jumped.

'You're going to be late!' she hollered, wanting to get going, wanting to get back, wanting something other than to sit here witnessing their shenanigans.

'Sure you don't want me to drive?' her son asked, yawning.

'No, I'm good.'

Enya and Aiden shared the car. It made sense.

Finally, they were underway. Holly had waved until she was no more than a dot in the rear-view mirror, and Aiden had nearly cricked his neck making sure he didn't miss a glimpse.

'Do you mind if I nap, Mum?' Without waiting for an answer, he settled back in the seat and folded his arms across his chest as he closed his eyes.

'Course not. You nap.'

She swallowed her disappointment, having planned the conversation she wanted to have, wanting his advice on so many things, her new business venture with Jenny, the damp patch on the kitchen wall, did he know where she kept the will in case of emergencies? Things like that. Nothing, she realised, that wouldn't keep.

The sound of her son's gentle snoring wasn't nearly as rewarding as the chatter she had envisaged. Their animated discussions in her head were always far more engaging than the reality. In them they reminisced, and he laughed, as they turned the clock back and she felt the warm glow of a memory that could sustain her in the early hours, when she might sit on the edge of her bed and breathe slowly in through her nose and out through her mouth. Woken and alarmed by no more than a text, a noise, a dream, a paper cut of worry . . .

He woke as she pulled into the car park.

'Shit! I'm cutting it fine!' He pulled a face, and she mentally pulled her hair out. 'See you in three weeks, thanks for dropping me off.' He leaned over and kissed her roughly on the cheek. 'Love you!' She could feel the imprint of it on her face and would treasure the contact long after he had gone.

'Love you, too. So very much,' she whispered into the ether as, with his bag slung over his shoulder, her boy ran along the covered walkway and into the terminal without looking back. With the confidence of youth, his stride that of someone who was sure of where he was heading and how he was going to get there. In that second, she envied him. Her life, her place in this world, felt watered down, diluted to the point where she sometimes gasped when she caught her reflection in the mirror.

A trick of the light . . .

She didn't leave immediately, but sat in the car, staring ahead. For someone who felt as if her life was stagnating, it was nice to see people travelling.

It was interesting, watching the bronzed and bedraggled returnees pulling cases on wheels, wearing jumpers loosely draped about their shoulders, shivering to confirm they had come from somewhere much, much hotter, as they clutched souvenirs and duty-free booze in sturdy plastic bags. If these travellers had arrived at the airport hand in hand on an excited high, this felt like the other end of the budget flight conveyor belt.

It was more than a little depressing. She had seen many couples over the years bickering on this very spot, no doubt travel-weary and miffed at the prospect of tackling the sunscreen- and sweat-soaked laundry that hummed in their cases. Plus, the thought of going back to work tomorrow without the joy of a holiday looming was probably enough to knock the gilded edge off their tan.

She was lucky on two counts: her mother's Irish heritage meant never having a tan to preoccupy her, and she and Jonathan had never stopped laughing, chatting, always looking forward, planning. It wasn't always roses and wine, of course not, there were days when she could happily have throttled him, and there were a thousand small things he did that drove her to distraction, but in the main, they were good.

More than good.

And then, as she did sometimes, her mind wound back to trips she'd taken years ago. The three of them, arriving at the airport, Aiden jumping up and down, so excited to be going on a plane, his little backpack bulging with comics, Top Trumps, sweets and puzzles to keep him occupied, and keen to hold her hand, always so keen to hold her hand.

'I do, I miss it. I miss it all. I miss being that important in his life.'

She felt the ache of longing for those times, wondering, as she often did, how time had passed so very quickly. Jonathan loved to travel, to sit in the sun, excited to swim, try new food, drink cold beer, and let the giddiness of a holiday change his whole personality, as he shook off the responsibility of the day to day and danced in the street, twirling her around and around.

'Shit!' Enya simultaneously swore and jolted in her seat, as her car suddenly rocked.

Almost instinctively, her hands grabbed the steering wheel. She looked up to see the front of the silver Mercedes crashing into the passenger door of her Audi. It made the loudest bang, so much so that several of the weary travellers stared and winced. Her face coloured under their scrutiny.

She wasn't a habitual swearer, but the shock fired the word from her mouth. 'For the love of God!'

Lost in daydreaming, the loud noise probably had more impact on her than if she'd been more focused on the world around her.

From her vantage point, she could now see the long legs of a man standing between the cars. This was the last thing she needed. Was her car invisible too or just her inside it, she wondered? Unbuckling her seat belt, she prepared for a confrontation with the navy-jean-wearing, car-crashing klutz.

Chapter Three

Enya stepped from the car with a small ball of fear and shock bouncing around her stomach. He had hit her little Audi!

'Ouch!'

He laughed, *actually* laughed, this not the reaction of one who was contrite, which would ordinarily have been a match to the tinder of anger growing in her gut. There was nothing, as far as she could tell, that was remotely amusing about smacking into her car with his weighty Merc. The conflict, however, arose because he was incredibly handsome. It was shallow, yes, but conflicting, nonetheless. And it threw her.

She ran the pad of her thumb over her wedding band. Her life was set, she rarely looked at a man, let alone studied one. But *this* man! Her stomach gripped and she tried to remember the last time she'd looked in a mirror, wondering whether she'd brushed her shoulder-length, dark curly hair, suspecting it was more bird's nest than glossy. His hair, in contrast, was grey, longish, and pushed back over his forehead with a defiant wisp of fringe that hung down over his eyes, which were bright with crinkles of kindness at the sides. He looked sun-kissed, his forearms brown, visible from beneath his navy T-shirt, the long sleeves of which had been pushed up over his elbows. His watch was bulky, fingers long, his manner most charming, yet not schmoozy or slick. He was simply open, smiling and a little taller than her.

Always a bonus.

His mouth was curved in the attractive crescent of someone who was happy despite their predicament. It spoke volumes about his nature. She felt a pull of desire deep in the base of her gut that was as unfamiliar as it was unwelcome. Tensing her jaw, she tried to lift the slight bulge of a double chin that had appeared despite her lean shape, a tiny resistant pouch that irked her far more than it should. It was an action designed to make herself more attractive, more attractive to *him*, and the fact that she felt the need to do so at all was unnerving.

Paying little heed to her chin area, he bent down and examined the door, which now sported an ugly V-shaped dent. 'I am so sorry! It was a second's lack of concentration, thought I could get around and bam! Entirely my fault. Are you hurt? Shocked, I bet.'

'No, no. I'm fine.' She was.

'Phew, no need to call the feds!' He was well spoken, not boorish or bullish, and sucked air through his teeth as he laughed.

'It's . . .' What did she want to say? *It's fine, handsome man . . . you can bash my car any day if it means we get to chat . . . you have lovely hair . . . I expect you smell of lemons . . .* Standing up straight, she wrapped her arms around her torso, tilting her head to one side now, a pose she considered quite coquettish, and one she had not used in an age. Who even was she right now?

'You should take my details and then if you want to go through the insurance . . .' He held her eyeline, still smiling.

'Yes, of course.' She glanced at his hands, no rings.

'I have a friend who owns a car dealership in Bath, it might be cheaper or easier to let him sort it out and I can pay the bill, protect your no-claims, whatever works!' He raised his hands as if signalling that he came in peace.

'Yep, whatever!' She laughed in a girlish way that made her cringe. 'My husband used to work in insurance.'

Why she felt the need to mention this, she was unsure; possibly to assuage the guilt and taste of disloyalty that was underpinning the whole encounter.

He pulled out his phone and tapped out a text with his index finger.

'My email, telephone number, obviously, and date and time of accident. That should cover it, shouldn't it? Ooh, I'll take a picture!' He pushed the phone to arm's length and clicked away. 'Do we need to do anything else?'

I don't know, do we?

She liked the way he didn't assume control or direct her in the way some men might.

'I think that's everything.' She nodded.

'Great. What number do I send it to?'

'Oh, it's zero, double seven, double three . . .' She reeled off the number, knowing Aiden always teased her for saying it in a way that apparently sounded most unnatural, but it was the only way she could remember it.

Her phone pinged.

'And thank you for being so understanding. I just wasn't concentrating.' He repeated the admission, then it was his turn to laugh in a way that she wondered if in hindsight might make *him* cringe. 'It's been quite the day and I was singing, loudly!'

Bizarrely, she felt the need to stow away the facts she'd garnered about him so far, more than a little fazed by her interest in the stranger. He'd had quite the day, she wondered why? He owned a nice car, was easy-going, handsome and did not, apparently, have the brain capacity to both sing and concentrate.

'What were you singing?' She was curious.

'The Mumbley Boys' song . . . erm . . .' he snapped his fingers, 'no, what are they called? Erm . . .' He tutted, looked skyward, and she felt unexpected flames of joy lick her consciousness. He was lovely. Lovely to look at, lovely company, and to interact with him at all was just – lovely.

It was surreal and surprising to realise that what she felt in that instant was desire, as a flame of want burned inside her that she had believed, prior to this strange encounter, to have been almost entirely extinguished. She felt her face blush at the silent recognition, wrestling with the mortification at the fact she felt this way at all. Her wedding band seemed to shine like a beacon.

'It's my car,' he explained, 'but my daughter's playlist. It's on my stereo and I don't know how to change it. I'm far better with my hands than technology. When the clocks go forward, I don't know how to adjust the one on the dashboard either, so for six months of the year I'm an hour out! Drives everyone crackers. Everyone apart from me,' he clarified. Another insight, he had a daughter. 'Her choice of music bothered me at first, every time I drove anywhere I was forced to listen, but I rather like it now. It makes me think of her, helps me understand her, actually. And I think it makes me trendy, and go-getting, in the way that she and her contemporaries are.'

'I think you'll find trendy is a word only used by those of us who are not.'

'That's actually probably very accurate. Were you ever trendy?'

'Oh, none taken, and no. No, I don't think I was. Or go-getting, come to think of it. Maybe once, for one night when I was seventeen.'

It was odd that she should think of that night now; she guessed it was because the feeling of desire, the thrill and the optimism were not dissimilar.

He laughed again; this time it was more natural. He leaned against his car and folded his arms across his chest, settling in, as if they were not in the short-stay car park at the airport and on a timer.

'That is as oddly specific as it is intriguing.'

'Mmm.' She wasn't about to impart the details of that fateful night to a stranger, no matter how attractive.

His phone rang.

'Ooh, better get that.' He took the call, and she shamelessly eavesdropped. 'No, no, love, I'm in the short-stay at the back! Thought I'd park up in case of any hiccups. Your purse?' He bent low and peered into his car. 'Yep, I can see it on the front seat. What are you like? No, no, stay where you are and I'll drive around and meet you at the front, there's a drop-off lay-by. Yes, absolutely sure. I'm on my way, hold tight!'

He pulled a face as he ended the call and she smiled, feeling instantly and profoundly embarrassed – had she been overly familiar, too flirty? She felt shame at the mere possibility running through her veins, wondering whose purse he was about to deliver, a wife's? A girlfriend's?

'Let me know what you decide about the insurance and whatnot,' he called as he walked back to his car.

'I will.' She kept her head down.

'And once again I'm so sorry! And even though I'm smiling, my apology is sincere, please don't doubt it!'

'I don't.'

'Better dash!' He gave a loud sigh. 'There's always a disaster looming, seems this one has been narrowly averted. It's been smashing talking to you.'

She looked up, noting how he seemed reluctant to look away, which was both exhilarating and confusing.

23

'You too.' She fumbled with the handle, also a little reticent to get in immediately, despite her reservation. Their first and last meeting she was quite certain, and something she would no doubt mull over at her leisure – if nothing else, to ponder the absurdity of it, yet there was no doubting the pull of attraction.

She was aware of him disappearing inside his Mercedes and as he wound the window down, the unmistakeable sound of Mumford & Sons' 'I Will Wait' floated across the car park. It was a rousing, passionate tune that filled her up and made tears rise in her throat and nose. A beautiful, powerful song that moved her in the way music did when you were raw or alert or hurting, and the right words and melody managed to convey what your heart and mind struggled to express.

With her phone in her hand, she saw the text he'd sent, all rather perfunctory and no name. Moving her fingers quickly, she saved it into her phone under the name HCK – Handsome Car Klutz. It felt fitting.

Back in her car, she took deep breaths and tried to calm her flustered pulse, doing her best to get a grip and to present as casually as possible to any onlookers. The last thing she wanted was to give any clue that she had got into a tizz over a brief encounter with a stranger in a car park. It sounded stupid when she recounted it in this way.

She held her tears at bay until she reached the dual carriageway. A quick glance at the back seat and she could see Jonathan looking less than approving.

'Don't look at me like that.' She sniffed. 'What am I supposed to do, Jonathan?'

His response came loud and clear into her head. 'Maybe stop crying and keep your eyes on the bloody road?'

She snorted her giggle and wiped her eyes and nose on the sleeve of her cotton blouse.

It was some comfort that three years after his death, he still had the power to make her laugh.

Chapter Four

Enya pottered in the kitchen, wiping the surfaces and topping up Pickle's water, the fact that Aiden hadn't texted to say he'd arrived safely occupying her thoughts. She wasn't sure if he'd said he would, not that it mattered; either way, her mind raced at all the unpalatable possibilities that might have befallen him. This alone enough for her to feel the initial flicker of concern and for her anxiety to spike.

She popped out into the back garden and took deep breaths, eyes closed, face tilted towards the sun, and it worked, as her breathing returned to its normal rhythm and her pulse slowed. The most amusing of her worries, with hindsight, was that Aiden had got on the wrong flight, *unlikely*, had found himself in a strange country where he'd promptly lost his passport, wallet and phone, *highly* unlikely. And was right now being held against his will in some godforsaken hell-hole of a prison and was only allowed one phone call, but all of his contacts were in his phone, which of course he had lost. This *extremely* unlikely as he knew their landline off by heart, it hadn't changed for the last couple of decades. But what if he'd had a bang on the head?

And so it went, the minutes ticking by and her catastrophising over the most bonkers of scenarios. Her mind was put at ease when a message finally arrived from Holly a little before bedtime. Five words that saw her muscles soften and her breathing restored to a natural rhythm.

SPOKE TO AIDEN, ARRIVED SAFELY! X

She was thankful in that moment for Holly Hudson and her considerate nature, and not exactly miffed that he hadn't thought to text his mother, but certainly aware of it. It was a simple fact of parenting she had had to accept over time, that just because her son occupied most of her waking thoughts and her every decision was based on his well-being, the same could not be said in reverse. This of course was absolutely correct, not that it made it any easier to swallow at moments like this. If Jonathan were here, he'd placate her.

'You know bad news travels fastest. No need to worry. He's fine, probably sleeping . . .'

She knew she had the capacity to get into a bit of a tizz over the little things. It had always amazed her late husband how the world could, in his words, 'be going to hell in a handcart', yet she'd still be overly concerned with the worry that, post-apocalypse, who would water her plants, unplug the lamps and gather the junk mail from the back of the door, knowing it to be a terrible trip hazard in an emergency.

My goodness, she missed him! Not always, not every second, and not in the way she had at first. Gone was the excruciating needle of loss that had sat in her heart, and how thankful she was for that. It had been exhausting and distracting to be so consumed by sorrow. What she now experienced was different, altered, one of the phases of grief no doubt, yet no easier to live with despite her understanding. It was a sensation she could only describe as pure anger, which left her feeling spent. She was furious, in fact, that he had got sick and left her here to battle on without him. Something he swore he would never do.

'It's you and me, Enya B, us against the world!'

And she had believed him.

One of the things she hated most about being a widow was the word *widow*. To use it had a strange effect on whomever she was talking to, as they either brushed it off with embarrassment, as if it were of no consequence, too awkward a topic to linger on, or they wrung their hands and crinkled their brow as they sought words of condolence that were usually pithy and clichéd. Prior to the demise of her husband, her own mental image of a widow was someone elderly, clad in black and fumbling with prayer beads as they sat on a stool outside their south-eastern European home in the sunshine, crisping the skin on the back of their liver-spotted hands.

Enya didn't own anything black, was inept at all things remotely bead related, wasn't that big on prayer, and her pale skin meant she was like a gecko in the sun, seeking out all possible shade. *Widow!* It was farcical! She shopped in Oliver Bonas, ate melting brie with spelt crackers, and did Pilates; she was most definitely not widow material.

It all felt monstrously unfair, and she was sure would have been slightly more palatable if she had been an ailing octogenarian, the natural order of things, even. But she had been fifty-two when Jonathan died. An odd, in-between age, really. She was decades away from going to bed at 8 p.m., celebrating a small tin of soup as if it were a decent dinner and being on first-name terms with the doctor's receptionist. Although she did favour a trip to a garden centre over the pub and had started to cut snippets out of magazines that she thought might be useful.

Maybe it was a slippery slope.

She wasn't sure how to 'be' much of the time. Being a wife had kept her mentally and physically busy. Plus, it wasn't a one-sided thing, her husband had been there for her too. Cooking, cleaning and caring for her other half was not a chore but rather a pleasant preoccupation. Similarly, considering what to cook, where to clean and when to care for him had kept her cogs turning.

In the last year or so of Jonathan's life, she had been fully immersed in nursing him, keeping up with the interminable regimen of pill swallowing, pillow plumping, the application of unctions, the ferrying to the loo, the ferrying back to the bed. A round trip that was a marathon, but with far less cheering, not much of a fanfare when they returned to the mattress on to which they both collapsed, and certainly no medal. Fetching drinks, ice cubes and morsels of food with which she tried and failed to tempt him to eat, the washing of his ailing body, and laundry . . . laundry after laundry after laundry. It wasn't so much the chore itself that felled her, but what it represented. A never-ending pile that at the end of a long day, or in the wee small hours, had the power to make her weep.

Now she was free, had been for some time, and yet it wasn't a freedom she had yearned for, quite the opposite. She had found comfort in her coupledom, just as she had in being a busy mum. She liked the routine and took enjoyment from the thousand small things Jonathan did to make her life better. Like picking her up if she was out walking in the rain. He would, if an unexpected downpour struck, drive her known routes until he found her, and always placed a bin liner and a towel on the passenger seat to save the upholstery from her wet bum. He willingly ran her reading glasses up the stairs if she settled down to read pre-sleep and had left them in the kitchen, understanding she might not want to leave the cosy spot. He used to hand her a cup of tea on a cold, dark morning and never baulked at having to de-spider the bath when the need arose. He was handy to have around, company. He was her background noise and without him her life seemed quiet. Their shared love and history made for a most companionable life; one she would have been happy to live until *her* final days.

Single was a term that she felt dismissed her twenty-four years of marriage, as if it had just been a phase. She didn't feel single; in fact, she still felt very much connected to her husband, ex-husband, dead husband. Even this terminology foxed her. Too young to hang up her hope and enthusiasm for the future and too old to know how to pluck a different life from the peg and wear that. It felt a lot like treading water, paddling around waiting for . . . she wasn't sure what, exactly.

Maybe this was at the root of her restlessness, the thought that she might simply idle forever, waiting and watching the clock, hoping to slip into a new identity and for it to fit her perfectly. Afraid of being forgotten, or worse, redundant.

Thank goodness for Aiden, who in the wake of his father's death had looked her in the eye and said, 'I'm so glad I've got you, Mum, no matter what happens I've always got you, haven't I?'

She had felt the swell of connection in her chest; to be so needed was the tonic she thrived on. 'Yes, of course, my love, always . . .'

It had grated every nerve in her body when family, friends and even well-intentioned strangers told her with confidence, *'Life goes on . . .'* or *'It will get easier . . .'* It wasn't her way to let irritation surface or let the big things knock her off course. Case in point being the time they were on a long-saved-for Caribbean holiday and a hurricane hit – Jonathan had told her to grab what was vital and to meet him in the lobby, while he, passports and credit cards in hand, went off to find out the plan. Enya had done as instructed and arrived in her bathrobe, clutching her pale-blue silk wedged espadrilles. They were her most coveted item and were indeed vital to her wardrobe. He had stared at her, mouth agape, when he realised she'd abandoned their laptop, phones and chargers – all still sitting on the bed, but as long as her shoes were safe . . . She told him that in the event of future hurricanes or any other epic disasters in which they found themselves while travelling, he needed to be much more specific.

Yes, her forte was internally panicking over the little things. Often in the early hours. The trouble was, she didn't always recognise they were the little things, allowing even tiny paper cuts of worry to grow in magnitude, before miraculously resolving to put it all out of her head and let peace reign, twelve minutes before her alarm went off.

How she loved those twelve minutes.

An outwardly calm, peaceful, largely unflustered woman, she therefore found it difficult to admit that as those platitudes about 'life' and 'time' were offered without any semblance of understanding as to just how her whole world had been dismantled, she had felt the urge to wallop the mealy mouth that said such things.

This fleeting desire for violence was rare. Thankfully.

She smiled now at the thought of Jenny explaining how she had wanted to punch Blake Dunlop in the mouth. Maybe they were more alike than she thought.

There had been no other disasters, man-made or otherwise. No more trips.

Her travelling companion had died and along with him her desire to step outside of the country. This too she held quietly inside, a new fear that she could quell by staying at home, close to all that was familiar. It was another way she was a little diminished, a little pared back.

The passing years had allowed for some clarity of thought about the whole matter of her husband's demise. Jonathan hadn't chosen to leave her, and she now felt guilty at having blamed him at all, remembering how he'd railed against the inevitable, fighting to stay present for as long as he could, knowing that a month, a week, a day could make all the difference. Also, with the lucidity of a mind that wasn't in turmoil, she understood that he had battled the inevitable for her, aware that he had probably hung on for longer than was comfortable, until she had found her brave voice and smilingly told him that it was okay, he could go . . . she'd be fine, they all would. And besides, he wasn't leaving her alone. She had her parents, Aiden, Pickle their cat, Holly, who Pickle worshipped with a seemingly ever-increasing devotion. And her older, more glamorous, less lanky sister, Angela.

These words and affirmations were easy, the problem being that much of the time, she wasn't fine, not at all, despite her assurances to the contrary.

The cat returned, meowing, and lolloped down on to her favoured patch on the floor. Jonathan had presented her with 'Madam Pickle Paws' the year before he was diagnosed. As if he sensed there might be a need in her life for the pretty-faced, smarty-pants tabby, who was aloof and far too fancy for small talk or slumming it. In the immediate aftermath of his passing, when Enya had howled into her pillow or lain in a heap on the rug in the small, square sitting room, quite unable to sit up or catch her breath, it was that little cat who would lie on her, purring gently, kneading her with her pickle paws and giving her love. Again, with hindsight, it would have been weird if Aiden, her then twenty-four-year-old, rugby-loving son, had done similar.

Also, she still had Jonathan.

Even though he wasn't technically by her side, she still saw him, sitting in his armchair or standing by the fridge, looking over her shoulder in the bathroom while she cleaned her teeth, and watching her take the secateurs to her shrubs and flowers as he stood on the patio. She still spoke to him, too.

Like her moments of feeling utterly flustered and anxious for no apparent reason, this too was a secret kept between her and Pickle. He never replied, not directly, what with him being dead and all, but he'd smile or raise his eyebrows and on the odd occasion, frown. And she did hear his words, knowing what he *would* have said.

Luckily, he had always been predictable.

Chapter Five

As Enya settled back against the bamboo and rattan headboard, happy in the knowledge that Aiden was in Rome, safely ensconced in his hotel and not chained to a grimy wall somewhere dark and dismal, she couldn't decide whether to read a book or watch something on her laptop, unable to fathom her mood. In truth, it was a little early for bed; she was tired, but not sleepy, desiring rest, but not escape.

It was moments like this she felt the whip of widowhood across her skin, and it stung. What she wanted was Jonathan by her side for a good old natter, or to speak to Jenny, who she knew was out for supper with Phil. Angela, her sister, also a good candidate for an uplifting chat, was currently in Portugal with her husband, Frank.

It was a rare and fortunate thing that she, Angela and Jenny lived happily in a triangular friendship. There was no jealousy if two were together and one was otherwise occupied, a treasured thing for them all. Angela and Frank had gone to stay with Enya's parents, who had retired a few years back to a new-build estate in the Algarve. Angela, who looked like their dad's side of the family, loved the sunshine, the cuisine, and her afternoon siesta, whereas Enya, who missed her parents dearly, was not a fan of beach life, preferring to be at home with her favourite mug, latest novel, her own bed, and Pickle to curl up to on the sofa.

'*Boring!*' was how Angela described her.

'A little homebody!' Jenny's slightly kinder suggestion.

They were both right, but she was resolute. Without Jonathan to accompany her on trips, to chat to at the airport, help put her bag in the overhead locker and give their destination to the taxi driver in his phrasebook Portuguese, it all felt like a bit too much.

The quiet of the house had a rhythm of its own, a singular note of silence that grew loud in her ears. She wished Aiden were in his room along the corridor. She wished Jonathan were downstairs checking the doors and windows, about to appear at the top of the stairs on the landing. She wished for a lot of things. Taking a deep breath, she tried to figure out how she had let her life bleed into other people's to the point where she now felt almost entirely lost without their definition of her. How had it happened to her that at almost fifty-five she was defined only as a wife and mother, or worse, a widow! How could she feel this lonely!

She figured there was no harm in trying Angela.

'Were your ears burning? We were just talking about you.' Angela answered the phone with this question.

'They were indeed, hence, the call.'

'Right, I'm putting you on loudspeaker. We're out for dinner!'

There was a vague rustling. Enya cringed, knowing her sister would have no qualms about broadcasting their conversation to whomever might be within earshot.

'No, don't do that, Angela! I wanted to ask you—'

'And why, *exactly*, shouldn't she do that, young lady?'

Enya closed her eyes; it was obviously too late, Angela had pressed the button. 'Oh, no reason, Mum! Just wanted to ask her some boring questions and thought I'd spare you all,' she lied, pinching the bridge of her nose. 'Have you all had a lovely day?'

'We have. Despite your dad having a bit of a funny turn.'

'I did not have a funny turn! Ignore her, Enya,' her dad growled.

'Not a funny turn?' her mum shouted. 'He's right, it's perfectly normal to have to pull over in the car and vomit on the verge for no good reason. I've told him to go to the doctor in the morning, but you know what he's like!'

Enya cringed, wondering if they were in a busy restaurant, but sincerely hoping they were the only customers, or that if there were others in close proximity, they were deaf.

'*He* can hear you, you know; I am right here!' her dad countered. 'As I say, ignore your mother, love. The reason I was sick was that *someone* insists on wearing that heavy perfume that makes me gag. We were in a very hot car at midday because Frank wanted to visit the Benagil Caves.'

'I only said I'd never been, and the next thing I knew I was being bundled into the back seat, don't blame me!'

'Hi, Frank!' she called above the din.

'And do I have to remind you, it's the perfume *you* bought me, Michael!' her mother shouted.

'I am well aware of that, *Linette*, but what I didn't do was sniff it first. Lord God, I wish I had!'

'Listen, folks, sounds like you're having a great time, but the line is really bad, crackly, so I'll say goodbye and call tomorrow, when we can . . .'

Enya ran out of steam and ended the call. It was quite possible they wouldn't even notice she'd gone but might in fact carry on squabbling and shouting for the world to hear.

Her parents had been married for sixty-two years, happily married for the first fifteen, apparently. Jonathan used to find it a source of much amusement that they so disliked each other that neither would give the other the satisfaction of a divorce and the opportunity to find happiness elsewhere, likening their marriage to a finger-trap puzzle where both were pulling hard. She wasn't so sure, but thought their bickering was in fact how they communicated, so used to the tussle back and forth they'd grown used to it, completely unaware of the toll it took on others. It was, at least, preferable to think of them in this way, irritated by the other, yes, but still happy, deep down.

She lay back and opened up her laptop, staring at the keyboard, and yet with the whole world at her fingertips, any number of movies to choose from, re-runs of shows she'd loved, and two episodes of *The Great British Sewing Bee* to catch up on, not to mention the endless digital rabbit holes down which she could wander, nothing, absolutely nothing appealed to her. Without the energy to seek entertainment, she closed down the screen and sank into her pillows.

Reaching over, she ran her palm over the mattress next to her. A cool spot, awaiting the warmth of a person who was not coming back. Not ever.

'How? How can you not be here, Jonathan? This was not the plan!'

She felt the familiar tightening in her chest and breathed slowly, wanting to keep the demons at bay, not to feel the panic that started in the floor beneath her and rose up like water, until she was engulfed, surrounded and certain that one more second of it would see her drown. These feelings too were something that she kept secret.

It was a delight to see Angela's number flash up on her phone.

'Oh my God! Sorry, Ens, I had no idea Mum and Dad were going to go for it like that. It's been non-stop all day, they're driving me nuts!'

'They're your parents, they're supposed to drive you nuts. It's the rule.'

She pictured Aiden leaving the car and walking to the terminal without looking back to offer a smile or a wave. It did feel a little like the natural order of things, the slow twanging of the frayed ropes that kept children and parents bound, so that come the inevitable, the loss was not half as acute as it could be. Unless they were taken too soon. Aiden had been twenty-four when he'd lost his dad, and this, she knew, was way, way too soon.

'If you say so.' Angela sighed. 'Frank's driving me mad too, moaning because he can't get the snooker on the telly, and the internet is slow and his knee is playing up. I honestly don't know why we bother coming away at all. I looked at a map today and saw that I could probably get a bus to anywhere in Europe – I was tempted to grab my water bottle and Kindle and leave them all to it. Not that they'd notice I'd gone. Not till someone needed a wet wipe or a mint imperial. I always carry both.'

Enya laughed. 'You can't jump on a bus or run away, because you're there checking on our parents. You're an angel. I can see the glint of your halo from here.'

'You're right, I really am!' Angela laughed too. 'Anyway, I'm hiding on the beach right now, said I was going to the loo, and I've snuck around the back of the café to call you. What's up, chick? And don't say nothing, we both know you only call late at night when something's bothering you.'

Enya felt the swell of love for her sister, who knew her well enough to understand a return call had been needed. 'It's been a strange day.'

'Did Aiden get off all right?'

'Yep, I dropped him at the airport, and he's arrived safely.'

'And Holly has managed to survive in the hours since he left, have we checked on her, sent a care package?'

She could hear the humour in her sister's tone. It was funny, this all-round concern for Holly, yet no one seemed to be checking on Enya, who had spent many, many hours on her own, trying to survive. 'Yes, she has, so far.'

'Good, good. So, what's up?'

Enya took her time, enjoying the connection that felt unrushed, as good as chatting face to face.

'I was in a minor . . . erm, car thing . . . car-crash thing . . . someone bashed my car.'

'No! Oh Ens! Are you hurt?'

Her lovely sister's concern was instant and obvious.

'No, no, nothing like that. I was stationary. He just . . .'

Hit my car . . . made me smile . . . I liked the look of him . . . liked talking to him even more . . . I'm aware I sound like some saddo who's been flattered by a wink from a passing driver as I stood at the bus stop . . .

'He just what, love?'

She had momentarily forgotten that her sister was on the end of the line.

'Oh! He drove into me, the . . . the passenger door in fact, there's a big old dent.'

'Jeez, well thank goodness no one was standing by your car, they'd have been squished!'

'Yup.' This a very Angela path to walk, straight to the worst scenario, the unpalatable. 'But they weren't. So . . .'

'Did you get his details?'

'Yes, he was a . . . erm . . . a man. A driving, man.' She pictured his tanned forearms, his chunky watch, the underside of his wrist, the soft fringe falling over his face.

'Enya, have you been drinking?'

She laughed loudly. 'No! I'm just thinking about the crash, although crash makes it sound so much more than it was, more of a bump, a bump with meaning. Not aggressive, more a second's lapse in concentration and then . . . bam! But it was odd, a strange encounter really. Not sure how to describe it without sounding like a loon, I wasn't going to mention it, probably won't tell Jen, but the man was . . .'

'Enya! You sound a bit giggly? Are you telling me you fancy the man who smacked into your car? Or am I reading too much into it?'

She could hear the excitement in her sister's voice and wondered if this was a good idea, to open up in this way.

'Fancy is a strong word.'

'Is it?' Angela laughed again.

'It wasn't that straightforward. It was nothing, but he was . . .' She ran out of words and smiled at the memory of him driving off with that song playing.

'Enya, I love you, but I'm tired. Mum will already have sent out a search party, Frank will be cursing me for abandoning him, and Dad will have nodded off into his pastel de nata, I'm plonked on wet sand and there's a young couple necking on a sunbed to my left, so I don't have time for the preliminaries, just tell me – and I know this is huge, but you *liked* this man, and then?'

'And then nothing.' She sat up straight and took a deep breath. 'You're right, it was huge. I mean it was nothing, but it was the first time I've felt, I don't know how to say it, like I wanted to spend some time with someone, I wanted to *look* at him. Wanted to touch him.' She felt the spread of a blush, this level of candour not something she was used to.

'So, you found him attractive?' Angela cut to the chase.

'I . . . I did. And it's weird and new and unwelcome and disrupting.' She used the words that didn't come easily.

'Only if you let it be, my love. Only if you choose to remain in your ice den.'

Enya jolted a little. 'What does that mean?'

'It means that you choose to hide away. Not physically, but you know how some women are really good at giving off warmth and come-and-get-me vibes?'

'Yes.' She knew women like that.

'Well, you're the opposite of that. You're an Arctic fox, cool, mysterious, and quite unapproachable, icy.'

'I don't think Jenny would describe me as icy!'

'Of course she wouldn't. You only reserve it for men! It's a skill. A superpower, you can repel an interested mate at fifty paces with no more than a raise of your eyebrow and a fixed expression of disinterest.'

'Really? An Arctic fox?' Enya wasn't sure if she was more offended by the analogy or her sister's choice of animal; surely if she was any animal she wouldn't be a fox, they were sly and wily, chicken nabbers.

'Or a penguin or any other chilly beast you care to name. Any creature who would undeniably benefit from popping on a woolly scarf and having a bowl of soup instead of standing in the cold.'

'Is that how you see my life?' It wasn't a pleasant thought.

'A little bit, yes.' Angela took a deep breath. 'When I call you on a Sunday morning and tell you where we've walked, any pub we've been to, the mates we've seen, trips planned, you reply with something funny that Pickle has done or tell me what Holly has made you as a gift, or you give me an update on how your seedlings have sprouted.'

'Because *that's* my life!'

'And *that's* exactly my point!' Angela pressed. 'You never used to be like this.'

'I'd like to see how many pub lunches you might fancy if you lost Frank.' Her fast and sharp retort one that she would undoubtedly ponder and possibly regret later. It was painful to hear her life described by the small things that had become the big things.

'Not many I'm guessing, for a while, but then I like to think I'd come out the other side and realise that I need to choose differently.'

'Now, why didn't I think of that? It's so obvious, Angela!' She comically smacked her forehead with her palm. 'I need to choose differently! Quick, pass my laptop so I can upload Grindr or whatever it is!'

'I don't think you'd get many dates on Grindr, my darling.'

'You don't know till you try!' Enya didn't want to think of herself as undateable.

'And don't be so defensive, I'm not having a go at you or criticising. I'm just saying how I see it, and I'm delighted at the thought that you might be putting your head above the parapet, getting out there. You're young and fabulous, and Jonathan wouldn't want you hiding in your snow den. He was many things, that brother-in-law of mine, but mostly he was generous and smart, and he loved you far too much to allow you to let life pass you by. That much I do know.'

Enya shrank down on to the mattress at the thought of her lovely husband, placed her hand on her chest and felt the throb of loss, like a drum, beating out its mournful rhythm that sat like background noise to her thoughts.

I don't want to have to put myself out there, I want you back . . .

'Would you say he liked you too, this man, did you get that feeling?'

Enya thought about this.

'I'd say possibly, yes. Not sure how to tell, he might just be nice to everyone. One of those people.'

'If you got the sense he liked you, he probably did. The question is, what are you going to do about it?'

'Oh, nothing! Nothing! God no!'

Just the thought was enough to invite her potential panic to lap at her heels. It was a frightful thought. She was not ready, not nearly ready. No way. She wanted Jonathan. She wanted him to be here, right now!

'Nope, don't be a pessimist! You have his number, are you going to call him?'

'No! Well, maybe, but only to sort the car repair, but even then, I'm not sure.' She closed her eyes tightly and wanted the conversation to end. 'I should probably let you go, poor Frank is alone with Mum and Dad right now.'

'Was he wearing a wedding ring?'

Angela, it seemed, was keener on chatting than getting back to the family dinner.

'No. But I was. I am.'

Enya closed her fingers around the gold band on her finger that was so much more than a sliver of shiny metal.

'The thing is, my love, he might right now be on the phone to his brother, explaining how he met a woman, a woman he liked and who he thinks might like him back, but he's unsure of what to do next, as she was wearing a wedding ring.'

'I guess so.'

'The only way to know one way or the other if he is attached, or to find out if it has legs, is to make contact. That's the advice from your big sister, who always knows best.'

'Oh yeah? Three words for you, Angela: warm ham sandwich!'

'Oh don't, it might have been nearly forty years ago, but I swear I can still taste it! Anyway, better go, you're right, there's bound to be something going on at the table that will need refereeing. Speak soon, be brave, I love you!'

'Love you.'

Be brave . . . if only.

Pickle, disturbed from her rest as Enya shifted her legs, looked less than happy, and coiled into a bun on top of the duvet.

'What's up, pussycat? You finding it hard to settle too?'

Pickle purred.

'Can you believe what your Auntie Angela said? You don't think I'm icy, do you, puss? No, you don't. It's quite insulting really. I'm warm, approachable. If I were an animal, I'd be a faithful hound or a sweet lop-eared rabbit. Anyway, if it is true, how in the world do I stop being an Arctic fox?'

She spoke into the ether as this thought persisted.

Chapter Six

Enya tried to sleep, figuring that if she faked it for long enough, the real thing might creep over her. Eyes shut, arms by her sides, lying back on her pillow, she did her best to smother the sound of that drum and let the quiet wrap her, but it was no use, the sandman had apparently left her off his list. Again.

Angela's words resonated; was she hiding in her ice cave? The question being whether she was indeed brave enough to do anything about it.

'Ugh.' She felt her stomach roll with sickness at the thought of speaking to him.

Her sister was right, there was only one way to crawl forward and that was to engage with Handsome Car Klutz directly, find out if he was married, interested, or was indeed just one of those people who was nice to everyone, or whether she was about to make a complete fool of herself. Although even if he was single, what did that mean, what would she do with that information?

'I'd do nothing, but at least it would be closure,' she reasoned.

With the phone in her hand, she lifted her finger, hesitating before she pressed the icon that would connect her to HCK.

'What should I say? I'll be subtle of course, see what he says, how he reacts and go with that. God, I feel sick! What if I make a monumental idiot of myself, what if I sound like a weirdo or desperado. How do I even broach the topic that I might have felt a little sexy at the sight of his wrist!' She ran her hand over her face. 'This is something I haven't had to contend with for decades!' Pickle's lack of response did nothing to settle her nerves. 'I guess if he is curt or cool, I never have to speak to him or of him again. It's not like I'm going to have to see him. I can always block his number, delete the contact, it will be as if it never happened.' She talked herself into it.

Consoled by the option of deleting all mention of him entirely, she pressed the button and instantly regretted doing so. Hunched over with embarrassment, with her toes curled and her face contorted, physically reflecting the agonising regret of her action.

If she ended the call, however, he would still see that she had called and that was almost worse somehow! She was unsure how something as basic as making a call to the person who had damaged her car could cause her this much angst. It was a huge relief when his answerphone kicked in. What she should have done was end the call, allow him to call back if he wanted or needed, but instead she listened, smiling, quite enamoured by the sound of his voice, which had the same effect as it had in real life, as her heart jumped in her chest and the tingle of excitement ran along her limbs, sending a blush of desire over her skin. And finally, she discovered his name.

Hi, you've reached Dominic's phone, leave me a message, and . . . you know the rest, I'll return your call when I get the message, which is likely to be weeks and weeks after you've left it, so . . . apologies in advance . . .

Dominic! So intent was she on listening that she almost ignored the beep, aware suddenly that it was recording, and she was doing no more than breathing and smiling. He might think it a crank call!

'Oh! Gosh! Yes, erm . . . it's . . . it's me . . . car park woman.' She cringed, *car park woman?* 'Just thought I'd . . . you know . . . doing some . . . some admin, car stuff, erm, anyway, it's me and so, yup.'

Hastily, she finished the call, threw her phone on to the bedside table, and wriggled down on the mattress, hiding her face under the duvet with her hand clamped over her mouth, breathing quickly through her nose, wanting to disappear forever. She felt Pickle readjust her position.

'You absolute dipstick!' she finally yelled at herself as she came up for air, 'you sounded like a babbling teen! Angela's right, when is the last time I stuck my head out of my ice den? He'll block *your* number! Delete all mention of you! You'll have to pay for the bloody door now, yourself, which is no more than you deserve. I'm dying of shame!'

Closing her eyes, she wished hard now for the escape of sleep, every muscle coiled, cringing at her entirely pointless and embarrassing message that Dominic would apparently not hear for weeks and weeks, and would by that stage probably have forgotten all about her! But sleep, it seemed, was still not on the agenda, as her cogs turned, her thoughts whizzed, and her interior monologue screamed negative confidence-crushing words at her!

Idiot!

Moron!

Car Park Woman?

What were you thinking!

Poor Jonathan, did you forget about him?

The truth was that in that moment when Dominic's voice had held her attention, she had in fact forgotten Jonathan for a second or two. With this realisation came the awful sense of failure, like she'd let her husband down, cheated, even.

'I'm so sorry,' she whispered.

Her brain noise was quieted by the sound of her phone buzzing. The breath caught in her throat, and as she reached for it, the name flashed up on her screen, HCK. Unsure if she should answer, she held the phone for a second or two. It would be awkward, of that there was no doubt, embarrassing too – what would they have to talk about? The initial fizz of excitement was now dulled when she pictured her lovely husband. She felt like a child who'd been caught with her hand in the biscuit tin.

'Hello?' Her voice no more than a shaky whisper.

'So, I've spent most of the day wondering what your name might be. I'd kind of settled on Maggie.'

'Maggie?' She laughed, as much with relief at the ease with which they had begun – that, and to be called Maggie was better than being called an Arctic fox or a penguin.

'Yes, not sure why, it felt fitting somehow, but how foolish do I feel, now I know your name is in fact Car Park Woman. Is it French? Hungarian? Dutch? I'm not familiar with it, I'm assuming Woman is your surname and is Car Park double-barrelled?'

'That's correct. Most people shorten it to the initials CP.'

'Ah, makes sense. So, CP, here we are.'

Enya smiled. 'Yes, here we are.'

She felt some of her confidence restored, enjoying the warm feeling in her stomach, a reminder of what this felt like, whatever *this* was, wary of adding words or labels that would sound as frivolous and ridiculous as they sounded in her head. She was a grown woman, not some teen hankering for company.

'How's the car, have you administered paracetamol, a bandage, spoken soft words of reassurance, offered sweet tea?'

'All of the above.'

He made it easy. Easy to chat, easy to forget her loneliness, easy to mask her loss.

'I see.' There was a beat of companionable silence. 'Well, that makes me very happy.'

'How so?' She sat up a little, all nerves withering, replaced with something that felt a lot like energy.

'Because if your car is comfortable and doing as well as can be expected, that means you haven't discovered any new or disastrous levels of damage that might necessitate the intervention of our insurance companies, which hopefully means you just wanted to talk to me.'

'I did. I did just want to talk to you.' Unsure of where this self-assuredness came from, in that instant she sounded as bold as she felt. This, however, was underpinned with the rumble of unease that she still hadn't established if he was free to be having this rather flirtatious chat at all, and that was before she could swallow the tang of shame at how she could say this at all – her, Enya Brown, Jonathan's wife.

'Well, I'm rather glad. I would have called this afternoon.'

'I see. And what would prompt such a call to a stranger?'

'Simple, really, I wanted to know about that one night, what happened? The night you thought you might have been trendy and a go-getter when you were seventeen.'

It was her turn to laugh. It was flattering and connecting, not only his interest but his recollection of that one brief conversation in the car park, seemingly as sharp as her own.

'Well, that's funny, as I wanted to know why you have had *quite the day*?' she quoted.

'You first,' he urged, and she could tell he was smiling.

'Gosh, it was a very long time ago.' Suddenly, she felt a little uneasy at being so candid with this man she knew nothing about, a complete stranger.

'I'm interested,' he stated, the words loaded.

'You are?'

'I am.'

There was something about the way he spoke that drew her to a place of safety. It smacked of promise, of connection.

'Take your time.'

She breathed out slowly and, as instructed, took her time, as if they were old friends or old lovers or, at the very least, better acquainted to the point where to share with him tales of one night in her seventeenth year, spent on the island of Mallorca, was no big deal. She turned her body towards the window, tilting her head away from the bathroom door where Jonathan stood.

'It was our last night of a holiday in Palma. The first time I'd been away without my parents, and they only allowed it because I was with my big sister, Angela, who had rather carelessly got food poisoning. I think it was probably the warm ham sandwich she ate on the sand, which had been wrapped in her towel for a couple of hours. Anyway, it was either a case of sit indoors and watch her face turn grey or pluck up the courage to go out on my own. So, I went wandering, which was most unlike me. I wasn't brave. I've never been brave,' she admitted, 'yet honestly? There was something about pushing myself out of my comfort zone that made me feel invincible! I remember everything about the evening. I've never thought I was pretty or attractive, not like Angela, who has fabulous bosoms.' She glanced down at her chest where her fried eggs sat, as perkily as they were able, inside her cotton nightie. 'She takes after our Nana Collins, who had melons, whereas I am more like our Nanny Jan.'

He laughed and she winced – how had she so quickly got on to the topic of boobies? She glanced over her shoulder towards Jonathan, who looked past her into the middle distance, and she felt a fine film of shame cover her.

'Anyway, I was always lanky and pale, but not that night. That night I was alone in a foreign land, all warm and glorious, with the smell of paella wafting on the breeze, pesetas in my pocket and strawberry lip gloss in my clutch. Angela had bought these silver platform shoes and was saving them for her last night – well, I couldn't let them go to waste, could I?'

'That would have been criminal,' he agreed, and it made her smile.

'Exactly, so I slipped them on and borrowed one of her off-the-shoulder T-shirt dresses, bouffed up my hair with enough hairspray to stop a gale, and off I went. I didn't walk down that strip, Dominic, oh no. I strutted. It was my catwalk; my moment, and I was on the hunt.'

She paused, aware that she had spoken his name so casually, like she used to when catching up with her husband.

'Oooh, remind me, Jonathan, to get the chicken out of the freezer . . .'

'Did I tell you, Jonathan, that I bumped into Phil in the garden centre?'

'What do you mean, terminal? What are you telling me, Jonathan?'

She did her best to shake off the suffocating feelings of loss she was trying to avoid.

'I felt simultaneously grown-up and scared, but it was a good scared – you know, the way you feel when you are about to test yourself but come out the other side with a feeling of having achieved something.'

'I do. I'm a keen sailor and when you really push a boat, test her, that's when you not only learn about the vessel, but about yourself too. If you race, which I used to, you can only win when you give over to that fear, resign yourself to the very worst thing imaginable and recognise that it's okay. No matter what happens, it will all be okay.'

There was a beat of silence while she let his words settle, as he perfectly summed up all she was trying to convey.

'Well, it was kind of like that. I heard a man whistle, calling to me from a bar where he sat with his mates. "Never Gonna Give You Up" was belting out of the speakers, it felt like a sign. I turned, and there he was, not a man at all and certainly not the swarthy

Spaniard that I might have imagined, but in fact Karl from Whitley Bay, who was celebrating his eighteenth. We drank sangria, smoked Marlboro Lights and our thighs edged closer together on a sticky faux-leather banquette. Honestly, Dominic, I thought I was Sheena bloody Easton.'

This time he laughed heartily, easily.

'We snogged on the beach, Karl and I. Snogged for an hour at least. A revelation for me, as I was never popular. I can't believe I've just told you that!' She screwed her eyes shut. 'You're the only person on the planet who knows this other than me and Karl.'

And Jonathan of course, Jonathan knows everything about me . . .

'Your secret is safe with me,' he whispered, his low murmur sending shivers along her limbs. It was a curious and unfamiliar reaction to a stranger, the overwhelming desire for physical connection that was like a spell.

'It was all rather anticlimactic after that. He went off to find his mates and didn't take my number.'

'What a rotter!'

'Not really. I didn't want a boyfriend or anything like that, too busy studying and playing hockey. Plus, this was the world pre-internet, mobile phones and messaging, it would only have fizzled and caused possible heartache. Far better that one night that is stuck in my memory, special because of that, no matter how dire. I learned two things that night. First, that clothes and shoes can really change the way you feel about yourself, which is why I always wear colour, it cheers me.'

'I noticed that today. You were . . . bright!'

'Ha!' He had noticed her, seen her! She liked the thought, *bright*. 'What was the second thing?'

'Oh, the second thing was that snogging, if you're doing it with the wrong person, isn't really much to write home about.'

'Poor Karl!' he laughed.

'Poor me!' she countered.

He laughed again, loudly and without restraint. It felt good to have him react in this way, a superpower!

'I grew up a bit that night. And looking back, I needed to. My parents were strict really. They didn't see me as an adult until I got married, which I did when I was in my twenties. And even then they would phone to tell me if there was a cold snap expected, reminding me to leave extra time in the morning to defrost the car.'

'I can relate.'

'I went back to the room to find Angela sitting on the loo while she threw up in the bidet in a room full of mozzies. She'd had to leave the windows open, apparently, to try and get rid of the smell. But nothing could dent that feeling. Like I was desirable, a go-getter, and excited for my whole life that stretched ahead.'

'They define you, don't they, those moments, those incidents that are unexpected, like jewels hiding in the gloom.'

Again, he summed it up perfectly. It was this conversation, this whole exchange, a jewel hiding in the gloom.

'Did you have a Karl from Whitley Bay night in your misspent youth?'

'No, he wasn't really my type. There might not have been a Karl but there was an Issy who was rather free and easy with her favours, as my mother would have said, a lovely girl who had a fondness for Land Rovers, I seem to recall.'

'And you had a Land Rover?'

'No, but my dad did, and so I *borrowed* it one night and went a-wooing!'

'Did it yield the result you were hoping for?' She smiled.

'It did indeed, and even the next day when I was getting leathered by my dad for taking his precious Landy for a spin without his permission, I couldn't wipe the smile off my face.'

'Worth it then,' she guessed.

'Oh, more than worth it. Issy married the son of a local farmer who, rumour had it, was a collector of Land Rovers.'

They both laughed in a way that was natural when two people were so well acquainted — and yet they weren't. No more than strangers. She looked back towards the bathroom door; Jonathan was staring right at her. It was as sobering as it was jarring.

'I should go, I should, erm . . .' Sitting up, she pulled the neck of her nightie closed.

'Oh, you don't want to know why I've had quite the day?'

'Sure, go ahead.' She spoke softly, turning her body away from the bathroom door. Speaking quietly, as if this might prevent Jonathan from hearing.

'In all honesty, it had been quite the day leading up to the unfortunate incident in the car park, but post that it really has turned out to be one to remember.'

He was charming, his flattery well received, and she felt a flare of joy at the admission.

'I signed the lease on a flat. A place of my very own.'

'Oh!' Embarrassment cloaked her; of course it wasn't her that had made his day one to remember. 'Well, that sounds exciting.' She meant it. A flat, *his* flat, single then. 'I'm not sure,' she coughed to clear her throat, 'not sure why you called me back.'

'I'm not sure why,' he hesitated, 'and everything I want to say is so clichéd that I don't want to risk it.'

'Probably best.' She closed her eyes.

'So, you were married in your twenties, and are you still, still married?'

It was the first time she'd heard a hint of nerves and was glad of it, giving the topic the attention it deserved.

'I'm a widow.' There it was again, that word, that dreadful, dreadful word. 'My husband, Jonathan, he died three years ago.'

As was her habit, she twisted her wedding ring with the underside of her thumb.

'I am so sorry. That must have been rough.'

'Yes.' She ran her hand along Pickle's back, glad of the company. 'And what about you, are you married, have been married?'

There, she had done it, asked the question on which everything else hinged. There was a second of silence before he spoke. 'I am married.'

These three words were rocks that he lobbed through the glass of her happiness, leaving tiny fissures and cracks that spread far and wide, after which the whole energy of their interaction changed, and she felt a little foolish for having been so open. More than a little foolish, mortified was more accurate.

Her tone and demeanour changed immediately. She sat up straight.

'I see.' Closing her eyes, she fought the embarrassing desire to cry, the drop in her stomach far greater than if she hadn't allowed herself the swell of excitement before. 'Well, I'll say goodnight, Dominic. It's been lovely to talk to you and it was nice to meet you ever so briefly, today, but . . . well, you can . . . you can text me the details of your friend's garage, or whatever.' She couldn't find the words to convey how his marital status was an absolute non-starter for her, and realised she didn't have to. 'I have to go now.'

'I . . . I understand, but before you go, can I just say that the picture you are painting of me right now is not a true one. I am married and I could have pretended otherwise, but I never lie, never, about anything.' She heard his lips, forming the words, sticky with nerves. 'And so believe me when I tell you that I've been, I've been treading water, for the longest time, not unhappily, not desperately, but just, idling. And I want more. I think I deserve more; I don't want to settle anymore! And today I signed the lease on a flat, so we can start to dismantle . . . everything.'

His justification was so predictable, possibly even untrue, that he may as well have added *she just doesn't understand me!*

'Well, Dominic, you don't know me, and I don't know you, and that's part of a much bigger conversation: what we want, what we deserve and what we settle for. And I am most definitely not the person to have that conversation with.'

In an instant, he turned ugly in her mind. His smile no longer enticing but rather forced, his floppy fringe not appealing, but probably cultivated to fall just so, a cad. And his friendly manner, no doubt well-rehearsed to snare unsuspecting widows who might be flattered by all that lovely attention.

'I understand, but—'

'There is no but.' She cut him short.

'Right.' He swallowed loudly. 'Good night, CP.'

She hated the way it felt, hearing their quickly established nickname, hated that she would never get used to the sound of it, hated the taste of disappointment that sat on her tongue and the deceit that coated her lips. She had been flirting with a married man. Flirting when she was still so desperately cut up over losing her husband, and he had a wife, *a wife*!

'Good night.'

She lay still for some minutes, letting the words of their conversation permeate. She was a fool, an easily flattered fool. Hopping out of bed to wash her face in cool water, it was as she stood over the sink and flicked on the light that she saw Jonathan, as ever, looking over her shoulder. His expression was thoughtful. She closed her eyes, unable to deal with his mood and obvious judgement, not when her own was so fresh and acute.

'I . . . I know. I know, my love,' she stuttered, 'time to climb back into my ice den.'

Chapter Seven

Enya plonked the three weighty shopping bags by her front door and flexed her palms, which carried the imprint of the handles, before fishing inside her handbag for her buzzing phone. A text from Jenny filled the screen:

I HAVE PROSECCO AND TIRAMISU. WHY DON'T WE EAT PUDDING LATER AND DRINK TOO MUCH. WE CAN DANCE IN THE KITCHEN. WHADDYA SAY?

She smiled at the prospect, thankful, so thankful for her friend, whose messages and visits were indeed bright jewels that brightened up the most ordinary of days.

AM COOKING FOR THE KIDS BUT COME OVER – AND YES, WE CAN HIDE THE TIRAMISU AND PLONK! I'LL DIG OUT MY ABBA CD!

Her friend's reply was instant:

ACE!

She was already looking forward to it and could hear the comforting notes of 'Dancing Queen' in her head. It helped calm the worry beginning to flare at the thought of the prawns that had been out of their freezer home for at least half an hour now. This was what Jenny did, made everything feel a little bit better. It wasn't lost on her how her friend put effort into being there, into thinking up weird and wonderful ways to give her something to look forward to.

Three weeks had passed quickly, it felt like mere days since she'd been feeling anxious about getting to the airport on time to drop her son off, and now she was feeling anxious about getting to the airport on time to pick him up. It had been easy to return to the predictability of life, a life edged with loneliness once Dominic's marital status had been exposed.

He hadn't been uppermost in her mind, not really, yet now, remembering the car-park incident, she thought about the lovely man who had bashed her door, the lovely, *married* man who had bashed her door. Her shame had faded a little and in its place sat the subtle ache of embarrassment at the fact that she had allowed herself to feel so giddy, so physically affected over the smallest and most minor of interactions. It wasn't typical for her, she was smarter than that.

'Morning, Enya!'

'Oh, morning, Maeve!' She felt the hint of a blush to have been thinking about HCK at all, not that Maeve had ever professed to have or displayed any mind-reading skills, but still. 'All okay?' Her lovely neighbour popped out on to the path that ran between their two houses from where they both accessed the bin shed, and what would in days gone by have been the coal store.

'It's so warm, not yet midday and it's this hot!' The older woman wafted her tunic.

It always fascinated her, the way people were keen to tell her what the weather was like when she was standing in front of them, as if she were not staring at the same sky, experiencing the same temperature, with her prawns slowly deteriorating and crying out for the chilly interior of her fridge as she searched for her key. Her bolder self, the one that she kept under wraps, wanted to say, *'Really? Warm, you say? Well, strike me down! And here's me in my snow boots and ski snood! But then I am part Arctic fox!'*

Instead, she smiled and nodded. ''Tis a bit.'

'Aiden's home today then.'

Maeve lived next door to the Hudsons and had watched the children on either side of her garden fences grow up and fall in love when in their late teens. The woman felt a lovely sense of connection to the two youngsters, and said often that when they got married, she wanted a front-row seat.

'Yes! I'm picking him up from the airport in a few hours. I've been and got all his favourite bits. Including prawns!' Enya laughed, hoping her worry might leach from her words and Maeve would advise her not to tarry and go get that seafood in the fridge. But no.

'Expect Holly has missed him, poor love. Three weeks! It's a long time.'

Try three years . . . 'Yes, although I think she's taken the opportunity to redecorate their bedroom.'

'She's a clever girl, has always been very clever.'

'She is, Maeve.'

The older woman would never, it seemed, forget that Holly, aged nine, had aced her cycling proficiency while Aiden had managed to fail his spectacularly and had stood in the front garden wailing loudly for all to hear before kicking his bike. Not his finest hour. A more churlish, overly proud mother might take the opportunity to point out that Holly would be struggling to pay her rent as she tried to get her home-made craft business off the ground, were it not for the hefty wage her cycling-proficiency-failing, bike-kicking, super-skilled son was bringing in each month as a robotics engineer. He was, however, and in fairness, still a bit wobbly on two wheels.

She could jest about it, but she did worry sometimes that he and Holly had rather fallen into their coupledom without testing the water; had they even dated other people? Not that she could recall. They did, however, seem incredibly happy, and that was what mattered.

'That's why I thought a lovely supper here might be a treat. Prawn cocktail to start!'

'Ooh, lovely. He'll be looking forward to some home-made grub no doubt. My Arthur never liked foreign food. I gave him noodles one night for his tea, threw the bowl against the wall he did! That taught me. Next night I went back to pie, mash and carrots. And do you remember the Jubilee street party when you tried to give him a taco! *"Taco! What the bloody hell is that? Are you having a laugh, it's cardboard!"* That's what he shouted. Oh dear, that put the kibosh on his celebrations. I had to quickly go find him a slice of lemon drizzle to calm him down!'

'Yeeeeees. I remember. Fun times.' She smiled, remembering Arthur's miserable, muttering fizzog that used to appear on this very path on bin day. 'Aiden actually loves Italian food and that's where he's been, Italy, so I'm sure he's been feasting on pasta and, and . . .' Her mind went blank. She couldn't think of any other Italian food. It happened this way sometimes, a thought hiccup.

'He wants to watch that waistline, his dad wasn't exactly a rake, was he? And he certainly doesn't take after his mum!'

Maeve laughed and Enya reminded herself that Maeve was older and therefore deserving of respect, and that Jonathan would no doubt have chuckled to hear their neighbour of thirty years talk about his ever-expanding girth. She also took little offence, aware that she was indeed a rake – tall and skinny and about as handy in the garden, her glorious dahlias proof of this.

'He was not. Used to say he was built for endurance, not speed.'

The irony wasn't lost on Enya that it turned out her husband wasn't built for endurance at all. And just like that, the thought of him, confirming that he was not inside waiting for her, kettle boiling, smile on his face, *ah the wanderer returns!* His favourite refrain. She felt the first flush of anxiety, starting in her feet and rising up the back of her calves; her head felt hot, her face clammy and, as ever, the fear of the panic made her panic.

'God rest his soul,' Maeve announced with sudden solemnity.

'Yep.' She turned abruptly towards the front door, wanting to get inside, away from . . . people. 'Anyway, Maeve, I'd, I'd better get this food inside.' Again, she plunged her hand into the plum-coloured Radley cross-body bag that Holly and Aiden had bought her as a birthday gift a couple of years ago and which she treasured, trying to locate her key. It was with blissful relief that her fingers touched the cool, slim metal.

Her neighbour stared at her with a slight look of concern.

'Give Aiden my love, won't you, and tell him, welcome home!' Maeve called over her shoulder as she ambled back towards her house, leaving Enya feeling a new wave of guilt at any negative thoughts she might have harboured.

Maeve was part of this small community in Mablethorpe Road, the cul-de-sac of Victorian railway workers' cottages in Watley Down, once a market town, now a suburb on the outskirts of Bristol, and the place they had all chosen to put down roots, see out their retirement or raise their kids. Each house had been remodelled, extended and added to over the years, but from the front they all looked identical, bar the variety of front-door colours. Theirs was a deep green; Jonathan had chosen it because it reminded him of steam trains and because the cottages had strong links to the railway. It had made sense to him at least. The houses were, she always felt, rather like the people who lived inside them, a surprise! No one really knew what went on behind each facade.

'I . . . I will, Maeve,' she stuttered, feeling sweat prickle her skin, 'and if you need anything, you know the rule, just holler or come right around the back, the doors are usually open!'

'I know that, my love.' Maeve ambled inside.

Enya rushed into the hallway and kicked off her sandals, not wanting to mark the freshly mopped oak kitchen floor of the open-plan kitchen-diner at the back of their cottage. An addition that had eaten up a good chunk of their back garden and their savings, but it was no loss. She didn't miss the slab of sacrificed garden and to sit of a summer's evening with the wide French doors open was a treat in itself. And when it rained, the water ran in tiny rivers down the windows and beat out a rhythm on the roof in a way that she found quite hypnotic. As for their savings, her husband's untimely death and his fastidious attention to their finances meant she need not worry about money.

The mortgage had been paid off, various policies now paid her a handsome monthly dividend and in a couple of years their pensions would kick in. It was, of course, no less than she had expected from such a cautious man, who had spent his entire career working in insurance. She wasn't super-wealthy, not by any stretch, but knew that not having to worry about popping the heating on and being able to go and buy prawns for her son's return was a lovely way to live. A privilege. Not nearly as lovely, however, as having her husband by her side and being encouraged to watch the pennies.

She leaned against the kitchen island and took deep breaths, head bowed, eyes closed, until she felt a little calmer. A glass of cold water helped too. Eventually, she took a seat at the kitchen table and placed her head on the tabletop, breathing slowly in through her nose and out through her mouth.

'What's wrong with me, Jonathan? I have never been the panicky kind and yet look at me!' She wiped her brow with her fingertips and took long, slow breaths, placed her hands on her thighs and waited for her trembling limbs to settle and her pulse to calm.

'Bloody hell,' she whispered, quite drained by the feeling, and she focused on the blue sky through the garden window. Something visual to anchor her, proof there was life outside of these four walls, and that the world kept turning.

It happened like this sometimes, as if an alarm had sounded and she was jumping into action as her adrenaline surged. A feeling not dissimilar to that bit in a dream when you wake just before hitting the floor or nanoseconds before the bogeyman grabs your ankles.

She hadn't told anyone about these episodes. It felt a little silly, embarrassing. How to explain that as she sat far from danger inside the safety of her pretty cottage, she felt terror leap in her gut as if she were on a ledge, about to jump, had seen the glint of a blade aimed right at her, was staring down the barrel of a gun or was about to be whipped up into the eye of a tornado.

It made no sense, not even to her. What did she have to feel afraid of?

It didn't help that she spent many a private moment panicking about it happening. Panicking about the potential panic that a panic attack would bring. And the fear of the fear of the panic, induced . . . panic.

Go figure.

'What do you make of it all, puss cat?'

Pickle looked up briefly at the question, as if to express her irritation at being woken from her warm spot on the kitchen windowsill. Here she languished, legs stretched out, tail hanging down towards the sink.

'Honestly, Jonathan, this cat! She's got several cushions, a bean bag, even a snuggle pouch, so many places to sunbathe, and yet she wants to lie there next to the taps! I just bumped into Maeve. She's got her finger on the pulse as per, knew that Aiden was coming home today, and that Holly would no doubt be fretting and in danger of figuring out what to do with that hand that is nearly always clamped to some part of our son's body.' She laughed out loud, feeling a lot better, as the panic passed. She stood and unpacked the shopping. 'Ooh, that sounded wrong, I mean his hand, thigh, arm, shoulder, you get the idea.'

She popped the prawns into the fridge first, breathing a big sigh of relief as she did so. She'd sniff them later to check they were okay, before dousing them in Marie Rose sauce.

'And please don't think I'm being mean about Holly, I love the girl,' she turned towards her uncommunicative, indifferent tabby, 'and I know Pickle does too. It'd be hard not to. She's lovely, sweet, she crochets me socks and scarves, brings me scented candles, I just . . .' Enya paused, holding the baby gem lettuce to her chest as she ordered her thoughts, whispering into the empty room as was her habit, as if Jonathan were still sitting at the table with his legs stretched out, displaying whatever novelty socks her sister had bought him for Christmas or birthday last, while he read the latest Peter May novel. 'I just worry sometimes that it's all they know. Each other. Their life is alien to me. I was thinking about it just a sec ago, they've hardly explored the possibility of other people, have they? I mean, you and I were young when we met, weren't we, but how can I put it? We weren't daft. We were inexperienced, yes, but I felt like we had our heads screwed on. We had a plan, didn't we, you'd finish your apprenticeship and follow your dad into insurance, I'd have our baby, wait till it was old enough to go to nursery and then work around drop-off and pick-up times. And it worked, didn't it? Sometimes, I listen to Holly talking about influencing this or that and followers and reels or whatever they're called and it's like she's talking a foreign language! How can that be a job? Taking pictures of her life and crafts and putting them on her phone? I just don't understand it. I want them to be secure.'

Her phone buzzed on the countertop.

'Aiden! Hello, lovey, how are you getting on?'

'Yep, not bad, just checked in, no delays, so I reckon through baggage and whatnot by . . . I guess, sixish?'

'Oh, that's smashing! I'll be in the usual spot.' It was so convenient having a local airport that was familiar and not too busy. 'Are you tired?' It was always her concern, he worked hard and never seemed to slow down.

'No, I'm good, I want to erm . . .' He fell silent, which was odd and uncharacteristic.

'You want to what?' she asked, knowing him so well that she was overly aware of his hesitancy.

'Nothing. Nothing, Mum.' He took a deep breath. 'Just . . .'

She listened, quietly, hoping her silence might help him gather his thoughts, spit out whatever it was he clearly wanted to say.

'We'll catch up on the drive home, maybe.'

'I'll look forward to that. Safe travels, love.'

'Yep.'

And he was gone. Enya held the phone against her cheek for a short while, wondering what her boy might want to catch up about.

'That was odd, he sounded a bit, don't know really, just not himself.' She spoke to Jonathan, who stared at her from the kitchen table. And as was the case since his untimely death, he said nothing.

Chapter Eight

With one eye on the clock, keen to leave on time, Enya wiped her hands on her jeans and put the lettuce in the salad crisper. Her phone buzzed with a text from Jenny.

FOR THE LOVE OF GOD, JUST TAKE THE GOODS, DON'T LET HER BRING THEM BACK HERE! I CAN'T FACE ANY MORE – WE'RE DROWNING IN SUGAR. WHY CAN'T SHE GET A DIFFERENT HOBBY THAT'S KINDER TO MY HIPS? DELETE THIS TEXT IMMEDIATELY!!!!!

Enya was about to re-read the message to try and make more sense of it when a knock on the door drew her from her thoughts. She dashed to open it.

'Holly! Hello, sweetie. Cup of tea? I was just going to put the kettle on.'

The girl looked flawless, subtle make-up, a shiny, swinging ponytail and toned legs snug inside her leggings. 'Ooh, yes please. I made these.'

She handed Enya a pale wooden tray lined with a red and white gingham cloth on top of which were piled generously sized, freshly baked blondies that smelled heavenly, and Jenny's text suddenly became clear.

'You clever old stick! They look gorgeous!' And they did.

It was a skill Enya both envied and admired, the way the young woman took such care over everything she baked, everything she made. It wasn't enough to whip up items that were moist, delicious and moreish, she would also set them on a cloth or in a basket with handwritten labels and flourishes of ribbon. Her knitted gifts too, always with a dinky label sewn into them, and delivered wrapped in brown paper and string that put her in mind of days gone by. It was beautiful and joyful and yet she couldn't help but wonder if maybe Holly had too much time on her hands. Not that she'd shared this with anyone other than Angela, who had sprayed her laughter and strawberry shortbread crumbs over the front of her dress at the very suggestion.

'The girl wants a baby, then we'll see who's got time for bloody knitting and titting about, she'd be too busy wiping arses, mashing carrots and crying from a lack of sleep!'

'Sounds like you might be wishing that upon her, Angela. Do I need to remind you we are talking about our little Holly Hudson, who we love dearly? And besides, Aiden has mentioned in the past that babies won't be on the agenda for a good few years.'

She had felt torn by the revelation, excited at the prospect of grannyhood, especially as it was a road she'd be travelling with Jenny, but also a little relieved that her son was giving himself time to get his life in order, to establish himself, hoping that in these discovery years, he and Holly would find some parity and that the beloved girl would settle down and show the streaks of independence that Enya knew were vital for resilience.

'Do I need to remind you that it was you who started it?' Angela had shoved the remainder of Holly's home-made shortbread into her mouth.

Enya smiled now to think of her sister, hoping she and Frank were having a better time on their break. The last time they'd spoken, it had all sounded a little fraught. A month was a long time to be holed up with their parents, even for Angela, the angel.

'They're Aiden's favourites!' Holly slipped off her Birkenstocks and Enya was grateful. 'I've missed him so much!'

'Well, I've just put the phone down on him. He sounded tired, but said his flight was on time. I'll pick him up about sixish.'

'He didn't call *me* . . .' Holly stared into the middle distance, as if it might be the end of the world. 'I would have gone to get him, but I've got this Insta Live thing and it's been arranged for weeks. I'm going to do it from your kitchen where the light is good, if that's okay?'

'Of course it is!' She had no idea what the event would entail and hoped there'd be no need for redecorating, which seemed to be Holly's current preoccupation.

'Thanks, Enya. It's a collab with an American guy called Columbus. He's super-talented and makes dog collars, pup jackets, cat clothes and stuff, but we think there's crossover – his demographic is, you know, cutesy, home-loving, slightly vintage, the DINK market.'

Entirely unsure of how to respond to the words that she recognised, but which made little sense to her, Enya smiled widely. 'Right. Good.'

She watched Holly make her way into the kitchen. Pickle immediately perked up and gave an elongated stretch, arching her back in a way that looked blissful, before hopping down to slink around the girl's legs.

'Hey, little Picks!' Holly dropped to the floor and patted her outstretched legs. Without the slightest hesitation, Pickle settled on to Holly's lap and closed her eyes as she was treated to back rubs, tummy tickles, paw holds and even kisses to the top of her pretty head.

'Did you finish the bedroom?' She placed the tray of blondies on the countertop and filled the kettle.

'Nearly! It looks fab, I'm just waiting for the knobs off the chest of drawers to dry, I've covered them in pages from old books and clear glue. The actual drawers I've painted in a tea colour, but with the edges distressed, and the knobs will just finish it off. The whole room has like a vintage ship's library vibe! I recorded a time-lapse video of the restoration, got loads of likes.'

Vintage was obviously the word of the day.

'Well, that sounds . . .' Enya tried to find the words that wouldn't dull the light of enthusiasm in Holly's eyes, while trying to disguise her own bewilderment as to why you might want to sleep in a vintage ship's library. If Enya had the time or inclination to decorate her own room, she'd do it in the style of a very comfortable bedroom, with the emphasis on extreme cosiness, but what did she know? Her taste was a little more eclectic. She bought things she liked rather than considering how it might affect the whole. Jonathan, she remembered, had reached for his sunglasses when she'd placed the bright, bird-embroidered cushions on the raspberry-coloured sofa. It was also more than simply not having the time or inclination to improve the house since Jonathan had died, but rather that she wanted to leave things just as they were. This so she could better picture him in their bed, on their sofa, standing right here, leaning against the countertop with his legs crossed at the ankle, waiting for the kettle to boil. She smiled at him, as Holly fussed over Pickle and the cat purred obligingly. 'It sounds very *you*, Holly!'

'I hope Aiden likes it. Mind you, if he doesn't, I can change it, a chance to make some content showing that you don't have to get it right first time.'

'Good point, yes!' She had no idea what she was enthusing over.

'I've missed him so much! Can't wait to see him!' Holly tensed her arms and legs and beat her feet on the floor with delight. She was giddier than usual, if that were possible. Pickle jumped off.

'Well, only a couple of hours or so and he'll have landed. I think even you can wait that long!' She grabbed the mugs from the wooden mug tree, feeling the unwelcome flicker of irritation at the girl's besotted display. It had been sweet at first, endearing, but sometimes it smacked of neediness.

'Only just, Enya. I hate being apart from him.'

'I know.' She smothered the unfavourable thoughts that it might be healthier if Holly were not so dependent; what right did she have to judge how they loved? 'Your mum's coming over later.'

'Yeah, she said. Just think, Enya, in a few months you'll be as boring as her, filling your time with flowers for weddings and funerals!' Holly teased. 'Although I can't imagine you two getting much done, you'll be too busy laughing and skiving off for cups of tea. The business will go bust, but at least you guys will have a good time watching it sink!'

'Ha! Your mum has it all very much under control. I'm going to be her apprentice, it'll take me a while to learn the ropes, but I can't wait.' She felt lifted at the prospect of the challenge ahead, knowing that Jonathan would be delighted that she was using some of the money he'd left to part-own her own business.

'Talking of weddings, d'you remember a while back I said I wanted a basket of sweet peas to carry up the aisle?'

'I do indeed.' It was also a little concerning that Holly had almost planned her entire wedding, despite the fact she and Aiden were not engaged and there had been no mention, as far as Enya was aware, of any impending nuptials.

'Well, I've changed my mind. I'm going to go for lavender with the odd blue thistle and gypsophila, lovely blues to contrast with Aiden's open-necked, natural linen shirt, what do you think?'

'Oh.' What did she think? *That to give so much thought to an event that wasn't even on the horizon was a bit previous.* 'I think whatever you choose, for whenever that is necessary, will all be perfect, because that's your thing, Holly – making everything look wonderful, inviting. You've certainly got the knack.'

'I need every little detail to be absolutely on point. I want people to take loads of photographs and when they go to work or the pub, to show everyone the pictures and say it was the best wedding they've *ever* been to.'

Pickle turned her head to stare at Holly, before wandering out into the garden. It was the first time Enya had ever stared at the little creature who sauntered off into the sunshine and envied her, wishing she could crawl across the floor and slip into the garden, off in search of peace and quiet, to feel the sun on her face, just for a minute.

Holly was now relaxing on the lounger, plugged into her phone and tapping her fingers in time to whatever played in her ear. Enya portioned the prawn cocktail on to beds of shredded lettuce in her mum's old green-glass trifle bowls and popped them into the fridge. The salmon en croute was prepped and Holly had strict instructions about when to shove it in the oven. The ice bucket, awaiting the rosé from the fridge, sat next to three wine glasses. She hated the lack of symmetry of the three glasses and placed a fourth on the countertop to make a square to help ease her mental itch and to make it seem, just for a second, that Jonathan might be joining them.

'Not that you'd thank me for rosé, more of a lager man, aren't you, love.' She smiled. 'Right, Holly!' she called out. 'I'm off! Back in a bit, don't forget to put the salmon in!'

'I won't!' Holly waved and settled back on to the lounger with a look of pure contentment. 'Tell Aiden to hurry back to me, I'm so excited!'

'Yep.'

'And tell him I would have loved to come and meet him, but this Insta Live with Columbus feels like a real opportunity to increase my following!'

'Sure!' Enya knew she'd do no such thing, as she had barely understood what the girl was saying.

The roads were kind, traffic lights in her favour, and she pulled into the car park a tad before six, thinking inevitably about HCK. Pulling down the sun visor, she checked her reflection in the mirror, noting the glow in her cheeks entirely in keeping with the flush of desire that had quite taken her by surprise some three weeks ago now. He really had been the most handsome man, Dominic. There was something about him, his face, voice and manner, that had stirred long-dormant feelings inside her. It felt both thrilling and disloyal to recall it, still with echoes of her own foolishness ringing in her brain.

It was an encounter that had unsettled her, to say the least. The car was booked in to the local garage to be repaired. She had decided after all to go via her insurance company, meaning she could avoid further contact with the married charmer who had won her over with such ease, and had left her punctured with holes of shame from which disappointment in her actions leaked. How could she have considered such a thing? A married man! The thought alone enough to make her shudder. And did he think she was stupid? He'd taken a lease on a flat that *very* day . . . yeah, right.

More than that, she loved Jonathan, missed Jonathan, and was without the heart space or mental capacity to consider anything else, and that was all there was to it.

A text came through from Holly.

SAMON ON CROOT IN. ALL GOOD X

'All good except your spelling, command of French, and knowledge of cuisine,' she whispered a little meanly, knowing

Angela would find that hilarious and dismissing her brief desire to show the message to Maeve next door. I mean, yes, it was all well and good being able to weave a bike in and out of traffic cones, but did it really make you gifted?

Drawn by a shape in her peripheral vision that was familiar, her heart lifted at the sight of her boy. Call it mother's intuition or just an above-average level of insight into the human condition, but he didn't look to be in any hurry to jump into her little Audi. The one with the ugly dent of a Mercedes grille on the passenger door. His demeanour not that of someone who had been away from home for three weeks and was happy to be back. Not that she was counting. Her heart flipped at the prospect that something might be wrong. Was he ill? He didn't look ill, but Jonathan hadn't looked ill either, until he did.

Oh God!

She watched, heart racing, as he stood under the covered walkway and stared into the middle distance, before running his hand over his face in the way someone did when they were either exhausted or trying to find an expression to go and face a situation.

'What do you think?' she whispered. 'Probably just very tired. Do you remember when he got back from cub camp and was too shattered to get out of the car, you had to scoop him up, lift him over your shoulder and cart him up the stairs, dumping him straight into bed in his little uniform, woggle an' all. He had muddy knees, a dry flannel, and a pristine bar of soap, after a week away. Said it was the best time of his life! Honestly, Jonathan, that feels like five minutes ago.'

She waved at her son, who narrowed his gaze in her direction then instantly straightened his shoulders and waved back.

He climbed into the passenger seat and closed his eyes, so distracted he didn't notice the ugly dent in their shared vehicle.

'That's better.' He breathed slowly through his nose.

'I know, air conditioning! Isn't it a marvel?'

She took in his profile, a little surprised as ever that the man with the two-day stubble, deep voice and hairy hands was her child. It was almost as if any time away erased years so effectively that she actually half expected him to be returning from cub camp with his unused flannel and unfeasibly dirty knees.

'Yep. Crap for the planet but lovely on a long drive, which is also bad for the planet, at the end of a flight, which . . .' He shook his head.

'You're right, of course, but if we look at our carbon footprint as a family, the fact that I don't go anywhere and haven't flown for yonks and don't plan on doing so any time soon, surely we are better than most?'

'Not quite sure it works like that.' He smiled at her. 'Hi, Mum.'

'Hello, love. Welcome home.' The dark bruises of fatigue beneath his eyes confirmation that her boy needed sleep. 'Good trip?'

He was always full of enthusiasm when it came to his career. Continually learning where and how the robotic surgery that was his specialism might improve the lives of people all over the planet, the planet that the air conditioning was right now damaging. The three-week programme in Rome was to understand the delicate nature of knee surgery that could, with a skilled practitioner, be directed hundreds of miles away from the patient via computer if the tech was used correctly. It had blown her mind to think of it. And not that she'd said it, but she wasn't sure she liked the idea of having her knee or any other part of her body operated on by a surgeon who could, for all she knew, be living it up on holiday, knocking back strawberry daiquiris and then swapping her bikini and sarong for scrubs to laser open a human. Enya had shivered at the thought. Progress or not, she wanted, should the need ever arise, to be able to look her surgeon in the eye.

'Erm . . .' He turned to look out of his window, and she felt the weight of the uncharacteristic silence.

'What's wrong, love?'

'Just give me a moment.' He turned down the whirring air con a couple of notches and instantly she lamented the loss of cold air on her menopausal face.

'You're scaring me!' She failed spectacularly to meet his request, as Jonathan's voice down the phone came to mind.

'. . . *just give me a moment . . . not sure how to say this, Enya B . . . I love you . . . you know that . . . but I've just seen Dr Birch . . . it's not good news, love . . .*'

'I want to get married.' He turned to her now, and a smile split his face in two, magically erasing all signs of fatigue as his features leapt to life. 'That's it!' He threw his palms in the air and let them fall into his lap as he exhaled. 'I want to get married, Mum. No, *more* than that, I *am* getting married!'

'My goodness, Aiden! You had me worried for a minute!' She placed her hand on her chest, where her heart did the rumba. 'That's wonderful! Absolutely wonderful! Oh my!' She laughed her relief into the confined space. 'As long as you're sure, and I only say that as your mum and not in any way trying to interfere, this is your life, your choices. But you need to be certain.'

It was probably a foolish thing to say he and Holly had grown up together; a couple since they were seventeen. She didn't want to meddle but was painfully aware that they still had a lot of growing up to do and that the dynamics of their relationship seemed a little out of balance. An image came to mind of Jonathan coming home to their little house as newlyweds when she'd served rice that had congealed into a solid lump. He had carved them both a chunk and eaten it with relish. It had been an in-joke ever since. '*One slice or two?*' they'd ask whenever they ate rice.

And she had learned, and they had grown together, figuring out as they went along; maybe it would be the same for Holly and Aiden. They had, after all, weathered him going off to university and her year at the local college, and had in the last couple of years built a beautiful home together in a flat on the other side of town with a view of the river. A home that now boasted a vintage ship's library in which they would sleep, one with knobs on the dresser covered in old books. She still didn't get it. Not that anyone would be discussing the décor of their flat once the date was set and the wheels were put in motion.

'I am.' He locked eyes with her. 'I've never been surer of anything in my whole life!'

'Oh love, I am so happy for you, and I know your dad would be too.' She pictured her planned evening with Jenny; they now had something to truly celebrate! Her gut gripped with excitement. 'But neither of us could match how happy a certain young lady is going to be. In fact, I suspect if you look under your bed, you might find pre-made wedding favours and several shades of toile from which she will make the bridesmai—'

'Mum.' He interrupted her with a slight shake of his head, and again the colour seemed to drain from his face, his wide-cheeked elation giving way to a rather grey pallor of sickness.

And she knew.

Before he said aloud the words that would cleave open Holly Hudson's heart, make a declaration that would drive an ice pick into the harmony of life in Mablethorpe Road, would mean strained conversations on bin day, put her business plans in jeopardy and scatter shards of glass on the floor of her friendship, she knew. Words that meant their lives would never be the same again because they lived in a connected bubble; a deck of cards that had stood proud for the longest time, and one that she was sure, in that moment, was about to tumble.

Her stomach rolled with nausea at the very prospect. She gripped the steering wheel, anything to try and steady her shaky hands.

Chapter Nine

'Oh God!' Her son exhaled and hid his face in his hands briefly.

'It's okay, Aiden, take your time. We can sit here for a bit. No need to rush.' Enya spoke slowly and softly, even though her mind screamed for him to get to the point and end the agony of her imaginings.

He nodded and gasped, as if it were difficult to get air into his lungs.

'I'm not sure how to feel or what to say,' he began. 'I'm really tired. So tired. Exhausted, in fact.'

Enya nodded, knowing there were no prompts to help him with this. He needed to find clarity and express what it was that occupied his thoughts. Her son took one deep, long breath and gave the words free rein.

'I met someone.'

'You met someone,' she repeated quietly, waiting for more, needing to hear him say it, to give her the details, as she tried and failed to mentally pave the fast-paced route from meeting someone to wanting to get married in such a short space of time.

'We were on the same plane. She was heading out to Rome to work for a fortnight but then took a few days' holiday so we could be together. She had to leave yesterday and the moment she went, I felt lost. I hated being there without her. She's . . .' He pursed his lips and blinked away the obvious emotion that rose at no more than the mere mention of her. 'Her name is Iris Sutherland, and she's' – he swallowed – 'she's like . . . she's everything.'

This was one of those times, and there had of course been others over the last three years, when she wished Jonathan were here to tag-team their response. It was a well-practised method, one with a hand on the tiller while the other acted as lookout, helping them navigate choppy waters as and when they encountered them.

'But . . . but . . . you can only have known her a maximum of three weeks, it doesn't sound like you, love. You're not spontaneous, you're considered, thoughtful, you don't make snap decisions, you never have. We sit for what feels like hours in a restaurant while you mentally tussle with whether you want the steak or the chicken! You take your time over things!'

'Until now,' he countered, 'and I know it sounds nuts, Mum, but after seeing her, *talking* to her for no more than an hour, if she had said, *Pack up, we're off to go and live in deepest, darkest Borneo*, I'd have gone. I'd have trusted the feeling in my gut, handed my life over to fate, and I'd have gone.' He shook his head as if it were a fact that he too was still trying to come to terms with. 'I mean, I'd probably have had to google where Borneo was first, but . . .' He smiled weakly then, as if aware, as was she, that his choice came with consequences and heartache that rather robbed the news of its glitter.

His words and intentions were utterly terrifying. Her son was declaring that he would run away with a complete stranger! He would willingly throw away the lovely life he had constructed, *they* had constructed, for what? Her second thought was for Holly, the girl who adored him, who had always adored him, Jenny's daughter. Enya felt the seeds of discord take root in her gut, aware that this was going to be one hell of a bloody upheaval for them all. She did her best to smother the flames of anger that flickered inside her, knowing they were as unattractive as they were unfair, but what the bloody hell had he done?

'Wow, I've never . . .' She didn't know if it was insensitive or helpful to admit that she had never felt that way. She had loved Jonathan, loved him still, of that there was no doubt. But that instant gut-pull of attraction that was strong enough for him to flirt with the idea of *destiny*, and the intervention of the universe? No, nothing like that. It was a concept that she believed to be utter rubbish. Bunkum. Something that only happened in movies and poems. It wasn't real. It couldn't be real! An image of Dominic, the grey-haired car klutz, floated momentarily into her thoughts. 'And you went from feeling like that to wanting to get married in *three* weeks?'

It was as close as she could get to screaming *ARE YOU ABSOLUTELY MAD?* Knowing that kind of reaction would help no one.

'Actually no, I pretty much felt like that after three days, less maybe, hours even! But as I said, it's not just that I want to get married, we *are* getting married. I spoke to her dad on the phone, bought a ring, and we've . . . we've set a date . . .'

'Oh my God, Aiden!' She closed her eyes and let her head drop. It was worse than she had thought, not just a possibility, but they'd set a date? Bought a bloody *ring*?

At this admission of all the things he had failed to do for Holly in the last decade, she felt truly sick. This was no flash in the pan, not a mere possibility, but was instead a crisis or, more fairly, a *situation* to be dealt with.

'I don't know what to say, love. I'm . . . I'm pleased for you, I guess.'

'Wow, Mum! Go steady with that enthusiasm!'

He huffed, sat back in the seat and her heart sank, wanting so badly to be the person who cheered him on, who championed him, but this was lunacy.

'I want to support you. I want you to be happy, I want that more than anything, but I'm also worried about how everyone will take the news.' She pictured having to tell Jenny and Phil and her throat constricted. 'And of course I'm a little heartbroken for Holly, more than a little.'

The thought of the girl sitting at home, so very excited for his return, did nothing to help ease her angst.

'I know, and it's not something I'm doing lightly. Obviously, I didn't want to tell her over the phone, it's been awful, texting her, telling her I was busy, making excuses.' He sighed and rubbed his eyes, and she could see that the deceit had not sat easily on his shoulders. Yet it angered her still; lying by omission had never sat well with her. 'But life's short, Mum. I think it's time we stopped worrying about how everyone else thinks and feels, and started doing what's right for us.'

It was her turn to stare at him, unsure exactly what he meant by this, but knowing she had to tread carefully. 'Aren't you worried that maybe what you feel is a reaction to the novelty of being with someone else?'

'No, definitely not.' He was adamant.

'You say that, but things can get, I don't know, a bit stale when you've been with someone for a long time, and maybe what you feel for, the girl, erm . . .'

'Iris.'

'Yep, sorry, Iris.' It felt bizarre, talking about her only child's *fiancée*, a young woman she would not have been able to pick out in a line-up and who she knew nothing about. Apart from the fact she too had spent time in Italy, and who at that very moment was walking around with an engagement ring on the third finger of her left hand that Aiden had given to her with a promise. A girl who had a date set for her forthcoming marriage and was probably already thinking about frocks and flowers for her big day. Enya felt the beginnings of a headache. This was a lot. 'Maybe, maybe what you feel for her is so powerful because it's new and exciting and a novelty, and it's probably a lot about sex, new sex, different sex.'

'God, Mum!' He pulled a face and turned his head to look out of the window.

'You know what I mean!' She didn't want to be talking to him about sex any more than he wanted to hear her talking about it, but it felt important for him to consider all angles and not jump into something he just might live to regret. A choice that could cause a bow wave that had the power to drown them all. 'I'm trying to say and do the right thing here. It's like walking a tightrope between encouraging you to live your best life and not wanting you to make a terrible mistake.'

'Dad always used to say the best way to learn was to make a mistake.' He looked right at her now.

'Yes! He meant by putting the wrong fuel in the lawnmower, losing your wallet, missing a flight, getting on the wrong train, failing your cycling proficiency – not going on a course for three weeks and coming back with a whole other life plan, with a date set for a wedding to a complete stranger you met on a bloody plane!' Momentarily she forgot to hide her concern and instantly regretted it.

'I knew you'd be like this!'

'Like what?' She did her best to hide her indignancy.

'Like . . . hoovering up my joy.'

'What a lovely thing to say to me,' she snorted. 'I am your flag bearer, your advocate and I always have been, and to say that is just, bloody horrible!' His words hurt; the thought that he might mean it hurt more.

They were silent for a breath.

'I'm sorry,' he whispered. 'I'm just so sad to be away from her, saying goodbye was horrible. And I know it sounds weird, but even though I'm here in this car, I'm still wherever she is, mentally. I'm still with her, does that make any sense?'

She looked into the rear-view mirror, where she could see Jonathan staring back at her. He looked less than impressed. She wondered if it was because she had allowed Dominic to creep back into her thoughts or because she seemed to be spectacularly messing up this pivotal conversation with their son.

'Not really. But no matter how sad you are, you can't take it out on me, because that's not fair.' She spoke frankly.

'I know. I *am* sorry.'

'That's okay.' She looked right at him, thinking how only three weeks ago she had longed to have his attention, a vital conversation like this, to feel needed, engaged, valued. What was it they said? Be careful what you wish for.

'We've hardly slept.'

She discreetly pulled a face, wondering if this was how he felt when *she* had mentioned sex. 'Well, I don't need the details.'

This not least because she loved Holly, loved Jenny and this whole topic felt disloyal. Her gut folded at the thought of her best friend, wondering again how on earth she would handle the news? Aiden, she felt sure, would make the hate list, probably knocking Poirot off the top slot, but they'd find a way through, they always did.

'How do I cope without him, Jen?' she had bawled after Jonathan's funeral.

'You'll cope because we are next door but one, here for whatever you need, whenever you need it . . .'

Aiden tutted, drawing her back into the moment. 'God, not that! Although yes that, but we just can't stop talking. About everything! I want to know what she's thinking. I love her opinions, her views, and we knew we had to sleep, but there was always something important to say, we didn't want to waste a minute of being together sleeping, so we'd sit up all night, watching the sun set and rise on the city. I won't ever forget a minute of it, not ever. We want to go back to Rome and take our kids when they come along.'

Enya twisted her body to fully face her boy, trying to accept that he was talking about forever, and kids! This from the man who had stated with confidence that babies were not on the agenda for a good while yet.

It was rare that she couldn't find the words.

'You're going to love her, Mum.' And there it was again, that beaming smile, like flicking a switch. 'She's beautiful, and smart and funny and it's like she's mine, like she was always mine and I was hers and we just didn't know it. But now we do and there's no way we want to waste a minute longer than we have to being apart.'

Poor Holly! She managed to swallow the thought and not let it leap from her tongue, knowing it might be incendiary in the midst of his admission of love.

'You said you spoke to her dad?' Enya carried the vague hope that the girl's family might be similarly concerned and would encourage the couple to slow things down. Maybe hoping, like her, that it would fizzle enough for them to see reason, to not jump in too hastily, but to give things time, to understand that this heightened feeling would not last, probably just an infatuation, an attraction, but certainly nothing with a foundation that would last a lifetime, because what the bloody hell could you learn about someone in just *three weeks*?

'Yes, her family seem lovely, *so* lovely! They're really excited.'
Damn.

'She's close to her cousins, who are in Australia, and I haven't met them yet obviously. Her nan is still alive and a right old character, won't leave her flat in Brighton, thinks it's dangerous to travel further than Horsham, they all sound wonderful. Her dad runs his own company. Her mum is Trish, she's already made me feel so welcome, just with texts and whatnot. They live in a little village on the outskirts of Bath with a view right over the city, it looks beautiful, I've seen pictures. They're all really excited.'

Outskirts of Bath, an hour away at most.

It was hard to control the misplaced surge of jealousy at the fact that the Sutherland family seemed to be well up on proceedings, and had probably celebrated the engagement of which she was unaware while she was cleaning out Pickle's litter tray, listening to Holly's plans for her bedroom décor, and fretting over her son's welcome-home dinner.

'We're getting married at their house in the garden, there's a side area with fruit trees and an incredible view. We're going to have a marquee, it's always been Iris's dream.'

'It all sounds amazing,' Enya smiled, more conscious now than ever of hoovering up his joy and hiding her feeling of despair at his news. News that would no doubt damage Holly and upset her best friend. 'So, when is the big day, what date have you set?'

'August the eighteenth. One month yesterday, four weeks!'

What the flippin' Aida!

Enya placed her hand over her mouth to stop herself from saying anything at all. *Four weeks!* She let the fact settle, already thinking about travel arrangements, frocks, and who would look after Madam Pickle Paws if they were away overnight? Immediately, she thought of asking Holly to look after her, and Jenny to do the flowers of course, before dismissing these thoughts as quickly as they had risen in her mind. Her pulse raced as the repercussions of her son's news, his change of heart, started to crystallise. It felt horrible, knowing she would be front and centre of this chasm, when she had done nothing to cause it and couldn't avoid it.

She and Jenny had always joked about wearing matching hats as mothers of the bride and groom. She now tried to imagine sitting alone among the fruit trees in the garden of a family who she didn't know, strangers, while Aiden married a girl who could have been anyone, a girl Jonathan had never met.

Enya started the engine, aware that the short-stay window was closing.

'Well, say something!' Aiden urged. 'What are you thinking?'

'I was wondering what your dad would say.' She spoke the truth.

'I think he'd say if you really love her then go for it, don't you?' He stared at her with such hope in his eyes that it was almost painful to witness.

'I guess he would, love.' She managed a thin, watery smile. 'What do you want to do now? Would you like me to find somewhere else to park, or shall I head home?'

He closed his eyes briefly and sighed, as he leaned forward in the seat.

'Let's head home. Is Holly there?' He swallowed.

She nodded.

'Okay. I've got to do this, and it's better for us all if I do it sooner rather than later.'

'Yep.' She smiled at him, doing her best to keep one hand steady on the tiller, while keeping lookout, and burying the crest of fear in her gut, as she pulled out of the car park.

Chapter Ten

Aiden, unsurprisingly, grew jumpier the closer they got to home. Shifting in his seat, he coughed to clear his throat and rubbed his hands on his trousers as he exhaled from cheeks filled with air. His nerves were a little contagious and as Enya parked in Mablethorpe Road, she felt anxiety flutter in her veins.

'Holly's probably in the back garden. I've cooked supper. But we don't have to eat, of course not, whatever you think best.'

She ran her hand over her forehead, feeling ridiculously concerned over the salmon that wouldn't keep. Not that it mattered, any of it, not in the face of the sledgehammer that was about to come down on them all. She stared at Jenny's front door, doubting they'd feel like dancing to ABBA and eating tiramisu once the news was out. Her lovely friend. How she wished, *wished* this was not about to be brought to her door.

'Right.'

He stared at the house, swallowing hard. She could only imagine the level of dread he was experiencing, knowing the daunting task that lay ahead. It wasn't as if he could take his time over it either, not with only four weeks to go until his wedding. A fact that still sounded like a bad joke, her sympathy for him a little curtailed when she remembered it, in recognition that it was a mess of his own making. There was also the smallest possibility that he might see Holly and change his mind. It would be fickle of him, yes, hard for her to navigate, yet still preferable.

It was Holly's squeal that focused her attention. Enya felt her stomach drop to her boots.

The young woman ran out of the front door and yanked at the door handle of the car. Aiden climbed out and caught his ~~girlfriend~~ ex-girlfriend, as she launched herself at him and wrapped her legs around him. 'I missed you! I missed you so much!'

Enya looked down the street, then at the dashboard, anywhere other than at the young couple, as Holly covered Aiden's face with kisses and held him tight.

She turned at the sound of a beeping horn. Phil – Holly's dad, Jonathan's old golfing partner and her next-door neighbour but one – sat in his car, beaming at the reunion.

'Put her down, son! You don't know where she's been! Welcome home, mate! Looking forward to a bit of "Dancing Queen" later, Ens?' He now addressed her directly and she lifted her hand in a limp-wristed wave of acknowledgement.

Phil yelled, Holly laughed, and Aiden stared at the man as Holly climbed down, holding his arm, beaming as if she'd won something glorious.

'He's home!' Holly shouted, jumping up and down on the spot.

'I can see that!' Phil tutted, eyes smiling, before he parked further along the road. Enya felt her insides shrink and sank down into the driver's seat.

She wondered if this was what it would feel like from now on in the street that was her haven; this discomfort that verged on excruciating. She wiped her face and tucked her hair behind her ears. Her heart broke for Holly, whose only crime was loving Aiden a little too much. Yet it was also full of worry for Aiden, who she could see was about to jump, trusting of the fall. It was a moment, among many others, when she wished with her whole heart that Jonathan was here to help navigate what lay ahead.

As Phil made his way along the pavement, arriving to slap Aiden on the back and receive a kiss from his daughter, Enya took the opportunity to creep from the car, smile her greeting as best she could, and slip inside her house. She actively avoided the man who would regularly pop in for a cup of tea, a sandwich or toast, seemingly always hungry. It might have been cowardly, but she felt quite unable to witness the affection Phil displayed towards her son, equally did not under any circumstances want to be around for the conversation Aiden was set to have with Holly. And crucially, she couldn't stand the deceit of perpetuating a grand reunion complete with freshly baked blondies and excited details shared of a redecorated bedroom. It felt much easier to hide in the kitchen. She put the radio on, hoping the chatter of Radio 4 might be enough to divert her from the fact that she thought she might throw up.

'I honestly don't know what to think, Jonathan, don't know what to make of it all!' She breathed deeply. 'God only knows how Jenny and Phil are going to react. What do I say to them?'

She ran her fingers through her hair at the prospect, but knew that it was really nothing to do with her or them; it was all about Aiden and Holly and how Holly was going to react to Aiden and Iris. It sounded alien in her thoughts. *Iris, and Aiden . . . Aiden and Iris . . .* nope. It was going to take some getting used to.

It became clear after ten minutes that the duo was not coming back into the house, a fact for which she felt nothing but sweet relief. Then the sound of a car engine. Sidling into the sitting room, she peeped out of the sash window, beneath her bespoke Roman blinds in grass-green and raspberry stripes, just in time to see her son in her little Audi perfect a three-point turn and drive out of the cul-de-sac. Phil was nowhere to be seen. Holly was in the passenger seat, but she couldn't see their faces. Had Aiden told her already?

Or had he indeed taken one look at the gorgeous girl and changed his mind? And then what would Enya do with the knowledge? What would Mr and Mrs *Sutherland* do?

It was bizarre and confusing how utterly complicated the whole situation felt in such a short space of time, and to think she'd spent the day fretting over supper and keeping the kitchen floor spotless.

'Sweet Jesus! What a day!' She decided to break with convention and poured herself a glass of the chilled rosé. Never one to drink alone, but if ever an occasion called for it . . .

Standing in the kitchen, she watched the sun set behind the old red-brick wall at the foot of the garden, noting how the bright-blue sky dropped a shade or two to take on an almost lavender haze, and the trees, as if startled by the change in temperature, shivered in the early evening breeze. Her stomach felt as if it were shredded. There was certainly no temptation to dive into the salmon en croute that now sat congealing on top of the range, or indeed the prawn cocktail that she had so fussed over.

With her phone in her hand, Enya tried to compose a text to Jenny, but was paralysed by doubt. To reveal the news if her friend was as yet unaware would be awful. To inform her unnecessarily, if Aiden *had* changed his mind, worse; how would she ever explain that? But worse still, the prospect of not mentioning it at all, making some quip about their planned night ahead, as if nothing was amiss, if Jenny *did* know. It was a minefield. Placing her phone on the countertop, she decided it was better to wait it out.

She took deep breaths, trying to quash the rising sense of panic, drank the cold rosé and cleaned the sink, fed Pickle, stacked the dishwasher, folded laundry into drawers, and in need of further distraction, revisited the mini crossword that she and Jonathan liked to finish as they ate supper. Her heart constantly jumped as she imagined Holly's face, as Aiden broke her heart.

'Five down, twelve letters, *unable to alleviate, often sadness,*' she read the clue aloud and studied the letters she already had. 'I, something, something O, something, something O . . .' She tapped the puzzle with the tip of her retractable pencil, her mind, much like the little squares she so desperately wanted to fill, blank.

The front doorbell rang. Had Aiden forgotten his key? But it was not Aiden on the step. It was Phil, and this time there was no air of joviality, no jolly humour or laughter, no quip about tiramisu. No hungry man in search of a snack. His eyes were small, lips thin, his face scarlet, he looked angry. It was everything she had feared and more.

'Where is he?' This his greeting, his jaw tense as he rocked on his heels, his shoulder twitching, hands balled into fists.

Her heart jumped now for different reasons, she was scared. 'I don't . . .'

'Don't give me that, where is he, Enya?' Uninvited, he stepped into the hallway and called loudly up the stairs, 'You can run, you little prick, but you can't hide!'

'Phil, for God's sake! I've told you – he's not here!'

His chest heaved and he breathed through his nose; it was frightening to be alone and this close to someone this angry, the man completely unrecognisable as the one she had encountered in the street earlier.

'Do you know what's going on? Have you heard what he's gone and done?'

'I know the outline, the—'

'Course you do!' He narrowed his eyes at her and took a step forward. It was at once accusatory and unpredictable.

'You need to calm down, you can't come into my home and talk to me like this, we're neighbours, Phil, we've been friends for a very long time.'

He ignored her and she felt the ripple of anger dilute the fear in her veins, knowing without doubt that if Jonathan were here, Phil would not dream of talking to her like this or intimidating her with his bulk inside her own home. His behaviour was also an indicator of what Jenny might be feeling, this thought more than she could handle. She felt tears prickle the back of her eyes. Jenny was her best friend, her very best friend. And Phil had been Jonathan's.

'I don't *need* to do anything. I've just had my little girl on the phone and she's,' he looked away and gathered himself, his voice breaking, 'she's distraught, her mother's with her. We can't leave her alone. And I want a word with that son of yours.'

'Phil, I told you, he's not here,' she repeated. 'Look, this is nothing to do with me and nothing to do with you or Jen. It's difficult, of course it is, but—'

'Difficult?' he spat. 'You should hear her, you should *see* her.' His bottom lip trembled.

'I can't stand to think of her so upset.' She meant it, *little Holly Hudson* . . . She fought to contain her own tears.

Phil ran his palm over his face. 'She's broken, Enya. Absolutely broken.'

He seemed to calm a little and she was thankful.

'I could fucking kill him,' he spat through gritted teeth.

'He's my son,' she reminded him. 'Jonathan's son.'

'I know, I know. And that's why we trusted him, why *I* trusted him. She can't sit up, can't speak. She's like a rag doll, limp, and her eyes are closed, and she's, she can hardly breathe.' He let his chin fall to his chest.

'I don't know what to say.' She spoke the truth, understanding his sentiment but first and foremost wanting to advocate for her only child. 'I'm as shocked as you are. I'm trying to remember that they are young and things happen, and I know it's hard but it's far better they go through this now and not when they are forty or fifty, when life will already be kicking them in the face. I don't think he meant for any of this to happen. Aiden's not a bad man, you know this. He's never played the field or treated Holly badly. It sounds like he just met someone and fell for her and that's that.'

Phil lifted his head and stared at her. 'What do you mean, he met someone? He's *met* someone? He said he'd changed his mind, just like that,' he clicked his fingers, 'after all those years, just changed his bloody mind!'

'I . . . I'm not sure, I . . .' It hadn't occurred to her that Aiden might not have told Holly the full story; she had assumed he would probably have given Holly the stark facts in the way he had her.

He raised his index finger and pointed it at her chest. 'You better tell him to keep out of my way, this is not over! This is *not* over!'

Closing the front door behind him, she walked back to the kitchen and half sat, half fell on to a bar stool, the sense of rising panic almost overwhelming.

Her phone rang. It was Aiden.

'Hello, love, where are you?'

'Just, just driving around, Mum.' He barely managed to get the words out, as distress made his speech stutter down the line. 'I told her, I told, told her that it was . . .' He broke away to cry some more.

'It's okay,' she lied, 'it's okay, love, let it all out.'

'I can't . . . she was so . . . I feel terrible.'

'I know, I know.' She closed her eyes and spoke softly. 'Come home. Come home and we can sit and chat. I'll make you a cup of tea.'

'I will, I'm, I'm just going to take a minute and . . . and . . .'

His tears, though hard to hear, were also strangely reassuring. Proof, as if it were needed, that he was aware of the hurt he had caused, acknowledging the betrayal of a wonderful girl like Holly.

His distress indicating that he had indeed been blindsided and not acted with ill intent. Confirmation that they hadn't raised a cold, indifferent rotter who could hurt a girl and feel nothing. He was kind and knew that the human heart was a fragile thing and that to discard one meant breaking it as surely as if he had thrown out glass.

'Just breathe, darling. It will all feel better in the morning. I promise.'

Not that she'd ever admit it, she felt ashamed, almost, that as her panic subsided, a soft glow of warmth replaced it at how much, in that instant, her boy needed her.

'I'll see you later. I need to tell you about Phil, he came over and I might have let slip that you've met someone.'

'I see.' His croaked response was hard to hear.

Enya went in the sitting room and sank down on to the sofa. Here she would await her son's return, while trying to order her own maelstrom of thoughts, and with one ear cocked for the sound of someone walking up the path. She prayed Jenny might come and see her so they could start the slow walk back to peace, to find a way forward. Conversely, she prayed that Phil would stay away, his behaviour had unnerved her. It was horrid to feel this vulnerable, this on edge. Jenny was an important part of her life, her routine; just the thought of not having her at the end of a phone was like a knife in her gut.

'God, Jonathan, what a terrible evening. I can't stand to think of Holly so upset, and Aiden sounded, don't know how to describe it, he sounded . . .'

I.N.C.O.N.S.O.L.A.B.L.E . . . ah, yes, of course he did.

Chapter Eleven

Enya had spent half the night agitated, awake and wishing she could talk to Jenny. With things unsettled between them, it was akin to pulling a loose thread on her life that allowed everything to unravel.

She held her phone and pondered the blank text, wondering what to send to her best friend that could possibly convey the overwhelming sense of panic and loss that whirled in her thoughts at the prospect of their friendship being damaged. The word *sorry* felt a little contrived and smacked of guilt that she was unsure she wanted to convey. *Missing you*, too trite, they'd only spoken yesterday when everything was fine, and any suggestion to meet up might imply that Enya saw her own need as greater than Holly's. She settled on a single red heart, instantly regretting that too – what did it even mean?

The read notification appeared, showing that Jenny had seen the message, but there was no reply. It felt like a punch in the throat.

She stared at her bedroom ceiling, worrying about Holly and picturing Phil, who had been so angry he'd looked quite different to the man she and Jonathan knew and loved. She dreaded seeing him again, knowing it was inevitable.

Aiden had arrived home last night as darkness cloaked the street, no doubt with the intention of slipping under Phil's radar.

'How are you feeling, love?' she'd whispered.

Her son had shrugged and leaned against the wall, unwilling to chat; and with a look of abject sorrow, stumbling with fatigue, he had gone straight to bed. She had then heard him moving around on the landing in the early hours and hoped that he might get some rest this morning.

Enya sat up in the bed, still with her phone in her hand. It was time for her Sunday morning call with her sister.

'So, let me get this straight.' Angela took a breath and Enya could picture her wearing her tropical sarong over her swimming costume, taking the call from the comfort of her sun lounger while Frank bobbed in the communal pool on his lilo. 'He's marrying this girl he's only known five minutes?'

It was typical of Angela to exaggerate.

'Three weeks, he's known her for three weeks, which I know is still very quick, but . . .' She felt the need to justify Aiden's actions, to defend him. Always. Even if she more than understood what Angela was driving at.

'What does she look like?'

'I don't know. Aiden said she's beautiful, but I don't have any more details.'

'And she works?'

'Yes, in marketing, not sure what that means, exactly.'

'Clever then. And did she have a fella that she had to dump?' Angela fired questions with her usual lack of tact.

'I don't know.' It hadn't occurred to Enya to ask.

'And what did Holly say, the poor love?'

'She's heartbroken, as you'd expect. Not that I've seen her.'

She felt the rise of sorrow in her chest at the thought of how Holly would be feeling, picturing her arriving here only yesterday with her tray of blondies and a spring in her step. A lifetime ago.

'And what about Jen? Have you spoken to her? She must be gutted!'

'No, I haven't.' This not an easy admission, cringing over her generic text that her friend had snubbed. 'I don't know what to say or how to say it. I sent a heart emoji.'

'I see.' Angela's lack of reassurance spoke volumes. 'So, is he getting his stuff out of the flat?'

'I suppose so, it's still all very raw and new, but they'll have to discuss the practicalities at some point.' She dreaded the process in advance.

'And Aiden paid the deposit, didn't he? Make sure he gets that back.'

'Honestly, I think that's the last thing on his mind.' She rolled her eyes.

'I suppose we'll have to start booking flights to get Mum and Dad over for the wedding, is it a secret or can I tell them? She'll have to get a hair appointment and find a dress . . .'

'Oh, God!' Enya honestly couldn't stand the thought of it all.

'Well, you can't spring it on them, they're old! You can't spring it on any of us, come to think of it, we have lives and things like this take a bit of organising. Unless it's going to be one of those awful dos where they nip up the registry office and we all shove fifty quid behind the bar of a grotty pub with a sticky carpet.'

'It's been sprung on me too, Angela! Don't forget I only found out yesterday, so don't start blaming me for any lack of notice, I have a life too!'

'You do?'

Enya heard the teasing in her sister's tone but wasn't in the mood for any discussion about her Arctic fox life today.

'It's a lot to get my head around. And I have no idea what kind of wedding,' she pinched the bridge of her nose, 'but Aiden said they would probably do it in her parents' garden among the fruit trees.'

'Oh, God no! That'll mean wasps.' Her sister sighed. 'Frank's allergic.'

'You can't have it both ways. You can either have your registry office affair with the sticky carpet to follow, or wasps, take your pick!' She hadn't meant to raise her voice.

'All right, no need to take it out on me!'

Angela was right, of course. Enya took a deep breath.

'It's all bloody awful! I'm trying to be happy for Aiden, of course I am, but I can't imagine what Holly is going through and Jen's ignoring me, I think. It's . . . bloody awful!' She could think of nothing more apt to describe the situation.

'Don't get your knickers in a twist, it's all going to happen or not and you getting wound up won't help or change a thing.'

Enya bit her lip, deciding not to point out that it was her sister's line of questioning and less than positive reaction that had caused her knickers to twist in the first place.

'Anyway, we'll be back on Tuesday, and we can discuss it all properly then. Right, got to go, I said I'd help Mum whitewash her veranda. Don't worry, I'll give Jen a ring.'

The fact that her sister and best friend were going to be in contact filled Enya with a sense of exclusion that felt like a stab in her chest, picturing the two women chatting, talking about her and Aiden and the whole sorry state of affairs, no doubt. It bothered her.

She didn't have an extensive network of friends, instead she was part of this close-knit trio, and to be on the outside was painful. Her old friend anxiety pawed at her, and she took a deep breath. 'Okay, say hi to everyone for me.'

'I will. Love you.' Angela ended their call in the way that was customary.

'Love you.' Enya looked up to see Aiden standing in the doorway, no time to give in to the panic that threatened her. 'Hello, love, how did you sleep?'

'Do you really think it's all bloody awful?' he asked with such desolation that she felt like the very worst parent in the world.

'I . . . I do a bit, yes.' She watched him walk into the bedroom and collapse on the end of her bed. 'Not the fact that you've fallen for Iris, although I admit, I don't understand it, Aiden.'

'You doubt how we feel about each other?' He looked crestfallen.

'Yes,' she levelled, 'not because you're being deceitful, but because I think it's more likely infatuation that can't help but wane. And I don't want you to get hurt or to hurt anyone, any more than you have to, and getting married quickly feels a little . . .' *Foolish* was the word she wanted to say. 'Risky.' Felt safer.

'It's real. I love her.'

'How can you know?' she asked softly.

'How can any of us ever know? Who can be one hundred per cent certain?' he countered.

'You can't, love, and that's why going gently is advisable.'

'Holly and I were going gently, and I wasn't happy. Well, I thought I was, but what Iris and I have is off the charts!' His tone was almost imploring.

'I guess I wanted you and Holly to go the distance because you would know each other inside and out, like it was for me and your dad. That shared history. Together for so long, so in love that we almost knew what the other was thinking. So in tune that we knew how to handle any situation just by looking at the other one. In sync. One team.'

The fact that she and Jonathan had gone the distance felt like a badge of honour, an achievement, and for her son to be throwing in the towel before he and Holly had even made it out of their twenties felt a lot like giving up on something solid for something new and shiny. She just didn't want him to make a mistake, although he was right, of course, there were never any guarantees.

'Iris and I are in sync.'

Enya could see this was an argument that she was in no position to win because her son was in no mood to listen.

'Yep.' She nodded.

'You don't believe me, that's why you said to Auntie Angela that you thought it was bloody awful.'

'I did say that, because Holly is hurt and it's your fault, your actions that have hurt her. You've cheated on her and that's, it's a lot.'

His head hung forward, in the way that it did whenever he was being admonished, reminding her so powerfully of him as a little boy that it was hard to continue.

'I also think that it feels like a pressure, this super-fast wedding, having to organise something that quickly. And, yes, risky.' She figured that if they were addressing the elephant in the room then she may as well discuss the entire herd. 'I can't imagine how Holly will feel when she finds out, and I just don't think three weeks is long enough to get to know someone, to have them figured out. Three weeks in a beautiful place like Italy, enjoying the sunrises and sunsets of Rome, is not real life. It's a holiday. To truly know if you want to spend the rest of your life with someone, you need to spend a wet weekend with them walking around Woolworths. You need to bicker, run out of money and steam, you need to nurse them when they've a cold and be disgusted by how they dunk biscuits in tea until they're mush and then eat them.' She looked across to the window where Jonathan now stood, smiling in recognition of his very unattractive habit. 'You should be with them long enough to feel exasperated by them, but also to build a connection that is strong, unshakeable, and I don't honestly think you can do that in three weeks.'

Her son took his time in responding. She worried she had gone too far, fearing him packing a bag and leaving her alone almost as much as she did the prospect of this rather rushed match.

'If you think this is easy for me, Mum, you're wrong. I'll never forget Holly's face when I told her that we were over. And I don't expect you to understand, I don't even need you to give us your approval, although I'd like it, we both would. But love doesn't need approval or permission, it just arrives, and we all have to make space for it. We *are* going to get married on August the eighteenth and we are going to be happy. I will spend my whole life doing my very best to make her happy. Or I'll die trying. It really is that simple.'

Enya felt his verbal elbowing, pushing her off the throne on which she had sat for most of his life, even when he was with Holly. He spoke resolutely and his meaning was clear: he had picked her, picked Iris Sutherland, who he had only known for three weeks, because he loved her, loved her so much he would die trying to make her happy. And for the first time since he had made mention of his plans and this new woman in his life, she felt a conflicting surge of optimism, knowing if they were going to succeed as a couple it was exactly this kind of grit, determination and strength of feeling that was key to making a marriage work.

'Well, all right then.' She sat up straight. 'I will try, Aiden. I love you, and I will try to support you in the way that you need.' She offered a small smile. 'I guess what I want to know is, when can I meet this girl?'

He looked at his watch and then back to her.

'She and her parents will be here by three o'clock.'

'Are you . . . is this a joke?'

She felt the first wave of panic, worried in tandem that Jenny, Phil and – God forbid – Holly might see them all arrive, while calculating that she had approximately four hours to shower, vacuum the house, plump the cushions, make cakes, and find some mascara that wasn't baked dry.

'Relax, they're not coming to see if you have dusty surfaces, they're coming to meet me in person and so that you can meet her.'

'Oh my God!' Her heart stuttered as she mentally located the Febreze and decided to iron her floral cotton dress with the beadwork at the yoke and the big sleeves; it was quite bohemian yet informal, cool, yet flattering. This was her son's fiancée who was coming to meet her, and she had no choice but to go with it.

'Are you saying I've got dusty surfaces?'

Chapter Twelve

Enya stared at the tray with the red and white gingham cloth and wondered if she were the worst kind of person, intending to offer Holly's home-made blondies to Iris and her parents with a cup of tea. Not that they'd know, not that Holly would, but still.

'I'm nervous, Jonathan.' She spoke as she put her mug into the dishwasher; the mug she'd put out for him she put straight back on to the shelf, before rinsing and folding the dishcloth neatly over the tap. 'I feel duty-bound to be a bit cool with the girl, feel like I owe it to Holly, and yet I know that's ridiculous. It's not her fault, is it? And if she's going to be our daughter-in-law, I want her to like us. I really do. What if her parents are awful, what if Jenny pops over and finds me sitting there having a cup of tea with her replacement like we're old friends. I know that would make me feel terrible. I don't do well with disloyalty. I guess it's nice Aiden wanted them to come to his family home, but I really wish they weren't.'

Her son was conspicuous by his absence. Knowing every square inch of the cottage, she could tell he was hovering at his window, this confirmed by the sound of the floorboard squeaks. She felt both aggrieved by his lack of visibility yet relieved too, as the idea of making small talk, of slipping up and accidentally letting him know that she felt nothing but dread at the prospect of meeting Iris and her family, was a worry. Or worse, her wish that she'd rather this wasn't happening at all. This was the exact situation in which having Jonathan by her side would have made a difference. He always knew when to make a joke, how to pick a topic that might engage everybody, and, if these failed, the ace up his sleeve: a tour of the greenhouse to have a little look at his tomatoes. His tomato crop was always a bit crap. She now suspected it was far more about having those stinky plants to talk to, or to prod and water when a distraction was required, than the embarrassingly small harvest they provided. Although it had been a never-ending source of comedy, his tiny toms that she supplemented with punnets from the supermarket. And the delightful ritual eating of the sparse fruit with declarations that it was quality not quantity that counted had never failed to be funny. She looked over at the sink and there he was, leaning against it. His presence yet lack of engagement a little irritating at times like this.

Aiden's feet thundering down the stairs told her it must be show time and she closed her eyes briefly and took a breath.

'Just got a text, they'll be here in five!'

He practically jumped on the spot with an energy that she hadn't seen in him since he was a child. He looked smart, had shaved, tamed his curly hair as best he could, was aftershave-doused, and wore his shirt, one that had hung pressed and ready in his wardrobe. He might have set up home with Holly, but his room here was just as he'd left it when he had shipped out two years ago. She kept it that way, for just in case. The two stayed over on occasion, and she now wondered if at the back of her mind she had always hoped he might come home.

'Are you nervous?' She filled the kettle in preparation and instantly regretted it; that was always a nice diversion if conversation was stilted or lacking, the old *off to fill the kettle* trick. It could buy as many as three minutes of face-to-face avoidance.

'A little bit, about meeting her parents, yes. I really want them to like me. But about seeing Iris?' He shook his head. 'Not a bit, just excited. Really excited. You're going to love her, Mum. She's amazing!'

So you've said . . .

'I'm sure I will, and I trust your judgement.'

'But do you really?' He looked at her quizzically, as if he, like her, recalled their earlier conversation.

'I do, Aiden. That doesn't mean I'm not concerned about the whirlwind nature of it all, and my doubts about what comes next, but trust you? Yes, I do. I've worried a little in the past that you and Holly maybe hadn't seen as much of the world as you might, queried if maybe it might be healthy to see other people before you took the big leap, but I didn't imagine this.'

It felt good to be entirely open, like redressing the layers of deceit that the Hudsons were dealing with, a little.

'I want to talk to you about Holly, and everything that happened yesterday, but not right now. I want to enjoy today.'

'Of course.' She forced a smile, and wondered how much Holly might be enjoying today. The tray of blondies sat like a sweet tempting poke in the ribs, making her presence felt.

The sound of a car outside saw her son run to the front door. In that instant Enya wasn't sure where she should be. In the kitchen? Her worry was that it made her seem too domestic and mumsy. Sitting on the sofa, reading? That might give the impression she was aloof, disinterested or, worse, lazy. She hated how much thought she gave to such an inconsequential thing and how much it bothered her. The kitchen was where she'd stay. She was, after all, both domestic and mumsy and knew there was no shame in that.

'Oh, this is so sweet, really cosy!' A woman's voice floated from the hallway, referring to Enya's home. 'We don't really have a hallway at The Mount, this is so cute!'

It spoke volumes. It was a nice thing to say, complimentary in its way, yet with distinct undertones of comparison. The Mount, the woman's house, was no doubt bigger, more contemporary, better. Enya stood tall and glanced downwards at the back door, where with horror she spied two slender turds in Pickle's litter tray. Her heart sank and she made the executive decision to get rid of them right now! Moving quickly, hoping Aiden took his time and showed them the sitting room, which was even 'sweeter and cosier' than the hallway, she grabbed the litter tray, ran towards the open French doors, and in a moment of sheer panic threw the whole thing, grit, shit, and all, over the fence. With her pulse racing, her face no doubt a little flushed, she hurriedly returned in time to see two women, Iris and her mother, who were identical in both look and dress.

She could now confirm to Angela that yes, Iris, like her mother, was indeed beautiful.

They had layered, buttery-blonde bobbed hair that fell over sharp cheekbones, an abundance of silver jewellery with turquoise stones sitting strikingly against their summer tans, and they both wore skinny cropped jeans with crisp white shirts. On their neat and well-pedicured tootsies, they sported leather sandals that suggested their feet, so delicately encased, would never be troubled by bunions.

Enya wasn't sure whether to curtsy in her frock with the voluminous sleeves and beads or run away.

It was always the way. She was quietly confident in her own skin, went about her routine without giving too much thought to her attire, ancient hairstyle and lack of make-up. Yet put her in the presence of a goddess and she shrank, dissolved inside, and morphed into her fourteen-year-old self who no one wanted to snog as she stood a full head taller than most of the boys; and if you were a girl no one wanted to snog, the popular girls did not want to be your buddy, fearing the lack of snoggability might be contagious.

'You must be Aiden's mum! I'm Trish.'

Trish was friendly, confident and with an air of someone who lived a golden life, and one who had invested in very good teeth. Her make-up was shiny and perfect. Enya cursed her own pathetic two coats of mascara, the ancient tube of which she'd had to spit into.

'I am, it's lovely to meet you, all a bit strange, but lovely!' She walked forward, and she and Trish held each other's hand. It was a moment of connection that set the tone. She just hoped Jenny wasn't anywhere close.

'I'm Iris.'

The girl – assured, calm, a little cool, and oh so beautiful – smiled. It felt only right to hug her. Enya took a step forward and opened her arms, when, much to her humiliation, Iris reached for her hand and shook it. It was a demotion. By declining the hug, Iris had made it clear that Enya was not someone she wanted to hold or be held by; a stranger, no matter that this was the girl who was going to marry her son.

Enya's heart hardened a little towards the girl, and flexed for Holly, who was affectionate in the way it was possible to be with such a shared history. Holly, who right now couldn't sit up, speak, or open her eyes, so great was her distress, a little rag doll, and who she guessed would probably welcome a hug right now.

'Hello, Iris. It's lovely to meet you.'

'Show Aiden's mum your ring!' Trish clapped, her glee evident. Her own mammoth rock glinted in the sunlight.

'Oh yes, of course.' Enya had quite forgotten this detail.

Iris splayed her manicured fingers and showed off the whopping gem that nestled on a white gold band. It was really something. She wondered how much of Aiden's savings he had blown on the impressive piece and cursed the fact that her thoughts had fled to what would happen if they didn't make it to the altar. Would Iris get to keep it? It was unkind and fatalistic, and she felt suitably ashamed to have mentally gone there at all.

The ring was a symbol, maybe a little gaudy for her tastes, but it was not her tastes that counted. Nor her opinion on the whole carry-on, apparently.

'The whole thing was pretty perfect.' She tuned in to Iris's slow rhythm of speech, her low tones, very different to the giddy way in which Holly spoke, chattering and laughing and hopping from topic to topic with such speed that Enya often lost the thread. 'We wandered down to the Spanish Steps area, and AJ had the whole thing planned.'

AJ?

'The jeweller had all these rings laid out on little silk pillows, waiting for me to try. I cried, of course. Pathetic, I know, but it was special. The boy did good!'

Enya stared at the statement piece that Aiden had planned. 'Wow! It's beautiful.' She turned to comment to her son, acknowledging that the boy had indeed done good, to give the approval he had already explained they were not seeking, when she realised he wasn't there. 'Where *is* Aiden?'

'Chatting to my dad outside.' Iris shook her head. 'I know they're going to get on. Which is both great and intensely annoying. My dad will steal him for hours.'

'I think that's lovely.' She found a smile, feeling suddenly outnumbered here in her own home. Even Pickle had done a runner, although in fairness she had left a parting gift. God, how she missed Jonathan.

'Has he told you all about the proposal?' Trish grinned.

'No! He hasn't actually.' She clicked on the kettle.

'We'll have to get him to tell you his version of the story,' Trish gushed, 'I'm never going to get sick of hearing it! We were watching TV, eating supper, the next thing, we've got madam here on the phone, and she's got this huge dazzler on her finger! We had a virtual toast – they had a bottle of champers at their end, and we did the same. I don't mind telling you, Enya, I cried too! Still can't believe it! My little girl is getting married!'

Enya could relate as she too felt like crying, picturing the joyful celebration across the miles while she had only got to hear of the impending nuptials in the car park yesterday. She felt left out, excluded, lost.

'Yes, it's all so exciting!' She hoped she sounded excited and not knackered and wishing she could curl up in bed.

'How long have you lived here?' Trish looked around the kitchen, taking in the island, the French doors, the pale oak floor, the Danish oiled wooden countertops, and cabinetry the colour of winter sage, with knobs in matt brass to match the taps, door handle and all the other ironmongery.

'A long time, we moved in when we got married and just, stayed!'

'You never wanted a bigger house?'

Enya stared at the woman, considering several responses, none of which she decided were polite to share.

'No. That's why we're still here.'

Me. Why I'm still here . . .

She busied herself with the fetching of cups from the cupboard of her unimpressive kitchen of her clearly inadequate home. The sound of men laughing came from the hallway and for a split second, as she sometimes did, she was relieved that Jonathan was finally home. He'd take over from here, maybe organise a greenhouse tour.

But of course, it wasn't Jonathan. This realisation one that never got any easier, the fact that he was never coming home.

'Here he is!' Trish shouted, as if Aiden were a special guest they'd all been awaiting. Her son stood tall for sure, and it was nice, they clearly approved and quite right too, he was lovely, and Iris was lucky, as of course, no doubt, was he.

With the stack of saucers nestling in her hand, she was about to place them on the counter, figuring if she couldn't impress her guests with the vastness of her palatial home, she could at least treat them to tea from her grandmother's vintage china, which only ever saw the daylight on special occasions.

It was as she looked up that Enya was torn as to whether she should scream or faint, deciding neither would be a good look when trying to appeal to Iris and her family, although it would be a story to tell her grandchildren, no doubt.

Chapter Thirteen

The two things happened simultaneously.

The china slipped from her fingers, clattering down on to the countertop, where she could see instantly that at least one saucer was now cracked in two. That wasn't, however, what caused the breath to stop in her throat. Aiden stood beaming widely with his hands on his hips, standing in her kitchen, next to none other than HCK.

'You are . . .'

She stared at him, wondering how he had found her, how she might possibly explain the arrival of the stranger to these guests on this special day and, more importantly, what would she say to Aiden? How, how could she justify the fact that this married man who she had met only briefly, and not by design, had found her home! And was here! Here, at this of all moments!

But of course, no explanation was necessary as her brain caught up and it all became horribly, horribly clear. She said nothing, waiting to see how he reacted.

'Dad!' Iris rushed towards the man and pulled him into the kitchen. 'This is Enya, Aiden's mum.'

'Enya.' He held out his hand, the way he said it almost with a sigh as if he, like her, the night before she had found out his name, might have been trying to guess hers. He set the tone, clearly not revealing that they had met, once, and spoken briefly on the phone.

'I'm Dominic.'

'Dominic.'

This the first time she would say his name to his face. She held his hand, and he shook it, gently. It was a confusing moment of contact that was as warming as it was awkward. She wondered if she were imagining the whole thing, the horror of holding his hand and feeling the visceral leap of want in her stomach, as his beautiful wife stood close by. His beautiful wife to whom he was evidently still very much married . . . his duplicity sickened her.

A loud banging on the edge of the wall gave them all a start. They turned to spy the elderly woman with a face like thunder.

Maeve stood on her patio, staring in. Her neighbour didn't wait for a greeting but launched into a loud and clearly considered monologue while they all stood transfixed by the septuagenarian with a litter tray in her hands.

'I don't know what's going on with you lot at the moment, I really don't. First I hear that Holly Hudson is having a breakdown, all because that wally of a son of yours has done the unthinkable—'

'He's not a wally.' This Enya addressed to the parents of the girl who her son, the wally, was all set to marry.

Maeve carried on as if she hadn't spoken. 'Then the next thing I know, I hear a bang, and someone has thrown shit and this cat toilet into my garden! It landed on my patio. If you think I'm touching those turds, you've got another thing coming. I like that cat, I do, but I'm not touching that! Heartbroken she is, bloody heartbroken.'

'The cat?' Dominic, it seemed, was having trouble keeping up.

'No, Holly Hudson.' Enya had turned and spoken curtly to him over her shoulder, unable to control the intense thrill she felt at no more than the sight of him, a reaction as instinctive as it was unwelcome. His married status put him firmly out of reach and she was now cloaked with remorse and guilt as his wife was none other than the beautifully coiffed and ever so slightly house-proud Trish. He smiled at her, as if taking the opportunity to do so while the rest of the gang were focused on Maeve while she spun her cat turd tale. Enya looked away, mortified, beyond mortified, and wishing she could run away.

'You were always such pleasant neighbours, quiet. But since Jonathan died, God only knows what's going on in here! It's not the first time I've had to deal with her turds.'

'Holly Hudson's?' Dominic inappropriately quipped.

'No, the cat,' Enya snapped before turning back to Maeve. 'I'll come and clean your patio. I am sorry, Maeve.'

'Well, I'm glad you all find it so amusing.' Maeve thrust the litter tray into Enya's hands. 'And as for you, young man,' she pointed a gnarled finger in Aiden's direction, 'you'll regret it! Mark my words, you'll regret it and I hope that when you do, Holly has run off with someone who deserves her.' Maeve turned on the spongey heel of her slipper and made her way back down the path, muttering. Enya couldn't quite make it out but was sure it was something about the ability to ride a bike.

The fact that Maeve seemed to have joined Jenny and Phil in the chorus of disapproval was a blow, and she felt further weakened by the prospect of interacting with any of them, wanting in that moment to hide away in her ice den. Forever.

'Are you okay?' Aiden's concerned tone was at once welcome and reassuring; suddenly, she didn't feel quite so outnumbered, while inside she raged with loneliness and fretted that this might be her life from now on, her whole life, spent in this limbo, hiding in her quiet, cold place.

It was only when she turned that she realised her son was speaking to Iris, who he now held in a close embrace, clasping her pretty head under his chin as if she had been in mortal danger and not just slightly embarrassed by their ranting neighbour's speech. Enya fought the desire to cry. And in fairness to Maeve, no one should have to contend with patio turds, or any other kind of turds for that matter, launched into their garden on a summer's day.

'Do you know what I think?' Trish asked loudly. 'I think we all need a little drinkie!'

Enya smiled at the woman, who, judging by the gleam in her eye and the excited change in her demeanour, might think this was the answer to many of life's curve balls.

'That's a very good idea.' Enya could only agree.

Trying not to look at her grandmother's broken saucer, fearful it could invoke further tears, another small part of her history destroyed, she went to the dresser where the wine glasses lived and hoped she might find five that matched. She closed her eyes briefly as she reached into its confines, catching her breath while she tried to reconcile the fact that Dominic, the Handsome Car Klutz, was in her house and that he was to be Aiden's father-in-law! It was surreal and awful all at once. She felt grubby, dishonest, and disloyal. He was Trish's husband, and she was Jonathan's wife, and she had chatted to him on the phone from her bed in a flirty manner. She cringed and wished she could fast-forward to the time they all left her less-than-impressive cottage.

'Everyone, please do go and sit in the lounge, get comfy! I'll bring the wine in.' She painted on a broad smile, wanting them gone from the room, needing a minute.

'Do you have any glue?' Dominic asked.

'Glue?' She stared, trying to see him only as Iris's dad or, more specifically, as Trish's husband.

'For the saucer.' He took the two halves into his hands and held them up for scrutiny. 'It looks like a clean break. I'm rubbish with technology but good with my hands,' he reminded her. 'So, if you have glue, I can fix this. No one will ever know.'

I'll know . . .

'That's very kind, thank you.' She thought it a good idea to have him preoccupied with the task, out of the way, even if it were for mere minutes. 'I think there's some in the shed. Let me grab the key.'

'Shall I take these through?' Trish picked up the tray of blondies.

'Oh, yes, please do.'

'They look wonderful, are they home-made?' It sounded like a challenge. Enya could of course answer with confidence.

'Yes, yes, they are.'

'Well, look at you, Mrs Bake Off! Could you give me the recipe?' Trish inhaled their glorious scent.

Again, Enya answered with the truth. 'I could.'

'I never make anything if it doesn't come wrapped in plastic, if it hasn't called to me from a shelf in Waitrose then we aren't eating it!' Trish's pride at the fact was more than a little surprising. 'I don't really cook,' she continued. 'I have a white kitchen and the thought of getting it messy or spilling something that might stain . . .' She pulled a face. 'I went through a phase of only serving pale food to ensure no nasty marks on my counter or linen. Do you remember that, Dom?' Trish fired a look at her husband, her tone a little challenging. It was uncomfortable, to say the least.

Dom . . . It was a witnessed intimacy that made Enya's gut fold with guilt; how deftly he had woven threads of trust and bound her with them. His manner, his smile, his easy nature, his interest. It had been slick and in that moment it was repulsive to her. She felt foolish. She was a fool.

'I do.' He bit his lip.

Trish laughed. 'We existed on a diet of rice, pasta, cauliflower, potatoes, cheese, milk, vanilla ice cream . . .'

Enya briefly caught Dominic's eye and looked away.

The woman wasn't nearly done.

'Bananas, parsnips, onions, noodles, chips, chicken, bread, bread rolls, cream, coconut milk, coconut flesh, erm . . .'

'We get the idea.' Trish's husband sounded slightly exasperated as he interrupted her flow.

'Oh, pardon me for breathing!' Trish narrowed her eyes at him.

Enya looked away. Not only did it feel intrusive to witness the exchange, but it was also quite alien to her. She and Jonathan had never spoken to each other like that. They were friends who loved each other and with that came a mutual and unquestionable respect. The Sutherlands' interaction was ugly and spoke of so much more than this brief irritation.

It was as Trish made her way towards the lounge that she stopped and turned, holding the tray of blondies higher.

'Just one thing, do they have nuts in? I'm allergic to some nuts.'

'Oh.' *Busted.* 'I can't remember.' She cringed.

'You can't remember if you put nuts into these home-made blondies?' Trish now narrowed her eyes in *her* direction.

'I can't, but I'd say it's not worth the risk. Let me go and find that glue!'

Trish took the tray into the lounge and, much to her mortification, Dominic followed her outside.

She felt flustered, complicit in something that was nothing, and at the same time cloaked in guilt at no more than letting a man, *this* man, into her husband's place of refuge and where she still liked to picture him. A sacred space.

'Gosh, it's beautifully organised.' Dominic admired the neat shelves that were stacked with clearly labelled boxes and tins, running his hand over the jars hanging beneath the shelves, whose lids had been screwed into the wood. 'You can tell a lot about a man by the state of his shed.' He smiled at her. 'You must miss him.'

'Why didn't you say, *Oh it's you, Car Park Woman*, when you arrived, why didn't you mention it?' She ignored his question, far from comfortable discussing Jonathan while standing in his shed.

'I don't know, CP. Why didn't you?' he countered.

Because I have felt flustered when I've thought about you, imagining you, wondering where you live, conjuring you in the early hours and this is not like me, not like me at all! You are a married man, and it goes against all I stand for! I'm struggling with how my son has hurt Holly, how can I have any legitimate stance on that if I do the same?

'Not sure. I didn't want to spoil the moment, I guess, everyone wrapped up with the kids' engagement.'

'Yes, that was it, same for me.' He smiled, as if he hadn't bought a word of it. 'Amazing to think that on that day, just three weeks ago, in a heartbeat that neither could have envisaged, two people were going to meet, and it was going to change their whole lives in ways they could not have begun to imagine. Their plans disrupted, their thoughts hijacked, their routine disturbed, their needs altered, their focus shifted, and it started with no more than a glance, a brief exchange, a shared understanding that all the planets were aligned and the universe was sending them this incredible gift.'

'How was it going to change their whole lives?' she whispered, hardly daring to ask, feeling an unwelcome and uninvited tremble to her limbs at no more than the proximity of him.

'Because they're getting married!' He smiled.

'Oh yes, of course!' She gave a small nod, understanding that he was talking about Iris and Aiden. This was what he did, wove a spell with his words, his manner. The skill was in not falling for it, keeping a level head.

'Think about it, one minute they were trying to find their seats on a plane, the next they're sharing an armrest and by the time they had landed in Rome, according to Iris, she knew. Just like that!' He clicked his fingers and she jumped. 'Do you think it's possible, to meet someone and fall, fall so hard that it leaves you with a kind of madness, with obsessive thoughts that take the rational you and leave you feeling hollowed out, exposed, vulnerable, but excited too, happy at the prospect of all that might lie ahead?' He stared right at her.

'I think . . .'

Enya wasn't sure if he was toying with her. What *did* she think? That if he had been single and free she would have given in to the madness the very day she met him? If, when she'd asked, he had replied, *No, no I'm not married*, she would have fallen so hard there would be no recovering from it? Possibly. But it was, she knew, no more than physical attraction, an infatuation, much as she'd described to Aiden.

She opened a little drawer on Jonathan's granny's old bureau, which was splattered with paint. Each colour told a story of a chapter in their life: the red of Aiden's ride-on fire engine that now languished in the loft. Pale blue that had been the colour of choice for their bathroom in the eighties, and droplets of the French grey that was actually closer to green with which her husband had painted the hall, stairs and landing when first diagnosed.

'*That should do you for a few years, one less thing for you to think about . . .*' he had stated, admitting to her, and possibly to himself, that all talk of recovery and plans for one more trip somewhere were lies.

She carefully removed the tube of glue and handed it to this man, a stranger who had certainly hijacked her thoughts and routine.

'Yes.' She held his gaze. 'I do miss him. I miss him very much.'

Chapter Fourteen

It had been two days since Enya had sat through the excruciating afternoon with the Sutherlands. She was exhausted, had barely slept trying to figure out the complex puzzle of it all, awash with shame that she was mixed up in the situation at all. To think her main concern had been Aiden and Holly. How she longed to talk to Jenny, to see Jenny, knowing that her friend offered the very best advice. With the whole experience bottled up inside her, their lack of contact made everything feel harder. She felt loneliness ripple through her veins and had barely ventured out, reluctant to leave the house for fear of bumping into Phil. It was a crazy state of affairs.

At least Angela was home, a sounding board and a friend, and she was in need of both.

Her sister sat at the kitchen table and slurped her cup of tea. 'There is nothing like a good cup of tea at home. The tea abroad is never the same, is it?'

'I guess not.' Enya fought to remember, another reminder of what she had lost when she had become a widow, those lovely experiences, mint tea in Marrakech, sardines in Lisbon.

'Even if you take proper teabags, I think it's something to do with the water.'

'Possibly.' Enya nodded.

Her sister's tan was deep, her hair sun-kissed, and she carried the languid air of one who was not yet revved up for life back in the real world.

'Mum looked old, I thought.'

'Ill or just old?'

Enya hated not seeing her parents frequently, but Jonathan had always reminded her that it was their choice to go sit in the sun and sip her inheritance through a cocktail straw on a nightly jaunt to the town square. Not that he begrudged them and neither did she. It beat popping on an extra jersey and dodging the rain in Keynsham while they watched daytime TV and went to bed earlier and earlier in the winter months. She shook away the thought that this was what her life had become.

'Tired maybe, and old, I don't think all that sun is good for her skin.'

Enya stared at her older sister, who presently resembled a burnished walnut and was about as wrinkled. 'Probably not.' She smiled to herself.

'So, tell me all about Aiden and Holly, what a bloody carry-on, Ens!'

'You could say that.' She took a chair opposite Angela and sipped her brew.

'Poor Holly.'

'Yes.' She disliked how Holly was cast in this way, a capable, wonderful young woman who was now to be pitied, it seemed, because of a choice Aiden had made. 'She'll be fine though, she'll come out the other end stronger and probably thankful. Who wants to be with someone if there's even the smallest possibility they want to be with someone else?'

'True.' Angela nodded. 'That's what Jenny said, pretty much.'

'You've spoken to her?' She held the mug between her palms and cursed the increase in her heart rate. It was awful, the feeling of exclusion, the grief at the prospect of losing her best friend, and this before she wondered what it all might mean for their business plans, the one thing that had been the light at the end of the tunnel when she considered losing her job of twenty-five years. Jenny had still not responded to her heart text, and it had left her at a loss as to how best to proceed.

'Mmm.' Angela swallowed. 'I hate feeling like I'm in the middle.'

'You're not in the middle! We're adults. And we've all been around too long to let this rip a hole in our friendship, haven't we?' The quaver to her voice indicated this was not a rhetorical question.

'We have, but you're my sister, my priority, yet Jen is my friend and I hate that I'm speaking to both of you and yet you're not speaking to each other, it's awkward. Weird.'

'Only if we let it be. I sent her another message after the heart, didn't know what else to do really. I think it'll be better when the dust has settled, when we're all a bit calmer.'

'And when d'you think that'll be?'

There was something in her sister's tone that suggested she might have a long wait.

'I don't know.' She held Angela's eyeline, this truth as sobering as it was unnerving. She missed her friend so much, hated the feeling of unease here in her own home. Hated that she had such a small circle, hated that Jonathan was not here to make everything feel a bit better. 'What did she say to you?'

'She's angry, so she said lots of things that I know she doesn't mean. Heat of the moment stuff.'

'Oh God!' Her sister's admission did nothing to allay her concerns. Enya wished she hadn't asked.

'Let's talk about something else.' Angela echoed her thoughts.

'You know I told you that Iris and her parents came over at the weekend?' She shifted in the chair, not sure if this was in fact a better choice of topic.

'Yes, what were they like?' Her sister's eyes blazed, she did love a gossip.

'Iris is lovely, beautiful. I mean, not overly warm, but she was probably very nervous. Her mum is glam, has an allergy to some nuts, and she necked a bottle and a half of sparkling wine and danced with her arms in the air to a song in her head, which was . . . interesting. Not judging, but . . .'

'Oh my God, you are *so* judging her! But carry on, I am here for this.'

'And Iris's dad.' She paused, and rubbed her tired eyes. 'Okay.' She put down her tea and lay her palms on the table. 'Do you remember I mentioned to you about that man in the car park?'

'The one who smashed your car in?'

'Well, he didn't exactly smash my car in but there was an incident.'

'I remember, you were giggly, said he was attractive; Alan Titchmarsh meets Gary Barlow.'

Enya stared at her with a look of utter bewilderment, and felt her face flush with embarrassment. 'I might have said he was attractive, but I swear to God I never mentioned Alan Titchmarsh or Gary Barlow, neither of whom I find remotely attractive.'

'You don't? What's *wrong* with you?' Angela tutted.

'What's wrong with *you*?' Enya countered as they reverted to their teenage selves, which happened on occasion.

Angela took a gulp of her tea. 'Okay, so maybe I might have fabricated the bit about Gary Barlow meets Alan Titchmarsh because actually that would be my ideal man.'

Enya pulled a face at her sister. 'Are you serious?'

'God, yes – I mean, think about it.'

'I'd rather not.' Enya sighed. Angela ignored her.

'Someone who can tend to your garden, trim your bushes while serenading you with a song they've written just for you.' Her sister looked into the middle distance, as if she were in her own world, a world Enya had no desire to enter. None at all.

'Anyway, the point I was going to make, and here's the kicker: the guy in the car park who I christened Handsome Car Klutz, HCK for short.'

'Obvs.'

'He's Iris's dad.'

'What do you mean, he's Iris's dad?'

'I mean, he is the father of the girl Aiden is going to marry!' A fact that was as confusing as it was mortifying.

'Flippin' 'eck! That's going to be interesting at the reception.' Angela smirked. 'What will you do? Play footsie under the top table?'

'No, don't start with that, it's not funny! I can't even joke about it. He's married, obviously. And that's it for me, I'm out.' Just the thought was shameful. 'And even if he wasn't, it's a non-starter. Not possible. I no doubt got the wrong end of the stick, that's what happens when you live the Arctic fox life and are entirely out of practice. He was probably just being nice to me, chatty. I'm sure he's nice to everyone.' She decided not to mention the undeniable attraction and the frisson of tension when he'd spoken to her in the shed. Jonathan's shed. She glanced towards the patio, where he now stood staring out at the garden. 'It was just one of those weird things where he was dropping Iris off to get on a plane, and I was dropping Aiden off to get on a plane, and our kids met and fell in love on that plane, and that's it, end of. It's those two we need to concentrate on and this . . . wedding!'

'Oh my God.' Angela put her empty cup down and placed her palms on the tabletop.

'What do you mean, *Oh my God*?'

'You say it's a non-starter, not possible, but I *know* you, Enya Brown. I know that look in your eyes. You *like* him, you like him, don't you?'

Enya thought how best to proceed; *with caution* came to mind.

'He's married.' She repeated, 'married. He's going to be Aiden's father-in-law. I've met him twice. I like him as a person, as a good sort for Aiden to get entangled with, but that's it. I don't know him! Nothing is going to happen and I'd rather you didn't mention it again.' She kept her voice steady, hoping not to belie the disappointment that tinged this fact or share her thoughts that he just might be a cad. A cad who had rather *conveniently* signed a lease on a flat, indicating he was moving out on the *very* day he met her, or so he said . . . She could smell the BS a mile off. 'I mean, my God, can you imagine what sorting through that situation would be like for Aiden?' His words came to her now, spoken softly in the midst of his grief.

I'm so glad I've got you, Mum, no matter what happens I've always got you, haven't I?

A knock put a halt to their chat. Enya's heart leapt as she opened the front door to Jenny and Holly! It felt wonderful to see her friend, to be this close to her. Jenny, however, could barely meet her eye and this swiped all possible joy from the reunion. It wasn't their presence that was disheartening, but rather the change in the way it felt that threw her completely.

Holly looked deflated, hollowed out and in pain. Her skin grey, her darting eyes swollen and red. Jenny seemed to have lost weight in the days since Enya had last seen her. Two bruises of fatigue sat beneath her eyes, and with her hands clasped in front of her, she looked like a stranger. There was nothing in her demeanour to suggest this was the same woman with whom she shared snacks at three in the morning, or who had suggested they dance in the kitchen full of plonk and pudding. But at least they were here, and that had to be a start.

'Oh! Come in! Come in!' She stood back to let the subdued twosome pass, simultaneously glad of her sister's presence while wishing she were not here, knowing her tendency to be blunt.

'Thanks.' Jenny gave her a small, closed-mouth smile that didn't reach her eyes; it was like a knife to Enya's chest and about as painful.

'Angela and I are in the kitchen.'

No sooner had Holly set foot inside the door than she started to cry. It was awful to see. She cried with her whole body. Shoulders heaving, posture cowed, head low, hands at her mouth, eyes raw and her mouth open, as she let silent howls of distress spiral from the purest kind of despair deep inside her and leave her body like smoke.

'Holly . . .'

Enya took her into her arms and held her close to her chest, as the girl fell against her, weakened, and altered. Gone was her effervescence, her irritating and unrelenting upbeat energy, her verve!

'The doctor has given her something to calm her down.' Jenny spoke with the quiet anguish of a mother whose child was hurting.

'Is he . . . is . . .' Holly began, her voice no more than a rough whisper, as if her distress had stripped her throat of its velvet and its volume.

'He's not here. He's at work. Come and sit down, love.'

Holly allowed herself to be guided to the table, where she stumbled before taking a seat opposite Angela, who, aside from reaching out to rub the girl's arm, thankfully stayed silent. Jenny too sat.

'Would you like a cup of tea?'

'No, thanks.' Jenny's speech was controlled, exact, with an undercurrent that left Enya in no doubt that things between them were broken, entirely broken. 'Holly wanted to come and see you.'

Jenny's words indicated that she would rather have not. This realisation was enough to flood Enya's veins with sorrow. She just about managed a life without Jonathan, but a life without Jenny too? She felt the rise of tears in her throat and the beginnings of panic.

'I'm so glad.' She meant it, having had no reply to the texts she had sent her, sending love and hoping she was doing okay . . . Enya had feared the longer it went on, the harder it would be to face each other. Not that this encounter was easy, none of this was easy.

'It just doesn't feel real.' Holly spoke again with that scratchy, barely audible voice. 'I don't want to see him. Well, sometimes I do, but I don't think I'm able to. But is he okay?'

Enya pictured her son jumping up and down on the spot at the prospect of Iris's arrival, how quickly his heart had moved on, forgotten. It angered and hurt her in equal measure.

'He's okay.'

'Good.' Holly took a deep breath. 'Good. I know we need to sort things out, like the flat and stuff, but could you ask him if we can do that in a couple of days, just give me a little bit of time to get my head straight.' Holly looked up to fully reveal her eyes, which were a little vacant and small, like someone had come along and erased her sparkle. 'Did I do something wrong, do you think?' Her question and the pitiful hum of sadness behind it was as moving as it was misplaced.

Jenny tutted, her jaw tense, as she exchanged a look with Angela.

'You did nothing wrong, Holly. You're wonderful.' Enya meant it, feeling a flash of disloyalty as rage sparked, remembering it was Aiden who had thrown the rock, caused the ripples.

'I've told her she won't always feel this way,' Jenny placated, looking only at Angela, as if it were easier to address her than Enya, the mother of the boy who had caused this. Enya wondered what Jenny would like to do to Aiden if her resentment towards Blake Dunlop, who had merely kicked an art project decades ago, was anything to go by.

'It's true.' She hoped her confirmation might help drive the message home.

'It's, it's not only that I lose Aiden,' Holly paused, 'but I lose you, this house, Pickle, I lose a decade of my life, and the way coming home to this street feels. I lose bits of my childhood and I lose the life I've built around us. I lose the future that I imagined.'

'That's not true. You don't lose me or Pickle, or this house.' Enya smiled at the girl, knowing this was a lie and that Holly Hudson did indeed lose all of these things. She also knew that her own loss was not dissimilar, Jenny's friendship something she prized highly, and their business venture, which had kept her upbeat, filling the void of her upcoming retirement, and yet now unlikely to happen. She took a deep breath, trying to stave off the panic that threatened.

'I think we all remember having our heart broken,' Angela piped up. 'It feels like the end of the world because it's supposed to.'

Enya stared at her sister, silently pleading for her to go gently.

'It's supposed to because the strongest things are forged in fire, Holly. You get burned but you emerge from the ashes stronger than you ever thought possible. Like a phoenix rising from the flames. That will happen to you, even if you don't believe it right now.'

'I . . . I don't,' Holly hiccupped.

Angela spoke with conviction. 'But you will. And when you do, you will not only have found strength, but power too. A woman who has gone through this is metamorphosed and the version of her who comes after takes no shit. She knows herself and she will never be beholden to anyone, she will never again put responsibility for her own happiness in the pocket of another. She is self-reliant and knowing, and in time you will thank him for the chance to change.'

Enya and Jenny stared at Angela, both more than a little taken aback by her wisdom. There was truth in it, yet Enya dared not admit she was still waiting to rise from the ashes, still bound in marriage to a man who had died, trying to find the wings that would give her the courage to take flight.

'Thank you, Angela.' Holly did her best to smile. 'Maybe I will have a cup of tea, Enya, if that's okay?'

'Of course it is!'

Enya jumped up, happy to have to fill the kettle, a diversion that she knew could buy her at least three minutes.

Chapter Fifteen

It had been an emotional day, a tiring one. Aiden had listened quietly when she recounted Holly's visit over supper. Losing his appetite, he had put down the fork and abandoned his pasta.

'I'm just not hungry right now, Mum. I couldn't eat a big dinner. Think I'll have an early night.'

'I understand, love. See you in the morning.'

And just like that her flames of anger at how much Holly was hurting, and the reasons for it, were partially extinguished. She was torn, feeling sorry for her son, who was guilty of being young and impetuous, while at the same time only able to imagine what it was like for Holly. It was a desperate situation that felt fragile for them all. Even trying to figure out how to successfully tread this middle ground was exhausting.

'What am I going to do, Jonathan?' she asked her husband, who sat in his chair, legs stretched out, as they watched *Death in Paradise* on the telly. 'And Angela can talk, but it's not easy. I feel like I'm adjudicating the whole carry-on, and I don't know how I manage it without you. I wish you were here. You'd know what to do.'

Desolation wrapped her tightly, threatening to suffocate her. She felt his absence, knowing she would give anything to feel his arms around her, his hand holding hers, just for a second. It was an unwelcome pull of emotion that made her cough and sniff, wary that if she gave in to them, those darn tears just might not stop.

As the credits rolled, she let Pickle out for the night, kissing her head and giving advice about not mixing with any of those rough cats who might try and lead her astray.

'Make good choices, little Pickle, and do not, under any circumstances, shit in Maeve's garden. It might send her over the edge and over our wall, neither of which we want.'

She planted another kiss on her cat's pretty head before letting her go, watching as Pickle slipped quietly into the shadows. Enya really did hope she'd steer clear of Maeve's house, unable to cope with another turd on the patio incident, fearing becoming another topic of discussion among the neighbours who used to be her friends.

She checked the doors and windows, clicked off the lamp and made her way up the creaking stairs. Her bones ached and she decided to take a hot, deep bath before bed. Their third bedroom had been indulgently converted into their en-suite bathroom, a fact that estate agents and their neighbours thought was crazy, as a three-bedroomed property was worth significantly more than a two. She and Jonathan had tried to explain that they had to live in the house and having a lovely bathroom as their en suite brought them more pleasure than if they hadn't made the conversion, safe in the knowledge that when they died, it would be worth more money on the open market. It was an odd concept to them, prioritising a future cash value over their everyday lives.

With a candle lit, and a liberal slosh of her favoured amber-scented bath oil in the water, she let her clothes fall in a soft nest by the bathroom door and climbed in. Eyes closed, she lay back and let the warmth calm her soul and soothe her body. It was here that she hovered for some minutes, entirely lost to the peace of it, able to switch off the tick-tick-tick of worry over her son's muddled love life, her guilt over her flirtation with Dominic, and the fracture in her and Jenny's friendship. A welcome hiatus from the shittiest of days.

Her phone, languishing on the sink, buzzed. It was odd to receive a call at this time of night and as ever she hoped there was no emergency, prayed her parents were okay, Angela too. Aiden was now struck from this mental worry list as he slumbered in his room at the end of the hallway, and she assumed that any potential threat or injury would be quickly heralded by a yell.

Stretching her arm, she managed to reach the phone. Without her glasses on, it was hard to make out the number.

'Hello?' she said as she lay back beneath the water.

'Enya, Enya, hi. It's Dominic.'

She felt her body shudder at the sound of his voice, sending goose bumps across her skin. It was an instant and automatic response to the sound of him. Guilt lined her throat as she managed to get the word out. 'Hello.'

Instantly, she placed one arm across her chest, hiding herself as if he might be able to see down the line, mortified by the thought alone. She wondered why he was calling.

'Hope it's not too late?'

Yes, because it's the hour of the call that's the issue here . . .

'No, no, I was just, just cooking.' She squirmed. It was the first thing that popped out of her mouth.

'Oh right, what are you cooking?'

'Spaghetti.' She closed her eyes and shook her head.

'Nothing like a bit of late-night spaghetti I always say, what sauce?'

'It's erm,' she looked around the bathroom, hoping for inspiration, 'it's erm,' she stared at the fancy glass bottle of bath oil, 'olive oil with garlic and lemon.' Her face twisted in cringing agony.

'Sounds delicious!'

'What can I do for you, Dominic?' Her tone now a little officious, urging him, the man married to Trish, to get to the reason for the contact. Her toes were curled with the stress of it all.

'Right, yes.' He paused. 'I thought I'd call because, well, how to put it,' he gave a nervous laugh, 'I wanted to. And I feel there are things left to say.'

'I thought we had agreed that it wasn't wise to call me. Not a good idea for us to speak like this.' Her voice was steady.

'I don't recall that.' He sounded sure. 'I know you said that it had been lovely to talk to me, and nice to meet me, and then there was a brief discussion about life in general – what we want, what we deserve and what we settle for, that kind of thing.'

'Oh, in that case, maybe I should have been more direct. What I meant to say was that I cannot become involved with you in any way because you're married. And that was before I knew you were married to Trish and that our children were getting married. Is that any clearer?'

She gave a long sigh, knowing the right thing to do would be to put the phone down. End the call and brave the inevitable awkwardness that would envelop them in the coming months when forced to face each other, and the memory of him speaking to her while she lay nudie-dudie in a deep bath rattled around in her head. Yet she didn't end the call because it was contact, it was someone, reaching out to her in this, the loneliest of hours at the end of the longest day. And it was him. She slipped deeper into the water. Hiding as best she could.

There was a second or two of silence; she heard him swallow, could hear him breathing. When he eventually spoke, his voice sounded pained and thoughtful, mirroring her own emotions that her rather abrupt words had failed to erase.

'It's hard for me to, to,' he paused, 'difficult for me to accept that we are—'

126

'There is no "*we*", Dominic!' It felt important to interject.

'And you're okay with that?'

She sat up in the water. 'It's not a matter of being okay with it. It's a case of accepting the facts and the many obstacles and barriers that are piled up, too high for us to overcome, to even get started. Because we haven't started. We are nothing. We don't know each other, strangers! A two-minute exchange in a car park that has been blown out of proportion for whatever reason. An attraction, yes, I'll admit, but no more, the kind of attraction that is always on a timer. No more.'

'I don't think you believe that any more than I do.'

'I don't, I don't know what else to say. A married man is a non-starter for me, that's . . . that's it!'

'Yet you don't deny there's something there. You feel the attraction too, you've just said as much, I mean how can you not, it crackles around us like electricity! I can't stop thinking about it.'

She lay back once again in the water, flattered no doubt, transfixed by his admission of the very thing she had felt too. But more than this, she was alert to the unalterable facts that would guide her, nothing else.

'And *I* can't stop thinking about how horrible it feels to be pulled into whatever it is you have going on, the whole *I've got a flat* ruse. I'm not stupid and it feels . . .' She ran out of words.

'You think it's a ruse?'

'Uh-huh.'

She heard him exhale loudly. 'Shit!' he spat. 'Really?'

'Yes.' She held her ground.

'It's not.' His voice now a little clipped, as if affronted by the suggestion. 'It's not. I signed the lease on the day we met, a small flat near a boat shed in a marina. I told Trish, and she has asked me to stay until after the wedding, to help everyone get through the next few weeks, as me moving out and planning for Iris's big day was a little more than she could cope with. So I agreed. We haven't told Iris. Don't want to spoil her moment. That's why I'm still going home, but the flat is real. My intentions are real. I don't know what else to say.'

Enya felt the uncomfortable gulp of sudden tears. It all felt a little more than she could cope with, on top of the shitty meeting with Jenny and the sharp cut of loss at what that meant.

'It's never about intentions, it's about action. Not that I'm telling you to act, nothing like that! But words are easy and I'm not,' – *strong enough, healed enough* – 'not ready to deal with words and the complexity of it all.'

Dominic was quiet for a moment and when he spoke his voice was calm, softer once more.

'You're crying because you know this *is* something, you know we're not nothing. And that's okay.'

'It's not okay,' she managed, 'nothing about this is okay.' *I am Jonathan's wife, still, very much Jonathan's wife . . .*

'I was listening to Iris telling her mother how when she saw Aiden for the first time, it was like everything she had known up until that point was thrown into doubt, her plans now chaos. Like something had been revealed, a secret world that had been waiting for her and the moment she had glimpsed it, she knew there was no going back. And I had to grip the steering wheel with all my strength and bite my lips to stop myself from yelling out that I knew exactly what she meant! Because it had happened to me too!'

'But it can't. It just can't, it's not real! How can it be?'

She had said something similar to Aiden, trying to help him understand that secret worlds and bright futures were what grew with time, they were where she and Jonathan had arrived eventually, but that whole instant love and a happy future concept? It was just that, a concept, an idea without foundation. And she would not give in to the novelty, not devalue what she and her husband had built by leaping at no more than a fancy for this man!

'No, Enya. No. You're wrong! This feeling, it's *something*! And I know you feel it too, you were receptive, you were lovely. How do we ignore it? What are we supposed to do, carry on as if it hasn't happened?'

'Yes, that's exactly what you're supposed to do.'

'What if I can't, what if I don't want to, what if I think I deserve this shot at happiness, and what if you do too?'

'No.' Her tears felt hot on her cheeks, clogging up her nose and throat. 'Just no! I don't know you and what I do know, I don't particularly like!'

'That's not true, I sense how you feel about me, I can see it. The way you look at me.' He spoke softly.

The way you look at me . . . It was undeniable, not that it made it any more real.

'I didn't like the way you spoke to Trish – snapped at her in my kitchen. It was unkind.' She spoke plainly.

'You're right, it was. I've thought about that too, a lot. I was thrown by seeing you, completely thrown, but more than that, the moment she suggested having a *drinkie*, I knew where we were headed, the dancing, the conflict, the slurred words, the aggression, the antagonistic cutting comments. Trust me, I've tried to help her make different choices, been trying for years. I'm exhausted by it. I wanted to disappear. I wanted to run!'

'It was still unkind.' She held steady.

There was a silent pause.

'I can't give you all the details in this one conversation, but I would dearly like the opportunity to talk to you about it. What I will say is that I'm so tired of not moving forward or making progress. When you popped up in the car park that day, it was like,' she held her breath, listening to his every word, 'it was like fate. I had no idea that I might ever feel this, this *pull*.'

Enya said nothing, but her heart skipped a little in her chest; it was new and enticing and not like her at all. She was not this person, not in the habit of feeling this way either. Her life was set, sedate, or at least it had been, until that one day when Aiden had got on a plane and changed the course of his life, and she had met Dominic, who was suggesting he could change hers.

'We haven't started, Dominic,' she said it again, 'we are nothing, and yet already I'm sitting here, crying in the bath, how can that be the basis of anything good?'

'It's already good, just knowing you are out there in the world is filling my crappy life with joy! I think we have potential, at the very least we have to explore this!' he pushed.

'There is nothing to explore, for a million reasons, but right up there is what it would do to Aiden and Iris. I could not, would not do that to them. It'd be ghastly.'

'I think you might have a million reasons lined up, but none of them can account for how I *feel* when I'm with you.'

It was as she opened her mouth to respond that she heard Aiden call out.

'Mu-um!' her son yelled and she jumped, sloshing the water over the side of the tub.

'Just a minute! I'm in the bath!' she yelled, fearful of discovery, a reminder, as if it were needed, that this was not a good situation to be in. It felt sneaky, deceitful, and she was right, nothing good should ever feel this way. She held the phone close to her face, whispering now, 'I'd better . . .'

'Yes, of course, of course.'

Without any lingering goodbye, she ended the call. And hopped out of the bath.

'Everything okay, love?' she called through her bedroom door, which she held ajar, doing her utmost to keep her voice steady.

'Yes,' her son shouted across the landing, 'have we got any crisps?'

She almost laughed at the request, thinking how their call was ended prematurely. Which was, she decided, probably a good thing.

'In the larder. Hidden from myself behind the breakfast cereal.'

Wrapped in her towel, her hair wet, she sat on the corner of the bed and tried to calm her flustered pulse, unsure what to make of her late-night caller and the unsatisfying way they had left things. So he had signed the lease on a flat, did that make a difference? Her phone beeped, a text.

HOPE YOU DIDN'T DROP YOUR SPAGHETTI IN THE BATH! I JOKE. IT'S LAUGH OR CRY, RIGHT?

Dominic . . . She had quite forgotten her lie and, not for the first time that evening, hung her head with something close to shame. It felt akin to being on a roller coaster, thrilling and terrifying in equal measure. Since Jonathan died, she had been waiting for her life to start, but knew no matter how strong the attraction, she could not easily jump from being Jonathan's widow, could not find pleasure if it was to be at the expense of another woman's happiness, and could not get involved with the man who was to be her son's father-in-law. It was sticky, complicated and unpredictable, none of which she needed right now, as she battled to heal the rift with Jenny and tried to advise Aiden on how best to proceed.

It was only when she looked up that she saw her husband standing by the window, facing the road, his back to her; his stance spoke of disappointment, and it was like a punch to the throat.

'I'm sorry . . .' she whispered, 'I'm so sorry.' But still he didn't turn around.

Chapter Sixteen

It was a busy day as ever in the offices of Greengate and Greengate, the two elderly proprietors who wore similar dark suits. No doubt expensive and tailored to fit when first made, but which now hung on their hook-shaped frames and were shiny on the arms and knees. They also both sported grey wiry hair that had barely thinned, with equal amounts of matching nose and ear tufts. As if their whole heads were full of the stuffing that found any old orifice from which to sprout.

Theirs was a fusty office with wooden desks, and creaking chairs with sharp mechanisms to adjust the height and tilt that could sever a finger with the merest glance. Chairs, like the men themselves, that were assembled long before the advent of health and safety. There was minimal technological intervention to their tried and tested processes. Paperwork was meticulously filed and crammed into dented filing cabinets. Here too, an overly loud clock, which required winding, ticked on the mantelpiece. It was now strangely silent to her, as if her brain had filtered it out or got so used to it; either way, it no longer troubled her.

Enya was at the beck and call of every request, every enquiry and at the mercy of the many letters, parcels and documents that needed signing for and distributing. Not that she minded the hectic work pace today, glad of the distraction from the distress that walking past Jenny's florist's had caused, the beautiful shop that she had thought would be her new home. Not only was her retirement now something she feared without any clue as to what came next, but it was hard to see how they moved forward when Jenny was avoiding her. Enya hoped her words had not been in vain when she said that time would help, that things would seem better when the dust had settled.

She had eaten her lunch at her desk, as was customary. Not that she had time for a break, but, spurred on by hunger, had unwrapped the food while she worked. One quick bite and she'd turned up her nose at the rather unappetising hummus and cucumber sandwich, which had been made in such a hurry with items grabbed from the fridge that she had given inadequate thought to the sog factor. Relief was to be found in the crunch of her Squares crisps, her one indulgence that went some way to restoring her mood. Aiden had, thankfully, left one packet. Not that there was much fun to be had in a break of any kind without catching up on funny texts from Jenny or letting her know an idea or a thought for the florist's. There they were again, those darned tears hovering so close to the surface. She missed her friend more than she could say, and had walked with uncharacteristic caution past the florist's, trying not to look in, wary of catching her friend's eye and having to cope with the rejection, knowing she was too tired to deal with it in a composed manner today. Her life would, she knew, be so much easier to understand if she had Jenny to comb over the facts with in the way they used to.

The phone rang non-stop. Only twenty minutes left until she clocked off and she was already picturing a gigantic mug of tea and a packet of custard creams. It was one of the few advantages of her widowhood, not having to consult anyone about supper plans. She was, if she so chose, able to snaffle biscuits on the sofa in lieu of a decent vegetable, like a teenager who'd been left alone to fend for herself while her parents were out of town. She would be lying if she didn't acknowledge a certain restlessness to her spirit today, as she replayed her conversation with Dominic over and over . . .

'. . . *knowing you are out there in the world is filling my crappy life with joy!*'

'Mine too.' She whispered the admission, knowing it wouldn't help in the long run to harbour these feelings she could never act upon, for what, a fling? Yet she couldn't help the smile that crept across her face, a visceral reaction to the memory of him saying these very words. To be wanted by someone, anyone, was flattering; to be wanted by someone like him, even more so. It was a lovely, secret distraction when she needed it most. All the glorious possibilities of what it might or could be were, however, elbowed out by the sharp reality of their situation. It was bittersweet even to contemplate.

The bell above the office door rang and she jolted, as if caught out, thankful that her thoughts were just that. She looked up to see Jenny and Holly standing in front of her. Her smile widened as a flare of happiness exploded inside her, flooding her with sweet relief! Jenny! Her best friend! Her heart lifted at the sight of her as she let her thoughts rush ahead; reunion followed by forgiveness. It was only as she imagined it that she understood how much she truly longed for it!

'Oh! Holly! Jen!' Jumping up, she walked forward and pulled the girl in for a tight hug. 'Oh, love.'

The young woman's demeanour had changed little since she'd last seen her only days ago.

It was hard to know what to say, how best to comfort the girl who sobbed against her. It was galling to see anyone so distressed, let alone Holly, who she had loved for the longest time, and who had for the last decade been as much part of her family as anyone else. Only she wasn't. Holly shared no blood and only had a seat at the table by invitation. An invite that Aiden had abruptly withdrawn. She caught Jenny's eye and felt the instant stab of dismissal as her friend blinked and looked away, as if they were strangers. Having misjudged the visit, Enya fought the desire to cry, to howl. This was not the kind of reunion she had envisaged. It made no suggestion of forgiveness, and the realisation left her quite bereft.

'She wanted to come and see you, but didn't want to risk coming to the house, in case . . .' Jenny let this trail, her tone laced with bitterness and anger that Enya wanted to address, to remind her friend that it was Aiden who had caused this, and yet it was she, Enya, who was suffering. There had to be a way to work it out, there absolutely had to be a way! But not in front of Holly, the girl had enough going on.

'I understand.' And she did. Letting her go, she studied the face of the girl who only a blink ago had been little Holly Hudson who lived two doors down. 'How are you?' It was a silly question, vacuous and inconsiderate, but just seemed to slip out, habit.

'I don't know.' Holly's voice no more than a whisper.

She looked shockingly altered in such a short space of time. Enya pictured the bounding girl who had clung to Aiden as he left for Rome, barely recognisable as this thin, pale creature, with a vacancy to her eyes that Enya recognised as the one that came with the most toxic combination of medication and grief.

'Sit down, lovey.' Grateful the Greengates were engaged with clients, she pointed to the two leather chairs by the door, fearful the girl might fall. Holly sat. 'And how are *you*, Jen?' She leaned back on her desk and folded her hands, taking the opportunity to try and build a bridge, as her friend took the seat next to her daughter and placed her phone and car keys on her lap.

'I'm . . .' Jenny, who also looked beaten by exhaustion, exhaled, stared at her daughter. Enya understood; when your child was this hurt, you felt every beat of it as if it were your own pain. Because it *was* your own pain. 'Holly wanted to speak to you.' Jenny changed tack, deflected. 'She wanted to speak to you when we popped by the other day, but Angela was there, so.'

'Any time, any time, my love, you know where I am.' She addressed the girl directly.

'I have something to say.'

Without preamble, Holly sat up straight and spoke with a clarity and strength to her tone that had been missing up until now. It suggested that she might be unable to cope with any more pleasantries exchanged; the formality a terrible reminder of how far they had drifted. As if she floated on Frank's lilo, but one pushed out to sea, the speed of the drift one of the hardest things to comprehend, cut loose.

Enya braced herself, expecting to hear a speech that would no doubt slash Aiden to pieces. It was not what she wanted, of course, but understood that it might be entirely necessary as part of Holly's journey to get it all out, to have her moment. She would, she decided, remain passive, neither condone nor counter, but instead recognise that when your heart was cleaved open it was easy to say things that would never otherwise find their way on to your tongue.

'Well, it's easy for you to say, Angela! Go for a bloody walk? Get some fresh air? Have a long bath? Is that going to bring him back?'

'No, love. I just thought . . .'

'Well, stop just thinking, and just saying, and come back and tell me how much walking you feel like doing when your husband is lying under a tree!'

Yes, she understood more than most.

'I'm pregnant.'

Enya felt the words ricochet off the walls and land in her chest like bullets.

'Holly!' It took a second for her to find the motivation to move. She felt almost breathless as she walked to her chair behind the desk and sank into it, not trusting her legs to keep her upright. 'Are . . . are you sure?'

'She's sure.' Jenny answered on her daughter's behalf, her lips tight and thin.

Enya felt torn; her instinct was to say, *Oh, God, no!* Aware as she was that if this news had come only a few weeks ago, they would be celebrating, rejoicing, delighted! She and Jenny, best friends, grannies together, before Aiden had hopped on a plane and diverted the path along which they had all been travelling for the longest time. Before he had fallen for Iris and broken Holly's heart. Pregnant Holly's heart.

Pregnant? It was a disaster. An unmitigated, complicated disaster, like flicking a match into a gas-filled room, like giving hungry foxes access to the henhouse, or throwing a lit firework into the fireworks storeroom. Enya did her best to contain these thoughts, keeping it together until she could go home and scream. If she had thought the whole state of affairs was complicated before, this was on a whole other level. How would Holly cope, how would Aiden? Would Iris stick around if there was a baby on the scene? *A baby!*

'Wow! Darling! I don't know what to say. I can't imagine how you're feeling, Holly.' Her voice, she was aware, sounded shaky.

'I was going to tell him the night he came home. I'd written a card, saying how our new bedroom was themed on a ship, going on a voyage into the unknown, as that's what we were about to undertake.'

Enya felt guilty for having internally mocked the theme and could now see it was as sweet as it was tragic.

'And is this . . .' how to broach the very delicate subject without being overt or suggestive, but the fact was that, at this juncture, Holly still had options, 'this is what you want? To have a baby?'

137

'Yes, it's what I want.' She watched as the girl who had spoken so definitively placed her hand on her stomach.

Jenny stiffened in her seat and at no more than the sight of her friend's straight back, Enya felt her hopes for reconciliation shatter and land like tiny shards on the carpet around their feet.

'It will all be okay.' With some of the strength returned to her legs, she walked to Holly and dropped down in front of her. 'We are all here for you.'

'Not quite.' Holly blinked away more tears.

Enya took the young woman's hand into her own; she smiled up at her, *a baby!* It felt surreal. She mentally tried to figure out how to make it wonderful, how to smother the doubt, the fear, the bloody nightmare scenario they all now faced.

'You're not all here for me, Aiden's not here for me.' It seemed the sound of his name was almost too much, and again she started to cry in earnest.

'He doesn't, doesn't know?' She spoke with hesitation, understanding that if he did know then it not only changed the manner of his infidelity, but also, more than that, it changed what she perceived to be the nature of the man himself, his integrity, his moral compass. It was already hard for her to justify the fact he had cheated on Holly, let her down, made rash decisions that had impacted her greatly.

Holly shook her head. 'He doesn't know.'

Enya felt the flood of relief.

'How far are you, darling?' It felt surreal, *a grandchild . . .* To think this was the very thing she had often dreamed of. She and Jonathan had discussed it, of course, but never could she have imagined the mess in which they now found themselves, nor envisaged a scenario where the news of her first grandchild would be met with such a complex mixture of emotions topped with sorrow.

'Ten weeks.' Holly looked at her mum, who smiled back. It was undeniably wonderful, no matter how terrible. 'I found out when

Aiden was away, didn't want to tell him on the phone, I wanted to see his, his face.' She hiccupped.

'You have to tell him.' She kept her eyes on Jenny, who gave a subtle nod, lips thin, eyes blazing, another indicator of how far their friendship had fallen. It broke Enya's heart a little more.

'Can you do it for me?' Holly whispered.

'Me?' She gasped.

'Yes, please, Enya, I can't do it.'

'I can, but, but you two need to talk. This changes things, maybe not the outcome or decisions made,' she trod carefully, 'but it means that you two have much more to talk about than the divvying up of the flat.'

'That's what I said.'

It was good to hear Jenny showing at the very least that they were on the same page for this, if nothing else.

'Can you tell him, and then ask him to come and see me so we can talk. I know we need to, but I want him to know the situation when he arrives, I don't want to have to break it to him. I think it's better he has a chance to get his head straight first, easier for us both. He doesn't want me, I accept that now. I'd hate to think he might feel obligated to be with me.' Holly shook her head. 'I couldn't stand that.'

It felt like compromise and Enya could only imagine what this young girl was going through.

'I can do that. Of course I can.' She squeezed Holly's hand and stood. 'I'll tell him.'

'Phil's going apeshit.' Her friend looked skyward.

'Well, Phil going apeshit isn't going to help anyone.' She spoke with a confidence she didn't feel, but knew she had to protect Aiden if Phil's rant in her hallway the other evening was anything to go by.

'Easy for you to say.' Jenny sighed and it was Enya's turn to look away, understanding that this was, after all, a mess of her son's making.

'I'll tell Aiden tonight. And will you be at the flat, love? Should I tell him to come and see you straight after?'

Holly nodded and there was the smallest smile on her mouth, as there always was at the prospect of seeing the boy she so loved. It was a terrible reminder of how Holly was still grieving the loss of her great love and, Enya suspected, the hope that it might all in fact blow over.

She raced home, pacing the kitchen, waiting for Aiden to come back while trying to make sense of Holly's news. The person she wanted to talk to was Jenny, the only other person on the planet who might just understand what she was going through. Without the desire to see another text message read and ignored, Enya decided to take stronger action. They were in this situation together and there had to be a way forward, there absolutely had to be. She loved her best friend, loved her so much.

With the notepad open in front of her, she sat at the kitchen table and took her time, letting the pen dance across the page with such sincerity, it was all she could do to keep her hand from trembling.

Jenny,

I'm still trying to process everything, as I imagine are you. My heart breaks for Holly, but I know she'll be fine, because she has you, has us and she is loved. My heart also breaks for me and you.

Truth is I miss you. I miss you so much. I guess I would have allowed doubt to creep in over whether Holly and Aiden would be together for life, only because of their age and lack of experience, which you and I have chatted about. But you and I . . .

She paused and took a moment to gather herself.

I would have bet my house that you and I could have survived anything. Our friendship is something I have always prized, never more so than when we lost Jonathan and there wasn't a day or night you weren't there for me. Something for which I will be forever grateful.

Our plans for the florist's, our cups of tea, the laughs, your three a.m. need for chocolate, all of it is what has sustained me.

To lose you feels . . . almost unbearable, it makes my stomach hurt, sends me dizzy. I can't sleep. The fact is the kids are having a baby and I think, no matter how we got here, it's a chance for you and I to find a way back to each other, because honestly? The thought of doing any of this without you – Jen, I just can't stand it.

I love you, that's it.

Enya X

With the letter inside an envelope and doing her best to ignore the quake in her limbs, Enya trod the path to the Hudsons' front door and popped the note through the letterbox. Her fingers grazed the handle, which she had touched a thousand times, walking into the place where she knew she would always receive the warmest of welcomes.

'Here she is! Hide the rosé!'

Movie nights, dinner parties, summer BBQs and birthday celebrations, even drinks on Christmas morning. This house almost as much a part of her life in Mablethorpe Road as her own.

She walked slowly home, knowing all she could do now was wait for a reply.

Chapter Seventeen

Enya fed Pickle and sat in the lounge, waiting for Aiden to come home, waiting for bedtime when she could curl up and try to escape in sleep, waiting for Jenny to acknowledge her letter, just waiting. Her appetite for a packet of custard creams now non-existent.

'What the hell are we going to do, Jonathan?'

He stared ahead, either deep in thought or still smarting over her bath-time chat last night. Whichever, it didn't feel good. Aiden's key in the door robbed her of the chance to ponder further.

'Hiya!' he called. He sounded happy, so happy, and she hated that she was about to take a knife to that balloon of ecstasy and pop it. Equally, it bothered her how unaffected he sounded while Holly was in turmoil.

'In here, love!' she called and sat up, settling her hands into her lap.

'How was your day?' He poked his head around the door.

'It was okay. Come and sit down.' She nodded at the chair next to Jonathan.

'I will, just going to get a beer.'

He was humming as he dropped his bag on the oak floor. Then the sound of him fumbling in the kitchen, opening the fridge door, the tinny drop of a bottle lid falling into the sink, and there he was, shirt undone at the collar, smiling, beer in hand, sinking down into the comfy seat with his legs stretched out and his breath even, looking and sounding so much like his dad that she had to look away.

'I spoke to Iris all the way home.' He beamed. 'I was actually glad to be sitting in traffic. How nuts is that? She was telling me this convoluted story about getting stuck in a rabbit hutch when she was a kid, her cousin had dared her to get in it and she did, but then she couldn't get out. It was so sweet; she was too scared to open her eyes and her dad had to come and saw the top off. We talk utter shite, but honestly, Mum, she's still the person I would rather listen to than any other. I can't imagine ever running out of things to say.'

She remembered being that way with Jonathan when they were brand new and their future lay ahead like a shiny thing, untarnished and precious. They'd talk until the early hours, caring less that their alarm was set for the working day, not wanting to waste a second on sleep. It was only in recollection that she realised they had grown quieter with each passing year. It was different when you knew what someone thought about everything, could predict how they would respond, even whether they wanted a cup of tea or not, no need for words. They simply moved together in an established dance, hand to hand, hip to hip, slipping against each other, and with no more than a look, a glance, a nod, a wink, in sync. *One team* . . . The truth was, she spoke to him more now that he was dead. Funny, that.

Her stomach rolled with nerves; she hated that she was about to hoover up her son's joy, to coin a phrase, in the most spectacular way.

'Iris and I have been talking about where we want to live, it's horrible being apart. Neither of us can stand it. And it seems the best solution, because I only have to go into the office two days a week and can easily commute, is that I move in with her. She has the annexe thing at her mum and dad's, a garden room, kind of. I'm going over tomorrow and will stay for a couple of days, to help with wedding planning and stuff, if that's okay? God, even saying wedding planning is like waaaaah!' He splayed his hand and raised his voice, giddy with it all.

She would have been hard pushed to remember the last time he had chatted to her like this, shared his life in this way. No TV, no background distraction, no phone in hand, no quick commentary or update as they collided in hallways or corridors, or shouted over shoulders as they left the house. It was lovely to hear him so happy, yet it was also another lifeline severed; he was leaving her, leaving the area to go and join Iris and her family in the annexe thing. It wasn't that she wanted to keep him tethered to her, of course not, but how she would miss him. His lust for life, now the thing that made her aware that he had, in recent months, been more than a little subdued. His words and energy, however, for a life that seemed to have cruelly cut Holly out, erasing her so quickly, made it impossible for Enya to share his enthusiasm, especially in light of the news she was yet to share. He didn't wait for her response.

'We're going to save for a deposit, Mum, and hopefully get our own place, I mean, that's the plan.'

This would ordinarily have been big news, something to be dissected and celebrated, with her predictable prompt about taking their time and going gently, but not tonight, not with even bigger news that would knock her son's proposed living arrangements into a footnote of insignificance. And, uncomfortably, she didn't entirely hate the fact that he was being forced back down to earth. It wasn't her belief that joy could be savoured when the trade-off was another person's happiness. That, she knew, was a price not worth paying. Plus, to hear him racing towards the next thing at a hundred miles an hour with this girl he had only known for five minutes would have been deeply concerning if she were not already wrestling with something far *more* concerning.

'What do you think?' He held his beer still, waiting for her to comment.

'I saw Holly today,' she began, keeping her voice level to give the subject the gravitas required. He breathed out through his nose, as if a little irked to have his bubble burst by the reminder.

'How was she?' He blinked.

'She wants you to go over there this evening, to talk about things, about where you go from here.' This a verbal stepping stone, leading towards the big reveal, a path she trod with caution.

'I don't see the point, Mum. I don't want to be mean to her or sound like a dick, but it's like, we've had that explosive conversation. We can't keep having it, it's just exhausting and doesn't help either of us. I've told her that she can stay in the flat, she can have everything in it we bought together, and I'll even pay the rent for the next three or four months while she decides what to do. I want her to be okay, I still care about her, of course I do, but—'

'Aiden.' Enya sat forward until she was on the edge of the sofa.

'What's the matter?' He too sat forward and put the beer on the end table, next to the lamp.

'Holly is pregnant.'

Her son laughed, letting out a low, long chuckle of disbelief, until he stopped laughing. He wagged his finger at her.

'That's not funny.' He licked his mouth and swallowed.

'It's true. She's pregnant, love. She came to the office with Jenny. They wanted me to tell you first and then suggested you go over to talk to her directly.'

'That's not,' he shook his head, 'that's not true. She can't be.'

'She is, darling. Ten weeks.'

As the colour drained from his face, she was glad he was sitting down, certain that had he been standing, he might have fallen.

'Is it true, Mum?' he asked again, his voice no more than a whisper.

She nodded, understanding what it felt like when despite the facts presented, your brain would not let you accept the reality.

'He's gone, Enya.'

'I think he might want some water; his mouth looks . . .'

'He's gone, my love. He's at peace.'

'I'll sit here for a while . . . in case he needs anything.'

'Why didn't she tell me?' he gasped. 'Is she okay? What . . . what do we do now?'

'I think you need to try and stay calm and not panic. It'll take a while to sink in, love. But talk to her, talk it out, make a plan.' As advice went, it felt as thin as it did clichéd.

'Does she . . . does she want to keep the baby?' he asked quietly, with a reticence to his tone in light of the topic.

'I think she does, yes.'

He breathed out, slowly. 'What do I say to Iris?'

Without a ready answer to this, she stayed quiet, watching as her son placed his head in his hands and fat tears dripped silently from the end of his nose on to the carpet.

Jonathan finally looked at her, although his expression made her wish he hadn't, suggesting she had been left with the hand on the tiller and they were now crashed upon the rocks. A failure by anyone's standards. She fought the temptation to yell at the man. *'It's all well and good looking at me like that, but what exactly am I supposed to do? I'm figuring this out as I go along!'*

Aiden abandoned his beer, quietly refused supper, and changed into his jeans before leaving to go and see Holly, making his way down the stairs and along the path with a walk of such sadness it was as if he were on his way to the gallows. As was always the way, she felt the weight of her son's predicament on her own shoulders. It was a night she knew she would never forget, not only as her brain tried to adjust to the fact that Aiden was going to be a dad, Holly a mum, but also it was the first time she hadn't known what to say to her son to make everything better while swallowing her own frustration at the gargantuan mess he had created.

Even when they had just lost Jonathan, in the midst of his grief she had found words of solace. It was easy; he would miss his dad, of course he would, but he could sleep knowing that he had been the very best son, how proud Jonathan was of him, and how deeply he had loved him. His time with his dad might have been cut short, but he could rest easy, knowing he could do so without regret. And what a marvellous gift that was.

This was different. An entirely terrible situation that for the want of a few weeks would have been nothing but cause for celebration. It was the cruellest trick of fate, and one into which she had insight. What if Dominic were single? What if they had met years down the line and his situation was changed, what if he were not Iris's dad, what if . . . *what if* . . .

'But now we know how fragile the threads were that kept them together, would it have been awful for Aiden to be locked into that relationship for life, Holly too?' She looked at her husband. 'Locked in, that sounds like punishment, and I don't mean it like that. What do I mean? And come to think of it, he's still locked in for life, isn't he, they both are? No matter who he's with or whatever happens next, this baby is forever.' She paused. 'A baby, Jonathan. I can't quite believe it.'

Pickle came into the lounge and hopped up on to the sofa, where she was absolutely not allowed to sit. Enya ran her palm over the silky back of her beloved cat, who now coiled into a loaf and purred in sleep.

She didn't feel like watching TV, wondering if the letter to Jenny had been a mistake, feeling as exposed as she did, vulnerable, not that there was a darn thing she could do about that now. She grabbed the latest Jill Mansell, a fail-safe good read, and settled back on the sofa. It did the trick, distracting her from the knotty ball of worries that seemed to be growing in her thoughts, until the buzzing of her phone pulled her from the pages.

The name HCK flashed up on her screen and again her heart stuttered. Her fingers hesitated for only the briefest of seconds before she placed Jill face down on the sofa, spine cracked, and reached for her phone.

'Hello?' She screwed her face up, she knew it was him calling and he'd probably know that she knew, yet the pantomime felt entirely necessary. The simple truth was, she had had the very worst day and wanted someone to talk to, someone who was alive, who might talk back. Someone who might say the things Jenny would have said to make it all feel a bit better, to make her feel less alone. Or someone like sweet Holly, who, it struck her then, was hiding away, usurped by Iris, hurt and lonely. And here she was, answering the phone to the man who was married to Trish, who would no doubt, if things were allowed to develop, feel usurped by Enya. It was sobering and unwelcome and instantly she regretted answering the call.

'Enya, it's Dominic.'

'Hi, Dominic.' She tucked her hair behind her ears and crossed her legs, as if by adopting this more businesslike stance, the encounter might be a bit more . . . businesslike.

'Hope it's not a bad time, would hate to interrupt your bath-time pasta-making?'

'Very funny. How was your day?'

She hated the casual nature of her enquiry, as if this were normal, as if it were okay, as if Trish were not at home, maybe tidying away the supper things or settling down to watch TV. Trish, who was about to become Aiden's mother-in-law.

'Oh, you know, the usual.' He took a breath as if he too were aware that she didn't know, because they were strangers. She had no idea if he ran marathons before breakfast or did macramé to fill the hours. 'It's been a quiet day really, and this is the best part of it, walking our dog, Fishstick.'

'Your dog is called *Fishstick*?'

'Yes.' He spoke without the tiniest whiff of irony. 'Do you find that amusing in some way?'

'No, not at all,' she mused, knowing if circumstances were different she'd have found it very funny. 'My cat is called Pickle – well, Madam Pickle Paws to give her her full but mostly unused name.'

'I see, it's full names you want, is it? In that case, I am walking Master Fishstick of Fowey, which is where he was born. Oh, hang on a minute, he's running towards a group of walkers and is yet to learn that not everyone wants to be bowled over, quite literally, by a hefty retriever who still thinks he's a puppy!'

She listened carefully as Dominic called, 'Sticks! Sticksy! Come on, pal!' Delighted that the mutt had a nickname.

'Disaster averted,' he breathed heavily. 'We like to wander the Bath Skyline walk, have you done it?'

'Erm, no, no I haven't.'

'I envy anyone that hasn't, experiencing it for the first time is the best thing!'

'I feel like that about books, books I love, it's with the smallest flicker of reticence that I recommend them to people, slightly envious, wishing I was about to dive in afresh.'

'The things we do . . .' He spoke softly, and she held the phone close to her face.

To hear his voice was like lighting a match under the fire of indifference she could construct when preoccupied with the routine of life, those busy times when he lived in memory only. There was undeniably something about him, his manner, even the idea of him pulled at her, made her forget the thousand reasons why she should do the right thing and end the call. It was as if her whole body bent towards the sound of his voice, her skin deliciously prickling in reaction to no more than the words in her ear. And the *way* he spoke to her, like he had done so a thousand times before. As if it were the most natural and obvious thing in the world for the two of them to leisurely interact in this way. A salve to her loneliness that allowed the embers of possibility to glow brightly in a future that looked a little grey without her friend, her husband, her job, her son living close by. It was hard to define and even harder to rationalise how solid this connection felt after only the briefest of encounters, how strong the physical desire for this man that she knew was at the root of this . . . this . . . whatever it was . . . which she would not allow to develop. A dalliance that would not, could not take hold.

'And how was your day?' he asked casually, and just the thought of the news that was another wrecking ball to a simple, uncomplicated life was enough for her to feel the gathering of tears.

'The usual,' she lied, knowing it was not her place to share news that might have the direst of consequences for the people they both loved. This realisation in turn filled her with fresh guilt, knowing she was talking about Holly Hudson and that there was a little baby at the heart of it. It was the first time she felt warmth at the thought, as the shock momentarily gave way to the golden idea of grandparenthood. *A baby*, a baby to keep her busy, to fill her day, someone else to love, to help fill the gaps. Although how that would work with Holly and Aiden still miles apart and the widening void between her and Jenny, God only knew. She prayed her letter might go some way towards starting the healing process, closing her eyes briefly, upset now at the thought that every silver lining seemed to be mentally balled and discarded as quickly as she conjured it.

'Our call was rather abruptly ended last night.' He kept his voice soft, adding to the conspiratorial air that required no such emphasis.

'Yes, there was a crisps location emergency.' She stopped short, remembering how uncomfortable it was to talk about Aiden, about Iris, a reminder that her attraction to Dominic was a doomed infatuation that could never take hold.

So, end the call then! came the memo from her subconscious, and yet she did nothing of the sort. The warmth in the base of her stomach encouraging just a few more minutes of contact, of company, before the long night ahead.

'Well, we had tears over whether crab and apple salad or sashimi tuna was the most appropriate starter for a wedding on a warm day.'

'I think either will be equally disastrous if left in the sun.'

It reminded her of the day Aiden came back from Rome, his words a tsunami of destruction in their little lives. That day, not so long ago, when she had been overly concerned about the health of her prawns. Prawns that had ended up in the bin when much, much bigger concerns swept that worry away like twigs in the kerb as a storm hit.

'My thoughts entirely.' He spoke slowly. Here they were again, chatting and in accord. 'I don't want to be pushy, but I did want to finish what I started to say last night. I'd planned it, practised it in my head, and so to be robbed of the moment felt frustrating.'

It was an admission of his vulnerability, practising his speech. There was nothing cocky or assumptive in his words, but rather it suggested a hesitancy and a desire to get it right. She liked it.

'As I said, I've been . . . I've been treading water, for the longest time. We, *we* have been treading water. And we're not desperately unhappy, there are no explosive rows, no anger. It might be better if there were.' He drew breath. 'It's more like we've run out of steam. Stopped on the tracks and there's no rescue in sight. We're stationary and therefore bored and frustrated. We snap at each other and it's ugly, I'm ashamed that you saw that. It's like we're waiting for someone to come along and show us the signpost of where we go next. Static. We skirt around the topic. Both admitting we're not happy, but the truth is it's more than that, we're done, and yet neither of us has had the courage to say it out loud, to blow the final whistle, not for the longest time, both afraid, I guess, of all that comes after. The disruption. It's why I took the flat. We agreed it's the physical separation that will ease what comes next.'

She thought briefly of her mum and dad, bickering the decades away.

'Yet you have the courage to say it out loud to me.'

She was aware that this knowledge came with its own set of consequences that could be either a burden or a gift.

'Yes,' he whispered. 'I do. I love Trish. That's the strange thing. And probably the most surprising thing to me. I might have assumed that to feel the way I do would mean falling out of love and that can quickly lead to dislike, irritation, all those things that slowly erode a shared life. But no, I still love her. Very much. But tragically, I love her like I love my brother, my great friend, my kids. I don't love her with a burning desire or, or a need to be with her, I'm not *in* love with her.'

His words at once filled her with elation and desolation, to be talking so freely and intimately about the woman she had met only briefly. It was both disloyal and riveting. He didn't sound like a man who was cruel or frivolous, quite the opposite. His words were considered and smart. It helped her understand the uncharacteristic attraction she felt for him. He loved his daughter; she remembered how the first time she'd met him he'd been waiting to see her safely boarded, listening to her playlist, wanting to understand her, and recognising that his child's lyrics of choice, no more than her favoured poetry set to music, was a way to do that.

It was beautiful. And he loved his wife. Ironically, just the kind of characteristics she would look for in a potential lover. If it weren't so bloody complicated and impossible it would have made her laugh, not want to cry.

'I suspect that you might be describing the majority of marriages after so long. Isn't it just standard practice that the sparkle wears off? As it's meant to. I can't imagine that level of passion or burning desire being sustainable, and isn't what replaces it more precious? That deep connection, the constancy?'

He gave a wry chuckle. 'Of course, but what if it's replaced with something less substantial than a deep connection? What if you're left with something that feels thin, diluted, as if you are both settling rather than finding the courage to live your best lives? And why should we settle? Why *do* we?'

'Convenience. Habit. Kindness . . .' The first three that sprang to mind.

'Life is short, Enya.'

'That much I do know.' She stared at the empty seat that Jonathan had vacated.

'Yes, of course. But why *can't* I feel this way? Why can't I grab this joy that is filling me up!'

Joy! She filled him with joy! This in turn filled her with something similar. She had quite forgotten what it felt like, the beginning, the excitement, the endless possibilities of a relationship that might just be the greatest love story ever told, or something that could crash and burn very quickly, and therein lay the thrill of it.

'Because,' she spoke plainly, 'it would cause the greatest upset to our children and would very likely come to nothing. It's a lovely, lovely distraction, but it would be a lot for our kids to pick through, would cause disruption, sadness, conflict, and I for one go out of my way to never do that to my son. He's been through quite enough.'

She made no mention of all he was about to go through.

'What if it was worth it?'

'It would never be worth that! I don't know what else to say.' This the truth, floored again, as she was by his frank and flattering admissions that she knew she would replay in the early hours, when her bed felt too big.

'Well, I do know what to say. I want to say that I'm entirely sick of not moving forward or making progress, of feeling stuck, and like Trish and I are simmering with nothing to light the dark winter mornings. I'm sick of it, and I think I deserve better, I think we both do.'

'That's . . . that's your right, your decision, but I don't really know you, Dominic, and so to be telling me this—'

'When you popped up in the car park,' he carried on, as if she hadn't spoken, and she held her breath, listening to his every word, 'it was like . . .' he laughed, as if he too remembered the way it had felt, 'it was like shaving decades from my jaded self. The way I felt, the way I *feel*, a little jittery, excited, it was like being seventeen again! I was excited! Properly excited, and not just in the way I am when my seedlings sprout or the boat gets a spring clean, but in the way that . . .' He appeared to have run out of words, words that mirrored her own feelings and which to hear aloud filled her right up. She felt light, excited, as her muscles contracted and her heart danced with joy.

'In the way that it felt when you borrowed your dad's Land Rover and went a-wooing?'

'Yes, Enya.' There was no hint of frivolity in his tone. 'Exactly like that. And what with having signed the lease on the flat, it felt possible! Everything felt possible!'

She wanted to remind him that signing a lease on a flat and being divorced or officially separated were very different things. There was no guarantee he would ever live in the place, or worse, what if he only intended to use it to conduct an illicit affair? It was a thought that horrified. Simultaneously, she wondered if Trish felt the same level of enthusiasm, and just picturing the pretty woman who had stood in her kitchen was enough to shape her words.

'I don't think it's a good idea for you to call me. Not a good idea at all. Not that I don't, or not that I haven't . . .' What did she want to say? Was she brave enough to voice the words that would end this lovely feeling of happiness, of connection to another human when she craved it most? Words that would shatter the frail and beautiful cage of happiness that she could feel forming all around her, around them. 'It's not fair on any of us.' She closed her eyes.

It was true, the thought of dumping this on Aiden when he was facing so much was unthinkable. Plus, if Iris didn't bolt at the news of Holly's pregnancy, then surely hearing her future mother-in-law had feelings for her father . . . Enya screwed her eyes shut at the mere thought. And then there was the sharp stick of betrayal that jabbed her awake in the early hours. She and Jonathan had created a wonderful life, and she had done her best to carry it on without him, but to change course, swap teams, fall into the arms of another man, do differently, then it meant he had really gone. It meant everything would change. It would feel like erasing all that they had built. She was the sole custodian of their old life, their old love, and to start over would be akin to abandoning it, abandoning Jonathan.

'Life, life is complicated enough right now,' she stuttered. 'For me to take a leap and go all in, I just can't. It needs to be easy, and this is far, far from easy.'

There was a silence that crackled down the line and her heart raced with lament, understanding it was a silence that would replace these calls. Jonathan, Jenny, Aiden to a certain degree, and now Dominic, the list of people who had slipped or were slipping out of reach was growing, a thought that was as depressing as it was true. She felt the clock of solitude beat loudly in her chest.

'Of course. I'm sorry. I just thought, I don't know what I thought. I guess I'm finding it a little harder to let go than I would like to admit.'

And just like that he was gone.

Gripping the phone like a preoccupied teen, she wondered whether to text, to try and explain that *if* things were different . . .

But the simple truth was that things were not different.

And that was that.

Chapter Eighteen

Aiden had arrived home after Enya had gone to bed, and she was unsure if it was a good or bad thing that there had been so much for him and Holly to discuss. She wanted him to support Holly, that went without saying, but was also aware of her son's fragility, having to navigate these new and uncharted waters while a storm raged. No matter it was a storm of his own making. Losing his dad had, unsurprisingly, changed him, forced him to grow up, and came with a tendency for him to bottle up his feelings and pretend, for her sake, that all was dandy. She knew him well enough to peer beneath the veneer of confidence that he sometimes presented.

In the morning he had left for work while she was in the shower. The only tell-tale sign of his presence a lingering scent of his cologne in the hallway and the carton of milk, left to warm on the countertop.

'I sometimes long for those days when I was a little bored! This is all too much for me, Jonathan.' She spoke to her husband, who sat at the breakfast bar on the far side of the island in the kitchen. 'I still love you,' she added, her voice cracking with emotion, 'you know that, don't you?', aware of the disloyalty of her thoughts and fantasies to which she was certain her dead husband was privy.

A brisk knock at the door pulled her from the conversation.

'Oh!' She clasped her hands under her chin and resisted the temptation to wrap her arms around the visitor, her eyes instantly filled with tears.

It was both a delight and a relief to find Jenny on the doorstep. Enya felt her smile bloom wider than her head as her breath came in long, slow bursts of happiness. She must have read the letter and here she was! Her best friend was *here*! Joy beat in her breast. It was all going to be okay; it seemed the dust, if not settled, was certainly settling.

'Hi, Enya.'

Her friend's tone, however, was less than effusive. Her manner guarded, arms clamped to her sides, the avoidance of eye contact. It was hard to read what was going on behind Jenny's facade. Enya figured it might just be plain old discomfort at how things had fallen off track for them, embarrassment, which, no matter how misplaced, she understood. But she was here now, and that really was all that mattered.

'Jenny! It's so lovely to see you! God, I've missed you! Come in, come in.' Enya stood back to allow her entry, like she had a thousand times before, but never with this weight of relief to her bones. They walked into the kitchen.

'I know Aiden's not here. Phil called him earlier. He said he was on his way to the office, and then away for a couple of nights. Phil's asked if he can see him when he's back.'

Jenny's tone was not that of the natural, smart, chocolate-hunting buddy who could make her laugh with no more than an anecdote about wanting to punch a child who had kicked Holly's art project. It was formal, stiff and a little foreboding, words issued from a mouth that was thin.

'Right.' Enya understood that her dream of happily rekindling their friendship might have been a bit premature. She folded her arms around her waist, her smile faltering, as her optimism faded.

Instantly, she felt protective of her son, knowing the prospect of his encounter with Phil would weigh heavily on him, and feeling raw and a bit stupid, having laid her emotions out in that letter that her friend had, thus far, failed to mention.

'I'm, I'm sorry about the other night when he barged in like that.' Jenny shook her head. 'I told him not to come over when he was angry. He shouldn't have done it, Enya. It was . . .'

'I get it, Jen. I do.'

Not only did she understand how hurt manifested itself in all sorts of ways, she also didn't think it was any woman's responsibility to apologise for her husband. She pictured Trish and Dominic bickering in this very room as if it were second nature and therefore mattered little who else was around, the norm. He was right, it was ugly.

Her neighbour looked a little beaten, and a little distant. Ordinarily, Enya would hug her, offer tea, get to the root of what ailed her, find words, and make a plan to soothe her pain. But today she felt entirely unable to do so, an awful marker of how wide the gap was between them and how quickly it had formed.

'Did you get my letter?' she asked, with the vague hope that she had not and therefore her rather cool demeanour could be thawed with no more than a repetition of its contents face to face.

'I did.' Jenny bit her lip, and Enya felt her heart sink and her throat constrict. It was the most awful feeling in the world, understanding that there was to be no reprieve, no healing. It was worse somehow, the indifference, when she had laid her heart on the line. She felt sick.

'I wish Jonathan was here,' Jenny sighed, 'he'd know what to say to calm Phil down, what to do.'

Enya nodded at this truth. 'Not sure there is anything *to* do, Jen. We just need to be there for them both and make things better, not worse.'

'Yep. I can't believe she's having a baby.' Jenny allowed herself a fleeting smile.

'We're going to be grannies.' Enya tried with the reminder to pull her friend closer. 'It hasn't sunk in for me really. I kind of vacillate between feeling overwhelmed with worry and delighted. Aiden went to see Holly last night.'

'Yes, she said.' Jenny took a moment. 'She was a little bit calmer this morning. Aiden told her he'd carry on paying the rent so she could stay in the flat if she wanted. He's going to take care of her financially until she can get on her feet. Said he'd go with her to her scans if she wants him to and that he'll be there for them both, always.'

Enya felt a swell of relief that in this sense, at least, he was doing the right thing, displaying the kindness that she knew was in his character and the sense of responsibility they had instilled in him.

'I keep trying to remind myself that he's a good kid,' Jenny closed her eyes and licked her bottom lip, 'despite wanting to throttle him, and feeling floored by this bloody mess, I try to remember that deep down he's a good kid.'

'They both are, and something I think about a lot is that even though I'm in my fifties, I'm still figuring life out one day at a time. No one tells you that, do they? You kind of assume when you're growing up that one day you'll reach a point and have all the knowledge, know all the answers. But it doesn't work like that, does it?'

'No, it certainly doesn't.' Jenny shook her head.

'And just when you think you might have a handle on life, something else comes along to pull the rug from under you and you're on your bum again, scratching your head and wondering which way is up.'

She thought of Dominic, *the way I feel, a little jittery, excited, it was like being seventeen again!* A shiver of misplaced delight danced along her limbs. How she wished she could talk to Jenny about it all, knowing how much she'd value her wise counsel.

'That's about the sum of it.' Jenny gave a short, unnatural laugh edged with fatigue. 'Anyway, I just wanted to come over and say that I'm sorry about Phil barging in and losing it like that and that it mustn't be awkward when we see each other, Enya, or bump into each other out and about, because that would only make things harder for the kids.'

'And you read my letter, Jen, all of it?' She hated how needy she sounded. 'It's just that, we've been mates for a long time. We have plans!' she enthused, one final roll of the dice.

'I did. I read all of it.' There was an embarrassed moment of silence as her friend declined to expand on the topic. Enya felt her breath coming in short bursts, fighting the desire to sob. 'Look, I'd, I'd better get back.' Jenny pointed stiffly towards the front door, choosing not to grab the verbal vine Enya had thrown her. Leaving their plans dangling and unresolved and her heart a little broken. It was painful and smacked of the awkwardness they had only just agreed to avoid.

'I just love you, Jen,' she sniffed. 'Are you sure you don't fancy a cup of tea? I've got chocolate!' Enya tried again, humbling herself because Jenny was worth it, her very best friend.

'No, thank you,' Jenny replied slowly and with a certain formality as she made her way along the corridor. 'What's she like?' Her words spoken as she faced the front door, avoiding eye contact. There was no need to clarify who she referred to. And there it was, the reminder of why they had been cleaved apart.

'Very different to Holly. Bit more, I don't know, serious, reserved, I suppose.' She felt the grip of disloyalty about her throat. 'I've only met her once, briefly, and what can you tell about someone after one meeting?'

'I don't know how my little girl gets over this, Enya.' Jenny reached for the door-knob. 'Truth is, I'm scared for her.'

'I'm scared for all of them.' She took a step closer to her friend. 'And, and I just want to say that we're more than their mothers, Jen, you and I. We're friends too, the best of friends, outside of them, away from them.'

'Are we?' The retort was sharp.

'I . . .' Jenny's reply had floored her. Enya didn't know how to respond, maybe they weren't, and this thought was the final knife in her gut. 'Jen . . .' Enya placed her hand on the woman's narrow shoulder, feeling a terrible level of guilt for actions that were nothing to do with her. Jenny gave an almost involuntary shrug. It was the final act of separation. Enya removed her hand, which felt like a slap across the face, her words now forced through a throat narrow with distress. 'No matter what happens, we're going to share a grandchild, a little one who will love having their nanas living two doors apart. I know I would have thought that was brilliant.'

'Really?' Jenny looked skyward, her mouth tense, as the last vestiges of pretence fell away. 'How exactly do you see that working, Enya? Holly and the baby in the kitchen, Aiden and his new wife in the lounge? Maybe you could make them all tea, offer cake?'

'Yes. That's exactly how I see it working, because it has to, because the thought of a little one being raised with this friction, this sadness and suspicion, it doesn't bear thinking about.'

'And whose fault is that?' Jenny fired.

It seemed her friend needed to dig a bit deeper to remember that Aiden was indeed a good kid.

'Not mine, Jen, and not yours.' She held her ground.

'I'd, I'd better go. And also, I wanted to say, that I erm, I appreciate the letter, but,' Jenny took her time, 'it would be easier for me, for us all, really, if we kept to ourselves.'

'What does *that* mean?' Enya swallowed the lump of distress.

'It means what I said, that we shouldn't be afraid to bump into each other, we live so close, but at the same time, we're all a bit raw, a bit bruised, and so I'd appreciate it if you didn't write to me again. I won't be coming for a cup of tea or bringing you flowers or texting you something funny I've seen.'

'Or letting me buy into the business?' She felt the solid future she had constructed crumble away, and with it came the uneasy feeling of panic that she recognised.

'It's for the best,' Jenny levelled.

'You're *unfriending* me?' she asked directly. 'Reducing me to neighbour status. Ending our lovely friendship?' She hated how her voice broke and the tears that now came with it. 'What next? Am I going on your hate list? Oh, Jen . . .'

'Not forever, I wouldn't think,' it wasn't quite the denial Enya had hoped for, 'it's just better this way. Holly is hurt, Phil's fuming and I'm—'

'Yes, Jen, do go on, what are *you* exactly?' Finally, the woman turned to face her. Her words were slowly and deliberately delivered, as Enya wiped the tears from her eyes.

'I am in the middle, Enya, holding steady the life raft on which everyone I love is resting and I'm bloody exhausted.'

'Me too,' she whispered, watching as her ex-friend and neighbour struggled with the door handle and made a mess of the simplest task, walking through the open door and out on to the path, faltering and threatening to trip as she did so. Enya understood, remembering in the wake of losing Jonathan, taking every step as if she had miscalculated at the bottom of a staircase and was unsure if she was safely planting her foot or tumbling into the abyss. It had taken months for her to remember how to walk properly.

She had quite forgotten this, in the way you did a toothache or an itch, erasing it from thought once you started healing. Not that she felt healed, not really.

163

Closing the door behind her, she made her way to the lounge and gently lowered the Roman blinds, wanting in that moment to shut the world out and to sit in the half-light, surrounded by the shadows of a life that felt as if it were falling away at the edges. In the middle of the neighbourhood that had once felt like her crowd but was shrinking by the day. Trying to picture what a life lived here without Jenny or, worse, having to avoid her, might look like. She sank down on to the sofa and curled her legs beneath her before firing off a text to Aiden.

EVERYTHING WILL BE OKAY. I LOVE YOU, ALWAYS X

It felt entirely necessary in that moment to tell him, understanding that the Hudsons weren't the only ones who were a bit raw, a bit bruised. And feeling so utterly alone, wanting to reach out to the person who was left in her corner, her son. What she wanted, more than anything, was to feel Jonathan's arms around her, holding her tightly, in the way that he did when things felt a little overwhelming. But no, the best she could hope for was to stare at him as he sat in his chair, legs outstretched, expression irritatingly impassive.

Enya hadn't meant to fall asleep, but clearly she had as she was now woken by the sound of a gentle knock at the front door. Her first thought, her hope, was that maybe Jenny, having considered their earlier conversation, had come to make amends, to explain that she'd had a rethink and that yes, a cup of tea would be lovely. Her heart lifted at the prospect. She would forgive her, of course she would forgive her!

It wasn't Jenny on the doorstep.

It wasn't anyone she might have expected or was mentally prepared to welcome into her home.

'Hello.' Dominic smiled at her.

'What, what are you . . .' She ran the tip of her finger under her eye to check for sleep, knowing there was a good chance of a cushion crease on her cheek and that her hair would have gone full bird's nest.

'I know you probably don't want to see me,' he began, and she felt her gut fold. The truth was she did, she did want to see him, knowing it was unwise, dangerous even and certainly futile. 'I'm not staying. I've taken on board what you said, about it not being a good idea for me to phone. I get it, but I can't stand the idea of drip-feeding snippets back and forth with the odd text or stolen message, and I can't abide the thought of all these thoughts spinning in my head wanting release. I just want the chance to say it all and to say it once. That's it. Just once. If you'll let me. I can do it here on the doorstep and then go. Five minutes.'

'I . . .' She was unsure of how to react, and she was a little bowled over by his presence, his face. 'Come in.'

It felt easier, safer, to have him on the other side of the door and away from possible public scrutiny.

'I didn't intend to—'

'Just come in, Dominic.'

She stood back, inhaling the scent of him as he moved in such proximity that touching him would have been easy. She quickly glanced up and down the street and was relieved that there was no sign of the Hudsons, and that Maeve seemed to still be keeping a low profile after the Pickle turd incident. He walked into the wide, pretty kitchen as he had only days before, and as if he had been doing so for much longer.

Despite her reservations, she felt the icy chill of Jenny's rejection thaw, and warmth spread through her bones at no more than the presence of him.

Chapter Nineteen

'Would you like a drink?' Enya reached for the kettle.

'I don't want to impose.' His expression was pained.

'I'm going to have one.' She lifted a mug from the shelf.

'Erm,' he looked at his watch, 'I try to avoid caffeine after four, keeps me up. Can I have water or juice?'

'Of course, and you can sit down. You're making me jumpy.'

'I'm sorry.' He ran his hand over his mouth and sat at the dining table.

'I have wine.'

'That would be lovely.' He allowed himself a small smile.

Wine with Dominic, she'd be lying if she didn't admit to feeling the tiniest frisson of desire grip her stomach.

'What's the time? I've lost track, a little.' She patted her wayward curls and wished she could pop upstairs to clean her teeth without seeming rude.

'Nearly five.'

'Goodness! I've slept for most of the afternoon, that's really not like me.'

'You must have needed it. You can't make your body do that. It's good to shut down and recharge occasionally.'

'I guess so,' she yawned, as her brain zapped back to life. 'I always feel guilty if I nap during the day. It was how I was brought up, to fill every minute with something productive, find a chore, keep busy.'

'I've never really understood that.' He watched as she walked across the kitchen to fetch two wine glasses and a bottle of her favoured rosé from the fridge. 'The guilt that comes with self-care. I say to Iris, put yourself first, then do what others need or want.'

'It's good advice, doesn't mean I know how to take it.'

'That's most advice in my case.' He laughed.

She placed the glass of wine in front of him and took a seat on the opposite side, glad that he hadn't sat in Jonathan's chair at the head of the table. It was one thing to have this man inside her house, but quite another for him to have sat there.

'Cheers.' He raised his glass towards her and took a sip.

'Cheers. Here's to a very unexpected visit.' She wanted to feel irate at the intrusion, but the truth was she felt nothing but delight to be in his company. Still reeling from Jenny's visit earlier, this felt like the opposite of exclusion. Her gut fluttered with the nerves of a sixteen-year-old on prom night and a flush of want that seemed to bloom whenever he was near. It was as addictive as it was hazardous, easy to misinterpret the physical attraction for something more.

'I like your home very much. The softness of it.'

'The softness?' She wasn't sure what he meant or whether it was a compliment.

'Yes, the cushions, linens, worn wood, glass, rounded chairs, lots of circles and tactile pieces. No sharp edges.'

'Not by design. It's a kind of mishmash of things I've acquired or inherited or fallen in love with.' She looked at the pink and green striped pleated lampshade on the tall red candle lamp. She and Jonathan had picked it up at an antique market in Wells. It had been the loveliest of days.

'That's why it works, it's personal, curated.'

'If you say so.' She took a glug of wine. 'It's also dusty, very dusty.' She felt the need to do this, using self-deprecation to smother any embarrassment, having found it hard to take a compliment since her teens, when an unhealthy pocketful of self-doubt had weighed her down. It hadn't been easy being the tall, lanky one in the pack. 'Okay, so five minutes,' she prompted, half in jest, happy to be in his company. His presence helping to dilute some of the hurt of Jenny's visit earlier, the moment her friend had shrugged free of her hand, something she doubted she would ever forget.

'Right, yes.' He put his wine down and took a deep breath. She liked the way he looked at her, as if she were something to be admired, *bright*. Compared to how Jenny could barely meet her gaze and the way Aiden sometimes rolled his eyes at her, it was lovely. 'I still find it quite extraordinary how we met in the car park before the kids knew each other, and here we all are.'

'It is extraordinary.' She too placed her glass on the table and toyed with the stem, grateful for the prop.

'A bit like Cupid was lining up his arrows and one accidentally caught us while aiming for the kids.'

'Is that what you think?'

His words so blatant. If he had been hit by Cupid's arrow then did he mean *love*, is that where his thoughts were heading? It was a thought that was both thrilling and ridiculous! But love didn't happen like that, no matter how strongly Aiden protested. It simply couldn't. She felt the slide of unease over her skin.

'No! Of course that's not what I think.'

'Oh.' She quickly took another sip, embarrassed to have let her thoughts gambol ahead, his denial causing a complicated response that was both a relief and a disappointment.

'I don't think there was anything accidental in it.' His tone was resolute, and she got the feeling he was testing the water. She remembered Jonathan doing something similar all those years ago.

'So if I did ask you on a date . . . what do you think you might say?'
'I think I might say yes . . .' she'd beamed.

'I always find it interesting how people meet, how they begin.'

'How did you meet your husband?'

She both welcomed and was made uncomfortable by the ease with which he asked. It was without awkwardness or any sense of competition, as if he were confident that that was then and this was now, and there should be no reason for any tension over the two worlds colliding. She figured it said more about her than it did him that she was not quite as comfortable with the topic, feeling so very connected, still, to the man she had lost.

'How did we meet?' It was an odd feeling, the rush of love she felt for Jonathan at the retelling of how they had started, while her stomach performed star jumps at no more than the sound of this man's voice, seated in front of her, where Jonathan had sat countless times. The simple truth was it was nice to talk about him, keeping him present in the way she used to with Jenny and Phil, laughing over his quirky sense of humour and the many scrapes they'd found themselves in over the years. 'My dad loves cricket. It's his passion, any cricket, international events, local park matches. He lives in Portugal now and spends the cricket season with one ear clamped to the radio. Drives my mum nuts. He loves everything about it, the sound of the ball hitting the bat, the gentle ripple of applause, the complexity of what at first appears to be a simple thing. I mean, you just throw a ball, hit a ball, and run up and down between some sticks before the ball reappears, right, how hard can it be?'

'Yep, that's pretty much it.'

She liked the grin that accompanied his response.

'He'd have you pinned in the chair for a good hour if he heard you saying that, wanting not only to explain the intricate strategy of the game, but trying to convert you to loving it too. He is quite the evangelist when it comes to his sport.' She liked talking about her dad too, promising herself to call him later. 'Anyway, he was asked to coach a local team of under-twenty-ones out Keynsham way where we lived. I got roped in to help with cricket tea, which I always hated, until that one day, when I pitched up and met a rather reluctant fielder, Jonathan Brown. I saw his name on a team sheet before we actually met, and it made me laugh.'

'Why?'

'Because that's the name of Paddington's brother!'

'Is it? I thought that was Michael.'

'Oh no,' she sighed, 'I'm sorely tempted to end this conversation right now and show you the door. Please don't tell me you are unfamiliar with the Brown family? And you're getting confused, it was Michael Bond who wrote it.'

'Yes, you're right. And confusion seems to be my current state. I spent an age this morning looking for the reading glasses that were on my face and which I was using to read the instructions on the back of a tin of varnish that were unfeasibly small!'

'Sounds like you might need new glasses.'

'Don't say that. Every trip to the optician is a reminder of my decrepitude. The way she shakes her head and writes me a prescription, it's never good news, is it? And don't start me on the cost of frames, which I assumed must be solid gold, but no, they're bloody plastic!'

It was her turn to smile. It was easy. So easy to chat to him, easy to ignore all the reasons why this was a bad idea. A reminder of what it felt like to share the mundanity of life with another, to have someone to sit alongside, to eat up the quiet hours in the day, someone who might run her reading glasses up the stairs when she settled down for a pre-sleep read.

'I avoid the doctors for the same reason,' he confessed. 'I have no interest in hearing what part of me is wearing out, failing or shrivelling.'

'Oh Dominic.' She sat up straight, her tone quite altered. 'You mustn't avoid going to the doctor! Please don't do that.'

'If we'd seen your husband sooner, well . . .'

'Sorry, Enya, I was trying to be funny. I'll go see the quack if and when I need to.'

'No, I'm sorry. It's absolutely none of my business!' She blinked.

'So, cricket.' He put them back on track, maybe, like her, unwilling to waste their time with any friction.

'Yes, his name stood out to me and when I walked into the cricket pavilion he was standing there, facing me, smiling, and he was tall, taller than me! And I said, *are you here for the cricket?* He was in full whites, cap in hand, and he shook his head and said, *cricket? No, what gave you that idea? I thought I was at the bus stop, does the three-four-nine not stop here?* I loved his humour, his sarcasm. And that was that, really. He cleverly befriended my dad and we just paired up! Happily paired up.'

'I think I'd have liked him,' Dominic added, without any sense of irony.

'Everyone did.' This the truth. 'So, how about you and Trish, how did you guys get together?'

She wanted to match his comfort in talking about their partners, almost as if in proof that they were doing nothing wrong and there was therefore no need to feel any guilt.

'Nothing so endearing as your story. Trish's parents were divorcing, and she got sent to stay with her aunt who ran the pub in the village where I grew up, just outside of Bath. The pub my friends and I used to frequent, where we'd glug strong cider and put money into the jukebox to listen to The Cure. She worked behind the bar, and she was beautiful and quite wild, which I found insanely attractive,' the way he paused suggested it might not now be the case, 'and when she and my mate Stu split up I offered her a shoulder to cry on and the rest is history.'

'Poor Stu!'

'Ha! Stu was our best man. And fret not, he is now married to Helen and has been for donkey's years. He's a photographer and is fat and content.'

'You make the two sound intertwined, maybe that's where I'm going wrong, I'm too skinny.'

'Are you not content?'

It was what he did, pulled her words and spun them into a wider commentary that she welcomed, showing his interest, a lovely distraction, a chance to help understand herself.

'I'm not sure. I'm aware that it's usually a yes or no answer, but it's never that straightforward, is it. Never that simple. I have these . . . these . . .' she hesitated, unsure why she wanted to open up to him, this stranger, with something that had dogged her for a while now, 'these kind of attacks.'

He sat forward, his expression one of concern. 'What kind of attacks?'

'It was the strangest thing. A few months ago now, I was walking in the park, and I thought I might be having a heart attack. In fact, I was certain I was having a heart attack.'

She paused to think about the moment, still carrying the echo of a trembling hand and disturbed gut.

'I've read about the symptoms, seen it countless times on TV and in movies, who hasn't? A fast heart rate, sweating, dizziness, mild confusion, a hot flush rushing over my head and body that made me want to drop to the floor. I figured that had to be it: my heart. *My heart!*'

'That must have been so scary.'

'It was,' she exhaled. 'I began to get flustered, wasn't sure what to do, fish my phone out of the pocket of my jeans and call an ambulance? I thought that might expend too much energy. Was I better off lying down and calling to the woman who had only just walked past, we'd had the briefest chat. I thought I might call her back and gesture that I was having a heart attack. I figured she'd know what to do. Not that she's a friend, but I know of her, she's local. Well, I was darned if I could remember her name. I knew it began with M and I went through them all!' she tittered, 'Marion? Margery? Mary . . . Nothing. It was bizarre, there I was about to possibly spend my last minutes on God's green earth and instead of my life flashing before my eyes or whispering something meaningful and life-affirming, I was entirely preoccupied with trying to remember the name of Michelle Johnson-Hughes and worrying, if you can believe it, about what Aiden would eat in the event of my demise.'

'You remembered her name eventually.' He smiled.

'Yes, thank goodness. It was as I thought about it that I realised my pulse had slowed and I wasn't feeling so faint. Then I wondered about what I might actually say to her, *I'm dying . . . Help me . . . Please tell my son there's lasagne in the fridge that wants using up . . .*'

She liked the way he laughed, liked feeling funny. It was the very opposite of being boring, she always thought, if you could make someone laugh like that.

'I of course survived and am now at liberty to enjoy the many other panic attacks that seem to strike at the most inopportune of moments. I sat on one of the little wooden benches that line the path and stared at the lake, taking a moment to breathe.' She took a deep, slow breath.

'And it went away?'

'It calmed, yes.'

'That was a relief.' He sipped his wine.

'I was equally as relieved I hadn't called Michelle over and informed her of my imminent departure. Not only would I have had to backtrack, no doubt sounding like a mad thing, but she's hardly discreet. News of my funny turn would be all over the postcode by now. It scared me, that's the truth.' She bit her bottom lip. 'That was the first one, the first panic attack,' she widened her eyes and shifted in her chair, 'and it's absurd because I'm not that kind of person. Yet I'm pretty sure that's what they are.'

It felt glorious and exposing all at once to have told someone, anyone. She had kept it from Jenny and Angela, not wanting them to worry about her any more than they already did, and she certainly didn't want to burden Aiden with them. There was also the unspoken belief that for her it meant anxiety, fear, a lack of control, the very opposite of the woman and character she did her best to portray. The fact she had chosen to tell Dominic wasn't lost on her. This sharing of a secret bound them closer.

'I wonder what caused it?' he asked softly.

Taking a moment, she stared out of the window towards the garden where the peach light of dusk made everything it touched beautiful.

'I don't know. We'd stopped on the path briefly, Michelle and I, chatting about nothing much in particular, as I say; we're not friends and she was talking about her husband who'd gone on a golfing weekend and her kids who were bringing friends home from school and I felt this . . . this . . . *fear* rising inside me.'

She cursed the thickening of her throat and the tears that pricked the back of her eyes.

'Her words made me,' she sniffed, 'made me ask myself, who am I now? Who am I if I'm not mothering Aiden and looking after his schedule and running him to school or picking him up or washing his clothes or a million other things that I liked doing, actually. I liked the connection, the way he needed me.' She swallowed, aware of delving into her inner monologue and sharing it with this man. 'And without Jonathan, not a wife anymore, just . . . me on my own. And my job is ending soon, I had a plan, but . . .' She didn't want to go into the detail of her and Jenny's split, knowing she'd cry, and she didn't want that. 'I guess I don't know how to be much of the time and that's terrifying.'

'I think you are so much more than a wife and mother. I think you're a wonderful woman who could set the world alight if she so chose. A woman who has the strength to grab any life she wants.'

Enya laughed softly, because it was cheesy, because it was embarrassing how much she was flattered by it and because it came from the mouth of this beautiful man who didn't really know her at all.

'I'm not sure about that.' She sighed.

'So, have these attacks happened since?'

She nodded. 'Often at night. I wake and I'm mid-panic – ridiculous, isn't it, safe in my bed while I feel like the world is ending.'

'It's not ridiculous. Not at all. I have insomnia and it's pretty much for similar reasons. A fear of what comes next. I guess that's why I asked if you were content?'

They verbally circled back.

'I suppose if I'm not content then it would be reasonable to assume that I know what I need in order to be so, what the *missing* thing is that would put a halt to my restlessness.'

'But you don't?' He held her eyeline, curious, interested, and it was nice.

'I don't. Not really, not without winding back the clock. And I guess in answer to your question, I'm content *enough*.'

'And that's all anyone can really ask for, to be content enough.'

'Ha! I hear your tone, Mr Sutherland.'

'Well, it's true! Why do we settle for mediocrity? It's as if we don't fully comprehend that this is our one life, not a rehearsal. And that's pretty much what I've come to tell you. I'm aware I've already had more than my five minutes.' He looked up, as if expecting her to end the conversation; she didn't, lost to the moment and enjoying his company. Moments like this were rare, however. These little pockets of loveliness when she got to feel . . . got to *feel*. 'I've been thinking about what you said about us being a non-starter, and I happen to think it was a moment when the stars aligned and the universe delivered what we both wanted, what we needed. Things like this don't happen to me, I can assure you. It's like . . . It's like you've put a spell on me. But in all honesty, it's not a spell I want to break. I like feeling this way, Enya. And on the day I got the flat, I was already feeling the most overwhelming sense of possibility and then you came along.' She liked it when he said her name, liked to hear the sound and see the shape of the word on his lips. 'I feel changed by no more than the prospect of spending time, even a stolen second or two with you. I can't remember what I used to think about before my head was full of you!'

She stared at him; this was uncharted territory, flattering and unnerving in equal measure.

'You don't know me. And I don't know you, not really.' Her words in contrast to the sweet nectar of delight that flowed through her veins. She understood how being this open came with consequences, letting the genie out of the bottle. It was a prospect as wonderful as it was frightening.

'Yet it's how I feel.' His gaze was unwavering across the table. 'How mad is that?'

'Entirely mad. And again, it's not enough to upend the lives of our kids for an infatuation, a crush,' she whispered, words that were easy and made no allowance for the way she studied his face, his skin, wanting to stare at him, to touch him, and for him to touch her.

'Even madder is the fact that if you gave me the green light, I would take you by the hand and we'd jump in my car and head for my boat.'

Or Borneo . . . without hesitation . . . He wanted to take her hand! Her ageing hand where the skin was a little wrinkled, the odd vein popped, and there was the silver scar on her finger from peeling potatoes. A hand that no one held anymore. It sounded wonderful and she wanted so badly to feel his hand on hers, to feel human with this, the most basic yet most meaningful contact.

'I mean, technically we couldn't go anywhere just yet,' he explained. 'Her name is *Foula Girl*.'

'Foula?' It wasn't a word she was familiar with.

'Yes, it's an island about twenty miles to the west of Shetland. My dad took me there when I was a kid and I dream of spending time there, it's remote with a beauty in its bleakness. And the most spectacular cliffs.'

'*Foula Girl*.'

'Yes, although she's a long way from home, holed up in a boatyard in Trowbridge right now. It's where the flat is too, a five-minute walk. Handy.'

'She's not in the water?'

'Not yet, she's been my life's work for the last eighteen months. She's my escape, the place I go to stop everything coming to a head. I've been buying time for us as a family, nothing more. Because pulling the plug on our marriage is not something I consider lightly. It felt easier, kinder to do it in stages, hence the flat. *Foula* is my happy distraction. A bare bones restoration, a rescue job really. She once raced the high seas and when I saw her,' he shook his head, 'it ripped my heart! But when she's ready, the moment her hull hits the water, we could up anchor and off we'd go.' He indicated with his arm stretched out, palm to the side, one eye slightly closed as if plotting a route. 'We'd just go!'

'Sail off into the sunset.' She felt the need to emphasise the corniness of his suggestion, no matter how her gut crunched, and her eyes widened as she pictured sitting next to him somewhere warm, watching the sunset, miles and miles away from Mablethorpe Road and all that ailed her. He, however, responded as if it were mere confirmation and there was nothing clichéd about it.

'Yes!' He banged the table and laughed, as if it were a possibility.

'This conversation is exciting, distracting, fun, but it's not that simple, is it? I can't imagine how such a thing might affect our kids,' she reiterated.

'I think they'd want to see us happy!'

She bit her lip, unable to tell him that there was a little more to it, that Aiden, the boy engaged to his daughter, was about to become a dad.

'I'm also an old stick-in-the-mud, I don't do well with change, it takes me an age to adjust. I'm still trying to get used to life without Jonathan. Still feel married to him and I think, I think that Aiden takes comfort from the fact that even though his dad isn't here, I am, holding the fort, keeping things the same. God, I even have a huge plant in the hallway that I hate. It takes up so much room, but because it's been there for so long, when Jonathan was here, I can't seem to throw it away.'

'Are you sure it's Aiden you do it for, keeping things just as they were?'

She stared at him. It was a fair question. And so she gave a fair answer. Her words when they came were delivered slowly.

'If I were to move on, what does that say about our marriage? I don't want my son, my family to think I didn't love Jonathan in the way I did because I hooked up with someone else. You read about it, don't you, people who remarry or have relationships, and some of the comments are always about how it's too soon, how *could* she, did she even love him? I can't stand the thought of that because I did love him. I do love him.'

'I think you might be overthinking it.'

It was her turn to give a wry laugh. 'Maybe. You and Trish, your situation, it feels messy.'

'I am determined for it not to be. I've never cheated on her, never, but something has changed, I've changed, and I just can't do it anymore!' He looked very close to tears, and it moved her.

'I don't . . . I don't know what to say, Dominic. I don't know how I'm supposed to behave because the last time anyone said anything remotely like this to me, and the last time I felt anything close to this, was at a time in my life when it was expected. We were in our early twenties and the sole objective for most of us was getting paired up, meeting someone, finding *the one* if you were very very lucky, but more than that we were all open to it! When your friends paired up and met their person, it gave you hope that it was possible it might happen to you too. But now . . .' she looked up, staring again into his face, taking the opportunity to study him in the way that she liked to do, a face that was still new and one that held her in its thrall, 'now it's different. I'm not that young girl anymore. I'm older, jaded, cynical even. I don't know how to start trusting you, how to start trusting anyone new. And I don't really believe in the fairy tale you describe, things take time, and yet I'd be lying if I said to hear you say those words didn't fill me with something that feels a lot like excitement.' She had done it, admitted to the fireworks that leapt in her stomach at no more than the sight of him. Looking up, she watched the genie swirl above her head. 'But the moment I think about you, I also think about Trish, I think about Iris, I think about Aiden, Jonathan. It's all so bloody complicated. It's one thing for you to move into a flat but quite another for Trish to find out you are with someone else. And that the someone might be me.'

She briefly thought of lovely Holly Hudson and her heart twinged.

'So, what do we do then?' His tone almost imploring. 'What happens next?'

'I . . . I don't know. Nothing, I suppose, we do nothing. What I do know is that Jonathan was my husband, *is* my husband. We took vows and I was his and he was mine and that's how I've spent most of my life, Dominic, and it's hard to see myself in any other way. And it would be hard for my son to see me in any other way.'

Dominic sat forward in the chair, his hands on the tabletop. She was overly aware that if she let her fingers creep forward, they would be touching. Quickly, she placed her hands on the sides of her chair and sat on them.

He swallowed and held her eyeline. 'But what if . . . what if you are *mine*, Enya? What if we don't let it be that complicated. What if we accept that you're meant to be mine, and what if every moment in your life up until this point was waiting for this, waiting for me!'

'I can't . . . I can't even begin to . . . I loved him. I love him.' She could now see Jonathan's face in his last moments. His hand inside hers, their wedding rings still glinting as if new and shiny with all they represented in their shared life and their shared love.

'Yes, of course, and you always will! And I loved Trish with every fibre in my being! I loved her, I *love* her still, but it's faded. It has run thin, dispersed, until in recent years all that is left is a hint of the rich and vibrant colour that was our new and exciting love. Why can't I reset? Why can't I choose you?'

She felt the watery contents of her stomach threaten sickness. It was a lot to hear, a lot to take in. 'Does Trish know all this?'

'She feels it the same as I do, she's not happy, I'm not happy, even if we rarely say it.'

'Why don't you say it?' She wanted the detail, knowing every bit of information was like painting by numbers, helping her build the picture.

'Because it hurts! It's painful and it smacks of failure. It's not what we're led to believe, is it? No one reads about the princess who rides off into the distance with her prince and has a few good years before everything gets toned down, their love becomes muted, and reaches the point where they'd rather potter in the garden than spend time together. It's supposed to be happily ever after, but that's not true, people change, people die! And what are we supposed to do? Put up with big plants in our houses that we can't stand for eternity? Cling to that feeling of how things used to be, hoping that we get a glimpse of it on our anniversaries or Christmas Eve after one too many? Is that it? Is that all we're entitled to?'

'Maybe, yes.' She remembered sitting in the car with Aiden, giving him advice on slowing down, explaining the kind of love that she and Jonathan had shared, together for so long that they almost knew what the other was thinking. So in tune they knew how to handle any situation just by looking at the other one. In sync. One team. How was it even possible to start over with someone new?

'No, Enya! It can't be, it's not enough, not *good* enough!'

'It was enough for me.' She spoke softly. 'Our passion became muted but evolved into something quite wonderful, maybe not the roaring wave but certainly a gentle predictable tide that was a lovely way to live. It was our happily ever after.'

'Really? Because it's not enough for me. Are you saying that when you find a pot of gold just lying there at your feet, as if it's been waiting for you all along, you don't think you have a right to dig it up, to hold on to it?'

'Not if it hurts other people or makes their lives more complicated!' She held his gaze and he seemed to shrink a little, getting her point entirely.

They were both quiet; it seemed that he, like her, was a little exhausted by the exchange in the highly charged atmosphere that had slipped from light-hearted joviality with alarming speed.

Her phone buzzed and they both jumped accordingly, as if discovered.

'It's Aiden! A video!' With something close to terror in her tone, she watched as Dominic sprinted from the table and stood behind the island, out of sight. She wasn't expecting a call and was as ever worried that something was wrong, urging her to answer.

There was no time for her to calm her racing pulse or to consider how she looked. She held up her phone and pressed the button, linking her to her son.

'Hey, Mum!'

'Hello, darling, I'm not too good with the old video thing, can you see me okay?'

She did her best to control the warble to her tone, wary of betraying the fact that Dominic was standing on the other side of the room. It felt awful, in the way anything deceitful did.

'Yes! Just hold your phone still, you're a bit shaky.' She gripped the phone. 'Anyway, Trish and Iris are here.' He moved the screen, changed the angle, and pulled it further from his face to ensure all three were visible. Enya felt her stomach shrink.

'Hello, everyone!' She waved.

'Hi, Enya!' Trish waved back and Iris smiled.

'We were just talking about colours for the cake ribbon, the chair bows, napkins, that kind of thing, and we thought it would be a good idea for you to be involved.'

'Oh, Iris, that's really lovely of you.'

She felt like crying, biting her bottom lip, reminding herself never to mention the pub Trish had worked in or the fact that Stu, Trish's ex, who was now fat and content, had been her best man. All knowledge that could only have come from one source, knowledge that she should not have.

It was the foulest pressure, hearing the sweet sentiment that indicated a kind nature from which her son would only benefit, all while the girl's father was in the wings, hiding in plain sight. She felt dirty and regretted inviting him in. She wished he would just disappear, imagining how quickly their smiles would fade if they knew who was lurking in her kitchen. Trish looked lovely, her hair shiny, lipstick just so, and Enya could only imagine what it would have felt like to be married to a man like Dominic, who was able to make a plan to dismantle his marriage, his family. Jonathan always put her first and would not have done a thing to cause her a moment of anguish or worry. Apart from dying and that was, in fairness, beyond his control.

How she felt about Dominic, this surge of unexpected joy, this perfect diversion, a new take on things, a lift from the predictability and mundanity of her waning grief, was no compensation for the knowledge that while she and this man sat and secretly sipped rosé in the dying light of a summer's day, his wife was at home, welcoming her soon-to-be son-in-law, smiling for the camera, and doing her best to show kindness to the boy's mother, a widow, who might be a little lonely.

'Oh, Enya, don't! You'll set me off! It's an emotional time, isn't it? Listen, we wanted you to know what we're up to, we've got samples!' Trish held a clutch of ribbons up to the camera, and teals, greens, golds and rose pinks fluttered in her palm. 'But we were hoping you might come over on Saturday. Nothing too formal, we'll have a BBQ, get to know each other a bit and we can go over wedding plans, what do you think?'

'I think . . . I think that sounds lovely.'

It was the last thing she wanted to do, enjoy the woman's hospitality, chit-chat about ribbon colours and cake. Realisation dawned then that one of the consequences of this . . . dalliance . . . emotional affair . . . whatever the label, it gave her something, many things. But it spoiled so much too. It spoiled the honesty she had shared with her son. It spoiled the planning for her only child's wedding, and it forever moulded the shape of her relationship with Trish and Iris. These women who had been chosen for her, one to be the wife of her son, and the other, should they so choose, grandmother to her grandchildren. She thought briefly of Jenny, her words still thumbtacks of pain lodged beneath her skin.

'. . . *it would be easier for me, for us all, really, if we kept to ourselves.*'

'Oh, look at you! Enya, please don't cry!' Trish smiled and Enya could only look away, filled with something very close to shame.

'Oh, Mum!' Aiden put his hand over his heart.

She did her best not to glance across the island at the man who was quiet, his expression troubled, as it should be.

It was definitive, her decision to end it now.

End it and walk away from whatever *it* was and whatever it could be.

Enough was enough.

Even if she considered his words that she was meant to be his, even if every moment in her life up until that point had been waiting for this, waiting for him, even then.

'Saturday will be lovely,' Trish continued, 'you're very welcome to stay over, we have spare bedrooms.'

'Thank you.' She had no intention of staying over but didn't want to quash the woman's kind offer so quickly.

'It'll be great to see you!' Iris leaned forward in her seat and Aiden smiled.

It was only because she knew his every expression, was in tune with every nuance, having studied his face since he was mere minutes old, that she could see the flicker of anxiety in his eyes, that his laughter felt a little forced, it didn't linger. It was easy to guess that he had yet to tell Iris that Holly was pregnant. Enya felt for him, felt for Holly too, for them all in fact. Three families who at no more than the whim of an airline computer allocating seating had seen their lives thrown into chaos, in this series of events that were, to quote the esteemed philosopher Lemony Snicket, most unfortunate.

'Have a lovely evening!' Trish chimed.

She nodded.

'See you soon, Mum!'

'Bye!' Iris waved.

Enya lifted her hand and ended the call. With the phone now face down on the table, she stared at the tabletop, unable to meet Dominic's eyeline as he quietly retook the seat opposite her. She thought she might throw up and clamped her hand over her mouth until the feeling subsided.

'This, this feeling,' she took a breath, 'this horrible sense of deceit, this is why you have to leave right now. This is why you can't be here, and why whatever this is has to stop. Has to stop right now.'

'We haven't done anything wrong, we—'

'No, Dominic.' Finally, she looked up and into his face. 'It's one thing to lie to other people, saying you are out walking, meeting a friend, working on *Foula Girl*, or whatever ruse you spun to come here today.'

He double blinked, suggesting she had hit the nail on the head.

'But it's quite another to lie to ourselves. You're right. This is not *nothing* and we *have* done something wrong. We are doing something wrong right now,' she tapped the blond Danish wood tabletop with her fingers, 'we're hurting people. Just by being here, and by not being there,' she pointed out of the window, 'we're hurting people. Our children are getting married! They don't need any more confusion. Can you imagine how this would hijack their big day, their plans? It would be so unfair. This has to stop before we say and do things we'll both regret.'

The words were easy. Coaxing them on to her tongue and allowing them to float out into the world, a lot harder.

Quietly, he pushed away from the table and stood. He placed his hands on his hips as he had in the car park, a physical action that was both alluring and commanding. His voice now a little less assured, considered.

'I'll leave. But I just wanted to say that this brief, fabulous thing that has occurred between us will stay with me. A warm place for my thoughts to reside on the coldest of days and nights.'

'For me too,' she admitted, not that he needed it confirming, aware as she was that what passed between them was beyond words, beyond definition, but was rather a feeling, a state of being – the strength of which was undeniable.

'I never meant to cause you any' – he looked towards the garden – 'discomfort or awkwardness. Never that.' He looked at her then, his eyes fixing her with a stare. 'And I mean no harm to Trish, the kids or anyone. They're my family—' His voice broke. 'I guess I have allowed myself a selfish indulgence, put myself first, which I don't think I've done, ever, not once during our marriage.'

'I can relate to that entirely.'

'Because we're those people, aren't we?' He found a small, doleful smile that didn't reach his eyes. 'I mean, you're right, I don't really know you, even though I feel like I do. But if I had to guess, I'd say you're a lot like me, smoothing the path for everyone else, removing obstacles or danger, content with the reward that they are well, happy, comfortable.'

'Yes,' she whispered. 'What I want or need doesn't count as much.'

It was true, she loved Jonathan deeply, and like him, adored their child, and their needs had always, always come before her own. The sweetest and most subtle martyrdom.

'Why is that, Enya?'

It was a realisation that made her incredibly sad.

'Speaking for myself, it has always been rooted in love. Loving those that love me a bit too much and not loving myself enough, I guess.' This the truth that caused her tears to form. 'Not, not a conscious thing, at all. More a slow erosion of myself, until I stopped considering what I wanted or needed to thrive and kind of . . . went with the flow. Then when Jonathan died,' she took a moment to gather herself, 'I sat very still for some time, it seemed like the best option to just sit and wait until the world stopped spinning. And in that stillness, I realised that the sun had disappeared, and the birds were quiet, the air had grown cool, and the moon was high, the sky dark. That's what happened to my life! That's what happened to me. I was twenty-one and the next time I looked up I was fifty-one, at that moment when day becomes night – you can't rage against it, can't turn clocks back or go outside and howl at the sky for one more minute of it. You can't because it's gone, and you are at the mercy of it. It was just like that. It *is* just like that. I just have to find a way to live with the new shape of me. I have to figure out who I am.'

'This, thing we shared, albeit briefly,' he paused, 'it felt like a marvellous opportunity, a chance.'

'Yes.' This too she couldn't deny, noting with conflicting sorrow how he spoke in the past tense.

'I should go.'

Reaching for his phone, which he deposited in his pocket, and grabbing his keys, which he held, she stood to see him out. Torn between wanting him to go immediately, to put them both out of the misery of this closeness, and not wanting him to go at all, picturing them on the sofa, her feet on his lap, chatting and happy.

Happy . . .

There were no words, as he walked quickly around to her side of the table and, with an urgency to his actions, took her in his arms. In that moment, she was the opposite of invisible. How she loved her husband, loved him so very deeply, but my God, caring for him and losing him had taken its toll. She fell into him then, fell into him heavily, landing hard with all her weight in his arms, her head against his chest. It felt wonderful to let someone hold her for a while, to take up the slack. Someone who wasn't weakened by illness or too frail to do the job or too sick to care, or too understandably preoccupied to notice that she needed to stay here a while. Someone solid and vital and present who held her upright, stopped her from falling down and slipping through the cracks, and where, in that moment, she wanted to stay forever . . . forever, as if she had finally found a place to rest.

There was no kiss, no progression, no harnessing of the physical energy that sparked around them, no discussion, no plan, no goodbye, for none were needed. Instead, after some minutes, he slowly released her from his fierce yet tender embrace, until eventually, still with the shape of him against her skin and the scent of him lingering, she opened her eyes at the sound of the front door closing. It would have been hard for her to describe her feeling of abject sorrow, the silence taunting her. She ran her fingers over the front of her clothes, as if touching the tiny particles of him that might still remain.

As she stood in the silence, her limbs shaking, and Dominic left the cottage via the front, she felt a breeze whip through the kitchen. It swirled around the room and out of the open French doors, disturbing the muslin drapes and rustling the blooms of the pale-headed tea-coloured roses that grouped around the arbour.

Rushing to the lounge, she stared at the sofa and the chairs, before heading upstairs to the bedroom, scanning the room and checking the small study area on the landing, then standing at the bathroom sink to look in the mirror. She even opened the front door, Dominic thankfully nowhere to be seen, as she stared at her little car. All of which were empty.

Back in the kitchen she whispered his name, softly, 'Jonathan?'

A futile call into the echoing quiet. She knew, knew that he had gone, could *feel* it. Understanding how impossible it would be to witness him in the arms of another, no matter that it was a gesture of goodbye, aware that any old fool would have been able to feel the emotion in it, to see the exquisite and all-consuming pain in their parting.

Jonathan, however, was not and never had been any old fool.

It was almost instinctive, as if at some deeper level she recognised that to be alone was the last thing she needed. Talking so openly to Dominic had reminded her of the unbearable silence of loss and she couldn't face it right now, couldn't face it at all. It was as if the scab that had formed over her grief had been ripped off, leaving her loss on her skin like a fresh wound, gaping, and the pain just as acute.

She grabbed her phone.

'Hello?'

'Angela.'

'What is it, love, what's happened?'

'Can you, can you come over, please. Can you . . . can you just come here?'

There were no further questions. No discussion of time or plan or logistics. No debate over whether the need to disrupt her evening was necessary or frivolous. Her sister responded in the way Enya knew she would, and her heart was glad of it.

'I'm on my way, Ens. Hang on, doll. I'm on my way . . .'

Chapter Twenty

Angela leaned on the outside wall and was breathing deeply as Enya opened the front door. Her face softened with relief.

'Just to be clear, you're paying for every speeding ticket and taking any points incurred on my licence. I made record time and even beat a fancy motorbike away at the lights.'

'There was no need for that.' She smiled, kind of glad that her sister hadn't spared the horses and was here, right where she needed her to be. It was reassuring. Jenny might not be coming to see her any time soon, but she could still rely on Angela.

'I thought there was every need for it, you sounded, I don't know, you sounded terrible.'

Enya nodded, unable to deny that she not only sounded but also felt terrible, weakened and disrupted by the afternoon spent. Having admitted to Dominic how she felt was exposing, and the way he had left her felt like the saddest ending of something before it had even started.

'Wine or tea?' she asked as Angela followed her into the kitchen. She had, as she awaited her arrival, swilled the abandoned rosé down the sink and popped the glasses in the dishwasher.

'Tea, but Ens, don't worry about a drink, please just come and sit down, I'm worried about you. My head has come up with every awful scenario you can imagine on the way here, ranging from you being diagnosed with something I don't want to hear about, to possible alien abduction.'

'You got me, it's alien abduction.' She pulled a face.

'Actually, no, we're not going to laugh our way out of this. I *know* you. I know what that call meant, you never sound like that, never ask me to come over, not since . . .'

'I remember.'

That last time, with hysteria edging her words, *Please, Ange, can you come here now, please just come . . . he's not got long, I can feel it . . .*

Angela reached for her hand and led her into the lounge, and she was happy for her sister to do so, wanting someone to take the reins, to care for her in the way Jonathan had when he was here and when he was able, before his illness robbed them both of so much. The sisters sat at either end of the sofa, their pace unhurried and the agenda unset, in the way it was when you were close to a sibling.

'I don't know where to start, really.' She pulled her knees up to her chin and wrapped her arms around her shins.

'Take your time. We're not in any rush.'

'I'm quite surprised by how my life has ended up,' Enya began.

Angela laughed out loud. 'Who isn't? I mean, good Lord above, do we ever get the life we envisaged for ourselves? If someone had told me I'd end up with Frank who was vice-captain of the football team when we were at school, I'd have laughed in their face!'

'You just laughed in mine,' Enya pointed out, half in jest.

'True, but that's because it's just as absurd! First, this is not how your life has ended up, because that would suggest it's the end and you are far, far from that.'

There was a second of shared knowledge where she knew that her sister, like her, was thinking that it had ended for Jonathan, a reminder there were no guarantees.

'Second,' Angela continued, 'the idea that things are set in stone, or that we have anything other than the smallest of control over how events turn out, is bonkers. Life is full of incidents, surprises, trip hazards and one-way streets! We don't ever know what's around the next corner, good or bad, so how can we picture a life that is an unwritten book?'

'I guess you're right.' It helped, a little, to think of it in this way, adding hope to a situation that only minutes before had felt hopeless. 'It's been a strange couple of days, that's why I needed to see you.'

'What's happened, my love?' Angela asked softly, the older sister falling into the role of matriarch as she always had.

'Holly's pregnant.'

'No!' Angela gasped.

'Yes.'

'Wow! Oh my God!' she yelled. 'I don't know what to say! Really?'

'Yep, she and Jen came into the office to tell me. I had to break it to Aiden. He's seen her and they have made some kind of plan.'

'Jenny never said – mind you, she's gone a bit quiet on me.'

'She's got a lot going on.' Enya decided not to divulge the whole sorry unfriending conversation and the dismissed letter, believing in the phrase 'least said soonest mended', and not wanting to affect Jenny and Angela's relationship any more than was necessary. She loved them both too much to allow them to experience the punch to the throat that Jenny's words had left her with.

'Oh, Enya.' Angela closed her eyes, acknowledging the less than perfect timing.

'I know.'

'Is Holly okay?'

'Not really, she's distraught, it's horrible to see. She's ten weeks, her hormones must be going haywire as well as having to deal with what's happened. Her whole world is spinning.'

Something she understood too well.

'And Aiden?'

Enya liked that Angela registered it would be impacting him too.

'Shocked, putting on a smile, planning the wedding and I think trying to figure out which way is up.'

'What did Iris say about it?'

'I don't think he's told her yet.'

'Do you think it'll affect the wedding?'

'I don't honestly know.' She pinched the bridge of her nose. 'Dominic, Iris's dad, came over earlier,' she whispered, understanding the level of subterfuge it implied and all the connotations of it.

'What do you mean, he came over?' Angela's tone and confused expression said it all.

'I mean he turned up! I opened the door and there he was!' She pointed towards the hallway. 'He wasn't going to come in, but I just . . .'

'That's odd, you have no contact and what, he appears suddenly like ta-dah!' Angela fanned out her fingers dramatically.

'Well, we have had some contact.' She hated the flush of guilt about her face.

'What kind of contact?' Angela held her eyeline.

'Just a couple of calls. *He* called me, both times, just before bed.'

'Wow!'

'That's your second wow of the evening.'

'Yes, I'm aware, but both with very different meanings. My first wow was as in, that's a surprise! A shock! Give me a second to take it in.'

'And your second?' She wasn't sure she wanted the answer.

'That was, wow, as in, I can't imagine sitting in the kitchen or reading in bed while Frank called a woman with whom he has a spark. Me planning what to make for his packed lunch, worrying about whether we've enough milk in, while he flirted with someone on the phone.'

Her sister's words settled like sharp things in her breast.

'It wasn't,' she shook her head, was about to deny the flirtatious suggestion, but couldn't, knowing she would only be kidding herself, 'you're not bringing up anything I haven't already thought or voiced. I know how it sounds.'

'Do you?'

Her sister's accusatory tone was less than helpful and the last thing she needed; it hurt, mainly because Angela only spoke the truth.

'I do, and just to bring you up to speed, he and Trish have agreed to part, he's taken the lease on a flat. All before us, before . . . before me . . . not that there's an us or . . .'

'I see.'

'Anyway, the last time we broached the subject, you were laughing about me playing footsie under the table with him at the reception!' Enya reminded her.

'I thought it was a joke, really. I had no idea that you might.'

'I haven't. I didn't. I *won't!* Anyway, it's all irrelevant because I told him not to call me and I made it clear he's not to come here, no contact. I won't see him again unless it's in a crowd or at the very least, a small group.'

'How do you feel about that?'

'Truthfully?'

'No, no, make something up to placate me. Of course, truthfully!' Her sister tutted.

She took her time, wanting to get the words right. 'I guess, I forgot for a moment.' She cursed the slip of tears down the back of her throat.

'You forgot what?'

'When I was talking to him, when I was with him – Dominic, I forgot that I was getting older, that I'm a widow. I forgot that sometimes I can feel so lonely it radiates like pain through my limbs. I forgot I'm getting close to the downward slope of my life. All the treacle I've waded through to get to this point, I forgot all of it. And you know that, that lightness you feel in your teens or your twenties, that sense of excitement fizzing in your blood and that the whole wide world was out there to conquer, that you could and probably would do it all and have it all once you got out of the blocks.'

'Yes.' Her sister nodded, her sharp edge now softened, her voice low, as if Enya's words had struck a chord.

'Well, it was just like that. And I liked it.'

'Of course you did, darling.'

'I just wanted to touch him, to touch his wrist, that little spot where all his veins gathered under the surface of his skin, the place where his watch rested. I wanted to touch his skin and for him to hold me. That's what I wanted, Angela.' Her voice was barely a whisper, but it felt good to say it out loud, no matter how cautiously.

'So if he's as free as you say he is, what's stopping you?' Angela held her gaze.

She took her time. 'I can't imagine Aiden having to deal with that on top of everything else. He and Iris have got some tough times coming up.'

'True.' Angela looked into the middle distance.

'Plus, Aiden is still mourning his dad, and this is his haven and I'm all that's left. How would he feel if I dismantled all Jonathan and I had, started over with someone new, anyone! Let alone his father-in-law! What would that look like around the Christmas table!'

'Well, that's just bullshit.' Her sister as ever pulled no punches. 'You can't put your life on hold for Aiden or your deceased husband! It's not practical, not smart!'

'I think it's smart not to rush headlong into something that might be nothing, to cause disruption for no reason.'

'Have you told Aiden that?' Angela raised her eyebrows. 'Sorry, that was below the belt. Carry on.'

'I just think, Ange, that we all have those attractions, those flickers of interest, all of us. It might be someone we meet or see on the telly or someone we walk past in the street. No one is immune, it's easy! That moment of instant attraction, it doesn't go away, does it, no matter how old we get. The lure of someone shinier than the dulled thing we have grown used to. It's exciting, enticing! The hard bit is remembering what's important and why we married or chose the person we're with. It's about understanding the difference between a fleeting moment of physical attraction and the deep connection to the person we've built a life with.'

'Yes, Ens, but if that person is no longer alive . . .' She let this trail.

They were both silent for a moment, as this fact settled.

'I need to focus all my attention on my son. He's going through a lot and what if this thing between Dominic and me is just a crush that would run its course, and quickly too. Can you imagine causing all that chaos, for nothing.' She shook her head.

'You think it's just an infatuation?'

'Maybe.'

'So why are you crying, baby girl?' Her sister reached for her hand. Enya hadn't realised she was and curled her fingers around her sister's palm.

'Because I can't stop thinking about every word he said and the way he looked at me and the way he makes me feel, made me feel,' she corrected.

'It's a big step. The first time, I'm guessing, that you've felt anything really, since Jonathan died, and that's huge, but also hopeful. It shows you're capable and that when the time is right . . .' Angela made a clicking noise, as if enough said.

'That's another thing, and kind of the reason I called you.' Enya bit the inside of her cheek, knowing this was a tricky subject for her to navigate.

'And there was me thinking the big news was your impending grannyhood and the fact that you may or may not have had a dalliance with your son's soon to be father-in-law!'

Enya gave a wry laugh. Her sister was right, it was a lot.

'So, tell me,' Angela encouraged.

'It's about Jonathan,' she began. 'I think he might have gone.'

She saw the flicker of confusion in her sister's eye. 'We know this, Enya. I was at the funeral.'

'No,' she shook her head, 'I mean, I can't see him, he's not here.'

'Do you mean . . .' Angela licked her lip, as if figuring out how to phrase it.

'I mean that I still see him. I still, still *see* him. All the time.' She couldn't think how else to explain it.

'You do?' Angela comically looked behind her as if half expecting him to pop up.

Enya nodded.

'What does he look like?'

'You know what Jonathan looks like!'

'Yes, but does he, erm, I'm trying to put it delicately.' Angela paused, and Enya laughed again.

'Well, that's a first!' Her big sister wasn't known for her tact.

'What I'm trying to establish,' Angela ignored her jibe, 'is does he look like he did before he died?'

Enya pictured him in his last days, a husk of the man he once was. Prematurely aged, with pale skin almost translucent, pulled over ashy bone, eyes sunken, mouth tight, lips diminished.

'Or is he . . . a ghost?'

Enya laughed again and threw her head back.

'For the love of God! What, like at Halloween with a sheet over his head? Actually, that's a good point,' she snapped her fingers, 'I should maybe lift it up and have a look, it might not be Jonathan at all! It might be Auntie Hilda, Nana Collins, or old Arthur next door!' She tutted and shivered at the thought.

'Well, I don't know! You say you *see* him, and so I wondered if you meant see him in a literal sense, or is it that you feel his presence, like a comforting force?' Angela wafted her hand above her head.

She knew her sister was trying her best and yet her tone alone was enough to make the situation almost comical.

'He looks like he did before he got sick. He looks really well, a couple of years younger, actually. And spruced up, but not fancy, the way he dressed on a Sunday afternoon. And it's not a presence or a feeling, it's actually him: Jonathan my husband. And he's always wearing the same thing.'

She looked over to the window where he often stood, in his jeans, the blue and white checked shirt he favoured beneath his navy V-necked sweater, dark socks, no shoes, hair recently cut, clean-shaven, and that expression that he wore, a happy face that said all is right in my world, because it was in the time before . . .

'I see. And does he, does he talk to you?'

'No. No he doesn't. But I talk to him all the time. I tell him what's going on, I ask him what to do and I share my worries and I like it.' She looked up at Angela, whose expression was serious, concerned almost. There was no sense of a comedic one-liner looming or that she was cueing up the next thing she wanted to say. Her sister was listening. 'He doesn't ever reply. He doesn't say anything. But he smiles at me, and he frowns sometimes. And I imagine his response in his voice and it's like chatting.'

'So come on, what do you think, Enya, why do you think Jonathan is loitering in your house?'

'Not only the house,' she explained, 'I see him in the car too, he sits on the back seat. Which is weird, because he was always either driving or in the front seat.'

'Why do you think he sits in the back?'

Enya shrugged. 'I think because I can see him there in the rear-view mirror, and it gives me comfort to know I'm not alone in the car on a long journey or driving home in the dark. It's like he's still looking after me.'

'Is that what this is about, do you think? Is he hanging around to look after you because, what, he doesn't think you can look after yourself?'

'Possibly. I mean, I think I'm doing okay. I think I *can* look after myself, but I must admit I get lonely. I miss him.'

Her voice broke. It was uncharacteristic and embarrassing for her to show this level of emotion, even with Angela. She thought she was over this, past it, but no. Her grief was a fluid thing, a shape-shifter that changed daily, hourly, even after three years of dedicated practice. One minute she could put his death to the back of her mind for a while and sing along to a song, or smell a flower, or sip coffee, and in that moment she felt bubbles of happiness float to the top of her life soup. How she relished those moments. At other times, her grief grabbed her by the ankles and pulled her so far down and down that she knew there was no further she could go. It was all she could do not to sink to the floor and weep. Weep for all she had lost and weep for that cold kernel of loneliness and despair that had taken root in her stomach.

'I don't know what to say to you, love. Apart from, three years is no time really, and it will get better.'

'Do you think I'm mad, Angela?' Enya asked softly, wary of the response.

Her sister took her time. 'Mad, no. Grief-stricken, yes. In shock, yes, probably, still. Confused, hell yeah! Trying to make sense of it all, definitely. And I think our minds are clever and complicated and do things to bring us peace and to help us get through. That's what I think.'

'Yep, I think you're right. And with Dominic,' she didn't want to lump the two men together in one topic, but it was almost impossible not to, not when they were, in recent days, so inextricably linked, 'it was like being shown through the keyhole of a door that has been locked for the longest time, a glimpse of a life that could be mine, if I had the courage to step inside. If things were different.'

Angela shook her head. 'I hear you, and it sounds lovely, sailing off into the sunset . . .'

It made her smile, that Angela should pick this particular analogy.

'But you're right, those kids are going to have enough to deal with without you pulling slats out of the fragile bridge that unites them.'

'I know.' She tried out a smile; the pain in her throat made it hard to swallow. Her sister spoke only the truth, not that she was any happier for hearing the obvious. 'It was nice to see that other life though, just get a taste of that golden feeling, for a second or two. You know the feeling I'm talking about.'

'Not really.' Angela shook her head.

'You can't have it all the time. It's too rare and precious and therefore all the more valuable for it, but it's like a, a golden moment that takes you by surprise. Like being at a great party or watching a sunset or when you were young and drunk or with a smashing boy or you'd stolen your sister's platform shoes, or a million other moments. Like when a song plays and you don't just hear the music, you *feel* it.' She placed her hand on her chest. 'You feel it and you close your eyes and you're part of it. A song that transports you, and makes you catch your breath and it's almost too painful to listen because it reminds you, not only of the person you were, or how you looked, and how you loved, but it reminds you of a time when you were full of hope.' She swiped at the tears that now coursed freely down her face. 'Full of hope that over the, the years gets chipped away by the knocks, and dulled through experience, and hidden under rocks that weigh you down. And just for a moment, in his arms, I *felt* it, Angela! I felt it all and he felt like mine. He did, he felt like mine.'

'And was Jonathan there then? Did you see him?'

Her sister's question wasn't barbed or harsh, but rather curious, asked gently.

Enya shook her head. 'No. And that's what I've been trying to tell you, that when Dominic left out of the front door,' she paused, knowing how ridiculous it was going to sound, 'I felt Jonathan leave out of the back.'

'Because you don't need him to keep an eye on you anymore, or . . .'

'Because I forgot to remember him.' She spoke the truth that was raw and painful to admit. 'I forgot to remember him.'

Chapter
Twenty-One

It was rare for Enya to have slept badly. Rarer still that she'd watched the hands of the clock go around until the early hours. Her mind, apparently, intent on forcing her to live the day about to dawn in a thousand different ways, predicting a thousand different outcomes, all with the most dramatic, terrifying, and humiliating of endings. The least scary scenario was her being run over by Trish, who chased her in a car. Once or twice, she enjoyed the luxury of brief slumber before a nightmare ensued, this time with Trish hauling her out of her house and inviting her to a duel. It would have been comical, the thought of the two of them, mothers of the bride and groom, to so debase themselves, had it not had its feet in the merest hint of possibility.

She had taken an uncharacteristic age to choose what to wear, desperately wanting to strike the right tone between *haven't bothered at all, I just rolled out of bed looking this way* and *I tried too hard and stand here in sequinned evening wear having totally misjudged the situation.* In the end, she opted for her comfy jeans, turned up above her ankle, new stone-coloured Converse that were gloriously fresh, and a short black and ecru checked smock from Toast that was cut generously and fell away from her body at the waist. It was as much about comfort as it was her look, knowing that to feel happy in her skin meant she was more likely to feel in control. Her curls were behaving and that alone was something to feel thankful for.

There was no way to wriggle out of the plan, agreed as it was that she would travel to The Mount, the Sutherlands' house that sat on the ridge of a valley looking down over Bath. The circumstances of the invitation were still etched in her mind, the memory of which made her flush with the uncomfortable warmth of guilt. The prospect of seeing Dominic again was not something she relished, not under these circumstances, where she was fearful of saying or doing something that might reveal their duplicity.

Just the thought made her feel grubby.

Aiden had not yet ventured home, having stayed with Iris all week, and, as he had the car, had agreed to collect her from the train station. Enya didn't mind the rigmarole, it meant she didn't have to worry about navigating the narrow country lanes, and she wouldn't have to arrive alone. A thought that for some reason always unsettled her, turning up somewhere new or unfamiliar. It was another thing that Jonathan did, offering her his arm whenever they arrived anywhere, as if he instinctively understood.

It broke her heart that she hadn't seen him. Not since the moment Dominic had left via the front door. She'd tried calling to him, writing to him and leaving a note on the kitchen table.

My love . . . come back to me . . . here I am . . . I miss you . . . come back to me, Jonathan . . .

She'd even howled her apology, crying as her bath-water grew tepid, and she felt the loneliest she had since he died, and the most alone. It felt like punishment for admitting to her feelings for Dominic and was a cruel lesson to learn.

For the last two years, Aiden and Holly had been ever present despite living across town, occasionally staying over, popping in for cups of tea, calling with innocuous updates on their day, all very mundane. Yet this contact, their voices and texts, the gentle oil that greased her cogs, had fuelled her will to keep going and had been the thing that got her up and moving every day. Cooking for them was a diversion. The sound of their feet running up and down the stairs, their laughter filtering back from the kitchen, even the nauseating smack of their smooching at every greeting or goodbye – they were the sounds of life that ushered out any threat of isolation. They meant that life carried on, and even though she might still feel every day as if she were wading through treacle, sounds muted, motivation a little lacking, these kids and their presence were a reminder that she was still there. Still human, even if she felt a little otherworldly, as if she were on the outside of the world looking in.

Jenny had been a huge part of that life, connected to her via their kids, but so much more than that, the person she called in the early hours, the woman who had made her tea when she'd arrived home alone from the hospital, having reluctantly had to leave Jonathan's body where it lay. Jenny was the person she texted with nothing to say, just because. She was her friend, her very best friend, and the loss of her cut her as deeply as any grief.

Hardest to accept was that her life, yet again, seemed to have changed all at once, given Aiden's understandable preoccupation with Iris. Holly, broken and in hiding. Dominic, at her insistence, closing the book on their story before it had started, and Jonathan . . . Jonathan gone.

As happened, sometimes she forgot to take a breath and felt the air jump in her throat. It felt a lot like sobbing without the tears, as her old friend panic paid her a visit. Leaning on the kitchen sink, she closed her eyes and took a minute until her breathing settled and the feelings of fear and anxiety passed. The last thing she wanted to deal with this morning was a panic attack.

Angela had been checking in with regularity, softly asking leading questions that without the intensity of the moment when Enya had called her were a little uncomfortable for them both.

'Have you *seen* anyone?'

'No. I haven't seen *anyone*.'

Whether her sister referred to Jonathan or Dominic was neither here nor there. Her answer was just the same.

A quick glimpse at the clock and she knew it was time to head off to the station, no more than a brisk fifteen-minute walk.

'Keys, phone, bag, purse, mints, water bottle, lip balm.' She still spoke aloud as if her husband were near enough to be kept informed. Running through her mental checklist to make sure all was in order.

Pickle was in the kitchen sun puddling, having found a warm spot on the kitchen floor.

'Pickle, I'm going out. I'll be back later. If you need a poo, use your tray. You've had your breakfast and I'll get your supper when I get home. You can go out via your cat flap if you want, but don't go too far. Be good. No parties. No running up phone bills. Do not open the door to strangers; if you hear a noise, call the police, and stay away from the drinks cupboard. There's money at the back of the tea-towel drawer for emergency taxis or a pizza. If you call me, I can be home in a flash.'

She smiled as she gave the same dire warnings her parents used to issue whenever she and Angela were left home alone. Angela's eyes would light up, as if their mother's words were a reminder that booze and pizza money were within reach, whereas Enya would simply make a promise, drawing a cross over her heart. 'Don't worry, Mummy.'

A good girl. Always.

Grabbing her Radley, she was about to shut the internal door when she heard a knock. It was an inconvenience, as well as making her gut bunch at the prospect of encountering Phil on the rampage. Or maybe it was Jenny, full of words of love and forgiveness? Still Enya hoped. It was, however, lovely to see this visitor, no matter how inopportune the timing.

'Holly, hello, darling! Come in, come in!'

She had been telling the girl to pop by whenever, explaining how she would always be there for her, and therefore felt unable to immediately mention that she was about to leave the house.

'Is . . . is he here?' Holly looked timidly towards the staircase, again her loss of vivacity shocking.

'No, my love. He's not. Come through.'

It was strange how, in such a short period of time, Holly moved through the cottage with hesitancy, as if she no longer had a right to be there.

'Do you want a drink, my love?' Enya pointed at the kettle.

Holly shook her head and Enya breathed out with relief that coasted on a trickle of guilt. 'Sit down!'

Holly sat at the table, and almost immediately Pickle jumped up on to her lap and nestled in for a cuddle. Holly held her close, kissing her head and running her hand along the length of her spine. 'I missed you, little Picks.'

'She's missed you.' It felt like the right thing to say.

'I was at Mum and Dad's, but Mum's fussing and driving me nuts. I just wanted to come over. Haven't seen you since you heard the news.'

'Yes, and wow, it's some news.' She borrowed a wow from Angela. 'It's wonderful, Holly, really. I know it's not the most ideal of circumstances and I can't imagine how much harder it's made everything, but in time it will only be wonderful.'

'Maybe.' Holly looked less than convinced. 'Have you and Mum had a falling out?'

A simple enough question, which revealed that Jenny might not have been entirely forthright with her daughter. As ever, Enya took Jenny's lead.

'Not really, no,' she forced a smile, 'it's just that things are a bit tricky for everyone right now, we're all getting used to this new state, and trust me, Holly, I wish we didn't have to.'

'Do you?' Holly asked, eyes wide, and Enya could only answer in truth without revealing the torment of having to exist with a foot in both camps, pulled brittle by the effort.

'I do.'

The girl beamed, as if this was all the inclusivity she needed.

'I want to ask how you're feeling, but I'm aware it's such a rubbish question to be asked when you're feeling low. What can I say instead?' She gave it a moment of thought. 'How about, I'm concerned for how you're feeling, I'm thinking about you all the time, sending you love.'

'Thank you, Enya.'

'I hope it helps, to know that.'

'It really does.' The young woman looked up, a chance for Enya to take in the dark half-moons of distress that sat beneath her bloodshot eyes. 'I thought when he found out I was pregnant, he might want to come back to me. I guess I hoped that.'

'Of course you did.' The girl's words were as pitiful as they were relatable.

'But he didn't.' Holly shook her head and buried her face briefly in Pickle's fur. 'I dream he's still mine, Enya, and there are brilliant moments when I forget what's happened, and I picture us with the little one, going to the park and playing on the Downs. But when I wake up and he's not there, it's like,' her face screwed up as if even the memory of it were painful, 'it's like . . .'

'I know.' Enya bent down and placed her hand on Holly's knee. 'I do know. I still get two mugs out in the morning when I make a cup of tea, I order a large cod and chips from the chippy because we always used to share it. I see a shirt and think, ooh I might get that for Jonathan. And I always put a glass of wine next to mine, for him. Lots of little things.'

Holly nodded. 'I get that. I suppose the difference is that Jonathan would never have left you. He loved you so much.'

Enya felt quite moved by the reminder, conflicted too for the way she had fallen into Dominic's arms so freely. It only ladled guilt into her veins, which already ran thick with the stuff. Not helped by the fact that it only mirrored Aiden's actions, his deceit, with which she was less than comfortable.

'But Aiden isn't dead, he just doesn't want me. And I don't want to say the wrong thing, but it's harder to understand in some ways, harder for me to get my head around. Not that I want Aiden dead, of course not, but I can't tell you how much it's hurt me, the fact that he's not gone, just gone from me.' Her words tailed off as tears robbed her of speech.

Enya wondered if Trish might have said something similar had she been party to her conversation with Dominic across this very table. Her gut rolled at the prospect of having to interact with her later.

'Oh, Holly.' Enya let her cry and rubbed her leg. 'I am so sorry, my love, but I'm going to have to go and catch a train,' she silently prayed the girl didn't ask where she was heading or why, 'but you can stay here if you want. There's no need for you to rush off, just because I have to.'

No sooner had the words left her mouth than she regretted them, entirely unsure of the right thing to do, to say, as again she faltered on the tightrope between supporting this young pregnant girl and loyalty to her son. The boundaries of their relationship had undoubtedly shifted, and she was unsure if she had overstepped them or where Aiden would draw the line. It was new and confusing, as she figured out how to pave this new path with the girl who was carrying her grandchild, a girl who was more than a little broken.

'Is that okay?' Holly perked up.

'Yup, uh-huh.' Enya grabbed her handbag, the one Holly and Aiden had bought her. 'You know where everything is. Help yourself to food, of course. Sit in the garden, nap on the sofa, cuddle Pickle, do whatever you want. Rest. Just shut the door behind you when you leave.'

Holly nodded. 'I will, thank you, Enya.'

'Any time – we love you Holly Hudson, Pickle and I. That will never change.'

She watched as Holly's head fell forward and she cried, almost silently, as if it were a natural state for her of late. It was a desperate and affecting thing to witness, realising in that moment that she had forgotten to add Holly Hudson to the list of people who had slipped or were slipping out of reach, and her heart lurched.

She wished it were possible to fast-forward a few months, to a time when things, hopefully, would have settled a little for Holly. This thought was immediately followed by the realisation that in a few months, Aiden and Iris would be married and Holly would be very pregnant. How would she face it all without Jenny on side? It was an unbearable thought. Enya suddenly felt the pull of exhaustion, realising that this state of high energy, a life with so many moving parts, where chaos seemed to reign, wasn't going to end any time soon.

'I really have to go now, my love.'

'It's okay.' Holly sniffed. 'I'm just going to lie on the sofa with Picks, and sleep.'

'That sounds like a good idea.'

And in this regard, Enya truly envied her.

Chapter
Twenty-Two

A march was now required for Enya to make the train, not that it mattered; she was glad that she'd been there to let Holly in, to make her feel welcome. She decided not to tell Aiden about her visitor, not today, anyway.

Her train was on the platform. She ran to avoid missing it and climbed aboard, a little short of breath, out of puff, yet with a sense of relief. It was everything she tried to avoid about travel; cutting it so fine, she now had to meander through the crowded walkways, sidestepping backpacks, suitcases and the protruding legs of those inconsiderate enough not to sit in a more compact manner. Her preference was always to arrive early, choose a window seat, adjust her clothing, take a deep breath, and familiarise herself with her surroundings before the journey commenced.

As the train pulled out of the station heading towards Bath, no more than a short hop really, she felt anxiety flare, and wobbled on her feet as it picked up speed. It felt easier to stand by the loo, resting her bum on the litter bin and staring out of the door window as the concrete of the station gave way to red-brick walls and pantile roofs, bigger and bigger gardens, then the light industry and sprawling estates of the suburbs, before finally her eyes danced across fields. Acres and acres of countryside where deer gathered, crops swayed, rabbits hopped, and the sunny blue sky sat like a backdrop to the kind of watercolour Jonathan would have wanted to hang above the fireplace, and she'd have wrinkled her nose at his chocolate box taste.

The view and the gentle breeze hitting her face from the slightly open window did much to ease her thoughts and meant it wasn't until the train pulled into Bath Spa station that the string of nerves in her stomach began furiously to knot itself. *How?* How was she to spend the afternoon with Dominic, in Dominic's home, with Dominic's family, smiling, pretending, knowing the way he felt?

The way she felt.

Even before she set foot in the place, she felt warmed by the prospect of saying her goodbyes, wanting it all to be over. More specifically, she wanted it all to be over and to have passed without incident. It all felt horribly sneaky, understanding that even the smallest interaction with the man meant other things were spoiled, the butterfly effect.

Aiden, she knew, deserved more, as did Iris. This was supposed to be a happy day of celebration and planning, and for that reason she pulled back her shoulders and found a smile that would do, before waving in the direction of her little Audi, which had pulled up on the cobbles, lights blinking, driven by her boy.

The sight of him, someone familiar, someone she loved, in the little car Jonathan had bought, was enough for her to feel the rise of emotion in her throat. As she approached, Aiden leaned over and opened the passenger door just as his dad would have done. Another little thing, a kindness, behaviour both witnessed and inherited that warmed her heart.

'You look nice.'

She jumped into the passenger seat as he indicated and eased out into the stream of slow-moving traffic. 'Do I?'

'I wouldn't say if you didn't.' He sounded a little snappy. He had always done this, vented his anger, frustration, sadness in the one place he knew he could do so freely – in front of her. Not that it made her feel any better to be on the receiving end.

'Well, thank you.' She meant it, unwilling to share the agony of trying to decide on an outfit, the kind of thing Jenny would have helped with. His words enough to untangle a couple of the smaller knots that took up space in the base of her gut. 'How are you feeling, love?' she asked cautiously, having picked up on the undertone of his words.

'Excited! Happy!' He shook his head. 'Overwhelmed! So many things, Mum.'

'You're not having second thoughts, are you?'

'No!' Both his tone and expression were emphatic. 'Why would you say that? Of course I'm not! Jesus! I thought you might be a little more on board by now!'

His foot on the gas, she knew, was nothing to do with the fact that the speed limit was more forgiving here, but rather in direct response to her words, which had clearly irritated him.

'I am on board! I only ask because you're flying high, sitting on top of a whirling tornado comprised of hormones and new love, excitement, sex and energy, and it has real momentum. And as your mum, and as your dad is not here, *I* am the person who has to provide the checks and balances. It's dull, I know. It's not fun. It's negative, all the aspects that you'd probably rather not consider, but it's my job to point them out.'

He sighed.

The truth was, she didn't want him to fall foul of the old infatuation trap, didn't want to see him act in haste and repent at leisure. The image of Dominic sitting at the kitchen table crystallised in her mind. 'You've got to be so certain with these things. Especially when people have paid a high price for your choice.'

Whether she was speaking to Aiden or reminding herself was neither here nor there.

'I get it.'

She watched his shoulders release some of the tension, as again he indicated and turned from the main road, travelling now up a steep hill with grand Palladian mansions on either side. It had been an age since she'd been to Bath and she had almost forgotten what a beautiful city it was.

Unsure if he did get it, she tried a new analogy.

'Where I work at the solicitors', I deal a lot with people buying houses. But of course, they're not just buying houses. It's never just bricks and mortar with an outside space if they're lucky. Never just that. What people are buying is where they will eat their meals, picturing themselves with their friends, partners, or the people they love around a table, laughing, playing board games, sharing stories. The hallways are where they imagine their children, grandchildren or pets running. It's never just grass or a patio or balcony, it's where they envisage summer days, lazy nights, weekends, flowers, footprints in the snow in winter, even a BBQ with a cold beer in their hand. I often have to speak to them, these dreamers, to give them details of a report or the results of a survey, which are not always what they want to hear. *Oh, I'm sorry Mrs Smith, but the kitchen you were picturing at Christmas, full of all the people you love, has actually got dry rot, and needs to be pulled down*, or *I'm afraid Mr Jones, the attic in which you imagined building your model railway and whiling away your retirement, hiding from Mrs Jones, was converted without planning permission so you can't set foot in it at all.* They don't want to hear it, any of it, but it's necessary to keep everyone safe.'

'Mum, please. I know you mean well, but even saying *second thoughts*, and the way you asked it – almost suggesting that I should be having doubts.'

'Of course you should be having doubts! Not because it's the wrong thing to do or because I have anything against Iris or even because of the whole Holly situation,' she pictured the broken-hearted girl, probably asleep by now, curled on to the sofa with Pickle, 'you should be having doubts because that's how you figure out whether it's right for you, working through all of your concerns and asking the difficult questions. That's how you get to a point where, as far as you are able, you can say with certainty that it's the right thing for you to do.'

'I know it's what I want. It's definitely the right thing for me to do. No hesitation, no doubt. It's her. She's the one.'

Enya nodded; she disliked how quickly this negative interaction had occurred, having sprung from the most promising of starts. Was Aiden right? Did she always hoover up his joy? Such a horrid phrase, unsure in the moment of how to support him unconditionally while harbouring doubts that what he and Iris felt for each other might not be a forever kind of love.

'Everyone's really excited to see you.' He threw her a branch.

'That's lovely. I'm a bit nervous, truth be told.'

'I knew you would be, but there's no need, Mum. They're really nice people. Not far now.'

He turned and smiled at her with the same expression he'd been wearing since he was a small child, a wide grin, bright sparkly eyes, with an openness to his joy that was infectious.

She wanted to ask him how Iris had taken the news of Holly's pregnancy, but with his previous comments at the forefront of her mind decided not to steer them back down a negative path, unwilling to wipe that smile from his face.

The car slowed. Engine running, they came to a halt in front of two wide wrought-iron gates set inside slate pillars, on one of which the name The Mount was written in a bold, clear script.

Aiden reached into the central console and produced a little black fob that she hadn't seen before.

'They've given me my very own dibber!'

Again, that grin like a child on Christmas morning who had in his hands the very thing he'd always wanted.

'How marvellous!' It irked her how chuffed he was with this little bit of plastic, and how seemingly impressed with the family who had entrusted him with it.

He pressed the button and the gates moved smoothly, making a satisfying clunk as they rested open, allowing access to the wide slope of driveway, which was edged in what looked like shiny chrome balls. Closer inspection would reveal them to be water features, each with a gentle cascade coating it entirely, the delicate trickle the sweetest music that cut through the floral-scented air. The grass on either side of the driveway was neat with sharp edging and considered and controlled planting. She couldn't wait to give Jenny all the details, before instantly striking this from her thoughts and swallowing the wave of hurt that swamped her even now.

It was hard not to compare it to her own garden, where wisteria climbed over red brick and hung in soft droplets of lilac when in bloom. The wild garden in front of the shed; an abundance of grasses, shot through with delicate-headed wildflowers, an all-you-could-eat buffet if you were of the bee kind. One entire bed given over to the roses that seemed more abundant year on year. Hers was a garden that was wild, directed to a degree, but untamed, and she loved it. This was a different thing entirely. She could only wonder at the amount of work it would take to keep nature so bound in straight lines and in such order. A battle, no less.

'Here we are,' he announced with pride, and she understood that already he felt at home. It was another paper cut of loss that she would no doubt analyse in the early hours, at 3 a.m. to be precise, when those thoughts insisted on floating to the top.

Slowly, they approached a row of garages to the right of the house, all with shiny black doors and what looked to be offices or at the very least storage above.

'That's where Dominic works.' He pointed to the windows.

'What does he do?' She knew he had his own business but hadn't got round to asking.

'He's an architect, a commercial architect.'

'Right.'

It made sense, his informed commentary on her home and taste. She looked away, not wanting another place to picture him during the day, uncomfortable at how easily she was slotting in the next piece of jigsaw that helped complete the picture of his life and how he lived it.

'So if he's as free as you say he is, what's stopping you . . .' She heard Angela's words and shook these too from her head.

As if to counter this thought, she pictured Jonathan, wondering if he might come back to her, praying he might.

It was almost comical, the way Aiden parked the little car between two whopping four by fours. There was no sign of the silver Mercedes that had been instrumental in her introduction to this man and his family. *The Mumbley Boys . . .* She ran her fingers over her mouth, as if to physically remove any hint of a smile.

'Hey!'

She heard the call as she climbed from the car and there was Trish, with Iris not far behind.

'Here you are!' The woman crunched over the immaculate gravel, her arms wide, clearly intent on coming in for a hug. 'You made it!' she trilled, as if Enya had had to trek across mountains or conquer shark-infested waters and had not merely hopped on the 2.15 from Bristol with the mild inconvenience of not having a seat.

'Yes, here I am! Your garden is lovely. It must be so much work.'

'Oh, it's endless.' Trish held her briefly and kissed her cheek in a way that was familiar and showy. Enya knew deep down that were the woman not attached to Dominic, she would have found her actions to be nothing but endearing, kind. 'Thankfully, it's not work I have to do. Goodness, I wouldn't know where to start! That's where Young Walter comes in, and this is absolutely darling,' she laughed, 'he's called Young Walter because, obviously, his father is Walter Senior and Young Walter is probably knocking eighty. But he never misses a shift, here at the crack of dawn three days a week. He works so hard, weeding the beds, cutting the grass, keeping everything ship-shape. He used to have a garden himself, but the word is that after his wife died, well, I think he lost his way a bit, unravelled, and moved in with his dad. His life seems very small, and so coming here, the routine, the regimen, the chance to get his hands in soil, we both benefit.'

Enya could only nod, feeling kinship with Young Walter, wondering, not for the first time, what her life might be like when in a few months there would be no need to order files, answer the phone, send out mail, open packages and generally loiter in that dust-filled office at the beck and call of Messrs Greengate and Greengate. Jenny's florist's had sat like a bright hope on the horizon, but now she'd have to come up with plan B. It was that or sink entirely. What on earth was she going to do?

'Enya! Hi!' Iris called confidently as she jogged towards her, and she too greeted Enya with a soft kiss that failed to reach her cheek, but instead hovered in the air. A kiss that was cool and contained.

Enya remembered when she and Jonathan were engaged, and his mother, Mrs Dorothy Brown, an aloof woman of the era when things were a little more formal, never said, *Call me Dorothy!* Or God forbid, *Mother!* There were a couple of years when Enya panicked every time she had to speak to her, what should she call her? To say *Mrs Brown* felt uncomfortably officious, and relegated Enya, placing her very much outside of the inner circle. She smiled to think of it now, her younger self excruciatingly pouring tea from a nervous hand, '*Would you like milk and sugar . . . Mrs, Dor . . . Mu . . .*' The woman did nothing to help put an end to the fiasco. Thankfully, when Aiden was born it simplified everything. Enya had by then grown in confidence, and would say with something close to assertion, 'More tea, *Granny Brown?*' Mrs Brown had given no indication she liked or disliked the moniker but was rather taken with her new grandson and that was all that mattered really. Different times.

'Hello, Iris.' She smiled at the girl whose face she had yet to learn. The girl her son had, without doubt or hesitation, chosen. The question whether it was a choice made in lust or love was still a concern.

'I can't wait to show you all the bits and bobs we've pulled together. We've got cake samples, the lemon is my favourite, but then I love all things lemon, sashes for the flower girls, tablecloths and napkins, which Mum and I can't agree on, buttonholes, place-card holders, and there's a menu for us to look at and I need to confirm the photographer.' Iris clasped her hands and smiled, calmly enthusiastic, it would seem, when it came to the impending nuptials. 'I don't know how people string out the planning for a wedding for a year or longer. Three weeks or so is plenty if you're willing to pay!'

Enya studied the face of her future daughter-in-law, looking for clues. Was she a little red-eyed, either from an emotional or disrupted night just spent? It was a relief to find that she looked as fresh as a daisy. And the way she held out her hand for Aiden to take as they walked back to the house together suggested that whatever he had said about Holly's pregnancy, he was most certainly forgiven. She was happy for him. For them all. If Iris had reacted badly and it had caused ripples or worse, it would have felt like the cruellest blow. All that heartache and disruption for nothing, everyone's happiness, Aiden's included, cut down to a nub, never again to grow with quite the same abundance, how could it? Her head swam at just how complicated it had all become.

'I can't wait.'

She matched the girl's energy, understanding that it was not Iris's fault that she had walked in at the third act, where Holly had been centre stage since curtain up. Not her fault at all. And for Iris to be so inclusive, so considerate, was every mother-in-law's dream, the alternative too horrible to consider.

'Come through! Thought we'd start with tea.' Trish led the way as they moved en masse towards the vast white box of a house, where huge windows gave sight of the immaculate gardens and the view from the back.

'Oh, my goodness!'

It really was the most extraordinary property, putting her in mind of an art gallery. She felt Trish's eyes on her face, clearly excited to take in her reaction to the space, which was almost cathedral-like. A vast, marble-floored cavern with white steel beams running across the roof in lieu of rafters and grand, modern chandeliers hanging down like an art installation themselves. There were no obvious walls that she could see, the staircase cleverly hidden via a box to the front that led to the upstairs rooms.

'I like your home very much. The softness of it . . . the cushions, linens, worn wood, glass, rounded chairs, lots of circles and tactile pieces. No sharp edges.'

His words made much more sense to her now.

The house was zoned with a white kitchen area at one end, and a huge fireplace that looked more spaceship than inglenook as it dangled from a white tube going all the way up to the roof. Deep-pile white rugs were strategically placed on the floor, and white bookshelves, home to hi-tech or funky *objets trouvés*, but as far as she could make out, no books. Two oversized white leather chairs with matching footstools were positioned to face the rear of the building, and this was where her eyes were now drawn.

'This is magnificent.' Enya shook her head at the wonder of it, looking out over the patio where a pink powder-coated table and seating for twenty was dwarfed by the garden beyond.

The house, its fixtures and fittings, might not have been to her taste, there was nothing sweet, cosy or indeed cute about it, but from this vantage point on top of the ridge, the park-like garden dropped away down the hillside, and it was as if the property were perched on a mountain top, with the wide sweep of the valley below. Dotted with full and ancient trees, it was like peering through clouds at the world below, the stunning countryside bisected by the River Avon, which sparkled where the sun danced on its surface. And the city of Bath itself, sitting in beautiful symmetry like pale Lego bricks with red roofs, nestling in the distance. The soaring Gothic arches of Bath Abbey rose into the skyline, and she could only imagine what it might look like after dark when the honey-coloured street lamps and the interior lights of all who lived below would glow like the dying embers of a fire, and just as hypnotically.

'It's why we bought the place. The view.' Trish spoke with a pride that was not overt or conceited, but rather with love for the spot she called home. 'There was an old house on the plot, a grotty thing really, all creaky stairs and dusty corners.' Enya caught Aiden's eye, wondering if he, like her, might think that creaky stairs and dusty corners would be preferable. 'Took us six years to finish the build. Would have been a lot quicker were I not married to a perfectionist.' Trish rolled her eyes.

'Where *is* Dad?' Iris asked, looking around as if he might be wearing all white and they'd lost him against the marble background.

'Three guesses!' Trish threw her manicured hands in the air and walked towards the kitchen, where an island, at least fifteen foot in length, housed a couple of stove tops, one gas, one halogen, and what looked to be a wood-fired grill and a small sink. Everything looked pristine. Enya remembered then that Trish didn't use the kitchen for cooking. She had thought at the time that Trish was joking.

'Not the boat!' Iris sounded exasperated.

'He said he had a couple of jobs that needed doing urgently, he'll be back in time to fire up the barbecue, don't worry.' Trish winked at her daughter.

'It's like having a demanding sibling who takes the lion's share of his attention.' Iris laughed, and they all tittered, but there was a low hum of pain behind her words. Enya understood his desire to halt the move into the flat until after the wedding, dismantling things gradually. Iris would of course take it hard. The thought of the girl learning that there had been any kind of fascination between him and her future mother-in-law was utterly unthinkable. She was glad she'd nipped it in the bud when she had.

'She's my escape, the place I go to stop everything coming to a head. I've been buying time for us as a family, nothing more. Because pulling the plug on our marriage is not something I consider lightly . . .'

Enya, in truth, felt nothing but relief, even with his words in her thoughts; an hour or so's grace before she had to face the man who occupied space in her head was most welcome.

'Aiden, can you go and put the awning up, sweetie?' Trish spoke to him with affection, indicating a closeness that made Enya feel a little excluded. While she wondered where to stand, whether or not she should take her bag off and where she might place it, knowing it would sit like a burgundy splat on this pale, pale landscape, her son strode confidently out of the back of the house. He pressed a button that controlled a wide sail-like covering, which appeared like magic and cast the spacious patio in shadow.

'Thought we'd have tea outside,' Trish added.

'That sounds lovely.'

'There's a side garden, Enya, an orchard.' Iris pointed in the general direction. 'It's flat and has a clearing. We thought it perfect for the ceremony under an open-sided marquee, just in case the weather is rubbish – we'll pretty it up, of course, with fairy lights and flower arches and whatnot – and then all round to the back garden with the doors fully open so the reception can happen out there or in here, people can wander, plenty of seating, bistro tables, candles in jars, flowers *everywhere*!'

'Tell Enya about the swans!' Trish laughed.

'Yes, swans!' Iris pulled a face. 'Mum thinks swans on the lawns, just wandering, something to amuse the guests.'

'Well, that sounds lovely,' she repeated, and cursed her nerves, which not only curtailed her vocabulary but also made her overthink every word. Truth was, she felt a little overawed by the overt display of wealth, uncomfortable in a way that was alien to her, and unsure of her role in the very grand wedding plans. She wanted to feel part of it, wanted to show willing, but the way the three interacted, her son walking around the house as if he had been doing so forever, the ease of affection between the trio, relationships already established when this was only the second time she had met Iris in person . . . She felt empty and a little surplus to requirements, awkward. This the exact situation when being able to exchange a knowing glance with Jonathan would have made all the difference. Just a look that said *in tune, in sync, one team.*

A darling retriever came padding over, tail wagging, before falling down into a heap on the warm floor.

'Ah, this must be Fishstick!' She bent down and stroked the handsome large head of the dog.

'Huh! Who told you his name was Fishstick? I always introduce him as Sticks!'

'I . . . I can't remember.' Enya felt sick and focused on the lovely, lolloping dog, anything other than meet anyone's eye. The thought of having to come up with a scenario that would only take her further along the path of deceit made her want to throw up. 'Not sure, but I think Aiden or Iris must have.'

Thankfully, no one seemed to pick up on it. Iris herself changed the subject. And Enya feared she might pass out with relief. She stood up straight, keen to put as much space between her and the dog that had nearly been her undoing as was possible.

'It's not going to be a big wedding, but we have about fifty coming, people we absolutely have to invite, immediate family, my closest friends, Mum's closest friends, that kind of thing. Thankfully, some people couldn't make it, what with it being short notice and the holiday season.'

'Yes, of course!' She hadn't considered this.

'We can't get married legally here so we'll have the ceremony and then the Monday after we'll go to the registry office, that's just going to be AJ and me and two mates to witness. I want the wedding at home to be the "*wedding*",' she flexed her fingers to put this in air quotes, 'and the registry office thing will be purely administrative.'

'That makes sense.' Enya swallowed this horrid new feeling of alienation that she was unaware of the detail. It was the opposite of how Holly and she interacted; Enya even knew what perfume the girl would have worn on her big day. The big day that never was. She felt the fold of exclusion in the base of her stomach at the thought of her boy getting married without her. 'Also, I wanted to say, I'd really like to make a contribution to the cost, happy to go halves or whatever works.'

It was far from comfortable talking about money in this way, especially as they were strangers.

'Oh goodness, no!' Trish answered. 'We only have the one daughter, her dad would be mortified not to do this for her. But thank you, Enya, bless you!'

There was much to unpick about the woman's response, not least the way she seemed to dismiss the fact that Enya only had the one son, and would have liked to have paid for something, anything! Also, the way she added *bless you* indicated that she suspected Enya might be incapable of making a financial contribution, what with her living in such a cutesy cottage and all.

'We need your invite list,' Iris continued. 'AJ's been useless – apart from his nan and grandad and his Auntie Angela and Uncle Frank, two mates from school, three from uni, Jim, of course, and a few of the rugby lads, and one from work, he's drawn a blank!'

Enya opened her mouth to remark that he'd forgotten Holly and her parents, so used was she to them being a pair, so entwined were their histories that it still felt most odd to think of them as separate. How she wished Jenny was going to be present, her ally in every situation, until now.

'We're a very small family.' She hated how apologetic she sounded.

'Yes, but your bestie, who's your bestie?' Trish asked, as she filled a glass kettle with water and set it to boil.

'Erm.' She looked out towards Aiden, who was securing the awning and adjusting a chair to make sure it was in line. *Jonathan . . . Jonathan was my bestie . . . but I've lost him. Jen was my next bestie, but I've lost her too . . .* 'My sister, I suppose. My sister, Angela.'

She looked around in time to see the lingering look of wide-eyed judgement shared between Trish and her daughter. Glad she hadn't yet discarded her bag, she gripped the handle, something on which to steady her shaky hands.

Chapter
Twenty-Three

The sun had dropped a little and a pleasant breeze blew up from the valley below. Enya had declined a second glass of wine and switched to sparkling water, not that it had dented the enthusiasm of the others, who had sunk a couple of bottles. The chatter had been about all things wedding, and now, as Trish ended her rather tense phone call, there was an embarrassed hush around the table.

'I don't bloody believe it, your dad's not coming back this evening, a problem with the boat. I don't know why he doesn't just sail off on the bloody thing and be done with it.'

'You don't mean that. Besides, you were always telling him to get a hobby, get out of the house, and now he has!' Iris spoke now in defence of her dad, and Enya saw the conflict. Iris had earlier lamented his absence and yet now represented him when her mum slated him. She understood more than most how exhausting it was to be so pulled in two directions. *Brittle.*

'Yes, you're right, I did tell him to get a hobby, but I didn't think he'd be out the house permanently! You were right, what you said earlier, it's like he's got another child or another woman, and her name is *Foula Girl.*'

Enya reached for her drink, keen to hide her face and become falsely preoccupied with her sparkling water, anything other than participate in the chat about Dominic's other woman. Or worse, give any hint that she had knowledge of *Foula Girl* . . . her slip-up with Fishstick earlier still sat uncomfortably under her skin like a tiny thorn.

'I can do the BBQ!'

Aiden spoke with an energy that Enya rarely saw when it came to chores around the cottage. He'd been like this all day, and she understood: his desire to be liked by his future mother-in-law, his need to impress Iris, to show her that she was making a good choice when it came to husband material. But she'd be lying if she said it didn't bother her. What would Jonathan say? He'd say, *It's good that he can be himself when he's at home with you, relax and not feel the need to perform.* And *it will all settle down here in time.*

Yes, it was good advice.

Yet she'd counter it with her concern that their son appeared to be marrying a woman with whom he didn't seem entirely at ease. She and Jonathan would no doubt argue a little about it and let it settle until they agreed and compromised. It was their way. Had always been their way. There was nothing they couldn't say, nothing she couldn't raise, nothing either of them had to hide. Until now, when she had felt a visceral longing for another man's body and had, at least once, forgotten her husband while enthralled with the man. It didn't feel good.

Any flicker of irritation, however, at Aiden's behaviour was smothered with the blanket of relief that she wasn't going to have to face Dominic. And with this relief, as ever, came the guilt that she had a need to feel this way at all.

With new bottles of wine now lined up on the table, she watched as Trish indulged, noting again how fond she was of the tipple and the speed with which she downed her glass, not judging, but wondering if maybe she wasn't quite as confident as she presented. If circumstances were different, she thought she might try to get to know the woman better. But how could that be when the memory of being held in Dominic's arms was still her most dominant thought? Trish, she knew, may not be smiling if she were aware of the situation, which meant every sip and every bite Enya consumed was laced with self-consciousness.

It had been the strangest of days. It still felt surreal that Aiden was getting married even as they picked ribbon colours, chose red velvet cake over Iris's favourite of lemon, based purely on the aesthetic, and selected fonts in which place names would be printed. It still felt otherworldly, the very thought that her son was marrying this woman he'd known for such a short time and, in doing so, joined their families together. Hardest of all was the simple fact that this union seemed to be roaring ahead with unstoppable momentum, and whether right or wrong, she wasn't sure there was a darn thing she could do to stop it.

Not for the first time, she thought of Holly Hudson and hoped she had found some time to rest.

The BBQ was adequate but not fancy, an overly burnt sausage, a dry burger and a basic salad, exactly what Aiden would have prepared on their rusty old BBQ by the shed, and not on this mega machine that resembled a large bullet and looked like it had fallen straight off the front page of a fancy garden catalogue. She was, however, grateful for their fabulous hospitality, the kindness.

Enya was tired and, with one eye on the clock, the moment the plates were cleared and having declined pudding, she said to the assembled, 'I really should be heading off. It's been a lovely day, wonderful in fact.'

'Thank you for coming, Enya. I'm so excited about everything, about the wedding, about our choices, about my dress,' Iris beamed, 'but I'm most excited about being married to AJ, our life together and getting to know you better.'

There was no doubt about it. Iris, who didn't have Holly's overly enthusiastic or sweet nature, seemed no less lovely. Certainly, she spoke of all the things Enya had ever wanted for her boy and yet . . . she couldn't help the underlying sense of frustration that if Iris Sutherland had been allocated a different seat, if she had missed the bloody flight, Aiden would still be with Holly. She, Jenny and Phil would be going crazy with excitement for the new baby, Enya would not feel the need to hide from Maeve like a criminal, Jonathan would still be around, and right about now she'd probably be ordering business cards for the new floral venture with her best friend. It wasn't Iris's fault, of course not, but still, this was her unpalatable truth.

'Can I help with the dishes or clearing up, before I leave? I don't like the idea of abandoning you with the mess.'

'Oh God, no!' Trish waved her hand. 'Don't worry about that.'

'Well, thank you, once again, and come to me next time.' It was a glib offer that she prayed she wouldn't have to honour. Just the thought of Dominic walking into her home was enough to unsettle her even further.

'We will, we will.' Trish nodded.

Aiden and Iris gathered salad bowls and dirty plates, ferrying them to the kitchen, as Trish leaned across the table and fixed her with a stare.

'I'm on to you!' Trish narrowed her eyes, her hot-pink lipstick, which sat a little proud of her lip line, curled into a sneer.

'Oh? What have I done now?' Her laugh was nervous, exaggerated and awkward, as her heart jumped up into her throat. She wondered if Trish was going to mention Fishstick.

Trish unfurled her index finger and pointed it towards Enya's face. 'You didn't make those blondies, did you?'

'Blondies?' It took her a split second to grasp the thread.

'You're no baker! You didn't even know the recipe!' The woman tutted loudly.

'You got me!' She held her hands up, like a comic cowboy who'd been shot by a pop gun where a little flag falls out saying BANG!

'I bloody knew it!' Trish stood and teetered on her wedged heel, leaning on the chair in front of her. 'What else are you fibbing about?'

'Oh, nothing else, just that. I am no baker and,' she thought hard, 'I know I said the swans sounded lovely, but actually, I think they might be a bit much!' She laughed, knowing how funny Angela and Jenny would find this in the retelling, before remembering all over again that she would only be telling Angela.

'That's what my husband said, but he's a shit. All this!' She let her arm fall over her head in an arc. 'And yet he'd rather be in a boat shed. Shall, shall I tell you a little secret?' Trish banged the table.

Enya gave a small nod, not sure how many more Sutherland secrets she could contain.

'I'd rather he was there too! He's got a bloody flat. He's off!'

Enya felt her legs jump under the table, *shit!* She did not want to be having this conversation, did not want to be party to any of it! Doing her best to look engaged without offering an opinion, she stared at the table.

'But don't tell Iris!' Trish put her fingers on her lips and sat down hard in her seat, leaning even closer, almost lying on the tabletop, until Enya could smell the sour notes of wine on her breath and seeping from her pores. 'I've got my eye on you, Enya!'

It was mere seconds before Iris's mother pulled her arms into a cradle on the surface and placed her head on them, falling into a sleep almost immediately.

Enya didn't quite know what to do, and so sat very still, wary of waking the woman and inviting any more commentary on her deceitful baking claims and petrified as to what else Trish might want to say. It was a horrible feeling, leaving her covered in a fine film of discomfort that she couldn't wait to shower off. Proof, as if more proof were needed, that to steer clear of Dominic was the right thing to do. To be in the middle of him and Trish was a little more than she could cope with.

'Oh, Mum.' Iris sounded neither angry nor surprised as she approached the table. 'Sorry, Enya, she's, she's got a lot on at the moment.'

'Honestly, Iris,' Enya placed her bag over her shoulder and wondered where her car keys were, 'it's been quite a week, and if I thought I could get away with a little nap on the table, I'd probably do the same. Anyway, I should be going.' She stood and declined to look back at her host, knowing that if she were asleep, snoring loudly, as Trish now was, the last thing she'd want would be an audience.

'See you soon, Enya,' Iris offered distractedly, without any suggestion of a hug or a smile, both of which Holly gave in abundance.

'Yes, see you soon.' Enya noticed how she kept glancing at her mother with something that looked a lot like concern.

Aiden followed her out to the car and handed her the keys.

'Will you be okay? You know the way?' he asked, as she climbed into the driver's seat and adjusted the mirror.

'Of course I will. I know the way, and if I didn't I'd use the sat nav on my phone. Easy. Will *you* be all right?' It felt a lot like abandoning him here, the same way she'd felt when leaving him at nursery for the first time.

He leaned on the open door and took a deep breath. 'Trish and Dominic have been arguing, not in front of me, but Iris is aware of it. It's hard for her, caught in the middle.'

'I can't imagine.' She put the key in the ignition, wanting desperately to ask what they were rowing about but knowing that was as inappropriate as it was unfair, as her motives were self-serving.

'It's weird for me, you and Dad were always so . . .' He looked into the middle distance and she saw a tendril of grief still present, waiting to wiggle through any gap it could find and take hold. 'You were mates, weren't you?'

'We were.' She blinked and glanced in the rear-view mirror at the empty back seat.

'I want it to be like that for me and Iris, it's important. The thought of living with the kind of tension that Trish and Dominic do, I couldn't stand it.'

'It comes with time.' This was the closest she felt able to come to saying *slow down! Be sure!* Knowing that would not land well. 'You'll lay the foundations, darling, on which your marriage will be built, open and honest communication and always love, they should be two of them. If you do that from the very start, everything else kind of takes care of itself.' She let this trail. 'How did Iris take the news about Holly being pregnant?'

It was then that he met her stare. 'I haven't told her yet.'

'Aiden!'

'I know,' he ran his palm over his face, 'she's just got so much on at work and what with the wedding planning and her mum and dad and—'

'You've just told me about the kind of marriage you want and keeping secrets is not the way to build honesty. You know this. You get married in less than three weeks! That's the kind of news that takes a while to percolate, you guys will need to work it through, you need to tell her right now! It's not fair on her otherwise, or Holly, for that matter. She needs to be able to call you or text you to discuss things and if she's a big dark skeleton in the cupboard, how will that make her feel? It's already going to be hard, love, you all need to come together to find a workable solution, otherwise, how will it be when the baby actually arrives? You're making a complicated situation worse! It's not on, Aiden! It's just not on!'

'You think I don't know all this?' He looked for a split second like he might be close to tears.

She toned it down. 'I know you've got a lot going on too. I know you'll be worrying about everything.'

'I am, Mum.' He spoke softly. She decided not to mention that it was a mess of his own making, wanting only to build a bridge and not alienate him any further, her son who right now looked more boy than man.

'But trust me when I say that if you also have to explain to Iris why you haven't told her, why you didn't tell her the very moment you found out, on top of the news itself, that will make it twice as hard. A double blow.'

'I'll tell her tonight.'

Enya stowed her bag on the passenger seat and climbed out of the car, wanting to hold her son in her arms. In part to feel him close and take comfort from it, but also to remind him that she was still here, would always be here. To her delight, he wrapped his arms around her and held on in a hug that was slow and heartfelt.

'I love you, Aiden.'

'Love you,' he managed, but still didn't let her go immediately.

'Three weeks is a long time. Long enough,' she whispered, unsure herself of what she was saying, *long enough to set ground rules, long enough to argue and come back together, long enough to change your mind . . .*

Finally, his hold on her weakened and she got back into the car.

'Text me when you get home.' He smiled, like her, no doubt recognising that it was usually her who issued this instruction.

'I will.'

'Oh, meant to say,' he pointed across the car, 'looks like something has clunked the passenger door, given it a right old thump. I only noticed it yesterday. There's a big dip in the paintwork and a dent below the handle. Have you bashed it, or has anything hit you?'

She felt her cheeks flame red. 'Oh, yes, don't worry about that. It was . . .' She shoved the car into gear. 'It's all taken care of, it's booked in for repair, no need to call the feds!'

She gave a nervous laugh and set off down the driveway, as keen to be gone as she was to arrive home, to get away from the vast house that felt nothing like a home. The house Trish and Dominic had built together, and which now had restlessness pooling on the immaculate floors and echoes of discontent bouncing from the white walls. A place where she had no desire to be, as she was inadvertently placed in the middle of it all. She hoped Trish would be okay, the woman's turmoil clearly hovering very near the surface.

Another quick glance in her rear-view mirror and there was still no sign of Jonathan; instead she pictured Aiden's expression of mild amusement at how she had damaged the car and not said so.

'Fucking hell!'

She banged the steering wheel in an uncharacteristic outburst. In that moment, feeling like she was losing control, in the eye of a storm that someone else had driven her into and with no one throwing her a rope, understanding that it was up to her to drive herself out of it.

Chapter
Twenty-Four

It was an easy journey home. Saturday night, and it seemed people were either staying home to enjoy summer in their gardens or had possibly already arrived wherever they were travelling.

Enya, calmer now, pulled up outside the cottage and parked in the road. The lights were on in the Hudsons' lounge window. She pictured them on the sofa, watching TV in the room she knew well, and felt the exclusion like a physical thing, an ache in her breast, knowing that after the day spent, in another lifetime she would have ambled up their path and knocked on the door.

'I need wine!' would be her greeting, and they'd laugh and sit on the sofa and Jenny would listen while Enya gave her every detail. Her friend would then come out with something funny and trite to defuse the situation and they'd eat toast and laugh, and no doubt end up making plans for their first joint window display, letting enthusiasm and giddiness overtake both their budget and their ability.

But this was not another lifetime, and Enya felt the creep of tears. It had been such a huge part of her every day, her best friend in this house along the street, somewhere else to go, someone else to talk to.

'I miss you, Jen,' she whispered into the darkness. 'It's not my fault! None of this is my fault!' Her breath came in gulping sobs, and she took a minute to calm herself.

Next door, Maeve's bedroom window was open. Enya remembered her remarking that, rain or shine, she could only sleep if there was a breeze to lull her into slumber and on a warm night like this, she more than understood.

It was the strangest thing, but for the first time ever, even in the immediate aftermath of losing Jonathan, she didn't want to go inside. The green front door seemed to have lost a little of its lustre. She wasn't keen on being met by the silence or the darkness. It had been one thing to be alone in the wake of her loss, but to now be truly alone without Jonathan's presence was a new low. A new level of loneliness. Allowing herself a moment of melancholic nostalgia, she pictured arriving home late on a Saturday evening when Aiden was little.

Jonathan would have driven, they'd usually go for a wander around the Bristol docks on a Saturday afternoon, grab a chippy tea from the Clifton Village Fish Bar, and then they'd eat their supper on a bench overlooking the Avon Gorge, before balling the vinegar-soaked and ketchup-splatted paper and shoving it into a bin so the car didn't smell.

They'd tootle home to Watley Down with stomachs full and mouths grease-smeared, enthusiastically singing along to whatever came on the radio. Lyrical accuracy optional. There were two rules that applied to these happy Saturdays. First, if they were mid-song when they arrived home, they'd have to sit in the car and let it finish. This fostered the belief that to switch off halfway through a song would bring nothing but bad luck. Second, when a great day and evening had been had by all, they never simply all traipsed in and went to bed. Instead, they made popcorn and settled down to watch a movie with Aiden wedged between them on the sofa.

Or they'd play Risk or Battleships at the kitchen table, her least favourite games. Not that she complained, happy to be inside this bubble of love, where the winner stayed on until the best of three revealed a champion.

Simpler times, a simpler life, now gone forever. How she missed it, all of it, picturing her son in that strange house on a hill, delighted with his bloody dibber.

She walked slowly up the path and into the house, checking the kitchen, where there was no sign of Pickle, before running the tap and gulping down a large glass of water.

'I wish you were here,' she said to her husband. 'I just miss you so much!' Her words echoed.

Having made sure the French doors were locked, she plodded up the stairs. Her body would only benefit from a soak in the bath, but with fatigue pawing at her bones and drawn by the thought of getting cosy in bed, she threw her clothes into a pile in the corner of her bedroom and slipped into her cotton sleeveless PJs. Placing her bag on her dressing table, she opened her bedroom window as wide as it would go, plugged in her phone, grabbed her laptop, and climbed on top of the summer duvet, which, despite its lightweight qualities, was still too warm for this August heat. Her bedroom door she left wide open, hoping a breeze might also waft in from the window on the narrow landing.

Resting the computer on her raised knees, she couldn't decide between watching a movie or going on to YouTube and searching for extraordinary baking. It was a secret pleasure, watching clever cake makers and confectioners creating all sorts of incredible towering, ornately decorated goodies that looked far too good to eat. It was a habit that visually satisfied her sweet tooth without adding sugar to her diet. A win-win. It also seemed funny and ironic in light of Trish's accusations over the great blondie debacle.

Her fingers hovered on the search bar and with the new knowledge of what he did for a living, able to picture him in his swanky home office, she typed in 'Dominic Sutherland architect', wanting to see the face of someone who was not hostile or retreating, someone who had actively sought her out, included her, bolstered her fragile confidence.

'I think you are so much more than a wife and mother. I think you're a wonderful woman who could set the world alight if she so chose. A woman who has the strength to grab any life she wants.'

The breath caught in her throat as his image appeared almost instantly. *About Us* – the section of his company website, and there he was, smiling, wearing a white shirt open at the neck. Enya ran her fingertip over his face and took in the array of letters below his name. Even in this corporate shot, he had the air of someone who didn't take life too seriously, as if he might have found having his photograph taken in this way a tad amusing.

The way her body reacted to his image was all consuming, a fierce attraction that she knew, if things were different, she would explore. But things were not different. She meant what she had said to Aiden, that these connections took time; what she felt for Dominic couldn't be any more than a physical thing, could it?

She enlarged the image until it filled the screen and took a screenshot, not entirely sure why, but certain it was a picture *she* would revisit on the coldest of days and nights. It would, she knew, be the closest she got to him, unwilling to embroil herself any further in the mess that was the Sutherland household. She felt for them all, quite unable to imagine a situation where she and Jonathan would have simply bickered and avoided each other. Equally, she had seen first-hand how being caught between her warring parents affected Iris, the girl her son was about to marry, and to add to *her* anguish, to create more drama, was something she would never do, knowing it would be Aiden who would bear the weight of his girl's unhappiness.

Her laptop shone brightly in the darkness and the image suddenly felt a little overwhelming, overt. A little like self-inflicted torture, being shown a coveted prize that she hadn't won.

She closed the screen down and was instantly and shockingly aware of the shape of a person in the doorway.

The scream that left her throat was loud and visceral – a call for help, as the very worst thing she had imagined since childhood was made real. A person in her room! Not only in her room but standing in the doorway, blocking her exit! And she was alone, without Jonathan, without Aiden, and without a way to avoid confrontation.

It was only when the person screamed too, as loud as Enya, if not louder, that she realised it was Holly, *Holly!* Her scream dried up as all the moisture left her lips, and she struggled to catch her breath; it was then laughter that filled her mouth, laughter flavoured with relief.

'Jesus Christ! Holly! You scared me half to death!'

'And you me!' The girl leaned on the door-frame and bent over, breathing heavily. 'I was calling your name, but only quietly as I didn't want to frighten you.'

'Didn't want to frighten me?' Enya placed her palm on her chest where her heart was yet to catch up that this was not a life-or-death situation. 'Call louder next time! Or better still, text me to let me know you're in the house!'

'I did! I texted you!'

Enya shook her head; she hadn't got the message or, more accurately, had not seen the text. A salient lesson to check her phone more thoroughly.

'Oh my God!' Holly sat on the end of the bed and they both let the sweet music of danger averted fill the air around them.

'Are you okay?' Enya managed.

'Yes, I fell asleep in Aiden's bed, and I didn't want to leave, so . . .'

It was as they chatted, allowing their pulses to calm, that they heard the distinct and loud knocking on the front door, followed by Phil's voice calling, 'Enya! Open up! Enya!'

'Shit! It's my dad!' Holly ran down the stairs while Enya grabbed her cotton dressing gown and popped it on over her summer PJs. She held her breath, wondering what Phil might have to say, wondering why he was knocking, considering their last horrid encounter.

Holly opened the front door and Phil rushed in, shoulders back, baseball bat in hand. 'Holly! What are you doing here? What's happened? We heard screaming!'

'Nothing, it's nothing, Dad, we're fine.'

'It didn't sound like nothing.' His chest heaved.

'I gave Enya a fright and she returned the favour,' Holly explained.

'Why aren't you at home?'

'I fell asleep.' Holly shrugged.

Enya watched from the stairs as Phil went briefly into the kitchen and back out again. 'Tell you what, it gave me a fright too,' he commented as he poked his head into the sitting room, checking the coast was clear, before finally coming to a stop in the hallway. She felt relief and something very close to hope to see Phil rushing to her defence when he thought it was needed. Nothing less than Jonathan would expect, and she was grateful.

'Shall I call the police?'

It was this question that alerted Enya to Maeve's presence, the older woman standing in her pale-blue nightdress on the front step with a milk pan in her hand and two curlers at the front of her hair.

'He *is* the police, Maeve.' Jenny's voice now, the woman just out of sight.

Jenny! Her best friend, here too! She felt the bubble of happiness in her stomach.

'I know that,' Maeve snapped, 'but does he need backup?'

Had there not been so much confusion at this late hour in their usually quiet cul-de-sac, Enya would have laughed out loud. Maeve had clearly been watching too many cop dramas on TV.

'What are you doing here, Holly?' Phil repeated.

'As I said, I, I fell asleep on Aiden's bed. Enya didn't know I was here – I crept into her room and scared her.'

'You could say that.' She trod down the stairs and switched the kitchen lights on. 'Would anyone like a cup of tea?'

It was the kind of situation Jonathan would have found hilarious. The three households standing in the kitchen in their nightwear, all except Phil, who wore a set of grey prison sweats that earlier in their friendship, before the great rift had occurred and all interactions were riven with fragile emotions, she would have asked if he'd stolen, a perk of the job.

Jenny took a seat at the kitchen table as she had a thousand times before and Maeve and Phil followed suit. It was a small act, this gathering, but spoke of reconciliation, of familiarity, and after the day spent at The Mount, she was entirely grateful. Just being in Jenny's presence was a reminder of how much they had shared, all the confidences exchanged over the years, the advice given and more laughter than this whole house could hold. Her best friend. Enya swallowed her tears. It was not the time for tears, it was time to put the kettle on.

Enya sipped the tea and felt the restorative nectar slip down her throat. It was good to know that in case of an emergency, she was guaranteed a decent turnout by way of response, although she was still a little unsure of what Maeve might achieve with her weapon of choice – the old milk pan that now sat on the table.

'How're you doing, Holly?' Maeve reached out and patted the girl's arm.

'I'm okay. All good, really.'

'She's getting there, aren't you, love?' Jenny added, and Enya felt the unspoken judgement of Aiden land all around them. He was, after all, the reason for this sorry mess in the first place. Not for the first time she felt conflicted, wanting to defend her son, but also uncomfortable with his actions.

'I've started knitting.' Maeve smiled. 'I'm making a shawl for the little one, and then I'm going to do a cot blanket.'

'Oh, Maeve, thank you.' Holly smiled back. 'I thought about knitting something but don't seem to have the energy for it.'

'Well, thank goodness for you, Maeve. I couldn't knit a stitch, but I'm good at playing hide-and-seek, and I can read a mean bedtime story.' Enya wanted to add her contribution.

'I bought a couple of nursery rhyme books this week.' Jenny beamed over the top of her mug. It was a second of normality, of ease, a reminder of their lovely friendship.

'We should make sure we don't get the same books, Jen. I've still got most of Aiden's from when he was little. All the classics, *Can't You Sleep, Little Bear?* and *Peepo!*' She felt it important to mention her son, keep him here in his home and in this scenario, despite his absence.

'Oh, she used to love *Peepo!*' Jenny smiled at her daughter.

'Do you think you're having a boy or a girl?' Maeve asked softly. 'We should do the wedding ring test.' She sounded very keen.

'The wedding ring test? I don't know what that is.' Holly flexed her fingers.

Enya, like all present, it seemed, was drawn to Holly's hand, where there was a distinct lack of wedding ring. Not that she gave a fig about the convention, but knew it had mattered to Holly, knew it *would* matter to Holly. That, and she carried the thought that another young woman would be getting the ring.

'We've been doing it for years!' Maeve chuckled. 'I remember sitting excitedly at the kitchen table while a knowing neighbour dangled my mum's wedding ring over my bump. Whether it spins in a circle or swings back and forth in a line lets you know whether you're carrying a girl or a boy. Oh, the elation, when I learnt my new baby was to be a girl! I instantly named her Felicity, don't know where I got that name from, and pictured the hours we would spend together; I'd plait her hair and help take care of her dolls.'

'How is Lesley doing?' Phil asked after Maeve's daughter, who lived in Northampton.

'Oh, it wasn't Lesley, turned out *that* baby was our Andrew: the six-foot plumber, father of one and a man who has never had the slightest interest in letting me plait his hair, or playing with dolls.'

They all laughed.

Phil smiled at Enya, and she felt her heart lift. It was how it used to be. He was a smart man who used to make Jonathan howl with laughter, and vice versa, and this small smile in recognition of Maeve spouting poppycock took her right back. A reminder of how much she needed her tribe, her friends, and how her life without them had made living here seem unstable and thin.

'We've always said we don't mind what we have, as long as it's healthy.' Holly spoke quietly, already halfway through her sentence, it seemed, before remembering there was no *we*.

'That's the spirit, love,' Phil took her small hand inside his and held it tightly, 'and I don't mind what we get, as long as it loves rugby. I've already been online and found a little Bristol Bears kit!'

Their laughter was now somewhat subdued, all possibly thinking, like she was, how matchday had always been a big deal for Jonathan, Phil and Aiden. The traditional fry-up, a pint or two, then off to Ashton Gate to watch the Bears romp home.

'Aiden not here, then?' Maeve looked towards the stairs, as if he might be hiding upstairs.

'No, he stayed at Iris's. It's been a bit of a day, full steam ahead wedding planning, I've eaten cake and deliberated over ribbons. I know I'm tired, I can only imagine how he's faring.' Enya took a large mouthful of tea, and it was only when she lowered her mug and met the gaze of four horrified faces that she understood how tiredness, and the relaxed nature of this gathering, had given her a false sense of friendship, encouraging her to speak without filter. Her tongue stuck to the roof of her mouth, and she knew instantly what she had done.

'Are you joking? He's getting *married*? To Iris . . . *Iris* . . .' Holly gripped the edge of the table as she breathed with her mouth open, eyes glazed with shock. Phil threw his arm around her. 'Enya! Tell me he's not getting *married*, he can't be!'

'Come on, love, let's get you home.' Phil helped his daughter from her seat as Jenny, in a trance-like state, stood.

Enya felt as if a hole had opened up in the universe and all the forgiveness and all the jollity had disappeared into it, aware that she had yet again messed up spectacularly. She sat still, numb with shock and self-reproach. Her neighbours, their heads shaking and with a low-level murmur of collective disapproval, walked towards the front door. Maeve carried the milk pan in her hand.

'What the bloody hell is wrong with him, Enya? *Married?* Does he get some kick out of what he's putting her through?' Jenny asked with a tremble to her bottom lip, all thoughts of reconciliation now scrubbed. 'It's cruel, cruel and unfathomable to me!'

'There's nothing wrong with him, Jen. He just met someone and has fallen for her and wants to be with her and they're getting married, in a few weeks, actually. And I know how hard this is, it's hard for us all, for me too.'

'Is that right?' Jenny snapped, clearly believing she had the upper hand when it came to the pain of this situation. 'All I can say is, God help *Iris*!' She spat the word. 'And now my daughter has a name that will taunt her in the middle of the night. So thank you for that too.'

Enya wanted to sob, this the first time she and Jenny had properly shared a cross word like this. She felt fatigue prod her in the ribs and knew that when she returned to the solace of her mattress, despite the excitement that had hijacked her night, she would have no trouble in nodding off. She was sick of being in the middle of so much drama at the Sutherlands' house and now inside her own, it was exhausting.

Jenny wasn't done. 'I mean, honestly, who the hell meets someone and wants to marry them in a few weeks? Who does that? It can't be real, can it? No one falls instantly like that, not in real life. It's not possible!'

'You don't think so?'

'Do you?' the woman countered.

'Jen! Are you coming?' Phil called to his wife, who gave a heavy sigh of disapproval as she left.

Enya, alone now, battle-weary and entirely sick of being on the receiving end of those judgemental tuts, sat back down and picked up her mug of tea, picturing Dominic as he'd sat at the table opposite her.

'I don't know – is the answer, Jen. I didn't believe it. When it comes to Aiden and Iris, who know so little of life, I just don't know. But when I think about how I've felt in recent times, I'm thinking that maybe it's entirely possible. Not that I can do a bloody thing about it!'

Chapter Twenty-Five

It was Sunday, the day Enya usually tackled specific jobs, like mowing the small rectangle of rear lawn, wiping down the windowsills, cleaning the car. All of these, for no legitimate reason, felt like Sunday jobs, but after the disastrous night she had just spent, despite getting a full six hours of sleep post the impromptu tea party, she was without the energy for much.

With the French doors open, the hanging baskets and planters watered and birdsong filling the garden, she took a moment to sit in the lounge, enjoying the cool air as the sun was yet to work its way around to the front. Yet not even this idyllic tableau could pierce the liquid distress that filled her stomach and rose up into her throat. It felt cruel to have been briefly gifted the company of her neighbours, and for things to have felt partially healed between her and Jenny, only for it all to be snatched away. She could only imagine the chatter across the fence, the shaking heads, the muttered commentary. But rather than hiding, wary and guilt-ridden, what swirled in her veins was a lot closer to anger.

She'd had enough.

She had spent the last few months wondering what her role might be, indeed who she was, but this, this isolation, now made her question whether she was even in the right place. It felt as if she were in freefall, as wary of the landing as she was fearful of the fall itself. But one thing was for sure. She was not going to be made to feel like a scapegoat, was not going to allow herself to be coated with the judgement of others, especially in her own bloody home!

Pickle sauntered in from the hallway, stretched and arched her back, front legs out, shoulders practically grazing the floor and her back legs almost on tiptoe, posing her back in an elegant slope that looked to be blissful. The cat closed her eyes as if to confirm this.

Right now, however, Enya's foremost concern was for Holly. It had been a careless slip-up, her words blurted softly without malicious intention, yet she knew they had landed sharply, injuriously. That was the trouble with lies and lying by omission: it was hard to keep tabs on who knew what and who was to be kept in the dark, and what it was okay to say and what it was not. It required greater brain function than she had to spare right now. The idea that she had caused the girl more than a second of heartache was more punishment than she could stand. Another example of the bloody chaos that Aiden had set in motion. The question now was what to do about it; she was unsure whether making contact and raising the topic with Holly might make things better or worse. But it was far from comfortable knowing she'd waved the girl goodbye yesterday without mentioning she was off to engage in wedding activities. It felt duplicitous, wily, and sly. *An Arctic fox.*

Jill Mansell provided the escape she craved for half an hour, and to lose herself in the beautifully crafted story saw her pulse settle, her limbs relax, and her thoughts unfurl. Her eyelids grew heavy, and it was one of those days when all alone and to nap for a while felt like the best thing. As the book tumbled to her lap from wrists gone weak with sleep, she heard a car door closing and opened her eyes wide.

A key in the front door told her this could only be Aiden. Jumping up, she raced to meet him in the hall. 'Hello, you!'

She gratefully received the graze of a kiss on her cheek, understanding in that moment that peaceful Sundays spent alone were not actually something to look forward to, but rather held a mirror up to the quietness of her life when he wasn't around.

'Well, this is a lovely surprise! How did you get here?'

'Took a cab from the station.' He sounded low and she guessed he had come clean about Holly's pregnancy, trying not to second-guess what had happened next, wondering whether he and Iris had leapt over this first hurdle hand in hand or whether the news had helped them apply the brakes. She hoped it was the latter, still worried that this first flush of infatuation and sex would quickly fade.

'I'd have picked you up, always call, you know I don't mind.'

'I know.' He made his way into the kitchen and she noted his lack of holdall, meaning it might only be a flying visit. 'Can I have some breakfast?'

'What do you fancy, scrambled eggs on toast?'

It had always been his favourite. There was the unmistakeable flare of love in her veins at no more than the prospect of cooking for him. A task she had bemoaned over the years, coming in from work to hear him and Jonathan duet, 'What's for tea?' It used to drive her crackers.

'Yes, great.'

He grabbed the juice from the fridge, gave the carton a rattle and, deducing there was less than a glass full, drank it straight from the spout. She'd been berating him for years about this but found it hard to fault his logic about saving on washing-up.

'It was smashing yesterday, that view!'

'Yeah.'

His rather succinct summary indicated there was much more to say, but she'd wait until he'd eaten, not wanting to disrupt his appetite, nor the lovely atmosphere, as she relished his presence.

She cracked three eggs into a ceramic bowl, discarded the shells and added the milk, which she measured by eye, next a generous pinch of salt, before she whisked it together. A knob of butter melted in the ceramic pan on the hob. Two slices of sourdough were duly popped in the toaster, as she turned down the heat of the melting butter and doled the mixture into the pan, agitating it with her favoured wooden spoon, watching as it began to solidify and started to form the soft creamy curds that her son would wolf down.

With the thick toast buttered, the glossy yellow eggs sitting in a mound on top and finished with a generous grind of black pepper, she set the plate on the table and sat down opposite, nursing a mug of fresh coffee – all the sustenance she needed.

'Don't know where Pickle's disappeared to, she was here a minute ago, she'll soon come back if she knows you're here.'

He nodded as he chewed his mouthful, crumbs in his stubble as he ate quickly and without consideration, not having to monitor his manners as there was no one else around. She wondered, again, despite the obvious display yesterday, if he felt sufficiently at home at The Mount to dive into the fridge or go ferreting for crisps late at night? His obvious hunger suggested maybe not.

How she wished Jonathan were here, he'd know what to do, one hand on that tiller and her, confidently beside him, keeping watch ahead. It was time, she knew, to grab the skipper's hat and do both. It was bloody time! She was not going to allow herself to sit meekly in her own home while her neighbours ran down her son, not going to *beg* when a heartfelt letter was rejected out of hand, and certainly was not going to allow Phil or anyone else make her feel afraid.

Aiden pushed the empty plate away from him. 'That was lush.'

'You're welcome. I wasn't expecting you today, not that it isn't lovely to see you, it is, always!'

'I just wanted to come home.'

'Ah, Aiden, that's lovely!' The warmth she felt at his words was just perfect; she decided to enjoy them, guessing the news that came next might not be so glorious.

'I wanted the journey too, sometimes it's good to just travel, isn't it? Sit on a train, sit in a cab, but almost submit to it, nothing you can do but go with the flow and think.'

Enya sipped her coffee and trod carefully. 'And what is it you're thinking about, love?'

He looked out of the window and sat back in the chair. 'The wedding, the details.'

'I think you'll be hard-pressed to find anyone, less than three weeks ahead of their wedding, who isn't going through the same thing. It feels like a pressure, but I can honestly say that every wedding I've ever been to, it doesn't really matter if there are cock-ups. In fact, some of the best weddings are the ones where things do go wrong.'

He nodded, but seemed preoccupied, only half listening.

'My cousin Laura, when her boy Jack got married, the band didn't turn up and so someone grabbed a couple of speakers and they put on a playlist and honestly, it was the best night ever, even your dad danced!' She pulled a wide-eyed face, knowing Aiden, like her, was aware of his lack of coordination on the dance floor. 'People were shouting out their favourite tunes and on they came! It was like a jukebox, it was fab.'

'Sounds it.'

'I guess what I'm trying to say is that it doesn't need to be perfect. Things never are.'

'No, they're not, are they?' He looked at her now and she tried to read between the lines. 'Things got pretty heated after you left yesterday.'

'In what way? Between you and Iris?'

'No.' He shook his head. 'Trish was really drunk, as you might have noticed.'

'I did, but that's her business in her home, maybe she was nervous or—'

'No, Mum. It's a regular thing. A fairly new regular thing by all accounts. I get the impression she's always been a bit of a free spirit.'

'. . . she was beautiful and quite wild, which I found insanely attractive . . .' Dominic's words came to her now.

'But Iris is worried about her, obviously, and when she tried to move her up to bed, after you'd gone, Trish got a bit aggressive and then Dominic arrived home, and he and Trish had a row. It wasn't great to see. She was screaming at him, about him not being there, about being distant, telling him to go, then asking him to stay. It was all a bit . . .' He exhaled. 'I didn't know whether to hang around and be there for Iris or to give them space, it was bloody awful.'

'It sounds it.' She felt sorry for them all and hated that she might inadvertently be a small part of it.

'I want to marry Iris, more than anything I want that, but if she said let's fly to Vegas and do it in our jeans, I'd like that even more.'

'It's your wedding too, it has to be what you both want.' She was desperate for him to get to the point of what ailed him and wanting so badly to warn him yet again to slow things down, to take the time to make sure it was really what he wanted.

'Everyone says that, don't they, but it seems to me that it's all about compromise and one of you saying yes to keep the peace or make the other happy.'

'I guess so.' Holly, she knew, had every last detail worked out; Aiden would merely have been required to turn up and say, I do! But it was not Holly he was marrying.

'How do I tell Iris that Holly is pregnant?'

'For the love of God! You *still* haven't told her?' She put her mug down, her voice raised.

'Does it sound like I've told her? I wouldn't be asking, would I, if I had!' He raised his voice a little.

Enya sighed. 'Your sarcasm is quite unbecoming.'

She was still a little startled at how it took no more than a light strike of a match to set things ablaze and how quickly the fire of disharmony took hold. It was a pattern that was tiring, and she was more than a little sick of being his verbal punchbag, his and everyone else's.

'And you're right, of course, silly old Mum!' She raised her voice. 'And so I guess my advice is the same today as it was yesterday and the day before that and no doubt it'll be the same tomorrow: tell her sooner rather than later as the longer you keep it from her, the less favourable a response you're going to get. I don't know how else to put it! Keeping it a secret only compounds the problem. And forgive me if I'm not mentally in tip-top form this morning. I had a rather disturbed night, on account of your pregnant ex sneaking into my room in the middle of the bloody night, when I was unaware she was in the house, which gave me a flipping heart attack!'

Her words, bluntly delivered, now coasted on pent-up anger; she was entirely over being shoved with the shitty end of the stick when none of this was her doing!

'What?' He screwed his eyes up in disbelief.

'You heard me, and when I screamed, Phil, Jenny and Maeve – who, incidentally, was armed – came running in and we all had a cup of tea in our PJs! That was until I inadvertently announced that you were getting married, and everyone rolled their eyes and left in a huff, like I was a toxic thing to be avoided! As if it's *me* that's caused this whole bloody pantomime. And it's not me, Aiden, it's nothing to do with me, actually, but you're not here, Jonathan's not here, and it appears to be me who is the sounding board, the kicking post, or the shoulder to cry on! And truth be told, I'm getting a little pissed off with it all!'

'You told them I was getting married?' This apparently what he'd chosen to take from her monologue.

'Yes, Aiden, I did. Because, as I might have mentioned, I am losing track of what you have said and what you are keeping secret.'

'I'm not keeping anything secret.' He sounded most indignant.

'You are though! You are!' She banged the table. 'You hadn't told Holly, the expectant mother of your child, that you're getting married in a matter of weeks and you haven't told Iris, the woman you want to spend the rest of your life with, apparently, that you're having a baby with your ex-partner, have I missed anything?'

'You make it sound so simple!' he barked.

'I need to, because it seems you are intent on making everything so bloody complicated! I mean, what's the plan? Wait until the child is a teenager then whip it out as a surprise one Christmas, ta-dah! Here's one I prepared earlier!'

Whether with nerves or at the end of his tether, Aiden burst out laughing, and she had no choice but to follow his lead.

'It's not funny!' she wheezed, as she howled her laughter, knowing it was that or sob.

'I know, I know.' Her son lay his head on his arms, as his shoulders shook. 'Oh my God, I know!'

They sat this way for a minute or two, both struggling for breath, beside themselves with laughter until it naturally subsided and the air around them was cleared of anger and in its place, the beginnings of peace.

'Mum,' he ran his palm over his face, 'I'm so tired.'

'Me too, love.'

'Why was Holly here in the middle of the night?'

'Well, it wasn't strictly the middle of the night, but I was in bed, preparing for sleep.'

'She broke in?' He stared at her, clearly hoping to be corrected on this point.

'No.' It was time for Enya to speak with the honesty she was keen for her son to foster. 'She arrived just as I was leaving to catch my train yesterday. I think she was trying to hide from Jenny and Phil, and I didn't feel I could tell her to leave, didn't want to. I'm happy she still feels she can come over whenever, and it will be even more important when the baby comes along.'

He gave a slight shake of his head, as if he was still finding it hard to accept that a baby would be coming along.

'I came home, didn't know she'd fallen asleep and went to bed, only to see her shadowy figure looming in the doorway as I nodded off. I screamed the place down!'

'Where was she sleeping?' he asked, his voice quiet, suggesting he could take an educated guess at the answer, especially as she lived in a two-bedroomed house.

'In your bed.'

'That's not,' he closed his eyes, 'that's not okay, not really. Supposing I'd come home with Iris?'

'This is *exactly* what I'm talking about, Aiden, setting the boundaries, having those difficult conversations that mean people aren't taken by surprise. They need to happen and soon.'

'Can I tell Iris the news over the phone, do you think?'

She answered slowly. 'Do you remember when Dad was ill, when we first found out?'

Aiden nodded.

'How would you have felt if I'd told you over the phone?'

'Terrible.'

'Exactly, and for me who was doing the telling, I needed to see your face, hold your hand, be there to help you digest it, to answer the hundreds of questions that I knew you'd have.'

'So I take it a text is also out of the question?' He beamed at her.

'No, I think that's a good idea, or better still, why don't you do it via a series of emojis?'

'Do you know, Mother, your sarcasm is quite unbecoming.'

'I need another coffee, and only because it's too early for wine.' She stood from the table. 'Can I get you one?'

'No, but I'll have some more eggs if there are any going.'

Enya grabbed the bowl and happily smashed eggs into it. She grabbed the whisk and vigorously beat them.

'You okay, Mum?'

'Yes! More than okay, why?'

'I dunno, you just seem a bit . . .' He stared at her hand, beating the eggs furiously as she gripped the bowl.

She stared at her son.

Dominic was right, she was a woman who could set the world alight if she so chose, and she did! She chose right there and then to step out of the shadows and go grab the bloody life she wanted, one where she was in control.

Chapter
Twenty-Six

'Greengate and Greengate, Enya speaking, how may I help you?'

She was certain that long after the firm of solicitors had closed its doors, she would still be saying this in her sleep. She'd only been settled behind her desk for a minute, Thermos mug of coffee in hand, mentally preparing for the day ahead. If calls started this early, it was usually an indicator that it was going to be a busy one.

'Enya, hi, hope it's okay to call, I got your work number from Aiden. I tried your mobile, but . . .'

'Trish, hello!'

Her heart jumped at the unexpected contact, remembering the way Iris's mother had pointed directly at her and slurred that she was going to be keeping an eye on her.

'My phone's probably hidden in my bag somewhere. And of course that's fine, call any time, although not after September as I won't be here anymore, none of us will.'

It was easy to trot out the words with a jolly undertone of relief, inviting comments about her becoming a lady of leisure and all other associated clichés. She'd had a plan to go into business with Jenny, invest, learn, and spend time with her best friend. It would have been perfect. The memory of Jenny leaving on Saturday night, spitting lava and hurt as she did so, still sat behind her eyelids. Her new stance to encourage strength and self-reliance made no allowance for the way her heart lurched.

The truth was, she would miss it here. All of it: the two sweet men who she had never grown close to on account of their position, hers, and the era they belonged to. She'd miss the generations of families who knew that if the Greengates were handling the matter, they were in safe hands. But mostly she'd miss the routine, the reason to leave the house, the walk to and from the High Street, even the sweet fatigue that came after a day of office work. It was therefore vital she found a new job and soon; whiling away her days in a melancholy state while she watered that infernal plant in the hallway wouldn't do at all.

'Yes, Aiden said retirement was on the cards.'

Retirement? It was one of those words that struck her as funny and entirely misused when it referred specifically to her. A word for old people, old people like widows.

'Is everything okay, Trish?'

'Everything's fine – well, as fine as it can be when you're running around like a headless chicken trying to organise a wedding in whistle-stop time and no one else on the planet seems to share your urgency.'

This Enya took personally; was it a dig, was she being accused of *not sharing the urgency*, let alone the workload? As per her new MO, she kept her voice steady, a woman in control!

'Can I do anything? As I've already said, I'm more than happy to get involved.'

She tried to strike the balance between offering help and forcing herself on the woman or making her feel like she was hijacking part of the process, while making it clear she was not about to let Iris's mother ladle guilt over her.

'Oh, let me have a think, maybe, erm, we might need a hand with collecting a couple of bits from Bristol when they're ready. I'm thinking the place-name holders that Iris has ordered and a board thing with pegs on for photos, that might be good.'

'Great, just let me know where and when and I'll go fetch them.'

'That'd be brill.'

There was a moment of awkwardness where Enya wasn't sure if she should fill the silence or whether Trish was about to speak.

'Reason for the call,' Trish swallowed, 'I was wondering if you fancied meeting up for a coffee?'

'Oh! I'd *love* to.'

This wasn't strictly true, she was about two parts trepidation and one part love at the prospect. Instantly, she wondered what Trish wanted to say and prayed it was not to discuss Dominic.

'Great, don't suppose you're free later, after work? I'm out and about and I could nip by, is there somewhere to go for coffee where you are?'

Enya looked out over the High Street, which might not have all mod cons but could boast a decent coffee shop or two, a deli with a reasonable cheese counter and a rack of crisps whose price tags could rival those of any fancy store, Jenny's florist's, of course, and a lovely bookshop. What more did they need?

'Yes, that sounds great. I wish I could say I have to cancel my many plans, but my diary is depressingly empty, as ever.'

'You should join a club.'

The woman's suggestion was a little left field.

'What kind of club?' She was curious.

'I don't know . . . badminton? Or, or do a class, pottery, or something?'

'Yes, I'll think about it.' This would make Angela roar, she was certain. 'Do you belong to any clubs or do any classes, Trish?' Her new assertive stance urged the question from her lips.

The way Iris's mother howled her laughter in response spoke volumes. 'Oh, God no!'

'So what time do you want to meet up?' Enya thought it prudent to change the subject.

'I can be with you by five?'

'Great, see you then.'

'Yep, see you then, Enya.'

No sooner had she put the phone down than it rang again almost immediately. 'Greengate and Greengate, Enya speaking, how may I help you?'

'Mum . . . Mum, it's me.'

'Goodness me, well, aren't I popular this morning! You got back to Bath okay yesterday? It was lovely to see you.'

'Yeah, easy journey. God, that feels like, I don't know, feels like it could have been weeks ago that we sat at the table and you made my breakfast.'

She could tell by his tone, in the way you could with someone you loved and were close to, that all was not well. 'What's up, kiddo?'

'Um . . .' He took his time. 'I told her. I told Iris last night. Told her about the baby, about Holly being pregnant. It was really, um . . .'

She heard him take a stuttered breath.

'It's okay, love. Just go slow, take deep breaths, and go slow.'

She had softened her tone and slowed her own pace, hoping he might follow suit, giving his thoughts a chance to catch up with everything that clearly whirred in his brain, while she braced herself to hear the fallout from his discussion with Iris, knowing it could be anything from complete forgiveness and understanding to 'the wedding is off'! It was impossible not to reflect on the fact that they had only known each other for such a short time and that the novelty of new, great sex, and all the excitement of the whirlwind could only carry them so far. Instantly, she felt mean for thinking it; maybe she was just an old cynic.

An old cynic with a whole marriage under my belt who understands what a lifetime of commitment means . . .

'I told her the moment I got back to The Mount. We went outside and I just said it. I told her that I loved her and that I never expected to meet someone like her. I said she was the single best thing that's ever happened to me, which is the truth. She was so happy, Mum, beaming at me, looking at me like she was looking *into* me. Do you know what I mean, when it's more than just a look, it's a connection.'

'Uh-huh.'

Enya pictured Dominic sitting on the other side of the dining table in the kitchen, and she understood. She did indeed know the look; a similar one she and Jonathan had perfected over decades of practice, a look embedded in trust, one that came with a shared history. Yet with Dominic it had seemed almost instinctive, an illusion no doubt.

'So, what did she say, darling?'

Enya trod the tricky path between wanting to give him time to speak freely while also acutely aware that she was at work. The clock was literally ticking, and Messrs Greengate and Greengate would at any moment be popping their wiry heads around the door to greet her with a joyous *Good morning, Enya!* before disappearing into their respective offices, where she worried one day she might hear a call for help as a teetering mountain of foolscap files actually toppled over on to them.

There were worse ways to go. She thought now of the lingering loneliness and her fading presence in her neighbourhood, a desperate concept. Wondering if it were possible that she might become smoke and disappear altogether, no more than *a trick of the light . . .* she would not let that happen. She would not, there *would* be a job for her somewhere after this, and never again would she be made to feel like a criminal in her own home. It bothered her still, Maeve's tuts of disapproval, Jenny's anger; it was as misplaced as it was infuriating.

'I was staring at her, and it was like I could see every bit of her face in detail, and she looked so happy. And just as hard as what I had to say was knowing how my words were going to make her feel. That I was going to deliberately pull the plug on her happiness. I was going to intentionally say something that would hurt her, the thing I'd sworn I would never do, and it was the worst feeling in the world.'

Enya bit her lip to avoid asking if it was worse than leaving Holly alone and broken while he chose ribbons and red velvet cake and pondered what music might be played as he tripped the light fantastic on the dance floor with his bride in his arms? But of course she didn't, because that was unfair and was only a private fleeting uncomfortable thought, the kind that was definitely best not to share.

'I told her I'd found something out, and the colour drained from her face. I don't know what she expected, but she knew instantly it was nothing good. I said, *Holly's pregnant*, and she laughed. She gave this kind of snort laugh, and I remember I did something similar when you told me, because it's so unbelievable that it has to be a joke, right? It has to be, Mum, because how can this huge sledgehammer come along and smash my happiness to smithereens, Iris's too? And I know what you're thinking, you'll be thinking, what about Holly's happiness, Holly's life, what about Holly . . . And you're right, I know you're right, but in that moment it was just Iris and me, and we are on countdown to this wedding just a couple of weeks away with so much to do. We're so excited. It's everything really, certainly her every waking thought. And it feels cruel that we now have to contend with this news.'

Knowing how quickly the wrong phrase or word when addressing her son could grow into a row, Enya trod carefully, yet spoke firmly.

'It's not contending with the news that's the issue here, Aiden. It's more than that. It requires a complete change of mindset. You're going to be a dad and that doesn't stop for the wedding or after the wedding or any time soon. In fact, it doesn't stop for the rest of your life.'

Case in point; she was on the phone to *her* child with one eye on the clock, worrying about him, trying to find solutions, doing her best to make everything feel better, and that child was hurtling towards thirty.

'I know, Mum.' His voice no more than a whisper and he sounded young, oh so very young. 'When she saw the look on my face she knew it was no joke and she kind of pulled away from me, even though we weren't touching. She pulled her arms in towards her body and pushed her legs together and moved an inch or two to the left so there was no danger of us making contact, of being close or of comfort being offered. Weirdly, I think that's what I'll always remember, not the words that cut the air between us, words that change everything, but the way she pulled away from me, shrank. It was as if she wanted no part of me, nothing.' His voice cracked.

'Oh, love. That can't have been easy, but at least it's done.' She would never admit that at the back of her mind was a ping of relief at the thought that if things really were done, she could take a breath, life could get back to normal, or as close as it could, and they could let the madness of the last few weeks settle. 'How are things now?'

'We didn't say anything for quite a while – well, it felt like quite a while, it might only have been minutes – and then she said, so what happens now? As though I knew the answer and wasn't trying to figure it all out as I go along. It's as if we've come to a fork in the road that means we might have to turn in a different direction from the one we were planning.'

'I guess that's true, in a way.'

'I don't want to be a dad. I don't want that, not with Holly and not now, I don't want any of it!'

To hear his blunt and emotional admission was both agonising and infuriating. Enya closed her eyes and spoke plainly, all worry about treading carefully now gone. There was simply no time for that. If she was grabbing the reins, so could he!

'Well, that, my love, is neither here nor there. The fact is, it's happening.'

Her words, harshly spoken, were intended to galvanise the boy into understanding, if not action. It brought her no pleasure to be the one pointing out that his options were somewhat curtailed when it came to his choices about parenthood, but she knew it was important for him, for Holly, and for the future.

'I'd better go.'

'Yes, speak to me later, Aiden. And it will all be okay, I promise.'

'You say that, Mum, and I want to believe you, I really do, but I just don't know how it will all be okay. There are no guarantees, are there?'

She pictured Jonathan studying images on his laptop, clicking on hotels in Andalucía, pointing out walking routes, cycle paths and which restaurants by the water had the best gazpacho and pescaíto frito. They had debated back and forth over dates, wondering whether it was better to go for one week or two, a self-catering apartment or a fancy hotel, should they hire bikes or drive and take their own? Like her, part of the fun of a holiday for her husband was the planning, the imagining, the anticipation of all they would taste, sip and experience. This the last trip they had booked and one they had never taken, because illness had drawn their focus and they had done the opposite of shrinking away from each other. They had huddled close, touching, together as one, to face whatever came next. One team.

'No, love, there are no guarantees.'

Her day passed quickly, and she was thankful. The shuffling of paperwork, filing of forms, making and taking calls, and even whipping up cups of tea, had all served to distract her from her thoughts about Aiden's call. Her brain too full to linger on any discord between him and Iris. As the clock now nudged five, she nipped to the bathroom and washed her hands, applied a little scent, dabbed on her lip balm, and ran her fingers through her unruly mop of hair. As her stomach bunched with nerves, she spoke to her image in the mirror.

'Why on earth did you say you'd meet her for a coffee?'

The answer was she hadn't felt able to say no, and now she had no option other than announcing a sudden mystery illness or migraine or hiding in the cupboard until morning. It was, she decided, far easier to give advice on facing up to a situation than it was to act on it.

That, and the cupboard was in fact full of stationery, no room to hide at all.

Chapter Twenty-Seven

Enya's phone beeped with a text from Trish; she was at Potters the coffee shop opposite the bookshop. Enya hastened her pace, not wanting to be late, and not wanting Trish to experience the same awkwardness she would feel if it were her sitting by herself waiting for someone to arrive. She wasn't very good at drinking alone or dining alone, not that anyone else seemed to give a fig, but a heightened level of self-awareness meant she found it excruciating. This too something she needed to conquer, but one step at a time.

It was oddly jarring to see Iris's mother in the place that was familiar to Enya, a little invasive for reasons she couldn't easily voice. This woman, whose daughter had, through no fault of her own, caused such ripples of disharmony in Enya's neighbourhood, her stomping ground. She looked behind her as she walked in, wary of seeing Jenny and of Jenny seeing her, not in the mood for confrontation today. Her heart skipped a little bit anyway.

Trish looked lovely as she raised her hand in a small wave. Her golden hair was neat, her make-up perfect, her nails a delicate shade of pretty pink. Enya stared at the beautiful woman and dismissed the uncomfortable flash of jealousy that sparked in her gut.

I am not that person.

She repeated this to herself as she smiled and made her way to the corner table, where two brimming, milky coffees bedecked with an arty fern shape in their foam sat next to a small plate of dainty macarons in lurid shades of green and purple.

'I got you a latte, hope that's okay?' Trish rose to offer a brief hug that squeezed the last drops of pettiness and spite from Enya's core.

'Any coffee is good coffee, thank you! And thanks again for Saturday, still thinking about that view from your garden, don't think I'd ever tire of staring at it.'

Not that I want to live in your house, with your husband, please don't think that, I most definitely do not! These the words she had to strangle in her throat to stop them from leaping out into the wild.

'Sorry the food was a bit lacklustre, and sorry I fell asleep before you left. I think it was the heat, it got to me.' Trish double blinked, as if acknowledging the lie and hoping Enya swallowed it.

'The food was fine, and don't worry, the heat does that to me too.' She sipped her coffee.

'This is a nice little High Street; I can see why you like it.'

'Yes, Jonathan and I have always felt happy to mooch around. It's small, familiar and has everything we need.'

'How did you guys meet?' Trish settled back to hear the tale.

'Oh,' she hated the thought of mirroring the conversation she'd had with Dominic, 'I went to a cricket match and there he was.'

Trish nodded. 'Dominic and I met in the local pub. Friends at first and then it was a rebound thing, a good rebound thing, as it turned out!'

Enya gave an unnatural laugh and stared at her coffee.

'The reason I wanted to see you,' Trish began, 'is that Iris told me last night about Aiden's ex, that she's expecting.'

'Yes.' Enya put the cup down and gave the situation her full attention. 'Yes, she is.'

'I've got to be honest, it's thrown me a bit. Not sure what to do with that news. I thought it best I talk to you, mother to mother.'

'Of course.'

Enya was relieved the topic was not Dominic, wary of what he might have said or let slip. This duplicitousness didn't sit well with her, yet neither did the fact she was once again in the middle of a discussion about Aiden and Holly and Aiden and Iris, just as she had been with Jenny and Phil. She couldn't catch a break.

'The thing is, Enya, Iris is my only child, and I care deeply about her happiness.'

'Yes, Aiden is mine, ditto.' She was not going to roll over.

'I'm worried.' The woman cut to the chase.

'I can understand that. I'm worried too.' She knew this was the time and place for honesty, around this subject at least.

Trish stared at her. 'What are you worried about, specifically?'

With the addition of the last word in her question, Trish had made it sound an awful lot to Enya like she had the monopoly when it came to concern. As was becoming more common with these interactions, it wasn't only what Trish said but how she said it that spoke volumes.

'Specifically . . .' Enya gave it some thought, knowing that with the wedding day looming, there was no time for tiptoeing around the topic, and she spoke directly. 'I'm worried that Aiden has made a rash decision based on hormones and not logic. I'm worried that he proposed without knowing his ex, Holly, was pregnant and might not have fully grasped all that this will mean for him, for them. I think Iris seems like a wonderful girl, *genuinely*,' she met Trish's eye, 'but I'm worried about how little they know each other, and how it would be easy to mistake infatuation or the attraction of the new for something that might not have longevity. But I guess, primarily, I don't want him to get hurt, to mess up, to live with regret or to be unhappy. What about you?' She took a sip of coffee.

'The same. But add to that the fact that the man my daughter has fallen for, who I think seems like a wonderful guy, *genuinely*,' Trish spoke sincerely, 'has got a girl pregnant and moved on very quickly. It feels cold and complicated.'

Enya's words, when they came, were unapologetic.

'It's certainly complicated, and I'm not here to defend him or make a case on his behalf, but I can tell you honestly that he is a lovely human. He's been with Holly – or *was* with Holly – since they were at school. Never a rabble-rouser, never stayed out late, got in trouble with the police, taken drugs, lied, none of that.' She decided not to mention the cycling proficiency incident. 'He was just a good kid. Loves his rugby, a cold beer, home-cooked food. He works hard and he's nice. He's studious, conscientious, quiet at first with strangers, funny, considerate. Takes after his dad.' She spoke without irony. 'I worried, in fact, that he and Holly were too stable, too staid. I felt they both needed to get out of their bubble a bit more, but I never expected him to come home and say that he'd met someone else. For him to express his feelings so publicly is a big deal for him. He's loyal, very loyal, and he had no idea that Holly was pregnant, and now he does, I know it will be torturous for him.'

Trish drew breath and settled her gaze on the middle distance. 'Do you think there's a chance he and Holly will get back together, if not now then once the baby arrives?'

Enya considered this for a moment. 'I don't *think* so, no.'

It was the truth. Yet there was a small part of her that acknowledged the possibility that when Aiden saw his child, and the infatuation with Iris had maybe dulled, he might be tempted to go back to all that was familiar, comfortable, and predictable, possibly the easiest route for all concerned. Especially as there would be a baby to consider, and assuming Holly might take him back.

The latter point dissolved in her thoughts. Of course she would take him back; whether she should or not was a whole other matter.

'That's not quite the cast-iron guarantee I was hoping for.' Trish raised her eyebrows.

'Oh Trish, how I wish we could have those cast-iron guarantees.' *It's you and me, Enya B, us against the world!* 'Honestly, I think if he'd felt the pull of duty that strongly, he'd have gone back to her the moment he found out she was pregnant. But none of us know how the human heart is going to react over time, do we?' She tried not to picture Dominic making admissions she would not act upon. 'I also know that Aiden's met with Holly, tried as far as he's able to smooth the path ahead, agreed to support her, now and ongoing. He'll take his responsibilities very seriously and I'm glad that he does.'

'I guess that's something Iris will have to contend with, the fact that financially her husband will be committed to paying for a child and all that comes with that.'

Enya felt the twitch of a nerve at the top of her cheek. 'I guess she will. I've always given Aiden the advice never to be beholden to anyone else financially, to always be generous yet considered with money, but to always make sure you can look after yourself.'

'Yet Holly is going to need *his* help financially?'

'Well, three things. First, that's between her and Aiden. Second, Holly is not my child, therefore I have no idea what advice her parents have given her. And third, he absolutely should, in my opinion, help out financially with this child he has helped create. As I said, he is a good person, loyal. Actually, four things – the final being it's actually nothing to do with me! Yet here I am, advocating for him, fighting his corner!'

'I don't think you like me much, Enya.'

The blunt statement made Enya sit up straight; it felt both goading and confrontational and yet was offered with a smile, almost in jest.

'I don't know you, Trish! Not really, not yet, and actually, I *do* like you. I also think that when it comes to something like finance and marriage,' she took a beat and considered what she wanted to say, 'it's something you work out, isn't it? Who knows what cards you're going to be dealt? When we were first married, Jonathan was an apprentice and I earned more than him. Then he qualified and earned more than me. We never made the other feel indebted, we just lived our life together. Then when he got sick, he earned nothing, but luckily for us he had always been prudent and we managed, more than managed.'

'I'm not looking for a meal ticket for Iris.'

'Then why mention it at all? I mean, supposing he and Iris had married, had kids, divorced, would you think it okay for him to stop supporting his kids if he met someone else?'

'No, I'd rather they didn't divorce in the first place.' Trish tutted her laughter. 'And that's not what I was getting at, I'm just worried for my kid.'

Enya smiled and tilted her head, *touché* . . .

'Iris might seem confident, worldly, but she isn't. There were eating issues when she was at school, and I worry it wouldn't take much to knock her off course again. We've worked so hard to make her better.'

'I'm sorry.' And she was, unable to imagine the horror of trying to manage that.

'I guess it's made me super-protective of her. You understand.'

'I do. I really do.' Enya calmed and felt herself warm to the woman, wishing Trish was an ogre. It would make the harbouring of thoughts of her husband that much easier and acting on them easier still. That, and with the knowledge of what Iris had already endured, she would never do anything to bring further upset to her door. 'I think your child getting married is a big, big deal. And when they're marrying someone they've only just met and barely know, it's super-scary, risky. Throw in something like an unexpected pregnancy and my goodness, is it any wonder we're both a bit jumpy?'

'You're right,' Trish nodded, 'you're right. I just feel like everything is slipping out of control. Everything's changing.' She looped her hair behind her ear.

'Well, I know how that feels.' Enya looked down the street to the sign that read 'Greengate and Greengate, Solicitors', knowing this too was coming to an end and her routine was once again changing, and all without the comforting presence of her best friend to smooth the transition. But she would be fine, she had to be.

'I don't want Iris to make the same mistakes I made; I just want her to be happy.' Trish blinked.

Enya stared at the woman. Was Trish saying she wasn't happy? She wanted the detail, but was in no position to ask, to probe, not when it would only be with the intention of satisfying her own curiosity. 'I think it's true that we learn from our mistakes.'

She hoped this was of comfort.

'That's what they say, isn't it, whoever *they* are.' Iris's mother sat forward in the chair and rested her elbows on the table, her hands clasped. 'I'm not happy. Haven't been happy for a long while really, and I suppose having Iris around as my little buddy, it's not only that I want to keep her safe, keep an eye on her, but I've relied on her too. The thought of her marrying anyone is hard for me, even though I want her to live her life, spread her wings, all of that stuff, but letting go isn't easy, is it?'

'None of this is easy.' Enya felt kinship with the woman, and couldn't have put it better herself, *letting go isn't easy* . . .

'I love my husband.'

Trish looked right at her. Enya felt her insides turn to liquid.

'I love him and yet I'm not *in* love with him, does that make any sense?'

Enya nodded and swallowed the boulder of guilt in her throat.

'I can't seem to get it right. He's not happy, I'm not happy, and that makes me feel worthless. Makes me hide my sorrow in a Prosecco bottle.'

They're not happy . . . they're not in love . . . Enya did her best to control the leap of something in her gut that felt a lot like the fireworks of possibility. It was indeed like being seventeen again, jittery, exciting. This she knew, however, was not enough to act upon, not enough to complicate Aiden and Iris's lives for something that could, in all likelihood, turn to dust. Her son and Dominic's daughter were getting married, and she could only guess at their reaction to her and Dominic hooking up. This was enough to temper her response.

'Mine's rosé.' She tried to show allyship, to let Trish know that you never knew what went on behind closed doors.

Trish gave a half-smile. 'I've tried so hard to be all he needs me to be, but . . .' She shook her head, as if it mattered not if Enya was present; either way, she wanted to say the words out loud. 'He's started to move out to the flat he's taken. Things are all on hold for a bit until after the wedding, we didn't want to spoil Iris's big day and the build-up.'

'I'm sorry, Trish.' She meant it.

'It's not a surprise, not really. We're very different people and we want very different things. It's like the bridge we used to rest on, that place we'd meet, the point of compromise, it crumbled away a long time ago, and so we both sit on opposite sides of the river, staring across the void, trying to figure out how to get back to each other, do you know what I mean?'

'Kind of,' Enya answered softly, kindly. 'Jonathan and I were always great friends. Things had certainly calmed between us, were more predictable, a little slower, but there was something comforting in that. But what you describe, it sounds lonely.'

'It is.' Trish sniffed. 'That's why I've clung to Iris, I guess. And I don't want her to marry someone who might not love her in the way she does him. Someone who might look at her as if she's a stranger, or worse, long to be with the mother of his child. I want more for her than that.'

Enya watched the woman's bottom lip tremble. She reached out and laid a hand on Trish's forearm. 'It's true what we said earlier, there are never any guarantees, are there? But I can tell you, mother to mother, woman to woman, that Aiden is a good man. And I hope, as much as you do, that he will be a good husband, and will do his very best to make Iris happy, always.'

'I believe you,' Trish whispered. 'I believe you.'

Chapter Twenty-Eight

Enya had enjoyed her day off. In this new spirit of self-reliance, she had spent it at The Mall, Cribbs Causeway, letting her thoughts settle as she trawled the racks in John Lewis and Oliver Bonas, wondering what might be suitable for a summer garden wedding. Unable to decide between a couple of frocks that had caught her eye, both long, loose and comfortable, one in cerise and one in tangerine. She decided to go back next week with Angela and get a second opinion.

Jenny would never say no to a trip to the shops, which inevitably ended with a noodle supper or an iced coffee, weather depending. Several women caught her attention, some looping arms with their friends, others laughing as they walked side by side in companionable chatter. Despite venturing out and making the trip alone, it made her feel both lonely and self-conscious and she left with her head down, fighting the frustrating desire to cry, as panic, her old friend, wrapped its tendrils around her throat. It was as frustrating as it was alarming and felt like a backward step.

It had been three days since she'd met up with Trish for a coffee and had decided against giving Aiden the details of their conversation, knowing that to hear so many doubts about him and his intentions, expressed by his future mother-in-law, would do nothing to bolster his fragile confidence. Trish, she knew, wasn't a bad person, but was just a mum doing her best, struggling to let go of her child, who clearly filled gaps in her life, and who she was worried might be about to make an emotionally costly mistake. If nothing else, Enya could certainly relate.

It was more than their discussion about the kids, however, that replayed in her mind. Her heart ached for the woman who had so eloquently described the lack of closeness, the loneliness that existed within her marriage. Confirmation too that Dominic had spoken the truth, his flat was indeed a big step towards dismantling his marriage. It made her feel sorry for Dominic as well, having heard first-hand that he wanted more, wanted to move forward, to feel energised, anything other than to feel that life was stagnating. Not that it was anything to do with her and not that she would be commenting to either of them. Knowing how they lived, however, made it easier somehow to check her phone at odd hours of the day and night to see if he had made contact. He had not, which left her with a complicated mixture of relief and disappointment swirling in her veins.

During gaps in her day, mixed with searching for Jonathan in the places she used to find him, she thought about how it had felt to be in Dominic's arms, the feel of him . . . the scent of him . . . and her gut twisted with longing, as if her body paid no heed to the practicalities her mind cast out. It was confusing to her, loving her husband so deeply, missing him with a longing that was acute, while allowing Dominic to nestle inside the cracks of her broken heart, helping it to feel whole again, just for a minute.

The Sutherlands were not her battle and certainly not her project. She had quite enough going on trying to figure out her own life. Although right now, in the blissful stillness of dusk, her only concern was what to watch on the TV, debating whether she could be bothered to stand up to go and seek cheese or ice cream, possibly both, and which of the fancy frocks she'd seen did she favour.

Pickle was curled against her on the sofa as a soft wind blew in from the garden, whistled along the hallway and glanced her face. She was thankful; the heat today, in this sultry early August, had been almost unbearable, without a breeze to stir the air.

The sound of a key in the front door heralded her son's unexpected arrival.

'Hello?' she called, as much to let him know where to find her as anything else, not that their home was vast or palatial with only two rooms downstairs, it was no The Mount, but still.

His walk was brisk, his face contorted, as he plonked down into the chair.

'All okay, love?' she asked, knowing it was not.

'Oh, everything's just peachy, Mum.'

At no more than the tone of his voice, Pickle leapt up from the sofa and, with her tail high in the air, made for a quick exit. Enya didn't blame her one bit.

She crossed her legs and sat still, knowing this was the lull before the storm, watching her son as his jaw tensed, his fingers flexed, and his foot bounced with energy.

'What's happened?' she asked softly, trying to calm him.

'What's happened is that the wedding is off.'

'Really?' Enya sat forward on the edge of the sofa, unsure if this was a tiff, pre-wedding nerves, or the actual break-up that she had considered.

It was conflicting; once more, she felt sad that the upheaval to all of their lives was for nothing, the damage to both Holly and Aiden and their lives as co-parents unfathomable. Yet now she also felt devastated for Iris, who'd had her dreams dashed, having got caught up in the whirlwind. Her primary concern, however, was for her son, who, like her, had felt the ground fall away in front of him, as a plan that he thought was solid coiled away from him, no more than smoke.

That was, if it were true the wedding really was off – or was this no more than the jitters, something to be resolved? Her head ached at the new drama, feeling quite unable to handle another slice of chaos.

Aiden looked close to tears and her heart lurched.

'It's been cancelled.'

'Cancelled? It's not like a theatre performance or a train!'

'Actually, it's exactly like that. Something that either through lack of interest, support, poor timing or a human or technical cock-up is no longer happening!'

'But—'

'But what, Mum? What now?' He sounded angry and she took a moment to remind herself that he was not angry with her but angry with the world, hurt, no doubt, humiliated, certainly. The last thing she wanted was for this to escalate into a full-blown row. This was, after all, his haven, even if it had, in recent times, pretty much stopped being hers. It was a fine balancing act, as she did her best to remain assertive.

'I'm just trying to understand what's going on.'

'You and me both. Iris and I have had a huge row and she said she didn't want to get married, and I agreed. I just blurted it out. It was like a thump in the gut to hear her say that, and so I jumped in the car and here I am.'

'I don't know if that was the best idea,' she ventured, 'you can't run out, run away, hide when things get tough. This isn't a soap opera, it's your life, and if you are going to spend it with Iris, you can't sort things out if you aren't present.'

She thought of Dominic, hiding in his boat shed, moving bit by bit into his flat so as not to detract from his daughter's big day.

She guessed this news might hasten that and felt another ladle of guilt at the fact that this was where her mind went. A quick sweep of the room and she double blinked, still no sign of Jonathan, even now, when she could really use the backup.

'I just wanted to come home.' He sounded young, so young, a reminder of his lack of life experience, of relationships.

'You can always come home, you know that. Whether you are twenty-seven or seventy-seven, you can always come home. Although come to think of it, when you're seventy-seven it will be your house anyway, or you will have sold it.'

'I came here for you to cheer me up.' He gave a wry smile.

'Oh, you should have said! I can do that magic trick if you like, the one you used to love when you were little, where I got you to close your eyes and count to ten, then I'd disappear by hiding in the cupboard under the stairs, and then you had to count to ten backwards before I reappeared in front of you.'

'Well, there's no point now I know how you did it. Where's the magic in that?'

It was her turn to smile.

'I wish I could make it all better for you, Aiden, I really do. What's happened to cause the big change of heart, what did you row about?'

'It escalated really quickly. I finished work, logged off my computer, sat with Iris on the terrace and she asked me what would happen if we were to have a baby and Holly asked me to have *her* child for Christmas, and I kind of froze and said we'd find a way to manage it. The first thing that popped into my head was that I could have alternate Christmases, one with Holly and the next with her, or maybe we could all go out together, and she went . . . crazy!'

'Right.'

Enya could see that for a young woman envisioning her lovely life with her new husband, the prospect of sharing him so uniformly with his ex would be far from appealing.

'I mean, what did she want to hear? That I'd tell Holly to get lost?' He snorted his disbelief that this could ever be a possibility. It was nice to hear this commitment, comforting.

'Maybe, and probably not in such a harsh way, but if I had to guess, I'd say Iris is looking for reassurance and that's understandable. Usually, this early in a relationship, you start to question if the person you've fallen for really is as wonderful as you first thought or were you just dazzled!' She couldn't help but return to the topic, knowing it was something she was still weighing up when it came to Dominic. 'It's that questioning and discovering the answers that builds a foundation, leads to longevity. I think it's all quite standard, but you guys are getting *married*. You're going from nought to one hundred very, very quickly. And I'm not trying to smash your dreams or tell you what to do one way or another and it's certainly not a *told you so* moment, but it's all quite predictable because you're moving so quickly.'

'That actually sounded a lot like a "told you so" moment in disguise.'

She pulled a face at him. Maybe it was.

'Anyway, you don't have to worry about any of that because we're not moving at all. It's done. She doesn't want to get married and that's absolutely fine with me.'

'It doesn't look like it's absolutely fine with you. Judging from your expression, it looks like the bottom has fallen out of your world.'

He looked up at her, clearly deep in thought. 'I just love her so much,' his voice quavered, 'I want to marry her, and I want her to want to marry me!'

Enya stared at her son's face, this the moment of crisis that, were it simply infatuation, might mean things unravelled quite quickly, his get-out-of-jail-free card, the instant where the scales fell from his eyes. The row that blew things up. It didn't seem to be the case – the opposite, in fact. He looked heartbroken, inconsolable, and like a man searching for the answers so he could put things right with the woman he loved.

'I know, love. So talk to her. That's the only way, talk to her!'

'I know.' He stood. 'I'm going to have a quick shower, change.' He plucked at his shirt. 'Nan called me earlier to ask what we wanted as a wedding present. I'll give her a shout.'

'Don't scare Nan with the detail, tell her you'll let her know. No need to say anything rash. A shower will make you feel better. When you come down, I'll make you something to eat.' Her son stood with a reluctance to his posture. 'This will all sort itself out, Aiden. I have no doubt it will have a different complexion by the morning.'

He gave a single nod before heading off to shower.

'Oh lordy,' she whispered, trying to understand how the prospect of her peaceful evening had been so ruined in such a short space of time.

She headed to the kitchen and outside, with the intention of diving back into the book she was reading. The garden such a beautiful haven at this time of year. It struck her then how easy it was to give the advice. Maybe it *would* be a good idea to speak to Dominic, to hear his voice, tie up loose ends, just to be connected, knowing how wonderful it made her feel. There was so much unfinished business between them it was excruciating. It sounded so simple and yet was anything but. The last thing her son and Iris needed was more complications. And what *exactly* did she want to talk to him about? She shook the idea from her head and listened to the voicemail her sister had left.

'Both dresses sound bloody awful, why can't you go for something more "mother of the groom" and less "hippy on a break from the commune"? I mean, seriously, cerise or tangerine? It's like you do it on purpose! I'll come over and we'll go find you something nice and suitable. Call me back.'

It made Enya laugh, she dreaded to think what something nice and suitable might look like to her sister, but suspected the word peplum might be used. She shuddered at the thought. Not that she needed a new frock now, not that anyone had to worry about her suitability as mother of the groom. As per her conversation with Aiden, there wasn't going to be a groom as there wasn't going to be a wedding. She'd wait, however, to see how things developed overnight before she broke the news, or indeed believed it to be their final decision, reminding herself that young people were gloriously impetuous, and that young love, for that was what it was beginning to look like, could be spectacularly volatile and that it might be a case of *all change please, all change!* before sun up.

Her phone buzzed in her hand. Angela, it seemed, couldn't wait to be called back. 'What the bloody hell?'

Enya drew breath. 'It's not you who has to wear it. Cerise and tangerine are my colours of choice, even if they're not yours.'

'I'm not talking about your hideous taste in dresses, I'm talking about the fact that I've just got off the phone to Mum. She's having kittens.'

'Well, congratulations to Mum! Siblings for Madam Pickle Paws!'

'There's nothing funny about this, Enya.'

Angela did this, took on the role of punisher and educator when the need took her. Being six years older seemed to give her sister a sense of moral responsibility and the belief that, as the elder, this was absolutely fine. Her sister wasn't done. 'Aiden just called her to say that the wedding is off.'

Enya looked up towards her son's bedroom window and shook her fist. So much for reminding him not to scare his nan with anything rash.

'Mum and Dad have paid for flights. They've organised for Benedita to come in and water the plants, they got her a key cut.'

Enya decided not to point out that they could easily ask Benedita not to water the plants, and that their neighbour having a key might not be a bad idea. As for flights, she would offer to reimburse them if they were out of pocket. She felt her anxiety rise as yet more administration and hassle fell on to her shoulders.

'Mum's really upset. She's booked her hair appointment, Dad went to the pharmacy and got extra tablets for travelling, they've bought insurance.'

'Angela, I get it.' She closed her eyes and did her best to control the irritability that flared at her sister reciting the many ways that Aiden had inconvenienced his grandparents.

'But *do* you get it, Enya? It's so bloody annoying, all this back and forth and for what?'

This a prime example of how the world and his wife saw fit to dump their anger and frustration on to her shoulders, and she was more than a little pissed off by it.

'I don't know for certain the wedding *is* cancelled. I don't know much! It might be a small bump in the road that they will get over or it might be the beginning of the end. But what I do know is that it's not my fault and it's really unfair for you to call and shout at me! Good God, I am getting sick of it! Literally, every conversation I have ends with me being either quizzed or berated for something that is nothing to do with me!'

'I'm not shouting at you!' Angela shouted, 'but I've had Mum on the phone shouting at me!'

'I see, so we have to pass it on, do we? Not sure who I should call, I'm trying to think who deserves a random pasting for absolutely no bloody reason!'

'I knew you'd be like this.'

'Like what?' It was Enya's turn to shout.

'Like it's all a big joke, like everyone else is in the wrong to be getting flustered, while you either just laugh it off or get defensive.'

Enya sat on the sun lounger and took a moment. Her heart jumped as she tried to contain it all, as yet again she found herself in the middle of a Venn diagram of shite where all the circles overlapped, and she was slap-bang in the centre of it all.

'I'm not laughing it off, Angela, but I might be trying to offer a bit of perspective. At the end of the day, it's about Aiden's happiness, his future, and if he and Iris decide not to get married, the last thing I will be worrying about is whether Benedita is or is not watering Mum's sodding spider plants.'

'Well, I'm not going to wait on tenterhooks while they decide whether it's a goer or not. I'm ruling myself out. I love my nephew, you know I do, but if you think I'm schlepping all the way over to Bath for the bloody wedding of the year if they change their minds again, you can think again. I'll explain to Aiden that his mother is a dipstick, refusing to take my concerns seriously, and I'll send his gift first class, but I'm not holding my breath.'

'Schlep all the way to Bath?' Enya laughed. 'It's only forty minutes on the ring road from your house and let's face it, you schlep all the way to Portugal for a free holiday and that's a lot further!'

'I go to check on my parents, unlike you, who can't seem to find the time, and for your information, it's only forty minutes when the roads are quiet. At rush hour it can take us fifty-five, especially up by the cinema when it's chucking-out time!'

'Whatever!'

'Whatever yourself!' Angela ended the call.

Enya stared at the phone, her blood bubbling with indignation and with the inexplicable desire to laugh.

As someone had pointed out to her quite recently, it was that or cry.

Chapter
Twenty-Nine

'Who were you talking to?'

Enya rubbed her eyes; she hadn't heard Aiden come down the stairs or into the garden, and the last thing she wanted to do was concern him or let him think that his pitifully small contingent at the wedding of the year, should it go ahead, was going to be even smaller. He did, right now, have enough to contend with.

'Only Auntie Angela.'

'Is she okay?' he asked, sweetly concerned.

'Oh, she's ace.'

'Mum.'

'Yes, love?'

He lifted the wooden bench and pulled the end around, so it was facing her, before sitting down. 'I want to be honest with you.'

'Well, that's always very much appreciated!'

Instantly, she wondered what he had been less than honest about and also noted her rather jolly tone, trying to mask her fear. Was Angela right, did she laugh things off?

'Christmas wasn't the only thing that Iris and I argued about, although that was the final thing, for sure.'

'What else did you argue about?' Enya did her best to control the quake to her voice, as she had the distinct feeling that whatever he was about to impart was not necessarily something she wanted to hear.

'Okay.' He took his time, as if digging deep to find the courage. 'This is going to sound nuts, or like I'm checking up on you, and I'm not, I'm really not!' He opened his hands out, palms facing upwards, as if to demonstrate that he came in peace.

'What? Just say it! You're making me nervous!'

'It's just that, I'm not that observant, but Iris is.' His mouth curved at no more than the thought of her, a good sign that this young love might not, after all, be dead in the water. 'She's pretty good at the detail and stuff.'

'Right.' She had no idea where this was heading.

'That time when we called you from The Mount, do you remember? Last week, when Iris and Trish wanted to show you the ribbon colours for the cake and talk about chairs and the decorations and stuff, when they invited you over for the barbecue. We FaceTimed you.'

'Erm . . .' She wrinkled her nose, did she remember that call? 'Yes, vaguely.' She did her best to keep her somersaulting gut at bay, blowing upwards with her bottom lip protruding, knowing she could at least blame the beads of sweat on her top lip on the intense heat.

'Okay, well, don't get defensive or mad.'

'Oh, my goodness! Don't you start! I do not!'

There was an uncomfortable beat of hesitation after she raised her voice. Aiden stared at her. 'Shall I come back later?' He gestured towards the house.

'No!' she inadvertently barked, and again rubbed her eyes. 'Just, just tell me what you wanted to say.'

'You were at the kitchen table.'

'I recall.' Her mouth went dry. Dominic had been so certain he was out of shot, out of range, but what if . . . She felt a little light-headed, a little nauseous; just the thought of having to conjure a lie to cover their deceitful tracks was awful.

'There was a bottle of wine on the kitchen table.'

'Guilty as charged!' She laughed, in the most natural fashion she could manage.

'And there were two glasses, two wine glasses.'

'No there weren't.' It felt easiest to say this, to deflect, to hold her gaze steady and not give in to the desire to scream that was building in her throat. Not that it felt comfortable or came easily to her, none of it.

'There were, Mum. Iris took a still, a screenshot, a picture.'

'She did?' Her voice was thin with discovery and guilt, and more than a little irritation at Iris's sleuthing. Her guilt made the whole topic most uncomfortable.

'Yep, and she's right, two wine glasses.'

'I must have used one and grabbed another and, what can I say?' Again, that laugh, she had no idea where it came from. 'I do it with coffee mugs and teacups, often have a couple on the go.' She sounded defensive and she knew it.

'They were both full of wine. I mean, sure, if one was empty and you misplaced it and filled another, but are you telling me you were drinking from two glasses at the same time?'

'No, Quincy, I'm not.' She drew breath. 'The truth is, it's what I do, what I've always done, since losing your dad.' This she felt the easiest lie, because it was rooted in truth and was, in short, nearly as exposing as the fact that Iris's dad had been hiding out of sight. It was everything she had feared and suspected might happen, Aiden and Iris falling out over the glasses that she and Dominic were drinking from; she could only imagine how much more intense their row, how horrible the outcome if they knew the finer detail, how much it would undermine their trust in her and Dominic. The irony wasn't lost on her as she continued to lie to her son. 'I place two mugs next to the kettle and I ask him if he wants toast to go with his coffee in the morning. I put two mugs down and ask him if he wants a biscuit with his afternoon tea. And I fill two wine glasses and for the seconds it takes me to pour, I imagine him sitting opposite me at the table or next to me on the sofa, and in that brief time, everything is restored.'

'That's really . . .'

'Really what?'

'Sad, Mum. It's really sad.'

The thickening in her throat confirmed that it was. Worse was her son's kindness, his empathy when she didn't deserve it, not when she wasn't telling him the whole truth. That and the fact that they were talking about the day Jonathan had disappeared and she missed him, missed him so much!

'I guess it is. I've never mentioned it because I don't want you to worry. Because despite everything, I'm doing fine. I really am. In fact, I've decided to do better – I'm okay! I never want you to hold back on living your life because you're worried about me. That would be the worst thing. But yes, you got me! Two wine glasses.'

Enya pushed her feet on to the patio, trying to stay grounded, trying to calm her flustered pulse. She braced herself for any questions.

'Well, that explains it.'

'Yes, it does.' She reached for her book, hoping that might be the end of the conversation.

'Can I ask you a question?'

'Of course.' She rested the book on her chest.

'Are you lonely?' His expression was almost tortured, and it made her heart swell, his love, his concern. It was true what she had said to Trish, he was a lovely human. The loveliest. And he deserved nothing but an honest response.

'Yes, I am. Not all the time. I'm not cloaked in it, or preoccupied with it, but when it strikes, I feel it acutely. Particularly recently, when I'm not only still grieving for your dad, but I've lost Jenny and Phil, Holly too in some ways. Maeve ignores me. You are understandably preoccupied, and I tend to spend most of my time trying to justify the actions of others. My job ends soon and the plan to go into business with Jen is now dust. So yes, I get lonely, and it's not a nice feeling.'

'When does it strike, of an evening when you're by yourself? Because I can make sure that I'm here more—'

'No, no love,' she cut him short, 'but thank you for saying that, for offering. That's exactly what I'm talking about when I say I don't want you to hold back in living your life. You don't want to have to come and babysit me of an evening when you should be out having fun. You're not responsible for me and I don't want you to feel that you are. And actually,' she paused, 'that's not when I'm loneliest. It's more when I'm in a crowd and your dad's not there. When I go supermarket shopping and realise I don't have to consider what I'm going to make for him or buy enough for two, or a million other little things that remind me he's gone.'

'God, that's really—'

'Please don't remind me how sad it is, I know it's sad! Death is supposed to be sad, isn't it? I think you'd be more worried if I were doing star jumps!'

She felt the desire to cry, not only in recognition of how sad she was at times, but because somewhere, deep down, she felt that Dominic, the Handsome Car Klutz himself, might just be the answer to her sadness, her loneliness, and yet it was not to be, could not be.

The novel fell open at a random page and she studied it intently.

'I just want to say three things,' her son began.

'Goodness me, Aiden, can't a woman read in peace?' She smiled; it was easy, she realised, to mask in this way.

'Apparently not.' He stared at her. 'The first thing I want to say to you, Mum, is that you have a lot of life ahead of you, and if you did want to see someone or date someone or even make a new friend, that would be fine, more than fine, it would be good. It's been three years and,' he swallowed, 'Dad would want you to be happy. I know he would.'

'Thank you.' She felt her throat tightening with barely disguised emotion; this permission, almost a suggestion, was generous and mature.

'The second thing is that you're holding your book upside down.'

She quickly turned it the right way and felt the burn of embarrassment on her cheeks, smiling at her lovely son. 'And the third thing?' she asked curtly to try and deflect, as was fast becoming her MO.

'Who's Quincy?' he asked, with a look of utter confusion.

◆　◆　◆

Enya climbed from the tepid bath and slipped into her pyjamas. It wasn't late but clothes felt like too much effort on this sultry night. Her cotton PJs and light dressing gown were just the ticket.

She stopped halfway down the stairs at the sound of voices floating along the hallway, Aiden's for sure, and a female voice. Iris, of course. She smiled; it sounded a lot like the choice between cerise and tangerine was back on. She'd leave Angela to calm down a bit and then text her good night with a smiley emoji. That should do the trick.

It was therefore a surprise when she entered the kitchen to see Holly sitting opposite Aiden at the kitchen table – a lovely surprise. Whether it meant they might rekindle what was lost or it was simply the two restoring bonds that would help them co-parent, it could only be a good thing. She breathed deeply, comforted by the familiar, relieved that they were being civil, thankful that it was not another drama-laden scenario, as she needed a rest from it all.

'Holly's popped in.' Her son sat back in the chair and folded his arms.

'I can see that! Hello, darling.' She walked over to the girl and pecked her on the cheek. 'How're you feeling?'

'Good! Actually, really good!'

Enya noted the bloom of health on the girl's cheeks, the perkiness to her posture and the smile about her mouth. It was lovely to see, yet was also a cause for concern. Enya hoped the upturn in Holly's spirit and demeanour was because she was calming, that the hurt of her break-up was softening, the emotional bruises beginning to heal, and not because she was in close proximity to Aiden. Because that might be a false dawn, and being offered hope and having it snatched away was, she knew from personal experience, often worse, harder to recover from. It was also unfair if he was, no matter how unwittingly, making an unspoken promise.

'I've got my first scan next week.' The girl beamed and pulled her shoulders in, excited.

'Oh, my goodness, that'll make it all seem real. Seeing that screen and having a photo to carry around. I've still got Aiden's, he looked like a big-headed alien.'

'Still does a bit.' Holly frowned at him, and Enya felt the icy point of recognition in her breast. She understood that this was all Holly had hoped for, Aiden, home alone, discussing the baby around the kitchen table.

'Just nipping to the loo.'

Her son left the table. It felt like Enya's opportunity to say something, to try and help set the girl's expectations, but she didn't know where to start. Wary of quashing the buds of reconciliation, if that was where they were heading, but also wanting to limit the potential for more damage.

The moment Aiden trod the stairs, Holly turned to face her, speaking quickly in no more than a whisper. 'He says the wedding might be off, that he's probably moving back home, what d'you make of that?'

It explained the girl's delight. There was no disguising the utter joy in her tone, the lift in her spirits; she was clearly delighted and equally consoled by the prospect.

'To be honest, lovey, I don't really know what's going on. There's been some kind of . . .' She didn't want to give details of the row, it felt misplaced, disloyal, and was not her story to tell. 'One thing I will say though, because I think the world of you, and I always will, is that even if the wedding doesn't go ahead, even if he and Iris decide to call it a day . . .'

'Do you think they will?'

It was clear she was only listening selectively.

'As I say, I don't know what's going on or how this is going to pan out, but I think you need to ask yourself, even if Aiden is free, would you want to be with someone who chose to end your relationship? Who left you for someone else? And just because he might be single again, and we don't know for sure, but *even* if he is, there are no guarantees that you and he would pick up where you left off. And you should question whether that's what you would even want.'

Aware that it was her son she referred to, Enya did her best to be open, honest, and only say what she would say to him face to face when she got the chance.

'What I want, Enya, is him. What I've always wanted is him. I'd take him back in a heartbeat. I love him.' Holly paused to gather herself, her eyes misting as she spoke. 'We're having a baby.'

It was as she opened her mouth to speak that Aiden walked back into the kitchen.

'I wanted to show you something,' Holly gushed. 'I've got a baby book! Well, actually, I *made* us a baby book!'

Holly dipped her head under the table to reach into her rucksack.

Aiden took the opportunity to face his mum and stared at her wide-eyed, as if he'd been cornered. Enya felt the smallest flicker of relief; at least he wasn't going to be fanning the flames of reconciliation, as managing Holly's expectations was still her biggest concern. His expression was that of a man who felt trapped, no doubt, obligated even, but whose heart was most definitely in the hands of another woman.

The baby book was duly deposited on the tabletop. It was as Enya might have expected, exquisitely crafted with care and attention to detail. A hessian-backed book with cream pages, each with space for a photograph or a pocket for a keepsake, and in the style of a scrap book; Holly's beautiful calligraphy graced each page.

'You can help, and we can fill in the gaps.' Holly took a gel pen from the front pocket of her bag and opened the book. 'Right, this is where we put any ideas for girls' names.' She tapped the pen on her cheek. 'I've already put Eloise, Jemima, Daisy and Amelia – are there any you'd like to add?' She smiled at Aiden, who looked a little pale.

'I don't . . . don't know, can I think about it?' His voice now no more than a whisper.

'Okay, let me know.' Holly turned the page. 'And for me this is a no-brainer, I was thinking for a boy, we should go with Jonathan Philip Brown, Jonny for short. I think your dad would have liked that and it means he's connected to our son, if it's a boy. We can tell him all about his grandad who was brilliant at Battleships, knew loads about music of the eighties, and was rubbish at growing tomatoes! What do you think?'

Enya smiled; she knew Jonathan would be touched, and that he'd find the summary of his life more than a little amusing.

'I . . .'

Aiden seemed to sway a little in his chair and Enya feared he might fall to the floor.

'It's all right, love. Take a deep breath.'

Rushing to the tap, she ran him a glass of cold water, knowing that this heat and being even a little dehydrated didn't help when you were feeling overwhelmed.

There was a knock at the front door.

'I'll get it.' She placed the glass on the table in front of Aiden and rushed to answer it. Her first thought was that it might be Jenny or Phil, come once again to retrieve their daughter, as they had on the night of the fateful scream and pyjama party incident. She wondered how best to greet them, and braced herself, deciding to be firm yet friendly, and not let herself be pushed around or derided in her own home. But no, it wasn't either of them.

'Iris!'

Enya felt her blood run cold, as she tried and failed to think of how to keep the two young women from meeting each other. Wishing for the first time that she did indeed have a bigger house, an east wing, or at the very least a network of tunnels down which she might hide. So much for a drama-free scenario.

'Can I come in?' Iris looked along the hallway, seeking out the man who she had argued with.

'Of course, of course.' Enya stood back.

It felt like the world turned in slow motion as the girl stepped over the threshold.

Chapter Thirty

Enya kept her sights on Aiden, watching as his face broke into a smile at the sight of Iris and then his eyes instantly widened with something close to horror as he registered the predicament.

It would have been hard to voice her biggest fear in that moment, but it was certainly screaming. She wasn't sure how she might react or cope if the young women in her kitchen started screaming, because that was what movies and the media told her might happen, that when women who loved the same man came face to face, they might scream, loudly. And while she feared it, she understood. It seemed the easiest of ways to stake a claim, to be heard. To be seen.

She blinked away the image of her and Trish, shouting until their throats bled and they were hoarse.

Holly, without a word being spoken, knew instantly who the visitor was and shrank back in her chair. Her demeanour altered; gone was her sparkle, her energy, as she folded her hands into fists and placed them on her thighs, head down, shoulders hunched, as if trying to disappear altogether. It broke Enya's heart to see this visceral display of raw pain.

'Can I get you a cup of tea, Iris?' she almost whispered. It felt the right thing to do, how she greeted anyone whenever they walked through the door.

'No, thank you.' Iris too kept her voice low, as if aware of the delicate bubble of glass in which they all waited, and that one loud noise, a single jolt, could see the whole thing come crashing down around them.

'Hi, Aiden.' Iris lifted her hand in the smallest of waves, and he gave a slow smile of response, closing his eyes briefly.

'Hi,' he managed.

And just like that, Enya understood that all was forgiven. The wedding was back on.

It felt like a privilege to witness the very thing he had described to her, a look that was so much more than just a look but was in fact a connection. She saw it, and she *felt* it. A look between two people so in love that they almost knew what the other was thinking. So in tune that they knew how to handle any situation just by looking at the other. In sync. One team . . .

Witnessing it had a strange effect, helping her understand in that moment that this was not a fleeting thing, was not simply impetuous infatuation, but was real. Her son was moving on to his next chapter, a complicated chapter, but a new chapter no doubt, and if he could do it, so could she. It meant not that she was redundant, but rather that she was free.

Enya noted the way Iris had called him Aiden, not AJ; not taunting Holly with their closeness, the use of a nickname. It was mature and kind.

The four stayed still, as if wary of movement, unsure of their next line in a play that was as improvised as it was unpredictable.

'You must be Holly.'

Iris took a step forward and Holly looked up, as if surprised that she could be seen, suggesting she had been wishing so hard to disappear that she might, just for a second, have believed it possible.

'Yes.'

The two girls locked eyes, taking the opportunity to unashamedly study each other.

'Do you mind if I sit down?' Iris pointed to the seat next to Holly, deliberately, it seemed, choosing not to sit next to the man at the centre of this muddle, understanding that it might be more than Holly, or Aiden for that matter, could cope with, the idea of him watching Holly watching them, while Enya stood by the island and watched them all.

'This must be as weird for you as it is for me.' Iris, her tone soft, addressed Aiden's ex directly and Holly nodded, silently.

'I want to say congratulations on your baby, but I'm not sure that's the right thing to say. Truth is, I don't know what to say, I don't want to get it wrong.' Iris swallowed, her voice low, and Enya felt her nerves from the other side of the room.

'It's fine to say congratulations. It's a good thing, a lovely thing.' Holly almost unconsciously ran her palm over her stomach, where a bump was yet to materialise.

'In that case, congratulations. Have you had morning sickness?'

'A bit,' Holly looked up, 'but nothing terrible. I think the worst symptom is that I've got an odd taste in my mouth. I love baking, but even the thought of cake . . .' She stuck out her tongue.

'I can't bake. I'm useless at anything like that.'

Enya loved Iris's words of self-deprecation and stared as Holly unfurled a little, sitting more upright.

'What's that?' Iris pointed at the baby book.

'I made a . . . erm . . .' Holly swallowed, 'a binder all about the baby, I'll update it when they're born. Milestones, that kind of thing.'

'What have you got so far?' Iris placed her arms on the table, as if settling in.

'I was just talking about names before you arrived.'

Enya noted how Holly had gone from talking about *we* and *us* to *me* and *I*.

'What have you settled on?' Iris smiled, her eyes still on Holly's face.

'Not really settled on any, but for a girl I like Eloise, Jemima or Amelia, I think they're my favourites.'

'I like Amelia, but they're all lovely. Don't you think, Aiden?'

'Yes,' he coughed to clear his throat, 'yes, all nice.'

'And what about for a boy?' Iris asked, continuing to engage.

Enya knew she had never seen such a display of confidence, of empathy. If she had harboured the slightest doubt about the girl, to see first hand the strength of her character made her heart bloom with affection for the young woman who would be her daughter-in-law.

'I was thinking to name him after our dads, so Jonathan Philip, but I'd call him Jonny.'

'Jonny's a good name. He could do anything with a name like that.'

'That's what my mum said.' Holly sounded young and sweet.

'So, you and Aiden were at school together?' Iris asked, as if unaware.

'Yes, feels like a hundred years ago.' Holly gave a small smile in Aiden's direction.

'What was he like, when you were at school?' Iris turned to face Holly, who looked up as if picturing that time in their lives.

'He was clever, quiet, nice . . . not trendy or that popular.'

'Well, thanks, Holly,' Aiden sighed, and the two girls smiled, almost laughing, but not quite.

Enya slipped into the sitting room, feeling it better that the three sat at the table and built bridges that might help them in the future, help them get to where they all needed to go. Bridges that might mean the baby who was going to enter their lives could never take a misstep or get lost when it came to navigating its parents' relationship, as there would always be something solid underfoot. The kind of bridges whose foundations would be laid by no more than looking at a baby book.

She sat on the sofa, wanting to weep for the three youngsters who found themselves in this uncomfortable, life-altering situation, moving bravely into the unknown, as must she. How she wished Jonathan were by her side, knowing that he, like her, would be feeling a new surge of optimism because of what was happening around the table. And also understanding that even in the trickiest of situations, there was always a way forward, if you worked hard enough at it. Opening her laptop, she looked at the screenshot of Dominic that she'd captured and felt warmth flood her being at no more than the sight of his handsome face.

It was some fifteen minutes later, maybe more, that at the sound of a chair scraping, Enya stood and made her way, as casually as she could manage, back to the kitchen.

It was Holly who now stood, placing her baby book inside her rucksack.

'I've got my first scan next week, bit nervous . . .'

Her manner was still hesitant, still subdued, but gone was the excruciating folding of her whole being.

'Oh, well make sure Aiden's got it in his diary, you know what he's like, he can meet you there. Is it at Southmead Hospital?'

'Yes.' Holly kept her head down but lifted her eyes to look at the father of her baby.

'I never mind going there, at least I can get a coffee while I wait. It's exciting, Holly.'

Iris had spoken plainly, her messaging clear; *there is a way to build a life, the three of us. I'm not going anywhere, and I understand that neither are you . . .*

'It is.'

'It must feel scary.' Iris stood. 'I can't imagine. But it will all work out. We were saying only earlier that when it comes to things like Christmas, we'll organise ourselves, do whatever's best, there'll be a way for us to make it work. To make everything work.'

Holly stared at the girl and jutted her chin, trying in vain to stop her tears, which fell in a thin stream over her cheeks. 'Be good to him, won't you.'

Iris watched as Holly put her rucksack on to her shoulder and continued to look at Aiden's face, as if unable to tear her eyes away.

'I promise you I will.' Iris swallowed and spoke softly, as Holly left the room.

Enya reached out and squeezed Holly Hudson's arm as she made her way towards the front door, opening it quietly and slipping out into the warmth of the summer's eve. Aiden almost rushed forward, as if it were a need, and took Iris into his arms.

Enya left them to it, knowing they would have a lot to unpick.

Peering out of her bedroom window, she watched Holly disappear inside her parents' house, and knew she would never forget the quiet, controlled interaction that had occurred in her home.

There had been a shift, not only for Aiden, Holly and Iris, but for her too, a reckoning of sorts, understanding that it was time for her new chapter. She just had to find the courage to open the book.

Pickle was on the bed and looked up, indifferent, it seemed, to her presence.

Enya lay on top of the duvet and waited for sleep. Her phone buzzed, a text from Angela.

I'VE HAD A THINK ABOUT OUR CONVERSATION EARLIER. I REVISITED THE LINKS YOU SENT AND WOULD JUST LIKE TO CONFIRM THAT BOTH OF THOSE DRESSES ARE ABSOLUTELY HIDEOUS. YOU HAVE NO TASTE. NONE AT ALL. WHAT WERE YOU THINKING?

It made her laugh out loud, this no doubt her sassy sister's way of saying that all was forgiven, and confirming her attendance at the wedding, should it go ahead. It was just what she needed at the end of this most extraordinary day.

Chapter
Thirty-One

Enya woke on this beautiful blue-sky day and lay very still, staring at the ceiling, a little unsure of how she should be feeling on this, her son's wedding day. Here she was, coming to terms with the fact that this was an event she had imagined since he was a child. Wondering who he would marry, where he would marry, would he marry at all? All these things were of course unknown, but one thing she would have said with certainty was that Jonathan would be by her side. Placing her hand on the cold pillow next to her, she felt his absence as keenly today as any since he had died, and yet it was without the melancholy that had dogged her since he had disappeared.

She simply wished he were here, knowing how much he would have loved it, all of it!

Witnessing the maturity with which Aiden, Holly and Iris had navigated the situation in which they found themselves had proved inspirational and helped her to see that no matter how differently things turned out from what you had planned, there was always a way to find the silver lining, to look forward. A way to make it work.

Sick of being held accountable for actions that were nothing to do with her, quizzed or confronted by everyone from her sister to her neighbours, she had taken control of how she was viewed and what she was prepared to tolerate. For too long she had been reactive, overly concerned with the little things, but not any longer.

If Jenny and Phil chose not to be part of her life, then so be it. Wishing for it and crying over it was certainly not going to change the situation; instead she would be civil, but try not to take the rejection personally, looking forward to her next chapter. Maybe she'd take Trish's advice after all and join a club!

Handsome Car Klutz continued to lurk in her mind, prodding her sleeping desires with all kinds of fanciful thoughts that weren't wholly unpleasant. Unsure whether it was widowhood, single life or simply her age, since losing Jonathan she had lost a fundamental part of herself. For some years now she had no longer seen herself as a sexual being, and the world, it seemed, had taken her lead. More often than not she felt invisible and, unsurprisingly, the addition of a cotton neckerchief, a fancy tasselled necklace or a good squirt of her favoured perfume didn't seem to enhance her visibility. But Dominic had seen her, and this meant she was not invisible, not quite.

Today, however, what she needed to do was go and watch her son marry his Iris and do her best to stay out of the chaos that was the Sutherlands' marriage.

'You got this!' she shouted, giving herself the pep talk, as she sat up to face the day. Of one thing she was sure: if the emotional highs and lows were standard when it came to wedding planning, then she was glad Aiden and Iris had crammed it into a month, uncertain if she had the mental reserves to withstand it a minute longer.

The pale-blue ankle-length dress she had chosen, with the help of Angela, hung pressed and ready on the wardrobe door. It was triangular in shape, with a high neck and an abundance of buttons. Her sister had pointed out that it made her look like a ward sister, or a matron, circa 1950. She had also added that this was a positive, as the last thing she wanted to do was look even vaguely attractive, what with Dominic being present and all. Maybe Angela had a point.

Enya hadn't seen Dominic since he had visited her weeks ago and there had been no phone calls, no contact at all. To say she was nervous about facing him was an understatement. Her hope was that enough time had passed to cool the embers of their burning connection, and that the openly stated admission that how they felt about each other neither could nor should be allowed to grow was something they both adhered to. Plus, today was not about them, not at all. It was all about Aiden and Iris, the people she would do her very best to protect, always.

Her parents had arrived yesterday and were staying with Angela and Frank. Having spoken to them both on the phone, she was excited to see them, and hoped they would manage to keep their bickering to a minimum. Aiden had stayed at The Mount, flouting convention; he and Iris had declared they'd rather not spend a night apart and planned on watching the sunrise so as not to miss a single second of their special day. It had made her smile, the cynic in her wondering if they'd feel quite so sentimental when their adrenaline flagged and fatigue hit, which, if she had to guess, might be around dusk. Not that she was anti this at all, hoping for a reasonable end time to the festivities and already picturing the bed she had only just vacated.

Having washed her hair yesterday, it had calmed and looked as passable as her curly mop ever did. Her mascara, blush, and nude lipstick sat on the kitchen table. There was something exciting about new make-up. With a mug of tea placed by her magnifying mirror, she dotted cream on to her face and neck and took a sip of that delightful first morning brew, when a gentle tap saw her head turn to the front door.

Holly stood on the doorstep with a pretty arrangement of flowers in her hands. It was instantly recognisable as Jenny's trademark style of weeping greenery, blousy-headed blooms, delicate petals, wisps of grass, and the scent! It was heavenly.

'Oh, Holly! They're beautiful!' She felt her heart lift at the sight of them, so much more than a simple bunch of flowers. It was a peace offering, it was recognition of the fact that Enya's son was getting married, it was forgiveness, and it was kind. As per her new, assertive stance and in the vein of self-preservation, Enya dared not let herself believe they were about to fall back into a close friendship, she'd make no mention of their joint business venture and she doubted there'd be any 3 a.m. calls for chocolate, but that was fine. This was a start, and today, it was enough.

'Mum was going to bring them down, but I said I wanted to do it.'

Holly was quiet, pale, her hair needed washing and she looked tired. Her voice carried the faltering air of someone who was struggling.

'Come in, love. I was just about to start my make-up; you know I'm not very good at all that.'

'Would you like me to do your brows?'

Holly had done this before; her steady hand, young eyes and attention to detail meant Enya had left the house with perfectly full arches over her eyes that reminded her of the brows of her youth, before she had recklessly plucked at them whenever the fancy took her.

'Yes, I really would. If you're sure?' Having done her best to shield the girl from all aspects of Aiden's life, let alone mention the wedding, this act felt intimate and was, she knew, the way it had to be, a life less deceitful, but one that was instead open and inclusive.

'I'm sure.'

Holly walked in and handed her the flowers.

'Tell your mum, thank you – they're stunning!'

Enya sat at the kitchen table, as Holly selected the eyebrow pen from her make-up bag. 'Tip your head back a little.'

She did as she was instructed and sat very still as Holly first gently brushed her brows, then artfully filled in the gaps with the delicate tip of the pen.

'There.'

Enya studied Holly's work in the mirror. 'Oh, that's much better, thank you. Cup of tea?'

'Please.' Holly sat at the table as Enya flicked on the kettle and shoved a teabag into a mug.

'Is . . . is he here?' The girl glanced towards the hallway.

'No, no, lovey, he isn't. He didn't stay here last night.'

Instantly, Enya watched her shoulders fall, her face crumple.

'I just, I just need to see him, Enya, I need to tell him things.'

'I know.'

'The last time I saw him was at the scan.'

'Yes, he sent me a copy. It was quite a moment. Did you get my text?'

'I did. Thanks.' Holly looked down, her blink rate slow. 'It was odd, really. It wasn't like it is in the movies, when a couple are excited and emotional and he's holding her hand, and they are both grinning at the screen.'

'I expect it's rarely like that, Holly. I don't think anything is like it is in the movies.'

Enya squeezed the teabag against the side of the mug and drizzled milk in as she stirred, before putting it on the table. Her heart flexed for the girl, who despite her fixed smile must be hurting.

'I guess not.' Holly took a slow sip. 'I can't tell you how I feel today, Enya. Can't explain to you what it's like, knowing the man I love, the man I've loved for most of my life, is going to marry someone else. It's like a bad dream that I can't wake up from.'

'I can't begin to imagine.' An image of Dominic, holding Enya close before letting her go, flashed through her thoughts.

'I'm glad you can't imagine because I feel like I'm falling. I've felt like I'm falling since the day he came back from Rome and told me that he'd changed his mind.' Holly looked directly at her now. 'How can you just change your mind, how does that happen after all that time? We built a life together, we had a home, a future, and then in the blink of an eye it was gone, all of it. And I remember as he was speaking I had to hold on to the arms of the chair to stop myself from falling through it and falling through the floor and the ceiling of the flat below and their floor, down and down through the foundations into the earth. I thought I might fall forever so I sat very still, and I didn't say anything at all, not at first. I couldn't. And by the time I found my voice, and knew what I wanted to say, the questions I wanted to ask, he'd been gone for hours. I'd watched him pack a little bag and walk out the front door, and even though I knew it was the last time he was going to do that, I couldn't believe it. It didn't seem real. I still don't believe it, even though I know it's happening, even though I know it's happened, and I know . . .' she stuttered, 'I know that today he properly stops being mine. He becomes hers in a way that he was never mine. Legally, and in the eyes of God if you believe in that, he is hers. Her husband and she'll . . . she'll be his wife and I'll . . . I'll just be Holly, his ex, someone he used to know.'

'You will never just be someone he used to know, not to him and not to me either.' Enya took the girl's hand into her own, understanding what it felt like to see your role, your purpose, so changed; it could leave you on the point of panic. 'You will always be our Holly Hudson and you will be the mother of my grandchild.'

Holly lowered her gaze and cried silently, her tears sparse, as if she had cried them all away.

'I want you to remember what Angela said, about how you will rise stronger from the ashes of this hurt. It's important, Holly, to tell yourself that what isn't meant for you passes you by. You'll look back at this terrible time of hurt and you won't forget it, never that, but you will be able to look at it objectively. I promise you that. You'll come to realise that you only want to be with someone for whom you are their number one. That's what you deserve, what we all deserve.'

Knowing she too deserved to be someone's number one, not the name in the phone that was called secretly while his wife was elsewhere, not snatched chats in the bath, but someone for whom you were a priority, who you made a supreme effort to be with openly, and not someone whose life was inextricably and complicatedly linked to your child's.

'I understand what you're saying, but today you'll watch Iris walk up the aisle, maybe, and she'll come to rest at the point where Aiden is waiting for her and he'll take her hand, not mine. They'll exchange vows, and you'll feel happy and glad because he's your son and you love him, and he loves you. I know how much.'

These words a precious gift that Enya would hold tightly.

'Then later, you'll hold Iris in your arms, even if only briefly, probably give her a kiss, tell her congratulations, and how beautiful she looks, and I'm sure she will. And even just imagining that, it's like another knife in my chest. I doubt there's much more room, to be honest. I look down and I see handles of daggers all over me, I feel their cuts, I feel the throb of the wounds where they have pierced my skin and stay lodged in my flesh, every word he spoke to me, every lie he told me, every promise he made, all of it plays like a movie in my head. And today is a big step towards erasing me. How can it not be? He will have a wife. You will have a daughter-in-law, and both of these roles have been mine for the longest time, within reach, almost.'

Enya found the girl's words profoundly moving, understanding that feeling of wounds in her chest from which all her sadness might seep, knowing that it *was* possible to heal, to start to take control, to hold the tiller and not to feel quite so petrified about the life that lay ahead, albeit a different life to the one you might have envisaged.

'I don't think Aiden lied to you, Holly. And a lot of what you say is true, but even when Iris is part of my family, it won't erase the fact that you are too and will always be.'

Just like I will always be linked to Jonathan, always be Aiden's mum, no matter what.

'Oh, but he did lie to me. He told me we were forever, he told me we had a future, he told me he couldn't live without me, couldn't imagine a life without me, but that wasn't true. I was just a placeholder until Iris came along.' The young woman raised her voice, as *her* hurt seeped from her.

'I am sure he meant every word when he said it, but that's life. That's how it works. We can only say how we feel and express what we want in that moment, but none of us knows what is around the corner, and sometimes things or people that we think are meant for us really aren't, not forever! I stood and made vows to Jonathan and never thought much about the *till death us do part* bit. Never thought he'd leave me.'

It was her truth and with it came a new level of clarity, understanding that death had parted them and that meant she was now allowed to feel again, to love again . . . should the right person come along. Someone like Dominic, knowing that what they shared was indeed a beautiful, bright thing, but no matter how strong the connection, it was impossible to pursue without causing ripples that had the power to damage, or at the very least confuse the lives of their children.

Enya smiled at the young woman with her whole life stretched in front of her.

'You're having his baby, Holly. You will always be the mother of his child, the mother of my grandchild, and I've loved you for a very long time, as did Jonathan.'

At this, Holly seemed to calm and take a deep breath. 'It's going to be a very strange family. I can't imagine him leaving his wife to come and see his baby. I can't imagine me taking the baby to where he and his wife live. I can't imagine any of it.'

While Enya was aware of Holly's needs on this difficult day, she needed to get ready. Being late was not an option.

'You've done an amazing job, my love. Thank you.'

She admired Holly's work as she applied the newly bought mascara to her lashes, liking the way they perked up and lengthened at no more than a touch of this magic wand. Her brows looked on point. She understood the appeal of make-up, yet rarely bothered, quite unable to find the motivation to put it on every day. This day, however, was a special one, and as the mother of the groom, she wanted to look her best, partly so that in years to come she could look back at any photographs of the big day without a shiver of shame, and partly, not that she'd admit it, because she was going to see Dominic.

'My advice, Holly, would be don't try and imagine it. Don't think about it. Just wake up every day and go through the motions until you're not having to go through the motions anymore, until you're actually living your life.' This advice came easily because it was what she had done every day since her husband had died and now understood that it went on, all of it. The wheels kept turning and it was up to her to find those pockets of joy where she could. 'You're young, you're wonderful and you're going to be a great mum. You will have a great life. A *baby*, Holly!' She allowed herself to picture the little bundle and felt the spark of excitement fire through her.

'You sound very certain.' Holly smiled at her.

'I am, because I know you, and I know Aiden, and no matter what mistakes have been made or how you have ended up where you've ended up, I know in the heart of both of you lies kindness and from that kindness everything else will grow. Trust me.'

'I do trust you, Enya.' Holly stood, as if she too were conscious of the time. 'I'd better let you get ready.'

'Don't forget to tell Jenny, thank you for the flowers.'

Holly nodded, and left quietly, and Enya hoped that what she had said was true, that from kindness, everything else would grow . . .

Chapter
Thirty-Two

Wary of crumpling her frock, Enya, in her jeans and a baggy linen T-shirt, carefully laid the pale-blue dress on the back seat, hoping to arrive with it crease free and to get changed just before the ceremony.

She jumped into the driver's seat and adjusted the rear-view mirror, staring into it in the hope that Jonathan might be there on the back seat on this day of all days, knowing she would give anything for one more glimpse of him, if only to say goodbye . . .

He wasn't.

What she did see, though, was the swish of the curtain in Jenny's lounge, as if someone was watching out of it, quickly hiding when she made her appearance. Still thankful for the gift of flowers, she wished her friend had waved, giving her the opportunity to wave back, to help smooth over the hurt. The flowers really had been the loveliest touch. Enya felt the rise of hope that if her friend had seen fit to send flowers, then maybe she was already slipping down the hate list. And that was good enough.

She pulled out of Mablethorpe Road and felt the tightening of emotion in her throat, her tears hovering near the surface that she managed to keep at bay, just. It had been a standard joke for years now, Maeve commenting how when Aiden and Holly got married, she wanted a seat in the front row, if not to be the maid of honour! Jonathan used to roll his eyes and they had all made light of it. The only question was the role Maeve would play, not whether Aiden and Holly would get married. That was a given. It was true what she had said to Holly, that it was just how life worked, and you never knew what was around the corner.

Aiden's wedding day without a fanfare on the street in which he had grown up, among the neighbours who had seen him take his first steps, parade in his first school uniform, join cubs, take his cycling proficiency, although the less said about that the better. They'd watched him and Holly fall in love, waved him off to university and welcomed him home with the degree scroll in his clever mitts. They had then stood at the side of a freshly dug grave on a hill with a westerly wind whistling over them and sung a soulful lament, as he had said goodbye to his dad, a man they all loved.

Today there was no bunting, no waving off, no guests in attendance, not that she expected such a thing under the circumstances. But there were also no cards of congratulation, no texts, no smiles of support, nothing, and all because there was no Holly Hudson with her bouquet of lavender with the odd blue thistle and gypsophila. And yet her memories of all of those milestones were still here, lurking in the cracks on the pavement and between the bricks of the cottages, proof that things might change but everything she held dear was still there, if you knew where to look.

If the last few weeks had taught her anything, it was that she couldn't, as she had assumed, rely on the all-encircling arms of her community, and that their love and friendship, which she had felt in abundance every time she had arrived home, come rain or shine, for the last three decades, had, in fact, been conditional. Another reminder that if she couldn't rely on them then she absolutely *had* to put her hand firmly on the tiller and rely on herself.

She put the car into gear and put her foot down.

Iris had asked her to arrive early.

'So we can have a celebratory glass of fizz and you can help me get ready and everything!'

Enya loved how the girl was excited to invite her, another act of inclusion that made all the difference, as it had to Holly on the day in the kitchen when Iris had shed her rather cool exterior and had shown the girl who would be mother to Aiden's baby such warmth. Enya knew she'd never forget it.

'Yes, good idea. Plus, you might need to talk down my nerves, Mum,' Aiden had chimed in without the slightest hint of any concern, as if there were not a single doubt in his decision to marry this girl.

Frank was driving Angela and Enya's parents. They had been told to arrive a little before 2 p.m. as the ceremony was to take place at three, just enough time for them *all* to enjoy a glass of fizz, comment on the breathtaking view and for her sister, no doubt, to make a faux pas to ensure Enya would spend the rest of the day on tenterhooks. She prayed her parents kept their squabbles to a bare minimum and that Dominic stayed out of sight. The chances of the latter were, she knew, slim, but she could wish.

The wide electronic gates were already open and two oversized urns sat either side of the pillars. They were generously filled to the point of overflowing, with white flowers, roses, dahlias, lilies of the valley and fist-sized hydrangeas. They really were something; Enya's first thought was to take a picture to show Jenny, but these were the last flowers in the world her old friend would be interested in.

'You can do this,' she whispered, reminding herself again that it would all be okay. Her son was, after all, inside this property. And it was his wedding day.

She drove slowly along the winding drive and arrived at the wide apron in front of Dominic's office where Aiden had previously parked. A young man in a neat white shirt, black trousers and taupe linen waistcoat made moves that left her wondering if he was indeed directing her to the parking area, or was practising for when he secured that job on an aircraft carrier and would be bringing a fighter jet in to land. His expression was solemn as he bobbed, bent his knee, arms extended and fingers pointing. She hoped he was doing it to make himself laugh, or even better to make his friends laugh in the retelling, otherwise he was going to be exhausted by the end of the day.

'Thank you!' She gestured and waved.

He responded with a salute.

Enya parked the car and made her way back towards the house with her dress over her arm and her beloved, rarely worn, pale-blue silk wedged espadrilles hooked on to her fingers, the ones she had saved from potential danger when she'd rescued them from a hurricane. A touch she knew Jonathan would appreciate.

The outside space was unrecognisable as the place she had visited only a couple of weeks before. There were walkways constructed out of iron arches, all decorated with more white flowers and miles and miles of festoon lights. At the entrance to the walkways gathered youngsters in the same uniform as the parking steward and each sporting a cheery grin.

'Do you know where you're going?' a smiley girl asked, making Enya immediately grateful for the small act of friendship. It helped ease her nerves.

'I think to the house, I'm the groom's mum.'

'Oh, yes, hello! You can go around the side and through the front door, someone will meet you there. Have a lovely day!'

'I will, and thank you.' Enya smiled and set off towards the house. She took three steps, turned a corner, and came face to face with Dominic on the path. 'Oh!'

'Hi!'

They spoke quickly and at once each took a step backwards, both looking at the ground, over the shoulder of the other, skyward, anywhere and at anything, rather than looking each other directly in the face. She felt self-conscious, awkward, and so very glad to be near him, which was as embarrassing as it was conflicting. Standing taller, she pulled her shoulders back, found a neutral expression, while doing her best to smother the rocket of desire that exploded inside her. There was no denying it, she really liked the person she was when she was in his company. It felt like shedding skin, like rebirth, like being seventeen and stealing her sister's fancy shoes. It was all of that and more.

'I think they're all in the, erm . . .'

'How . . . how are . . .'

Again, they spoke in unison, neither giving the other a chance to respond, both with bodies turned in the direction they intended to head, as if unwilling to linger. Exactly like that, as if there were fire at their heels, and to interact in even the smallest of ways might mean danger! They rushed on, neither looking back, each desperate, it seemed, to be gone from the other, while her stomach and the flush to her cheeks told a very different story.

'Shit!' she whispered under her breath, far from enjoying the unease that now clung to her skin, wary of giving herself away on today of all days.

The grand and palatial house was a hive of activity. Here too the cathedral-like ceiling had been artfully strung with festoon lights and everywhere she looked, displays of white flowers were crowded into glass vases, each giving off the most stunning scent. More iron archways formed tunnels that led from the back of the house to the vast canopy of a marquee through which the view could be appreciated.

The marquee itself was home to white wrought-iron tables, bistro style, and informal seating with chairs for up to eight people. The floral displays here were on another level. Like something from a magazine, as huge orb-shaped displays hung from the ceiling. There were at least four aproned florists, one on a stepladder, fussing, clipping, and tucking blooms into position. The tables themselves held a single glass hurricane lamp with a pillar candle, and each seemed to sit inside a floral nest.

'Here she is!'

Enya turned at the sound of Trish's voice calling loudly.

The woman threw her hands in the air, swaying slightly from side to side, suggesting Dutch courage might have been imbibed, and Enya's heart lurched for her. Remembering their chat in the coffee shop, understanding how when you were unhappy, even a glorious thing like your only daughter's wedding was just a hiatus from the life that she would wake up to tomorrow.

'Enya! Oh my God! Can you believe this?'

'It's incredible!' She didn't know what else to say. Hadn't known what to say the first time Trish had stood in her kitchen and been joined by her husband, as the penny dropped . . .

'We've been up since the crack of dawn, I'm already knackered! Can I get you a drink?'

'No, thank you, my bladder is quite temperamental, and I've sunk at least two pints of tea today.'

'How about some champagne?' Trish beamed, as if for this kind of drink, Enya and her bladder might make an allowance.

'Do you know what, I will, but after the ceremony if that's okay. I've got to pace myself.'

The look on Trish's face was one of disappointment.

'Come and see the kids! And I can show you to the guest room where you can get changed.' Trish linked her arm and led her around the back of the house. They nipped past the marquee entrance and took a winding path that seemed to run along the edge of the garden, almost hidden by the immaculate lines of pleached hornbeams through which they now wandered, Enya's dress still dangling over her arm, shoes on her hooked fingers and her bag over her shoulder.

'Are they nervous?'

'No, don't seem it, I am! I'm the one worrying about the details and the timing. Iris is more like her dad, calmer, laid-back.'

Enya nodded, not wanting to talk about Dominic at all.

Up ahead she could see a single-storey building that almost disappeared into the landscape. Its flat roof was grassed and the walls a pale timber, the only windows on the front. Vast dark-framed doors were a mini version of those at the back of the main house but did the same job, opened up the entire house, blurred the boundary between the outside and the in. The terrace here too was smaller, more intimate, with two Adirondack chairs positioned to take in the view, which from here was no less stunning.

'This is where Iris lives, well, Iris and Aiden now.'

It was no wonder to Enya that he'd been home so little. His childhood room with board games piled up on the shelf above the bed must seem quite unappealing in comparison. And of course, he wanted to be where Iris was. This she understood entirely. He was no longer a child, but a man, about to become a married man, and a father soon after.

Enya was in awe of the design and size of this clever secret building. It was far from the *annexe thing* that Aiden had inadequately described, and that she had envisaged.

'Enya!' Iris leapt from a high leather stool, one of four that sat by the counter that was part bar, part island.

315

'Hello, love!' She welcomed the kiss Iris planted on her cheek, a subtle change in their dynamic that she truly appreciated. Enya took the chance to study her happy, pretty face. Her make-up was subtle, her hair as she always wore it in an immaculately blow-dried bob, and Trish was right, she appeared to be anything but nervous.

'See, I told you,' Trish laughed, 'cool as a cucumber.'

'To be honest, I don't see what there is to be nervous about!' Iris shrugged. 'I'm at home. The weather is great. My dress is amazing! The only people who are coming are those we love. I'm marrying the love of my life, and we have strawberries and sorbet for pudding! It's a perfect day!'

'Well, when you put it like that.' Enya laughed too.

'Even my dad has promised not to run off to the boatyard.'

'Oh, that bloody boat!' Trish added through gritted teeth. 'Anyway, I'm going to love you and leave you, I need to do a few last-minute bits and bobs, see you in a sec.' She turned to Enya. 'If you need anything at all, just text me and I'll be right over.'

'Thank you.' Enya was touched that on this day when Trish had so much to do and think about, she was so very considerate to her.

'Mum!' Aiden came from a room at the back and into the open-plan space, resplendent in rugby shorts and an old Bristol Bears T-shirt of his dad's. Her breath caught in her throat at no more than the sight of it. He rushed forward and wrapped her in a brief, tight hug.

She smiled. 'Mind my dress!'

He took it from her and disappeared along a corridor, returning empty-handed not a minute later.

'Did you hang it up?'

'No, I shoved it in a corner on the floor. Oh, is that what you're wearing to the wedding?' He pulled a face of mock horror and pretended to dash off to retrieve it. 'Yes, I've hung it up.'

'Thank you.' She studied his face; he looked so happy, so assured, it was wonderful!

'Come and sit outside.' He took her hand and led her back out to the terrace, her hand in his.

'This is a beautiful place, Aiden.'

'It really is.' He let his eyes sweep the view.

'How're you feeling?' She kept her voice low and soft.

'I'm just excited, so excited! Jim's in the shower. I've seen his speech, it's not too bad, had to make a few changes, remove the odd anecdote. I didn't think Nan would appreciate the tale of me trying to wax my arse, that kind of thing.'

'Probably wise.' She smiled.

'I'm looking forward to the day, Mum.' He bit his lip, and double blinked.

'But?' She turned to face him.

'But I'm really, really missing my dad.'

'Oh, love.' She retook his hand and held it tightly. 'Me too. But you know what, he'd say don't let sadness cloud this special day. He'd say that to both of us, he'd say, dance and laugh and make the best memories!' She knew he'd mean every word of it. 'I've come to realise that the lovely memories we have of *him*, they're everything, and even though he's not here, we have joy ahead of us, so much joy! There's room in our hearts for everything we've already experienced, and everything that is still to come. It's magic.'

'I know you're right.' He held her hand with equal pressure. 'I know he's dead. I know I can't see him. But it's like I think I might bump into him or he's working away or the reason he's not with me is because of logistics or circumstances and not because he can't and never will be with me again. But on days like this, moments like this, the big stuff, when I look up and he's not around, that's when I realise that it's real. He's actually gone, because if he could, he'd be here, wouldn't he?'

'He absolutely would, but he was always so proud of you and today is no exception. He'd be so proud of you, Aiden.'

'Yep.' He let go of her hand and wiped his nose on the back of his arm. 'This has come around quick, hasn't it?'

Staring out over the valley below, she did her best not to cry. The third time today she had felt the urge to give in to the emotion that threatened, understanding that, just like Jonathan, no matter where her boy lived or what direction his life took him in, he would always be her son.

Yes, it had gone quick.

'Nearly there! One more push, Enya, that's it, lovey! One more . . . that's smashing. Oh, here he is, a boy, you've got a lovely little boy!'

Too quick.

Chapter Thirty-Three

Enya smiled at the excited high-pitched chatter she could hear loud and clear floating under the door of the bathroom as she cleaned her teeth. Slowly, she applied her lipstick, taking care to blend it with the lip brush as she listened to Iris's bridesmaids, who sounded positively giddy. It only helped build the lovely atmosphere.

She had to confess it felt a little odd, being in this pleasant yet strange environment, interacting with people she barely knew, alone in this minute, on her son's wedding day. This was his home, yet she didn't know where to find a mug for coffee, or where his bedroom was, or even if there was a number for a landline. There was a lack of familiarity quite alien when it came to her child, who for most of his life had been within reach. This was a new era and one in which she was certain he would thrive!

As would she.

She thought of Jonathan's mother who had, throughout their married life, been a little cool, a little off, wondering now if Granny Brown had felt the same level of redundancy that had dogged her in recent months. The confusing tumble of emotions where delight at what lay ahead for her boy was edged with the fear of being forgotten, even if only a little bit. Not that she would ever have been remote and judgemental like her own mother-in-law, never that. In fact, she looked forward to growing closer to Iris. This in turn made her think of Holly, who had predicted this very thing.

Of one thing she was sure: it was time. Time to build her own life, looking forward instead of back. Enya blotted her mouth on a tissue and stared at the face in the mirror.

'Enya Brown . . .' She reached out and ran her finger over the face looking back at her. 'That's who I am. I'm Enya Brown. And I have a whole lot of life ahead of me!'

Enya smiled. Saying it out loud anchored her, reminded her of who she was, what she was worth and what she still had to look forward to.

'Mum!' She started as Aiden called, interrupting her thoughts, knocking forcefully on the door. 'Auntie Angela, Uncle Frank and Nan and Grandad are here. I've just found them a seat and got them a drink. I told them you'd be with them in a minute!'

'Righto, thanks, love!'

It was the encouragement she needed to get a wiggle on, worrying not only what her sister might be saying but equally who she might be saying it to.

She left the bathroom in her finery, her favourite shoes on her feet, shoes that she had worn countless times when she was on Jonathan's arm. It helped make him present.

'Enya, you look gorgeous!' Iris called from one of the bar stools, where someone seemed to be rubbing a product into the ends of her hair.

'Thank you! I can't wait to see your dress.'

'Not long now! I've just sent Aiden and Jim back up to the main house so we can get ready in peace. Also, the plan is that you, Mum, Dad and I will meet at the entrance to the tunnel to go through the walk-in plan and the details.'

'Walk-in plan?' Her heart rattled, not only at the thought of being centre stage, but also that she might mess it up, get something wrong and spoil Iris's vision for her special day.

'Yes, don't worry, nothing too complicated.'

Phew!

'It's just a nice way to connect our families and add a modern twist.'

'Great! I'll see you there then, lovey.'

Enya made her way back along the secret path and turned right into the marquee. A few of the tables were occupied by young people, sipping drinks as they took in the view. It could have been any swanky venue on the Riviera, as sunlight warmed the space. It did something to her, seeing her parents, her sister and Frank sitting there all dressed up, waiting for her, waiting for Aiden. It gave her an emotional jolt in the way that something or someone familiar in an alien landscape often does. She hadn't banked on this high level of sentiment hovering so close to the surface.

'Nu-urse!' Angela called loudly, making Enya wish she'd never agreed to the dress that made her look like a matron. 'I've finished!'

A man on an adjacent table laughed loudly. Enya tutted; the last thing she wanted was for Angela to find an audience, understanding that there'd be no quieting her if that were the case.

'You can cut that out. If it wasn't for you and your intervention, I'd be wearing cerise or tangerine right now,' she whispered when close enough.

'You look lovely, darling. Give your mother a kiss.'

Enya did just that, holding her mum close, inhaling the familiar scent of her, and noting that her sister had been right, their mum did look old.

'Hey, Dad.' Her lovely dad stood and with misty eyes looked her up and down as he always did after any time apart, as if he couldn't quite believe she was there, he missed her that much.

'Ignore your sister, you look lovely.' He hugged her tightly.

'I always ignore her.' She took a seat at the table.

'This is some place,' Angela widened her eyes and sipped what looked like a cocktail of some sort, 'how much do you think it's worth?'

'I really don't know, Angela, perhaps you should ask Trish.' She pulled a face at her sister and hoped her sarcasm might shut her up.

'I just had a quick look on Zoopla,' Frank spoke with his eyes on his phone, 'closest I can find in the postcode went for two point four million last year, but it didn't have as much land and the house didn't look as fancy.'

Angela made a whistling noise.

Enya felt her face flush red and was about to make her thoughts known when Trish appeared. She looked lovely in a teal coat dress with a delicate feathered fascinator to match.

'There you are, Enya!'

Enya gave Angela a withering look, silently encouraging her to keep schtum, as whatever she might want to say about her online house snooping was not anything Enya wanted to hear. Today or any day, come to think of it.

Angela seemed to understand and closed her mouth.

'Trish, this is my family, Aiden's auntie and uncle, and his nan and grandad.'

'How lovely to meet you all! A proud day for us all!' She smiled at each of them in turn and it made Enya feel even more uncomfortable at how they had been discussing the value of her house. 'We can have a proper chat later, but right now I think we're required by the bride, and in a short while everyone will be asked to go to the side garden and grab a seat, as that's where they are having the actual ceremony.'

'And it's all legal, is it?' Frank spoke directly. 'I didn't know you could just get hitched anywhere, in my day if it wasn't done in front of a vicar or at the local registry office then it just wasn't legit.'

'Oh, I can assure you it is all very legit.' Trish nodded, her mouth smiling, her eyes not so much. 'They are doing the legal bit on Monday at the registry office, no one is going, just them and two friends as witnesses, so don't worry, we've thought of everything.'

'Did you know about this?' Angela looked at Enya, who prayed she wasn't going to make a scene.

'I did.'

'So, what are you saying, no aunties at the *actual* wedding?'

Enya swallowed her desire to scream, remembering quite clearly a conversation when Angela had declared her horror at the prospect of a registry office wedding, *'one of those awful dos where they nip up the registry office and we all shove fifty quid behind the bar of a grotty pub with a sticky carpet . . .'* She let her eyes sweep the magnificent setting, where a small army of staff in the standard uniform criss-crossed the vast space. They carried trays of fluted glasses, ice buckets full of champagne, some held trays of dainty canapés, while others gave directions, directing newly arrived guests to the side garden and the marquee where they were invited to grab a drink and take a seat. Not a sticky carpet in sight.

'This *is* the actual wedding, Angela. And you're here, as am I. On Monday it will just be Iris and Aiden and their two friends, a quick ceremony, in and out, and then I think they're planning a pub lunch.'

'Well, I've heard it all now!' Angela pulled a face and Enya did her best to ignore her.

'Shall we go, Trish?' Enya walked briskly, wanting to put as much distance between her and her sister as possible.

'Yes, see you all in a bit!' Trish waved. Enya locked eyes with her dad, who gave her a small smile of understanding. She was glad he was there.

'My sister.' Enya shook her head. 'I knew she'd worry if she thought there might be a secret ceremony she's missing out on!'

'I get it.' Trish stopped on the path. 'I totally get it. I'm saying I'm fine with it, because I don't want Iris to worry or give it a second thought, but truth is, I'm absolutely gutted not to have been asked to the registry office. I cry every time I think about it.'

'Oh, Trish!' She placed her hand on the woman's arm.

'It's ridiculous, isn't it – as Iris says, a quick in and out and nothing to it, so why has it upset me so much?'

Enya took her time forming a response, warmed by the woman's honesty, her vulnerability. 'I understand completely, and I guess it's because that's the actual moment they'll be officially married, and we won't be there. And probably because our babies are getting married at all, our little ones, all grown up and gone!'

'I guess so, and also it's the final thing, isn't it. Once they're married, my husband will ship out. The beginning of the end.'

Enya nodded. She hadn't considered this glaring fact and she felt for the woman, knowing what it was like to wake up in a big bed all alone and not to hear the sound of her husband pottering.

'I envy her, you know.' Trish looked into the middle distance. 'I envy her that new start. She's at the beginning, when everything feels possible. But it doesn't last, does it? The gloss quickly wears off and you realise that marriage is not all it was cracked up to be, not all you thought it *might* be, all it could be, and it's bloody disappointing.' Trish took a long breath through her nose and pulled back her shoulders. 'Anyway, we should get going, don't want Iris wondering where we've got to.'

'Absolutely!'

Enya walked slightly behind Trish on the path, feeling more than a little saddened by her words. The one thing she could say with certainty about her marriage to Jonathan was that it had bloomed into a beautiful, deep, loving friendship, which was more than she had ever thought it could be, and the only real disappointment was that he had abandoned her too soon.

'There you are!' Iris called.

'Oh Iris! Oh, my goodness!' Enya took in the stunning gown, which was long and draped and simple yet stylish, the folds of ivory silk falling as if contoured exactly to her shape. 'You look stunning!'

It was an odd sensation, this beautiful girl who was in a short time to become her daughter-in-law, yet Enya viewed her with a certain detachment, admired her as she would any other beautiful bride, for she was indeed beautiful. The fact was, she had met Iris only a few times, exchanged no more than a handful of sentences with her. They were, in so many ways, strangers. Yet the way she had witnessed her talking to Holly, reassuring and including her, and how ecstatically happy she made Aiden, were indicators that led Enya to believe that in time they would become close. In fact, she was certain of it.

'Doesn't she just.' Trish reached up into her sleeve with her fingers and fished out a cotton handkerchief with which she blotted under her eyes and nose.

The bridesmaids wore spaghetti-strapped slip dresses in a similar fabric, the colour of a blushing peach, dresses that were elegant yet without the delicate ruching and draping that gave Iris's dress its structure.

'Where's Dad?' Iris looked around; Trish did the same. Enya was only relieved by his absence. Bumping into him on the path earlier had been bad enough; she feared it would be that much worse to have to face him in company.

'Who knows?' Trish shrugged. 'But my guess is, as he can't be working on his boat, he'll be online reading about his boat or watching tutorials on how to fix something on his boat or buying a part for his boat.'

'Okay.' It might have been her wedding day, but this didn't appear to stop Iris from issuing calm and considered instructions to make sure the ceremony went exactly how she wanted it to. 'Here's the plan. Enya, you are going to walk with my dad, the two of you will pair up here, and follow the bridesmaids, who will follow Mum, who'll be walking with me. Aiden will be waiting with Jim by the celebrant at the spot where the ceremony will happen. The guests will all be seated on either side. The chairs are in a slight arc.'

Enya felt light-headed, her mouth suddenly a little dry. She didn't want to be disagreeable or seem rude, but . . .

'I thought, thought your dad would be, erm, walking with you, to the, the service area.' She heard the falter in her tone and so smiled to show that all was well.

'I guess traditionally, yes, but Aiden and I discussed it, and neither of us wanted you to be on your own. I know this is a day of celebration, but I also know it must be a hard one without Aiden's dad here.'

'That's . . .' She didn't know what to say, didn't know how to politely suggest an alternative.

'Don't overthink it, Enya,' Trish chimed, 'it's my honour to walk Iris up the aisle. She means the world to me and it's symbolic, one of the last things I can do before she starts this new life with Aiden.'

With Trish's upset fresh in her mind over not being invited to the registry office, and her admission over Dominic's imminent departure, Enya felt well and truly backed into a corner.

'Then when we get to the spot where Aiden will be waiting, Mum will stand back a little, but next to Aiden, so she can properly see me. You will stand back a bit, Enya, but next to me so you can properly see Aiden, Dad will be next to Mum. It'll all become clear and Rhona, the celebrant, will be on hand to guide anyone to where they should be standing, and if it's not smooth, it doesn't matter, nothing does!' Iris beamed.

'Well, look who's decided to turn up?' Trish sniped.

Enya turned to see Dominic. He was wearing a pale-blue linen blazer, almost the exact shade of her dress, navy chinos and a white open-necked shirt. He looked fantastic and there it was again, that darned firework. She thought about Frank scrolling property sites on his phone, Angela speaking overly loudly about the price of the house, any unpalatable topic to lower her mood, in case there was the faintest chance that her less than demure, less than mother-of-the-groom thoughts might be glimpsed in her face.

'Sorry, Iris. I'm here now.' Dominic addressed his daughter directly and the look on his face indicated he either hadn't heard his wife's dig or was a master at ignoring that kind of comment. 'A minor emergency. Someone needed a pump for a flat tyre, I've been rummaging in the garage. All sorted.' He smiled at his girl. 'You look . . .' He shook his head, as if no words could adequately convey his pride, his love.

His voice filled the space. Enya looked right at him, damning the fact that just the sound of him was enough to fill her with a heady cocktail of desire, longing, and regret. An unwelcome and potent mix. He might not be for her, Iris's dad, Aiden's father-in-law to be, but she would forever be grateful to the man who had both *seen* her and made her feel seen. He would never know, and she could never convey, just what this had meant at a time when she so desperately needed to shake off her cloak of invisibility.

'Right, Dad, so as I told you earlier, you are to walk with Enya behind the bridesmaids, Mum and I will go in first, it means Aiden and I get a second or two together just to take it all in before we start, and you know where to stand?'

'Yes.' He nodded. 'I know where to stand.'

'Great. And also remember,' Iris now addressed them all, reminding Enya of a teacher giving a last-minute instruction to her less than reliable students, 'this is not a conventional wedding. There are no hymns, no singing, it's not overly formal. We keep it fun, we enjoy the music.'

'Some of which I've chosen.' Dominic beamed, clearly delighted to have been given the task.

'Yes, and I should warn you, Enya, that Aiden has picked some of his dad's favourites too for this evening.'

'Thank you for the warning. I went waterproof just in case.' She pointed at her lashes, and noted how Dominic stood to one side, almost with his back to her, his head tilted as if he might just be employing the same avoidance tactic.

'We nearly forgot the buttonholes!' The florist Enya had seen earlier up a ladder now approached with a shallow box containing the small bunches of flowers. They were neat and delicate, with fronds of whisper-thin fern to break up the white miniature roses, lilies of the valley and sprigs of elderflower that were tied with rough twine. 'Can I leave you to it?' She handed over the box to one of Iris's bridesmaids and rushed towards the main house, suggesting a floral emergency that required her urgent attention.

Trish selected one and pinned it to her dress. 'Do you need a hand, Enya?'

'Oh, thanks, yes.' She lifted her chin as Trish pinned one of the pretty little sprays on to her dress; the scent was glorious.

Dominic stood tall, as if he expected his wife to attach his. She did not.

'Would you do the honours?' He addressed Enya directly and held out his buttonhole.

She nodded and took the flowers from his palm. Careful not to let her fingers anywhere near his. Her shaking hand a giveaway. The only saving grace was that Trish and Iris paid them no attention. Enya lifted his lapel, feeling the heat of his body near her palm, as she pinned the flowers into place.

'There.'

She patted his jacket and let her eyes glance up towards his face. A face she hadn't seen this closely since he had fled from her kitchen and she had stood there bereft, staring at the space he had occupied, as if the shape of him lingered still.

His expression, she feared, matched her own; it was that potent mix of longing and regret that, had it been expressed in music, would have been loud and building, a crescendo that carried you along with its passion and its beauty, a trailing rapture that could pierce her very soul. Feelings that had the ability to floor her, to be her undoing, and her salvation. A moment of connection, knitting all the strands of desire and roping her to him, this man who had come into her life in the most unconventional of ways and had turned things upside down.

'Thank you.' His voice held the distinct huskiness of all it tried to contain.

They stared at each other and in that moment, she knew that this was no infatuation, no glossy novelty that would wane as quickly as it had grown. It was something deeper and more profound. This realisation only served to pierce her heart, understanding that the facts had not changed, that Aiden and Iris were about to embark on a complicated journey with Holly's baby at the centre of it and the last thing they would need was her confessing to her feelings for Dominic. It felt cruel. She reminded herself of the advice she had given Holly:

'. . . *none of us knows what is around the corner and sometimes, things or people that we think are meant for us really aren't, not forever . . .*'

'Okay, here we go!' Iris turned to face her entourage, her face split with a smile of pure elation. This girl was ready, more than ready, to march up that aisle and grab the future she wanted.

Trish raised her arm and Iris slipped hers through it, just as the music began to play loudly. It wasn't what Enya had expected, no hymn, no mournful lullaby or thought-provoking melody. No slow evocative ballad with words of love and tenderness, nothing like that.

Instead, it was instant and booming, an explosion of strings, guitar, banjo and bass! It was energetic and life-affirming and entirely rousing. All present jumped on the spot, moved their shoulders, or tapped their toes or stepped gaily from foot to foot, arms moving, heads nodding, mouths preparing to sing along. It was a sound that encouraged movement and participation, it encouraged life!

And then came the slowing, hypnotic and clear voices of those very clever Mumbley Boys.

Enya felt the beat in her breastbone and breathed in time to it. She stared ahead as the bridesmaids, with their bouquets held aloft, almost danced down the tunnel and then the aisle in a slow yet intricate step.

The music was loud in her ears, as Dominic came to stand next to her, close now. She could feel his presence, could smell his cologne, and she remembered what it had felt like to fall heavily into his arms on that day, for that brief time when she found a place to rest.

He reached down and took her hand inside his, where it fitted neatly, entirely, and where her fingers curled naturally around his.

She turned her face to look at him and he did the same, as the music built into a crescendo that carried her along with its passion and its beauty. He spoke five words, five words said clearly and with resolution that would become indelibly etched in her brain, there for perfect recall whenever she closed her eyes.

'I will wait for you.'

That was what he said, and she got the message loud and clear. If only it were that simple. Then the last gentle squeeze of her fingers before he let go of her hand and offered her his crooked arm. She placed her hand through it. Both looked ahead, as they walked through the flower arch, along the tunnel and into the marquee, surrounded by flowers and love, music and an atmosphere of infinite possibility, before they came to rest on the designated spot and separated, coming to a standstill opposite each other. Their children, hand in hand, beamed into the face of the other as if they had struck gold and been brave enough to claim it as their own. And while her heart sang for her son and this joyful union, her eyes were firmly fixed on Dominic and his on her.

'Wowee!' Rhona the celebrant spoke breathlessly as the music came to a close and everyone clapped, everyone! This at the commencement of the ceremony because, unbound by tradition, it felt like the right thing to do. There were even one or two whoops and hollers from the assembled. 'Now that's how you start a wedding!' Rhona began, to much laughter. 'So, good people, we are here today to celebrate the love of Aiden and Iris and I would like to start by telling you a little story.' Another ripple of laughter made its way around the marquee. 'Sometimes it's the smallest things in life that can turn into the biggest things. A tiny twist of fate that means the universe puts something or someone in your path that is meant for you, meant to be yours.'

Dominic allowed himself a small smile, which Enya matched.

'This is one such love, which started with a lingering look, a feeling, an indescribable and instantaneous connection that took them both entirely by surprise! But standing here today, can you imagine if they had *not* acted on this moment, can you conceive of a world where they might have denied the pull of destiny and not leapt! Surely that would have been the biggest tragedy of all, and surely it would have been to the detriment of their happiness. And that has to be the goal, right, to be happy?'

'Yes!' came calls from the crowd.

'When two people are shown a path that leads directly to happiness, do they not have a duty to walk it? And what would be the end result if they didn't? I shall tell you,' Rhona paused for effect, 'it would be the biggest missed opportunity of their lives!'

Enya, listening intently to every word spoken, felt the slow, warm creep of tears across her face. Once she started crying, it was like removing a stopper and she really could not stop. It felt monstrously unfair that she could not walk the path that led directly to happiness. Dominic, it seemed, understood as he too let his tears fall freely. And there they stood, facing each other, almost oblivious of everyone else present as they cried, hearts rent, their pain evident.

It was clear to her, the great love story was Iris and Aiden's, and for her to act on any feelings towards Dominic would place the young couple, with all the challenges that lay ahead for them, under the most enormous strain. Walking that path, acting on these feelings that she was certain were real, had the power to cause turmoil, division, and pain, the very opposite of what she wanted for them. She loved her son and was too fond of Iris to do anything of the sort.

Trish, staring at her only child who stood in all her glory, cried too, but Enya suspected for very different reasons.

'I'd like to ask you this question,' Rhona took a breath, 'what is living, if it isn't to grab those glorious moments of joy when they are presented to us and to stuff them into our pockets, *knowing* that joy, that *love* is what will sustain us on the darker days and in the challenging times. What is living if it is not that?'

Enya finally managed to look away from Dominic's face, staring at her pale-blue silk wedged espadrille shoes, where a blot of tears sat. It would stain, no doubt, leave a faint salty water mark, but one she would treasure because it contained all that was in her soul, as her heart, full of heaviness, seemed like it might fall right out of her chest given all she felt and all that could not be . . .

Chapter
Thirty-Four

Enya exhaled into the cool winter morning and plonked the three weighty shopping bags by her front door, flexing her chilly palms, which carried the imprint of the handles, before fishing inside her handbag for her key.

It had been twenty-six weeks since Aiden and Iris had married, and it had passed quickly. It felt like mere days ago that she'd been feeling anxious, trying to imagine her son married to Iris, and trying to get her head around the fact that Holly Hudson was having a baby. Now she was feeling anxious about Holly's due date and when the baby, her first grandchild, would actually arrive.

She thought, not for the first time, about Dominic, still in her phone as HCK, the lovely man who had bashed her door on that day long ago. Iris's lovely dad, who had, eight weeks ago now, finally moved from The Mount into his flat in the marina to be near his beloved boat *Foula Girl* and was, according to Iris, in his element, as he read guidebooks and nautical charts, planning eventually to escape the worst of the British winter by port hopping around Europe, sampling wine, eating local food, getting a tan, and generally enjoying life.

Iris spoke about it with a certain solemnity, her mouth a little wobbly, and Enya got it, knowing how her own parents' bickering had taken a toll on her and they were still together. Trish had, according to Aiden, found a thousand reasons why Dominic had to stay a little longer, a fact that was as sad as it was desperate, and not for the first time Enya felt nothing but empathy for the woman. She knew more than most how hard it was to let go.

'He's gone, Enya.'

'I think he might want some water; his mouth looks . . .'

'He's gone, my love. He's at peace.'

'I'll sit here for a while . . . in case he needs anything.'

Enya was, however, happy for Dominic, even though they weren't in touch; it sounded like a nice way to live, the planning for his great adventure, and she too had found the ingredients to living a happy, fulfilled life. She read a lot, walked a lot, and worked three days a week in the bookshop on the High Street, impressing the customers and staff alike with her knowledge of growing dahlias, her proficiency at photocopying, and the speed with which she could complete the Rubik's cube.

Aiden and Iris had settled into married life. As a couple, they seemed invincible! It was as if they had known each other for a lifetime, so easy were their interactions, so in sync their pace and habits. It seemed her son had taken her advice, laying strong foundations on which his marriage was to be built: with open and honest communication and love, always love. To be in their company was a reminder that sometimes you needed to be brave, to cast a stone, cause a ripple, to effect the necessary change. Easy to say, but a whole lot harder to observe when human emotion lay at the heart of such a decision. In the wee small hours, she often wondered how Trish would feel if Enya followed *her* deepest desire, how Aiden and Iris would. No matter how she sliced and diced it, it all felt too risky, when the ripples of their lives had only just dissipated and the water was, for the time being, calm.

And she was happy! Better. Untroubled by the panic attacks that had so thrown her off course.

Iris continued to display her smart, quiet confidence, which was as endearing as it was impressive. The kind of attitude that would only help when it came to navigating the choppy waters of step-parenting and effectively, inadvertently, finding yourself in a marriage of three. The young couple were still living in the annexe at The Mount, a situation Enya didn't see changing any time soon, their lovely home with the incredible view that changed over the seasons.

Trish relied heavily on Iris. And according to Aiden, fluctuated between feeling angrily abandoned by Dominic's relocation but also wildly relieved at times, as if happy to live without the stress of their strained existence. She had also stopped drinking and was concentrating on her fitness.

Enya wished her well, knowing herself what that feeling of abandonment was like, remembering how angry she'd been at Jonathan, and how much it had hurt. It was also clear that she might have been a symptom of Dominic's unhappy marriage, but was not the root cause. For the Sutherlands, the waning, the distance, and the slow erosion of their connection to the point where they had lost momentum and were idling, these things had occurred long before he had inadvertently bashed her car door one sunny summer day.

'Morning, Enya!'

'Oh, morning, Maeve!' She felt the hint of a blush to have been thinking about HCK at all, not that Maeve had ever professed to have or displayed any mind-reading skills, but still. 'All okay?' Her neighbour was on the path between their two houses.

'It's so bloody cold, not yet midday and it's freezing!' The older woman narrowed her shoulders and pulled her woollen scarf closer around her neck.

'*Really? Cold, you say? Well, strike me down! And here's me in my string bikini and sarong!*'

She smiled and nodded. ''Tis a bit.'

'Holly's due date then.'

'Yes, it's come around quickly, hasn't it?'

Enya was pleased to be able to chat to Maeve with such ease. The frostiness that had settled in around the time that Aiden had met Iris, when Enya had rather unforgivably showered the old lady's patio with cat turd and litter, had thawed considerably. To the point where to chat like this on the path, or in the High Street, meant anyone looking on would not suspect there had been any awkwardness at all. Time, it seemed, helped to heal old wounds and life did indeed go on.

Sadly, it wasn't the case when it came to Phil and Jenny. She and Jenny acknowledged each other with a civility that spoke of reticence on both sides. It was a great shame to have lost the comforting ease of a lovely, lovely friendship that had meant funny texts, shared laughter, and someone to chat to when her day was less than full. She missed it, missed her. Knowing her friend would find it funny to hear of her dating disasters. The blind date at the local bistro where 'Call me Maurice!' had spoken at her for two very long hours, mainly about his love of golf, his favourite golf courses, the best weather for golf and how he'd finally improved his swing. And Scott, who had turned up to the park, where the plan was to walk around the lake with his very large dog, Boomer, in tow. A dog who curled its lip any time she approached, barked at the birds who were simply minding their own business and, as a finale, did a very large turd on the footpath. It was at this point, as Scott turned to inform her that he'd forgotten the poo bags, that Enya gave her excuses, took the short cut, and made her way home. Never to see Scott or Boomer again.

Phil did his level best to ignore Enya. If they happened to be in the street at the same time, he would employ obvious, almost comical diversion strategies, designed to suggest he had no idea she was there. These included paying close attention to his phone, as if what was on the screen was of the utmost importance, whistling loudly and looking in the opposite direction, flinging his car keys in the air and concentrating hard on catching them, and – quite possibly her favourite – engaging with any stray cat, dog being walked, or bird resting on a hedge, other than be forced to acknowledge her presence. She thought he might have got on well with Scott.

Every time Phil ignored her in this way, she wondered what Jonathan would make of it. This behaviour from the man who had been his chum, the one he had eaten breakfast with before a beloved rugby match, the one he shared beers with at every summer barbecue, the one who, every time he appeared on their doorstep in his police uniform, would see her husband yell:

'No need for physical violence, put the cuffs away! I'll come quietly!' or *'They've finally caught up with me, Ens! Take the money and run!'*

She knew Jonathan would find the whole thing disappointing, as did she. It had been her quiet belief that Phil's hostility would thaw, that he would eventually become tired of having to work so hard at ignoring her, thought there might be an event, a catalyst, whereby he would simply let down his guard and they could all relax a little, but no. She had tried initiating conversation, waving from the car, smiling as she walked past, but nothing, it seemed, was going to be enough to wind back the clock on their friendship.

'And she's living back at her mum and dad's.' Maeve drew her attention, nodding her head towards their neighbours' house.

'Yes, much better for when the little one arrives and nice for Jenny to have them both so close.' Enya found a smile and showed it widely.

Maeve took a step closer and lowered her voice. 'Holly told me that Aiden said he'd pay for her to stay in the flat if she wanted, pay for her to be there with the baby, but that she'd prefer to be back home. Easier for her to set up her little business and save.'

'Yes, that's right.'

She didn't want to discuss the detail with the woman, who was, it seemed, already remarkably well informed. Holly had mentioned, during one of their catch-ups over tea, that Maeve was always full of the most probing questions. It had become less odd, opening the door to the girl without Jenny barrelling in after her, laughing at something and nothing. Enya couldn't be prouder of the girl. The business she was setting up with Columbus, the lovely American, was already showing promise.

'Well, I thought that was wonderful of him really. And I suppose things happen, don't they, Enya? People fall in and out of love and it just happens, especially when you're young.'

She knew it was as close as their neighbour was going to get to expressing understanding, even support, for her son, and it was welcomed.

'That's right, Maeve, it just happens.'

. . . *even when you're not that young.* This she kept to herself.

◆ ◆ ◆

It had been a long day at the bookshop, where she had laughed till she cried working with youngsters whose energy was infectious. Now, as the darkness drew in and the cold grey dusk threw its blanket over the street, her desire to curl up in a den and hibernate with a book was strong; she had rather learned to love the downtime, finding peace in the quiet that used to pain her. Pickle too was reluctant to head out into the wintery eve, preferring her spot on a cushion, coiled on the chair in the hallway, surveying her kingdom.

'I thought it was nice for Maeve to say that about your brother earlier.' She spoke directly to Pickle, who, as ever, ignored her.

With the small watering can in her hand, Enya paused, standing in front of the vast devil's ivy that unfortunately continued to thrive, but instead of watering it, she placed the can on the window sill and hefted the heavy pot into her arms, balancing it on her knees as she wrestled the front door open.

Carefully, she lifted it on to the front wall, and tomorrow she'd add a Post-it note, *free to good home.* The hallway seemed lighter, brighter, and she chuckled all the way up the stairs, wondering why she hadn't done it sooner.

◆　◆　◆

Whether it was the knocking on the front door or the buzzing of her phone that woke her from her slumber, it was hard to say, as both things happened simultaneously. Enya answered the call as she grabbed her warm dressing gown. 'Iris? Is everything okay?'

'Yes, we're at the front door, we've been knocking for a while, Aiden forgot his key!'

'I didn't hear! Hang on, lovey, I'm on my way.'

Mere seconds later, she opened the door to find Iris and Aiden both shivering a little, but smiling.

'What's going on?' She blinked as they walked in and headed for the kitchen.

'I'm not staying, Mum. Holly's gone into labour and so I wanted to drop Iris off here and I'm heading over to the hospital. Jenny and Phil are with her, but I thought I'd be close, sit in the waiting room.'

'Yes, of course. Oh, my goodness! That's exciting!' Her energy soared, banishing any night-time brain fog, as she pictured the little baby that was making its way into the world. 'Are you okay, Aiden?'

She didn't really know what she was asking but was aware that this was a lot, knowing that to go and sit with Phil and Jenny at this time of high emotion took some guts. Things between her son and Holly's parents were best described as civil, yet without warmth. She was thankful that the sniping and sharp intakes of breath that had occurred at the mere mention of Aiden's name had subsided.

'Yeah, bit nervous but fine. Just hope Holly's okay.'

'She's in the best place.'

Again, she had no idea if this was true, but it felt like the right thing to say. It was most odd, this high occasion, a moment she had known would come yet had been quite unable to imagine, her son dashing off to be with Holly, leaving his wife behind. Yet here they were.

'I was going to go with him, but I think it will be tense enough without throwing me into the mix.' Iris laid her hand on her husband's arm, anchoring and reassuring him with no more than the lightest of touches. It was a lovely thing to witness.

'We can have a nice cup of tea,' Enya suggested.

Yet again, Iris was handling herself with grace and wasn't allowing sentiment to cloud the practicality of what would indeed be a very tense time. Her behaviour displayed a maturity that was as impressive as it was endearing. A generosity and an understanding heart.

'See you in a bit!' Aiden planted a big kiss on his wife's cheek and smiled briefly before dashing down the path back to their car, which had been left with the doors open.

'What time is it?' Enya rubbed her face.

'A quarter to one.' Iris yawned. 'Shall I make the tea?'

'Yes, lovely.'

It felt nice, having this time alone with her daughter-in-law, who pottered in the kitchen as if it were any other day or night. The two had fallen into an easy friendship over the months, very different women but with one all-encompassing thing in common: they both loved Aiden.

'What a week!' Iris yawned once more. 'I wanted to tell you in person, my mum has met someone.'

'Met someone?' Enya was a little floored by the news.

'I'm pleased for her.' Iris nodded, her smile sincere. 'I honestly believe it's for the best, in the long run. I can see that Mum and Dad just couldn't find a way to be happy. I get it, even though for me it's the saddest thing. They had a lovely home, time that was their own, they're in good health, and yet it counted for very little. It made me think that if they can't be happy together with all of that, then they're probably better off apart.'

'Yes, it is the saddest thing. But it will all work out; these things always do.'

'It's weird for me, Enya, the next time I see Aiden, our lives will be different.'

'I guess they will.' It was hard for her to know what to say, quite unable to imagine sitting at home with Granny Brown while Jonathan went off with his ex to welcome a child. Her body gave an involuntary shiver at no more than the prospect.

'I think Aiden's very lucky to have you.'

Iris placed the teabags into the mugs and held Enya's eyeline. 'I'm lucky to have him. I thought it was all absolute fantasy, you know.'

'What?' Enya had, in her half-awake state, lost the thread a little.

'Love at first sight, that instant attraction thing, being struck by the love bug, catching Cupid's arrow, whatever you want to call it.' She pulled a face.

It made Enya laugh. 'What changed your mind?' she asked, keen to hear Iris's story, to learn a little more about her.

'I'd been going out with a guy I knew from Bath, Jake. We saw each other occasionally. He was one of those men who on paper should have been gold. Like, whoa! He was good-looking, musical, funny, loved to travel, and was lovely, he *is* lovely. But there wasn't that . . .' Iris, almost inadvertently, ran her palm over her stomach, as if this was where the magic, the whoosh, the instant and all-consuming pull of love was most felt. Right there in the base of her gut. 'That moment when I felt . . .' She sighed. 'Do you know what I mean?'

'I do,' Enya whispered, not wanting to stray into waters where she might let slip her feelings for a man Iris knew better than most.

'My friends were talking about diamonds and hen dos, only as a joke, but there was a subtlety to it, as if we were all aware that we were of that age! Jake and I weren't even exclusive or anything like that. I kept him at arm's length really, as if I knew he was only a rehearsal, and I didn't want either of us to get hurt. I said I'd see him when I got back from Rome, but I don't think I gave it that much thought. And then,' she let out a low laugh and shook her head, as if the facts were still a little hard to understand, 'I was sitting on the plane, I hate flying,' this she addressed directly to Enya, curling her top lip, 'the air was a little thick, I wasn't comfortable at all, and I remember thinking that it was only a two-and-a-half-hour flight, even I could stand that. I got my water bottle out of my bag, stowed my book in the little pocket of the seat in front, I looked out of the window at the tarmac, and I now know those were the last three things I would do as the old me. Those simple actions before my life was changed forever.'

Iris paused to pour the hot water into the mugs.

'And I guess the weirdest thing for me is that I never saw it coming. I would have thought that with a monumental change right around the corner, destiny about to smack me in the face with a plank, I would have had some kind of warning, an inkling, an idea, but no, nothing. In fact, all I was thinking about was that I'd nearly managed to get on the plane and leave my purse behind.'

Enya felt the full blush of embarrassment on her cheeks; yes, she remembered the purse incident.

'I had to call Dad, who'd dropped me off in the car park, luckily he was still there. He ran it around to the front of the airport. I dashed out from check-in to pick it up. So, that's what I was thinking about; two things really, one how disastrous my trip might have been without access to money, credit cards and all the other things that make life possible. And two, how lucky I was to have my dad. Because he's that kind of guy, Enya, he's that kind of person. He's smart and reliable. And Aiden's like that too, kind, and reliable, just ask Holly.' She let this settle but spoke without malice or irritation. 'He sat down next to me, and I could barely speak. I've never experienced anything like it. It was as if I *knew* him, there was this bizarre feeling of familiarity. Thankfully, he spoke to me, and that two-and-a-half-hour plane journey lasted about five minutes. After we landed in Rome and stood in the aisle, waiting to get off the plane, I felt this kind of panic that I might never see him again, and even though he'd told me about Holly, I stopped him and said, what do we do now?'

Enya hadn't heard this detail and was moved by the beauty of it, both respecting and envying the girl's bravery.

'He turned to me, and he said, *"we figure it out"*. That was it, we figure it out! And I didn't let go of his hand and we walked like that down the steps, through the terminal, into a cab, not wanting to let go of each other's hand, not wanting to waste a second! And it's still like that, I just want to hold his hand while we figure it all out.'

'Well, I don't know why I'm crying!' Enya swiped at the tears that had gathered. It was a heartfelt admission on this night when emotions were already running high.

'Because it's beautiful,' Iris acknowledged. 'I trust him, Enya, without doubt, I trust him.'

'This, this can't be easy for either of you, Holly having a baby. It's only been an idea up until now, but very soon, that baby will be a reality and it's not going to be easy. But I think the strength of what you share is the key to making it all work.'

Iris handed Enya a mug of tea and the two walked into the sitting room, taking a seat at either end of the sofa, sharing a closeness both physically and mentally that she could not have envisaged when they first met.

'If I had the choice, I would of course prefer that Aiden was not about to become a dad with another woman. I considered bolting when I found out. It was hard for me. But it boiled down to the most basic of things really, in that you can't help who you fall in love with, right? And I'd fallen in love with him, deeply, devotedly in love. So, the only question I had to ask myself once the shock had subsided was, would I rather be with Aiden who was going to become a dad, or would I rather wave goodbye and walk away. Did I want him, want *us*, at any cost or was him becoming a dad a cost too high to pay?'

Enya sipped her tea.

'It never felt like an option, not really. Not when I broke it down like that, because there's nothing I wouldn't sacrifice for him, even becoming a parent for the *first* time together, because that's a milestone already reached for him.'

'You're not only smart, but very generous with your love, Iris.'

'I guess I've seen my mum and dad up close for so long, I know how I want marriage to work for me.'

'I think we all do that to a degree, my parents bicker constantly. I don't think they have the first clue about how soul sapping it is to be around, how horrible for anyone in their company.'

'I might prefer it!' Iris gave a dry laugh. 'The worst thing for me was the simmering, silent animosity between my mum and dad. Sometimes Mum would yell or make a comment, but most of the time they were quietly brooding, and the atmosphere was awful. It's been that way for as long as I can remember.'

'They clearly both love you very much.' She felt the need to offer the salve.

'They do, I know that,' Iris jumped in, 'but it's still horrible, knowing they both have this incredible capacity for love, for happiness, yet they just couldn't make it work with each other.'

'I think people find fulfilment in many ways, and maybe just because one area of their lives is less than perfect . . .' She let this trail, feeling entirely uncomfortable at the topic, knowing she might have had a hand to play in Trish's brooding of recent times that Iris had found so interminable.

'When I was sixteen, my friend gave me these incredible shoes,' Iris smiled at no more than the memory, 'high heels, with an open toe and a dainty bar across the instep. I loved them. They'd been her mum's and were a size five. I'm a six, but my brain refused to accept that they did not and would never fit me. I tried forcing them on to my feet, cut my foot actually. I steamed them to stretch them. I dieted, thinking I might be able to shrink my feet. I put plasters on my toes and tried to stuff them in. I even sat one night with a pair of scissors.'

'You weren't going to snip off a toe or two? No shoe is worth that!'

Iris laughed. 'No, but I thought I might be able to make a few incisions in the leather to allow them to stretch, which of course would have ruined them entirely.'

Enya thought of that one night, the memory of which she had shared with Dominic: her Mallorcan adventure, when she had felt trendy and go-getting with the aid of her sister's stolen silver platforms.

'I got a bit obsessed until I woke up one day and realised there would be other shoes. I took them out of my wardrobe and put them in the charity shop in town. They went straight into the window, looking beautiful! And I remember feeling relief that the problem had gone away, but also good that someone else with size five feet would probably love them very much. It also made me think of my mum and dad, holding on to things that weren't good for them, a relationship that wasn't healthy. Even then I could see that, like those shoes and my feet, they just didn't fit.'

Enya remembered the way it had felt to fall into Dominic's arms, even if only briefly. The utter peace she had felt at the contact and the way they had fitted together perfectly.

'So what do we know about your mum's new man?'

'Not much, he's called Neil and likes running and yoga. That's all I got.'

'I'm pleased for her, Iris.'

'Me too,' she managed, before yawning. She placed the half-drunk mug of tea on the end table.

Enya grabbed the soft blanket from the arm of the sofa and spread it over the young woman's legs, watching as she snuggled down and rested her head on the cushion, her eyes fluttering as the day and night caught up with her and sleep claimed her.

'Sweetest dreams,' she whispered, hoping the words might land in her ear.

Enya finished her tea and lay back on the sofa, resting her eyes, just for a second, so happy that she and Iris had shared this closeness and that her approach to the new baby meant it might just all work out after all . . .

When she came to and glanced at her phone, it was a quarter to five in the morning. Iris was deep in sleep. Not wanting to wake her, Enya carefully stood and closed the sitting-room door, before quietly creeping into the kitchen.

Frustratingly, she saw she had a missed call from Aiden an hour ago. He hadn't left a message. She was silently debating whether to call him back and risk interruption of any kind, and thinking about what might be best to text him, when she heard a faint tap on the front door. She walked softly along the hallway, wanting to let Iris rest, before opening the door to her son, who had clearly been crying.

'Darling!'

She opened her arms as Aiden stepped up into the hallway and let himself be held. Enya's heart raced, trying not to jump ahead, her gut a jumble of nerves as she tried to work out if they were happy or sad tears. Eventually, he pulled away, wiped his face on the sleeve of his jacket and, following her lead, tiptoed into the kitchen. Here, too, she quietly closed the door. Aiden spoke, instantly putting her out of her misery.

'A little girl. We've got a little girl, Amelia Jennifer Enya Brown. Seven pounds, three ounces. Mother and baby are doing well.'

His words sounded a little rehearsed as they coasted out on a wave of pure emotion.

'Oh, Aiden!' Enya placed her hand over her mouth and tried to order the complex range of emotions, but delight at the fact her name would form part of this little girl's identity was certainly right up there.

'She's beautiful, absolutely beautiful. Holly was amazing – I mean, really incredible.'

'Were you with her?'

He nodded. 'Didn't think I would be, but it all felt very natural. She wanted me to go in and I'm glad I did. It was a privilege and wonderful and overwhelming and a million other things!' His tears came again, and he pinched his nose.

'What did Jenny and Phil say?'

'Oh, they're beside themselves, as you can imagine. Jenny was in the room with us, Phil was close by. When I left, he was holding Amelia.'

'Amelia.' She tested out the name that had already been used a couple of times, the name of a little person who had newly arrived on the planet, her granddaughter! It was surreal, she couldn't wait to meet her, spend time with her! 'I'm so excited!'

'I wish Dad—' He broke away, no need to expand on the words that she felt keenly.

'I know.' She closed her eyes for a second.

'She's got hair, Mum, lots of dark hair!' He reached for his phone.

'Oh my God! You took pictures!' In the shock and surprise, she'd forgotten this would be a thing.

Aiden opened his phone and handed it to her, his smile wide as he flicked through, refreshing his memory with the images of his daughter.

Enya gasped. There she was. A tiny blanket-wrapped bundle of perfection with lots of dark hair and a tiny rosebud mouth.

'You had hair like that.' She sniffed.

'Your hair!' He laughed.

'Yes!' She smiled, knowing Amelia would likely spend her teenage years wrestling with her mop, before coming to love her wild hair in her twenties, when her confidence would bloom; hair that Jonathan had loved, and how he would have loved this little one.

'I need to sit down.' Aiden seemed to sway a little and took a seat at the kitchen table, where he put his elbows on the table and rested his head in his hands. 'I'm exhausted.'

'I bet you are. Do you want something to eat?'

'No,' he shook his head, 'maybe later.'

Enya took the seat opposite him. 'Iris is asleep on the sofa, you can either join her or go up to bed for a bit?'

'I feel strange,' he whispered.

'You're bound to.'

He looked up at her, his eyes tired and red, yet with a sparkle of delight to them. 'I loved Amelia the moment I saw her, felt like I wanted to protect her always, want to be there for her.'

'Yes, it doesn't go away, that feeling.'

'I'm trying to get it all straight in my head.' Aiden bit his lip; blinking hard, he rubbed his eyes. 'I love my wife,' he whispered.

'I know that.' She reached out and briefly squeezed his arm.

'But I love Holly too, how can I not? I've always loved her and now she's given me Amelia,' he gulped.

Enya felt her stomach jump, wondering where this was heading, fearing the turmoil his words might unleash. She stared at him, unwilling to offer comment until he had finished.

'I love them both. But I don't love Holly in the way that you need to for a marriage to work. I just don't. Not in the way I love Iris.'

Love but not in love . . . a phrase that both Dominic and Trish had used in confidence.

'Right.' Enya exhaled, unaware that she'd been holding her breath.

'Do you think it's possible to love two people at the same time in two completely different ways?' he asked, with so much hope it was quite moving.

Enya pictured Jonathan, her beloved husband, who would have so relished this day, Amelia Jennifer Enya Brown's birthday! And Dominic, who she still liked to picture the first time she saw him, in his jeans, navy long-sleeved T-shirt, and that beautiful song playing on his car stereo. The words of which had taken on even more significance since Aiden and Iris's wedding day.

'I do, my love. I honestly do.'

'Aiden!' Iris called as she ran into the kitchen. 'I didn't hear you come back!'

Enya watched as he jumped up to embrace her.

'What did we get?' Iris asked, while gripping him tightly, and Aiden held the back of her head in his palm.

'We got a little girl, Amelia, and she's perfect.'

'Of course she is.' Iris kissed his face. 'Congratulations, my love.'

Enya looked away, as if the interaction was not something she should be witnessing. Another life-altering minute that would shape this young couple, laying good foundations for a lovely future.

A knock at the front door drew them all.

'It's like Piccadilly Circus!' She tried to lighten the atmosphere as she went to get the door.

Her heart thudded in anticipation when she saw that Phil was standing on the step.

'Enya!' he almost shouted, even though they were no more than feet apart, his grin wide, his hands joined together as if in prayer. 'Oh, my Lord, you should see her! She's beautiful! Absolutely beautiful! A little smasher! And Holly was a bloody superstar. I can't believe she's here! I'm a grandad! You're a gran!'

'Yes!' She smiled. 'I am.'

'I've left Jen with the girls, she's a wreck, of course! But what a day, Ens! What a day!' Phil took a step inside, and Enya stood back to let him pass. 'What would Jonathan make of all this, eh?'

'He'd be over the moon, Phil.'

He reached out and placed his hand on her arm, the man who had been her husband's good pal, her friend too, and who now saw the occasion of their granddaughter's birth as a catalyst, an opportunity to turn back the clock. A chance to recapture the closeness they had shared, to reach out the hand of love and friendship, and make sure that the safety net that would hold

Amelia fast was strong and reliable. A safety net that would be there for all of them, each holding a corner, with space enough for any of them to take a rest should the need arise.

'I've got loads of photos!' Phil took his phone from his pocket and made his way into the kitchen.

Aiden released Iris from his embrace and reached for her hand. 'Phil, this is Iris.'

'Pleased to meet you, love.' Phil smiled directly at her, before turning to Enya. The interaction she had been quietly dreading was speedily done, over, and had passed without anguish. 'He did good today. That boy of ours. He did really good.'

Enya swallowed the lump of emotion that had risen in her throat. There it was, confirmation that her son was back in the fold, forgiven, and with it, she felt the encircling arms of the street of her community around her, holding her tight. 'Cup of tea, Phil?'

She went over to the kettle, glad of the diversion and the opportunity to gather herself, welcoming the three minutes it would buy her.

Phil studied the pictures on his phone and did his best to halt the tears that gathered. 'Ooh yes please, Jen said she'd come straight here when she leaves the hospital.'

'Right.'

She felt the rise of joy in her stomach, *my friend is coming here . . . my very best friend . . .*

'Couple of rounds of toast wouldn't go amiss, Ens!' Phil shouted.

Enya laughed and went into the larder to fetch the bread.

Chapter Thirty-Five

Enya lay back in her bath and let the bubble-filled water warm her limbs. There was something about a hot bath on a cold night that felt extremely indulgent and the most luxurious thing. It had been quite a day. Aiden and Iris had left shortly before midday, heading home via the hospital so they could see Amelia.

She had worried about what the presence of Iris at the hospital might mean, concerned that the love and camaraderie that had wrapped them all that morning might only have been a hiatus as they were all swept up in the moment, and that in the cold light of calmness, Aiden's welcoming back into the fold, and certainly his wife's appearance, might have been a little less convivial.

The photographs that pinged repeatedly as they arrived on her phone allayed all of her fears. There was Holly, holding her baby. She looked tired, but her expression was close to rapture; then another of Holly and Amelia with Aiden and Iris on either side. One picture of Aiden holding his baby girl, gazing into her eyes, was the first she decided to have framed, and then another of Iris with her stepdaughter and a wide smile on her face, and finally one of Holly, staring at her daughter as if she had won the greatest prize.

The photos were lovely, more than she could ever have hoped for; they were in fact everything. She couldn't wait for tomorrow when she got to meet Amelia for herself.

Jenny had arrived, walking slowly into the house, before the two women stood in the hallway wrapped in a warm and lingering embrace. Each holding tightly on to the other, as if relieved to have found their anchor, something to hold on to when for the longest time they had been adrift. It was only when they let each other go that Jenny smiled up at her. 'Hello Nan.'

'Hello Nan!' she echoed.

Her phone, now resting on the sink, buzzed. It was no doubt Aiden, Phil or Jenny with a tiny update, not that she minded, any detail could feed her thoughts for hours. Stretching her arm, she managed to reach the phone. Without her glasses on, it was hard to make out the number.

'Hello?' she said as she lay back beneath the water, smiling, waiting to hear another breathless account of the little girl's perfection, and her heart sang!

'Enya, Enya, hi. It's Dominic.'

She felt her body shudder at the sound of his voice, sending goose bumps across her skin. She sat up and leaned on the back of the bath. This the first contact they had had since their kids' wedding day, when they had, after baring their souls, studiously kept out of each other's way.

'Oh, hello!'

'It's been a while.' He kept his voice low, and she wondered where he was and if he was wary of being overheard, instantly wondering if he, like Trish, had found someone. The bile of envy tasted sour.

'Yes, it has.' She moved in the bath and the water sloshed around her.

'Ah, forgive me, it seems I've interrupted you again as you're making pasta!' He laughed gently.

'You have, actually.' She smiled, delighted, and perturbed by how easily his words, his manner and any shared recollection pulled her into his thrall. How effortlessly they slipped into conversation.

'I spoke to Iris; she tells me that congratulations are in order.'

'Yes, a little girl, Amelia.'

'Well, that's all good. Have you seen her yet?'

'No, tomorrow. Can't wait.' She felt her muscles tense in excitement at the prospect.

'I bet. And Aiden and Iris seem to be handling it well, taking it in their stride.' His words a reminder that they were joined together by these kids and would always be on the lookout for them.

'I think they're remarkable.'

'Me too.'

'And Holly, all three of them. It's not an easy thing to navigate.'

There was a pause, as if both aware that when there were three with a vested interest, three people with a heart connection, it was often far, far from easy. It was as if now the pleasantries were out of the way, the conversation could turn to matters of a more personal nature.

'How have you been?' he asked softly.

They were four simple enough words and yet the answer was anything but. How had she been? She had been thoughtful, determined, proactive, busy, and happy!

'I've been good, actually, better. No more panic attacks.' She updated the one person she had confided in.

'That's good! Really, really good . . .' He faltered. 'You sound settled.'

'I am,' she answered with confidence. 'Is everything okay, Dominic? I guess I'm just wondering about the reason for the call.

Not that it isn't lovely to hear from you, it is, but I can't imagine you just calling to congratulate me on the birth of Amelia.'

'No, not the only reason, you're right, but it felt like a good opportunity. The real reason is, I wanted to tell you something.'

'What did you want to tell me?' She held the phone close her face, listening intently.

'I wanted to tell you that *Foula Girl* is finished.'

'Well, that's, that's really something. I know it's been a labour of love for the longest time.'

'She's been more than that, actually. She's been a lifeline, a distraction when I needed it most. Something to pour all my energies into, something that's given me hope.'

'I'm glad for you, Dominic, happy that you've had her to rely on.' *At a time when you were lonely and struggling, something I entirely understand . . .*

It was her unspoken words that rang louder.

'That's the thing about a boat or car or a plane when it's a restoration project, it's not only about the hours you spend completing fiddly, time-consuming and sometimes utterly draining projects, it's not even about the nights you spend dreaming about how she'll look or what it will feel like to travel in her. No, it's much more than that. It's about a promise, a promise of escape and the fact that the thing you're lovingly investing your time in is the thing that will take you away from whatever it is you need to run from, whatever it is you're trying to escape. And that car or that boat, they become intrinsic to the plan, to your dream. I'm sure I'm not the only one who tells *Foula Girl* what's in my thoughts, what my plans are, she knows it all.'

'What are you trying to escape from?' She asked the question already able to at least half guess at the answer.

'My old life. The way I've been living for so long, the dissatisfying drudge. I've told you before, I'm sick of running away from everything, sick of hiding, sick of everything being just about good enough. Instead, I'm going to start running towards things, running towards the horizon. Running towards my future. Running towards a life that I believe I'm owed! A life I'm still young enough to enjoy.'

'Well, I for one wish you nothing but success and happiness, Dominic. I hope you find what you're looking for, and I hope all that running doesn't tire you out so much that you don't have time to enjoy the journey.'

A journey that I once thought I might take with you, oh lovely man. But one that I believe comes at a cost that is too high for our wonderful children to pay . . .

She heard the brief flare of his laughter and pictured him smiling in the way that he did, and her heart flexed at the memory of it.

'Did you hear that Trish has met someone?'

'Iris mentioned something. When did it . . . Is he . . . I mean, you don't have to talk about it, don't have to give me the details. It's none of my business, after all, nothing to do with me.' She wondered for whose benefit she had added the last sentence.

'I want to talk to you about it. I want to give you the details, it's important that you know.'

Enya listened intently as he quietly spoke words edged with emotion.

'She's seeing a guy she met online, met him not long after the kids' wedding actually, but has kept things quiet, kept it to herself for obvious reasons.'

'And how do you feel about it?' She cringed, unsure if this was the right thing to ask. It felt like a loaded question.

'I feel strangely sad, because it makes everything final. It takes us to that next phase, and an ending of anything is always a hard thing, even if it's something you've longed for. Change isn't easy for us humans.'

Enya made a murmur of agreement; wasn't that the truth.

'I feel happy too, because I want the best for her, she deserves happiness. It's the new start we both need, the momentum we've been looking for. He seems like a reasonable man; he makes her laugh and sounds solid and decent. But there's also this tiny bit of jealousy, which I know is ridiculous! I don't even know if I should be saying it out loud, but he's going to live in the house I designed and built, and even though our marriage is dead in the water, she's been my wife for a very long time. She'll always be the mother of my child, and so yes, a tiny sliver of jealousy. Is that odd?'

'No, I think it's honest.' She liked his openness.

'The point is, Enya, what I want to say is,' he hesitated, 'I'm going to run towards the life I want, and I want you to run towards it with me!'

She let out a burst of laughter, surprised, flattered and utterly unprepared for the sudden request. It was what he did, went from nought to a hundred with an enthusiasm that was infectious.

'You want me to take your hand and you want us to figure it out . . .'

'Yes! That's exactly what I want. I'm launching *Foula Girl* in the next week or so and then I'm going. I'm actually going! I can't tell you how long this has been in the planning in my imaginings, and the fact that it's arrived is like a dream come true. I feel happy! But I know I'd be a whole lot happier if you were to come with me. I think about you all the time, have done since the day in the car park.'

Her second snort of laughter was almost a visceral reaction. He made her self-conscious and elated all at once.

'Please, Enya, please just say yes, lock up the house, let someone look after Pickle, pack a small bag and come and jump on this boat with me, come and jump on this adventure with me!'

'Sail off into the sunset.' He made it sound so simple, when the reality was anything but; how on earth would Aiden and Iris react? And what of the life she had built here, her new job, feeling more at ease in her neighbourhood, the ebb of her paralysing grief for Jonathan, and now the chance to rebuild bridges with Jenny and Phil. She smiled to think how far she had come since the dark days of panic and fear at what the future might hold, not to mention the arrival of Amelia.

'Yes! Sail off into the bloody sunset, why not?'

'Because . . .' Enya took her time, knowing her words were some of the hardest she would ever have to deliver, knowing that to speak her truth meant hurting someone who was very important to her, someone who had the potential, in fact, to be everything, 'because Holly has just had a baby. Because Aiden and Iris are newly married. Because I have responsibilities to these people and because I love my home, love my life!'

'What, and you can't dispense your wisdom from a boat? You can't be on the end of a line twenty-four-seven to answer any queries or be there with words of encouragement? You can't do that while at the same time finding your own path to happiness? It sounds a lot like self-imposed martyrdom when you put it like that.'

'And when *you* put it like that, Dominic, it lets *me* know that you don't truly understand my role here. Yes, I can be on the end of a phone, but that won't help when Holly needs a babysitter or to escape from her parents or to take a moment of rest. Yes, I can dispense wisdom to Aiden down the phone, but it won't let me look in his eyes and understand that what he's saying and what he's feeling are very often not the same two things. Our kids are young and fresh and trying to figure so much out. I need to be here. More than that, I want to be here! I really do!'

'I think, Enya Brown, that you and I could be one of the great love stories. I think we could make each other incredibly happy for the rest of our lives and these kids on this new adventure – that's the short term. They won't always need you in the way that you see it, not like they do now.'

'Then I guess I'll have to rethink my life as I go along, won't I, and I'm prepared to do that, Dominic.'

My hand firmly on the tiller . . .

'And I wonder where I'll be then. Wherever it is, know that I'll be thinking of you.'

The way he softly whispered this made *her* wonder if he had said this aloud or whether she'd actually imagined it.

'Right, I have to go, Dominic, I have to go.' The weight of his words fell heavily on her shoulders; she had heard enough.

'I'll think about you, Enya. I'll think about you often. Every time I see a perfect sunset, every time I wake to a crimson dawn on a day full of promise, I will know that the only way it could be bettered was if you were by my side. I think I could love you, love you deeply . . .'

Enya held her breath. He had said it, broken the boundary, smashed the glass and let the words fly high above them, from which there was no going back.

'It's you and me, Enya B, us against the world!'

'Actually no, that's,' he sounded a little angry, frustrated, 'I *know* I could love you. I know it, and the fact that we can't be together for whatever reason, whatever blocks you're putting in our way, feels like the cruellest punishment.'

Enya could barely speak. He didn't get it, didn't understand the havoc such a love, were it allowed to flourish, would wreak on their children! It was a complication she could not, would not bring to their door. His words, however, she would replay when she woke on a cold winter's morning and pictured him staring at a perfect sunset or waking to the crimson dawn on a day full of promise.

'Goodbye, Dominic.' Her voice no more than a scratched whisper, clawing its way from her distressed throat. 'Goodbye . . .'

Chapter Thirty-Six

Enya leaned back against the wall, creating as much space as possible as Holly walked in with possibly the most ornate cake she had ever seen. The girl had made it herself, obviously, and it was worthy of a place on any shelf in the finest patisserie imaginable. The kind of cake Enya liked to ogle on her fancy cake programmes. It was Holly's way; she had a gift, presenting everything she made with so much love and care.

'You are such a clever girl, Holly!' Maeve called out from her comfy chair in the corner of Jenny's kitchen.

Columbus, who it seemed found nearly everything funny, laughed as he clapped. He put Enya in mind of a golden retriever, in that he had an abundance of blond hair and was never in bad humour. She liked him enormously. They all did, Holly included . . .

Holly's meticulous attention to detail certainly seemed to be a contributing factor to the fabulous homewares and lifestyle website she and Columbus had set up, which was proving to be extremely popular. Enya had even made a couple of purchases, including the fancy-pants collar that Madam Pickle Paws now wore around her neck.

Phil whooped and hollered his delight at the sight of the cake, made for Amelia's 'welcome to the world' party. Angela and Frank, Aiden and Iris too, all looked on with delight, utterly besotted with the beautiful baby girl who was pure magic! She had brought love, light and joy when they had needed it most.

The plan was for Enya and Jenny to each look after her one day a week, but the two had already discussed how they might spend these days together, sharing the childcare while taking it in turns to tempt her with glorious morsels for lunch, reading her books, washing her little clothes, and letting her rest within their warm embrace. The little girl felt like the glue that would repair the cracks in their lovely friendship. A friendship she truly relished and one, having tasted life without, Enya knew she would cherish, as they healed together.

The biggest surprise to her was Iris, her beloved daughter-in-law. Iris was a generous spirit; her kind nature and her unconditional love of Aiden meant she built a bridge that led to Amelia with every word she spoke and everything she did. Enya was beyond thankful for her, understanding how a young woman of a different nature might have made things far less harmonious.

Trish had only recently, and surprisingly, become engaged. According to Iris, the teetotal couple seemed to enjoy nothing more than attending exotic yoga retreats, and then holding dinner parties during which they could tell you in great, great detail all about their latest adventure. And where they served bright beets, scarlet peppers, turmeric-scented dhals and any number of healthy dishes that could, with no more than one small slip of a spoon, stain a pristine kitchen if you weren't careful.

She hadn't heard from Dominic since that night last month when he'd been about to launch *Foula Girl*, chasing his dreams and following his path to happiness. Not that she didn't think about him from time to time, of course she did, and suspected she always would. But the fact was her life was here, here with these people with whom she mattered, all staring at her beloved granddaughter, who was passed around, sleeping soundly, wrapped tightly in a blanket of adoration.

'I'll cut the cake!' Jenny called as she grabbed the knife from the utensil pot, before she and Holly grappled with the vast confection, taking it to a safe spot on the counter.

'A big piece for me!' Angela yelled. Enya shot her a look. 'What?' Her sister pulled a face. 'It's not every day I become a great-aunt!'

Iris came and stood next to Enya, while Phil and Aiden did as they often did, sat in front of Amelia, staring at her as if they still couldn't quite believe that this little angel was real and was theirs.

Iris nudged her with her elbow. 'One month old, can you believe it, Granny Brown?'

Enya laughed at the nickname, which she knew Iris and Aiden had picked just to annoy her. She refused to rise to the bait. 'It's gone quickly.'

'It has. And I wanted to say,' Iris licked her lips, 'you know we're okay, don't you?'

'Yes.' She studied her daughter-in-law's face. 'I know you're okay. Is this your way of telling me you're *not* okay? Because it's an odd thing to say, so now you've got me worried! Should I be worried?'

Iris laughed out loud. 'I'm saying we're *all* okay.'

'Well, good.' Enya stared at her, waiting for her to get to the point.

'I remember when I was learning to ride a bike, I was about five, Dad bought me a fabulous little pink bike with a basket on the front, streamers on the handles and stabilisers. I took to it like a duck to water, riding up and down the drive, going around and around inside the house, which was a building site in those days, but I absolutely loved it! That taste of freedom, I felt like I could go anywhere, see anything, be anything! It was just brilliant.'

Enya narrowed her eyes at her daughter-in-law. 'I feel like there's a moral message here, some kind of allegorical tale developing, and I'm waiting for it to land.'

'And you'd be correct.' Iris smiled at her. 'Dad wanted to take the stabilisers off, and my mum railed against it, *'No way!'* she yelled. *'She's too little, she'll fall over! She'll scrape a knee, break a bone, go through a window!'* I just remember all these terrible scenarios being bandied about, making me feel scared – was that what would happen if my stabilisers came off? My dad went along with it for a while, but I was getting faster and faster, and more and more impatient, until one day he took the bike to the garage with me following him. And he pulled those training wheels off. He put them in a box, and he said, *'You don't need these, Iris, you're going to fly!'* I got on the bike, and he was holding on to the back of the seat. I remember how it felt very different. Initially, I lost quite a lot of my confidence – gone was that feeling of invincibility, like I could go anywhere, and take on the world. I felt a little anxious, a little wobbly, but I was okay, because my dad had his hand on the back of that seat, and I knew as long as he didn't let go I was always going to be all right and we raced up and down the drive, which is quite a way.'

Enya laughed. She'd been along that driveway, and it was quite a way. The thought of an exhausted Dominic running with one hand on the bike was funny.

'Then after a few turns, I looked around to smile at my dad, and realised he wasn't holding on anymore, and I don't think he'd been holding on for quite some time. I hadn't noticed. I was just flying! Going along on my own, at my own pace, free! And it felt wonderful.'

Enya noted the glint of tears in Iris's eyes and sidled closer to the girl she loved.

'I realised years later that the reason my mum wanted me to keep those wheels on was only in part because she thought I might break a bone or go through a window. It was far more about keeping me little, keeping me small.'

They both almost instinctively looked over at Amelia.

'She didn't want me to grow up that quickly. She wanted me to be dependent on those training wheels, wanted, I guess, for me to be dependent on her, she loved me that much, I was her purpose.'

'Okay,' Enya nodded, 'I understand the analogy. I can even imagine the scene. And you are one of the most beautiful and independent, free-thinking, strongest women I've ever met. It's my pleasure to know you, and an even greater pleasure that you're married to my son. I guess what I'm struggling with here, darling,' it was her turn to nudge the girl with her elbow, 'is where the moral message for me is among all this? Are you saying I should get a bike?'

Iris turned to face her. Her voice was low, her tone level. 'I spoke to my dad.'

'Oh! Good, good! How is he?'

Iris held her gaze. 'I spoke to him about you.'

Enya felt her legs sway a little; she took a stuttered breath and shrank back against the wall, grateful of the support.

'He told me how he felt, told me that there was this, this spark between you, Enya.'

'I don't . . .' She shook her head; it was exposing and embarrassing and all the things she had worked so hard to avoid. 'I . . .'

'Please, please don't deny it. If it was a terrible issue, or a bad thing in my view, do you think I'd mention it?'

Enya undid the top button of her blouse and pushed up the sleeves of her Fair Isle jersey, suddenly feeling a little too hot as she struggled for breath. 'Nothing, nothing happened, it was just, I don't know how to describe it.'

'I think it's an opportunity, Enya, for you both. For two of the people AJ and I love most in the world. It could be wonderful, we just want you both to be happy. No, *more* than that, you both deserve to be happy.'

Enya wondered if she might actually faint.

'Dad told me he's carried you in his thoughts since he first met you.'

'He, erm, I don't know what to say.' Enya ran out of words and fanned her face with her hand.

'I believe him, I think whether you're present or not, he's thinking of you. So I guess my question is, are you ready to take off your stabilisers? Are you ready to chuck in your training wheels?'

'I don't know,' she whispered, staring at the girl who was encouraging her to seek out her happiness. 'The last thing I want is to make life difficult for you and Aiden. Supposing, supposing I did take off my training wheels and crashed and burned, what does our family life look like then? What would happen at Christmas, birthdays, all the times we would have to be together, it would be excruciating!' She spoke quickly, as flustered as she was overwhelmed.

'I can't imagine, Enya,' Iris levelled, 'I can't imagine having to spend time in the company of a couple who once shared something but had to find a way to make it work when it all fell apart. Nope, I can't imagine it at all.'

Enya watched as Iris raised her glass of water towards Aiden in salute, who winked at her in return as he turned to chat to Holly and Columbus. It struck her then that these youngsters who she had felt instinctively she needed to protect at all costs, they could actually teach her a thing or two. They were marvellous. She felt the flare of emotion in her throat and a tingling in her toes at just the possibility of chasing that kind of love.

'You are so very wise, Iris Brown.'

'I am. And I'm saying that you can let go of the saddle now, because we're not going to fall, Aiden, Holly and I, we're going to be okay, and you're going to be okay, I promise you.'

Enya stared at the girl, letting her words settle. It was a thought as scary as it was exciting, the prospect that she might actually be free to run towards the horizon.

'I don't know what to say to you, Iris. I just don't know what to say.' She felt a little dizzy as her head swam; it was a lot to digest.

'You don't have to say anything, just promise me you'll think about it. And even if my dad is not the answer. Even if he's not what you're looking for. Even if the timing is wrong for you both, or you've had a change of heart, or he's had a change of heart, that's not really the point.'

'Isn't it?' she asked, genuinely perplexed now.

'No. You've come so far, even in the short time I've known you, I can't imagine what it must have been like having your life turned upside down, losing Jonathan. But it's about finding the courage, Enya, it's about finding the courage to begin this next chapter.'

'I've never been overly courageous.'

'I don't believe that, not for a minute. You've never once not been there for Aiden or me or Holly, or Amelia, never judging, always positive and honest! I think you're quite wonderful.'

'I would hate Trish to think—'

'It's irrelevant what my mum thinks,' Iris interrupted, 'she's happy, and she will be happy, no matter what. Whether Neil is forever or not, she's finally found her stride and if that all goes pear-shaped, then she will have to pick herself up and dust herself off, it's what we do.'

'I really hope you're right.' She pictured the woman on the path in her beautiful teal coat dress who had cried and spoken so openly.

'She's at the beginning, when everything feels possible. But it doesn't last, does it? The gloss quickly wears off and you realise that marriage is not all you thought it was cracked up to be, not all you thought it might be, all it could be, and it's bloody disappointing . . .'

Enya knew it would take a while to let the words her daughter-in-law had spoken permeate. Words that effectively stripped her of her last coat of armour, the protective shields she wore around her heart and her body. This was why she had held back, fear of making life complicated for these very smart kids, and letting Jonathan down, of devaluing their precious love by moving on.

'Where have you always wanted to go, Enya?'

'Oh, well, lots of lovely places. Jonathan and I used to travel a lot and always had our next trip lined up, he'd even booked something, but we never got there.'

'That's a shame.'

'Mmm . . .' She nodded. 'Jonathan was always a great organiser, he liked to pair the food with the place we were going, he'd even look at the menus of restaurants we might visit and choose what he was going to have before we'd even set foot in the country! It was quite comforting knowing what was ahead of me, knowing what the plan was.'

This metaphor for life wasn't lost on her.

'You should go. You should go and see some of those lovely places.' Iris spoke with conviction.

'What, just pack a bag and up sticks?'

Iris pulled a face and nodded. 'Yes. That's exactly what you should do. Aiden and I can come and stay here while you're away – to be honest, you'd be doing us a favour. I don't want to hear one more tip from Neil on how I can get more protein into my diet, and the sight of my mother doing the downward dog on the terrace in all weathers is enough to put Aiden off his muesli. Plus, we can then look after Pickle, and Aiden will be down the road from Holly and Amelia.'

'It sounds like you've given it quite a lot of thought.'

'Not at all. It's just popped into my head!'

'You're a terrible liar, Iris Brown.'

'I am,' Iris admitted, 'and so are you.'

The two women shared a knowing look. And it was in this moment that Enya felt the pull on her back at the spread of her wings, as slowly she rose from the ashes, feeling a new wave of energy. A shift had occurred, and she felt imbued by the courage to finally take flight.

'I have a map, Enya.'

'Oh? What kind of map?'

'A map with all the places my dad will be visiting and when he will be there. An itinerary, if you will.'

She couldn't help the tears that found their way to her cheeks, it was overwhelming. 'You do?'

'I do.' Iris leaned over and kissed her warmly on the cheek.

'Cake!' Holly yelled as she shoved a large plate with a gargantuan wedge of lemon drizzle on it under Iris's nose.

'Oh God, Holly, do you know what, I'm not being rude, but for some reason I am completely off lemon. I mean, I *love* lemon! I love the smell, the taste, I love everything about lemons, but just recently, even the smell, I mean, just the sight of that cake, it makes me want to throw up!' Iris pulled a disgusted face and placed her hand on her stomach.

Holly pulled the plate away and stared at Enya. 'Is that right?' she asked with a sly smile around her mouth. 'You'll have some, won't you, Enya.'

She took the plate. 'I will, my darling, you are the most sublime baker. I do love you. I do love you both.' Her words coasted on a sweet river of emotion, recognising how very lucky she was.

The girls smiled at each other, one of them more knowingly than the other, as Iris sipped at her glass of water, trying to get rid of whatever was ailing her. Enya beamed at Amelia, knowing that to have a sister or brother so close in age would be the most marvellous thing.

Iris went to stand next to Aiden, who was chatting to Columbus, while Phil tucked into his cake. Enya looked around the room, taking in these people who made up her small circle. Her friends, her family. And as Holly placed a plate in front of Maeve, and Iris palmed circles on Aiden's back, and Jenny rushed over with a napkin to wipe Amelia's face, and Angela filled her cheeks with cake, and Frank laughed at her antics, she realised that Iris was right: whether she was here or not, they would all be fine.

Absolutely fine.

Epilogue

It was early evening, and to walk in the warmer climate, having left the spring frost of Blighty behind, felt like such a treat, as if to be in sunshine was doubly welcome when everyone else was reaching for bed socks and hot-water bottles. She could see why her parents loved this country. It had been nice to see them, although how Angela managed a full month in their company was beyond her. An angel indeed.

'Don't lie in the sun! You'll only go pink and peel! And don't leave any sandwiches in your backpack, take it from one who knows.' Angela's kindly parting advice. It made her laugh even now.

It had been a wrench to leave Amelia, knowing that any time away and she would miss the changes that seemed to occur daily. Holly had promised to keep her up to date with pictures galore and FaceTime calls whenever she fancied.

Iris too had promised to let her know when her morning sickness subsided. It was beyond thrilling, another baby on the way! Trish was beside herself, on the phone several times a day with ideas on everything from nursery décor to a birth plan. Not that Enya begrudged her a moment of it, understanding the incredible, life-changing thing it was when your baby had a baby. A thing that meant the world to her and Jenny, a special bond they shared.

Aiden had driven her to the airport, arriving early to pick her up. He had beeped the horn. 'Get a wiggle on! We need to go!' he yelled through the car window, and, 'What'll happen if you miss your flight?'

'I'll just get the next one.'

She'd beamed at him, this boy of theirs who made her proud every day, a wonderful man, a great dad and so, so in love with Iris, it warmed her heart to see.

Her stomach now rolled with anticipation, proud of herself, having successfully booked her trip, jumped on a plane. She had even managed to shut the overhead locker and grab a cab, all without Jonathan by her side; she felt invigorated, strong!

With her blue silk espadrilles in one hand and her knapsack in the other, she walked barefoot along the edge of the Marina de Vilamoura on Portugal's Algarve coast, breathing in the heady scent of this place where inland its history could be seen in every gnarled brick, every inch of cobbled floor and on every fresco of a saint that adorned the walls. Here, restaurants aplenty, all with outside seating, were starting to fill up for those looking for a late lunch, and the hum of conversation and the smell of food was strangely welcoming.

It took her back to that one night when she was seventeen, and rather than sit indoors and watch her sister's face turn grey, she had gone out on her own. Her sister might not have been smart when it came to ancient ham sandwiches, but the words she'd spoken to Holly played in Enya's thoughts.

You get burned but you emerge from the ashes stronger than you ever thought possible . . . and when you do, you will not only have found strength, but power too. A woman who has gone through this is metamorphosed and the version of her who comes after takes no shit. She knows herself and she will never be beholden to anyone, she will never again put responsibility for her own happiness in the pocket of another. She is self-reliant and knowing.'

How she loved this thought, a woman who was metamorphosed, as without her training wheels she ventured forth.

The sound of a guitar being played beautifully filled the air. She was alert, energised and alive, in the way it felt when you were about to test yourself but come out the other side with a feeling of having achieved something. Like standing on a ledge with the sparkling water below, knowing the swim will be worth finding the courage to jump.

You would have loved this . . . She spoke to Jonathan in her mind.

Looking up, she took in the big, big sky, feeling free, free, and happy. Her pace was measured as she strolled along the marina, taking in the tall masts of the ships, the varied ensigns fluttering in the breeze and the sound of the water lapping at the dock.

It was as if she sensed his presence before she saw him, standing at the back of his beautiful wooden boat, concentrating on coiling a rope and laying it flat on the aft deck. She looked at the bigger, more modern yachts between which he was moored.

'Excuse me,' she called, 'but I was just wondering, are you going to be able to manoeuvre out of this spot? It's just that I seem to remember you're not too good at judging distances, especially when trying to move into or out of a parking space, a one-second lapse in concentration and bam! Who knows what might happen?'

Enya felt the breath catch in her throat as he whipped his head around and stared at her.

'Enya . . .' he breathed, and there it was, that pull of desire deep in her gut.

Calmly, he put the rope he was coiling on to the deck and walked towards her.

'Permission to come aboard?' She lifted her shoes in her hand and took a step closer.

Reaching out, he grabbed the knapsack and took her hand, holding it tightly inside his before lifting it to his lips and gently kissing the back of her fingers; the touch of his lips lit a fuse that sparked along her limbs and set fireworks off in the base of her stomach.

He helped her climb down on to *Foula Girl* and stared at her, as if hardly daring to believe that she was real. She inhaled the scent of the man who was familiar and yet still a stranger in so many ways.

'Here you are!' he whispered, as if, deep down, he had been expecting her.

'Here I am.'

His tan was deep, hair longer, his smile and easy manner just the same. Her heart danced, as it had a habit of doing when he was close.

'How . . . how did you know where I was?'

'Well, I might have been given access to a map with your whereabouts and plans on it.'

'Iris?' he asked, eyes brimming with emotion.

'Yes.' She smiled. 'Iris. Although Aiden helped me plot and suggested this was as good a place as any.'

'Our kids are having a baby!' he sniffed.

'Isn't it wonderful?' She laughed, and fell against him, gripping his linen shirt and closing her eyes as he put his arm around her, letting her rest for a while . . .

'I can't believe you're here.' He pulled her towards him, holding her close. 'You told me that when Jonathan died you sat very still for some time, and that it seemed like the best option to just sit and wait until the world stopped spinning.'

'That's right.' She nodded, staring at the beautiful man in front of her.

'You told me that for you, the sun had disappeared, the birds had gone quiet, the air had grown cool, and the sky had gone dark.'

'Yes,' she whispered. It sounded bleak, and so very sad, a reminder of how far she had come, how she now viewed the world differently.

'Well, this is where our next adventure begins. We will seek out the sun, listen for the birdsong and bask in the warmth, the light. That's what we will do, Enya. That's how we'll live, and we can do it safe in the knowledge that all the people we love and all the good things in our lives are still there, waiting for us.'

'I don't doubt it.' She breathed against him. 'I've been thinking a lot about what Rhona said, that when two people are shown a path that leads directly to happiness, they kind of have a duty to walk it. And that if they don't, it just might be the biggest missed opportunity of their lives.'

'She's right.' He ran his finger over her cheek.

'I don't want to miss the opportunity, Dominic, I want to walk that path,' she whispered. 'I think I knew we'd find a way back to each other when the time was right, I knew it.' She stared at him now, speaking the truth without reservation or concern, understanding that love, when it came, didn't need approval or permission, it just arrived, and all you could do was make space for it. For there was no doubt in her mind that this was indeed love.

'I knew it too. I told you I'd wait for you. I've been looking for you, always looking for you. I could feel it here.' He touched his fingers to his heart, and she felt her whole body yield with longing.

'I like being with you.' She stared up at him.

'Well, that's lucky. What's the plan?' he asked.

Enya shrugged. 'I guess we take it one day at a time, right?'

'I guess we do.' He smiled at her.

'I used to think about you before I fell asleep and then when I woke up. I always wondered what you were doing and whether you might be thinking about me,' she confessed, feeling her words spiral up into the big blue sky.

'Yes, Enya. The answer is yes. I was, I was thinking about you, dreaming of you. I only wanted to sail away with you. I do, I *want* so badly to sail away with you, and every time I look up, I want to see you. Because even if we lived from now until eternity, it would still not be enough.'

'Is this real?' Reaching out, she let her fingers graze his face; his gaze was intense, and she had never felt less invisible in her whole life.

'It's real. There is nowhere else you should be.'

'Okay, Dominic, let's do this. Let's jump.'

'You have no idea how I've longed to hear those words!' He sighed. 'We'll figure it out, one day at a time. I want us to find our happy, our ever after. Do you trust me?'

She took in the man who had told her once that you could only win when you gave over to fear, resigned yourself to the very worst thing imaginable, and recognised that it was okay. No matter what happened, it would all be okay in the end.

'I do.' Staring at his handsome face, she felt the flames of joy lick her consciousness. He was lovely. Lovely to look at, lovely company, and to interact with him at all was just lovely. 'I really do.'

With her heart full, she let her eyes sweep the harbourside. Couples walked arm in arm, families chattered as they sauntered in the afternoon warmth. Sweet music floated on the air, and the boats, moored uniformly, bobbed on the water where the sun's diamonds danced on its surface. Content in the arms of this wonderful man who was giving her a second chance at love, a second chance at life!

It was as she let her eyes sweep the dock that she saw him. The breath caught in her throat and her legs threatened to give way. There he was, Jonathan, on the far dock, hands in pockets, smiling, smiling right at her. His expression one of pure love. He winked at her, and she got the message, he was happy, happy for her. The two of them as ever in sync, one team.

She gasped, fixing him with her gaze as she raised her hand in a gesture of goodbye, and just like that he vanished. She felt nothing but grateful for this final glimpse and the feeling of peace that filled her right up. How thankful she was for all the wonderful years they had spent, the gift of their son and the love that had bound them, would forever bind them.

Narrowing her eyes, she looked to the left and right, but he was gone.

Gone.

No more than a trick of the light . . .

If you enjoyed *Ever After*, why not read *This One Life*, available now.

Prologue

'Where's your sock?'

Marnie looked down at the little girl who, as ever, had rushed out of the school gates, keen to be free of the building that held her prisoner between eight fifteen and three fifteen each weekday, with an hour off at lunchtime for good behaviour. Not that her behaviour was particularly good, if Marnie were to believe what was written in the end-of-term reports or the snippets of tight-lipped disapproval that were traded on parents' evening.

'Disruptive!' the teacher had called her.

'Enthusiastic,' Marnie had countered.

'Noisy!' was another one.

'Confident?' Marnie preferred.

'Always asking questions . . .' The woman had spoken with a sigh.

'And how very fortunate are you to have such an enquiring young mind among so many dumdums . . .' Marnie would never back down in defence of the child, who had experienced more than most. Marnie was her champion, her flag bearer, her support system and the one who would love her till her last breath on earth.

The teacher had stared at her with a look of resignation. As if she understood that there was no force more powerful than a besotted matriarch with a fearless mouth.

She smiled at the haphazard jumble that gambolled towards her; sweater in her hand, one frayed sleeve trailing on the floor, the book bag open with loose sheets of paper threatening to fly away at any moment. Shoulder-length dark, dark hair that was partly over her pretty face, and a healthy splatter of whatever red stuff she'd had for lunch on the front of her white polo shirt.

This was Edith-Madeleine, aged seven, named after both of her great-grandmas, but known simply as Edith. Edith was the child who would fall off the wall, tumble into a pond, spill her drink, drop her ice cream, get her clothing snagged in a bush, and drop or slop whatever she was carrying. She was also loud – a glorious bundle of infectious energy.

'I've still got one sock!' Edith beamed as if this was compensation enough, lifting her foot to show that, yes, there was one slightly grubby knee-high sock slouched down around her ankle.

'Fancy-pants houses!' she shouted, changing the topic entirely, and pointed at the restored Georgian splendour of a row of terraced properties that were close to her primary school.

It was another world, one of high-end opulence – neat topiary set in square slate planters, glossy front doors, polished brass steps and an abundance of ungraffitied red brick. Large sash windows allowed tempting glimpses of oversized lamps, occasional tables, wide squidgy sofas and daring art. A fancy-pants world indeed, and one that Edith liked to point out as they walked past. It was a part of their walking home ritual that never failed to amuse them both.

Beneath Marnie's laughter, however, was the tremble of recognition, aware as she was that this glimpse into a life beyond their means had the power to unsettle as well as amuse. It could place spikes among the soft acceptance of life. It could sow a seed of discontent that was hard to uproot. A bit like looking at what you might have won in a game show before it was whipped out of sight. If only they had been luckier . . . got the answer right, or – as was the case with the upmarket houses they peered into – been born into a family like that. Marnie understood that dissatisfaction with your lot in life could be the most destabilising thing of all. Far better, in her opinion, to live contentedly with all that was familiar.

She chuckled. 'Yes, now, back to your missing sock. I can see you've still got one, darling, but what I'm more concerned about is the foot without a sock – the sock that's missing.'

'Oh!' She watched the little girl's expression of surprise, as if genuinely not understanding which sock they were referring to. 'I had to use it for something.'

'Right.' Marnie opened her hand as she turned to walk away, knowing that the child would slip her hand into hers, just as she had since that very first day of school nearly two years ago now. The time had flown and yet not a day passed when she didn't thank her lucky stars and all of heaven and earth for the chance to mother this amazing tiny human who was sunshine itself. A second chance, almost, and one she had never expected. Marnie braced herself for what came next – usually a convoluted, unimaginable story to explain a situation.

Edith did not disappoint. Skipping now, she pulled Marnie's arm up and down as they made their way along the uneven grey pavement.

'I found a mouse.' Edith looked up and grinned, little animal lover that she was.

'How exciting.' Marnie did her best to hide the shiver of revulsion at the thought of the tail on such a creature. She'd never been too good with tails, or anything that scampered, preferring the lumbering gait of a big old dog like Frank, who had been her childhood love. He had been as stinky as he was ungainly, but how she had loved him.

'Well, I didn't find it, Travis found it.'

'And he told you where it was?'

As was her habit, Marnie tried to jump ahead. 'Yes, but it was dead.'

It was a fascination how the child's face could go from triumphant to devastated in such a short time.

'Oh, well, that's very sad.' She squeezed Edith's sticky little hand.

'Anyway, I told Travis we should give it a fumeral.'

Marnie suppressed her laughter. It was close enough, and who knows how long the stinky little thing had been dead for. Maybe *fumeral* was actually very appropriate.

'That was a great idea.'

'We were going to tell Mr Lawal, but Travis said he might not let us bury her on school property.'

Her . . . ? All right, then.

'Travis is smart.' Smarter, Marnie hoped, than his dad, Travis Senior, who was currently serving an eight-year stretch for conspiracy to commit fraud. His mother lived three floors below them in the flats. A nice lady who looked far, far older than her years. Not that stories like hers, like theirs, were unusual in their little slice of East London – far from it.

'We named her Minty and found a place to bury her by the football posts. And then' – Edith swallowed, catching her breath; she did this sometimes, spoke so quickly that she ran out of steam – 'I said we couldn't just put Minty in the dirt! We needed something to wrap her in.'

'Ah!' Marnie could see where this was going.

'So I took my sock off and she fitted right into the foot bit like it was a little mouse pocket! And then we dug a hole and put her in it, and only Travis and I know where Minty is buried and I might visit her sometimes.'

'Well, you can't say you didn't do your best by her at the end.'

Edith nodded. 'We sang a little song.'

'Oh, you did? What did you sing?' She was curious.

'We were going to sing a hymn, but we didn't know any, so we sang that song . . . erm, I think it's The Beatles? The one about my troubles being far away. But it made me a bit sad because Minty's troubles weren't that far away, because she died . . .' Edith sang the lines, right there in the street – suddenly, loudly, tunelessly and with gusto.

It made Marnie's heart swell.

'Well, that was lovely.' She knew her husband, Doug, would be delighted that Edith had chosen a song from one of his favourite bands. 'I'm sure Minty would have loved her send-off.' She couldn't wait to tell him all about it when he got in from work.

'What's for tea?'

And just like that, the subject was changed and Edith was thinking about grub.

'Macaroni cheese.'

'Yes!' Edith did a little hop with pure delight and it warmed Marnie's heart. This was the child's nature: sweet, excited, and happy with whatever fell into her lap. The fact they'd had macaroni cheese for the previous two nights, as it was cheaper and easier to make a big old trayful and eat it till it had gone, was neither here nor there.

'Have you got any homework?'

'Nope. Just reading.'

It delighted Marnie how Edith so loved books that compulsory school reading didn't feel like homework at all but was simply one of her joys.

'I think it's Pop's turn to listen.'

'But he always falls asleep before I've finished!'

Marnie laughed at this truth. 'He works hard up the market, baby girl, and when he sits down at the end of the day, it's like his body switches off so he can get up early and go do it all again tomorrow.' She hated that this was his routine, wishing for him

– wishing for them *both* – that things might get easier as they aged. Not that they were ancient, far from it, but she noticed them both slowing down a little, with a reluctance in her bones to rise on a cold day or to tackle steps at speed.

'Can I go to work with him at the weekend? I can help!'

'I'm sure he'd love that. Have you been practising your calls?'

'I have.' She watched as Edith took a deep breath. 'Get your pots and pans here! Your buckets, your bowls, your drainers, your tea towels, your pegs! Come on, lay-dees!'

Marnie doubled over with laughter, unable to contain herself as the child did her best to imitate the male voice that called this very patter to the crowds.

'Did I do it good?'

'You did it very good,' she had to admit. 'Reckon you'll do Dougie out of a job at this rate!'

'He could have a rest then.'

The sweet sincerity of her words was as touching as it was kind.

'Yes, he could, my lovely one. Yes, he could.'

'Afternoon, Marn!' Mrs Nelson, in her familiar wrap-around pinny, called from the doorway of her flat as she tottered along the path with a bulging bin bag in her hand. Marnie noticed how in recent years the elderly woman had grown a little unsteady on her feet.

'Afternoon, Mrs Nelson. Do you want me to take that out for you?' It wasn't far to the communal bin store, but if it saved the old lady a job . . .

'No, you're all right, love. It's the only exercise I get nowadays!'

Marnie Woods had lived on the Brenton Park estate since she was a child, taking over the lease from her mother when she died almost twenty years ago now. The casual observer might see the grime, the grotty communal walkways, the urine-scented lifts, the graffiti, the large dumpster from which garbage overspilled, the abandoned rusting cars and vans, the kids clustering in the foot of stairwells smoking pungent weed, and the loud, loud fights conducted in several languages that were the inevitable consequence of living in such close proximity, the uneven paving stones, and the clots of dog shit peppering the thin grass wherever it sprouted. But Marnie knew better than to be fooled by such aesthetics.

She more than understood that what the untrained eye did not see was what made the place remarkable: the kindness of neighbours, the strong bond of those who had grown up there and the sense of pride that, when the chips were down, they rallied together. All anyone had to do was ask that young woman on the fourteenth floor whose baby son was proper poorly, something to do with his liver, just how their community worked. The Residents' Committee had figured out that if each flat gave a couple of quid, the little one could have his mum on hand for gruelling treatments, and they could travel by cab. Nearly everyone had given and it had been perfect. The woman and her family, having only arrived on the estate eighteen months ago, had felt the arms of her neighbours around her. It didn't change the bowed stance of deep worry that aged her, nor the blank-eyed stare of impotence that she wore as she walked to the shops or took the older kids to school, but Marnie hoped, in time, it might act as a balm of sorts. To know that they were thinking of her. To know they had her back.

'Where's your sock, Edith?' the old lady hollered as she held the dripping bag at arm's length.

'Oh, me and Travis had to bury Minty, who died today. We put her in my sock and dug a hole by the goalpost on the playing field. But that's a secret, Mrs Nelson. We don't want anyone else to know in case they dig her up.'

'Sweet Jesus! Who'd dig her up?' Mrs Nelson shook her head at the horror of the idea. 'Anyway, I'm sorry for your loss and may she rest in peace. I'm assuming she was a creature small enough to fit in a sock?'

'She was a mouse, Mrs Nelson. At least, we think she was a mouse. She'd gone a bit flat and a bit . . . dusty.' Edith wrinkled her nose.

'Right! Well, that's enough detail for us all. Let's get you home!' Marnie pulled a face at her neighbour, who laughed.

'We're having macaroni cheese!' The child danced on the spot.

'Good for you! Reckon I'll be skipping supper tonight. I've a head full of images of Minty that are enough to put me off eating for life!'

'Sorry about that, Mrs Nelson.' Marnie was sincere.

'No, don't be sorry. I could do with losing a few pounds.' She patted her ample tum.

'Only on your body and your wobbly neck thing, Mrs Nelson.' Edith patted her own chin. 'Not on your legs! Your legs are like little sticks!' Edith offered the compliment that was anything but.

'Mrs Nelson, I . . .' Marnie felt her face turn puce as she searched for the right words.

'What is it they say, Marn? Out of the mouths of babes . . .' Mrs Nelson suppressed a laugh.

'Something like that.' She smiled at the old woman who trundled to the bins. Marnie couldn't wait for Doug to get home. He was going to howl at this.

'Do you think Minty is in heaven?' This was quite a standard conversation twist for Edith; the verbal darting left and right, up and down.

'Well . . .' Marnie always trod carefully, not wanting to destroy any hope that the little girl might carry, but also unable to lie outright. 'I think the truthful answer is that I don't know. And I think what counts is that you gave her a lovely funeral, which was a very kind way to say goodbye to her.'

'But do you think she's in heaven?'

'What do you mean by heaven? What do you think it is?' Marnie stalled.

'Mouse heaven! Where there's all the cheese they can eat and tiny mouse cafés and little mouse swimming pools and mouse sweetie shops and mouse hotels and mouse motorways where they drive tiny cars to go to mouse cinemas, and mouse chip shops and mouse pubs . . .'

She got the idea. This too was a familiar topic for Edith: what happened when people died. Where did they go? Where did they live if they didn't live with you anymore . . . ? All pieces of the puzzle the child was trying to figure out.

'I think you have a wonderful imagination! And how great to think of Minty in her tiny car, pootling up and down the motorway to visit swimming pools and cinemas.'

Edith wasn't done. 'I think cat heaven – where there are cat beauty parlours and cat shopping malls and cat beaches and cat sunglasses shops and cat restaurants – would be mouse hell, because if Minty turned up there by mistake, she'd just be a snack, wouldn't she?'

'I guess she would!' Marnie chuckled. 'You amaze me, Edith Woods. You're quite right, you know; one person's heaven could be another person's hell, and that's very smart.'

'Like Pop with prawns.'

Marnie laughed harder and squeezed her hand. Her beloved girl. It was a fact in their home that she and Edith loved a treat of a prawn cocktail or a prawn sandwich, but her husband found them to be slug-like and would heave at the sight of them.

'Yes, like Pop and prawns.'

The beep of a horn was loud and drew their attention.

Marnie smiled at the sight of the battered blue van pulling alongside them as Dougie wound down his window. She was always pleased to see the man she so loved, who now winked at her. And still, after all these years, his flirting fired a spark inside her.

Edith shook her hand free and ran to the van, poking her head through the window to give her pop a big kiss on the cheek.

He beamed. 'Hello, little sausage.'

'Are you coming up? Have you finished for the day?' She pointed up along the walkway overhead to their flat on the seventh floor, sounding quite adult, as was her way.

'I have, my love. I got off early – not much doing, I'm afraid.' A look of defeat flashed across his face that tore at Marnie's heart. 'I wondered if I'd see you on your way home.'

'And here I am!' Edith jumped up and down on the spot.

'What happened to your sock?' Dougie looked quizzically at her bare leg.

'It's a long story, my love. A *very* long story.' Marnie pulled a face and he nodded his understanding; long stories and the scrapes Edith got into were not strangers to him.

'We'll save it for when we get home, then.' He reached out and ruffled Edith's hair. Still the little girl bounced, her energy unmatched. 'See you in a minute, Marn.'

'Bye, love!'

They stood and watched the van as it drove towards the car park.

'Do you think Pop might like to see Minty?'

Marnie stopped short on the pavement and stared at the child. 'Please tell me you're not thinking of digging her up, are you, Edith?' She kept her tone stern, her gaze level.

'Course I'm not!' They walked on in silence, approaching the concrete steps that would eventually take them up to their floor. 'But if I did, I'd probably be able to get my sock back . . .'

Chapter One

Edith-Madeleine – who, aged twenty-nine, chose to be known simply as Madeleine – stared at her reflection in the vast gilt-framed mirror that filled the space between the marble sink and the ceiling. Turning first to the left, then right, she studied her profile in the flattering light, liking the slight curve of her bust inside her ivory silk shirt, which sat crisply over her lace bra. The top two buttons were undone to reveal her bronzed décolletage. Next came close-up scrutiny of her understated make-up, using the tip of her French-manicured finger to remove a fleck of mascara that had found its way to her highlighted cheekbone, and carefully wiping the corners of her mouth to make sure no spit or matt 'café au lait' had gathered there. Her teeth were white – *white* white. Her chestnut hair hung in artful waves around her face and her navy cigarette pants, paired with nude heels, elongated her slender legs.

She smiled twice, and laughed once, making a mental note not to open her mouth too widely or to wrinkle her nose – both habits she had worked hard to eradicate. Next, she moved closer to the mirror and whispered, 'Nyor-keeee. Nyo-kee. Nyoki. I'll have the gnocchi. No!' She shook her head, and took a beat. 'The gnocchi for me, please.'

As the door opened, allowing noise from the restaurant to filter in, she straightened and reached into her Lulu Guinness clutch for her perfume – Angelique Noir by Guerlain. The bottle felt reassuringly expensive as she spritzed her wrists and behind her ears.

A glossy blonde woman walked in and halted. 'Oh! Your scent! That's utterly divine! Love it!' She inhaled deeply.

Madeleine gave her customary half-shrug of indifference while inside firecrackers of joy exploded in her gut.

She walked quickly from the bathroom, making her way back to the front of the restaurant, where she waited in the marble-floored foyer. The maître d' approached, as she had known he would, having been so accommodating when she'd rushed in and asked to use the loo before taking her table.

'Hello again, madam.' He gave a slight bow; she liked it.

'Hello.' She glanced at his face before looking past him into the dining room, where intimate tables were set with starched white linen and silverware. The whole place carried an air of refined sophistication.

'And you're having lunch with us?'

'Yes.' She looked back at him. 'Table for two, under the name Woods – Madeleine Woods.'

He walked to the lectern, where a bespectacled girl stood with a pen in her hand and carried an air of authority. The gatekeeper. Ignoring his colleague, he ran his finger down the computer screen and beamed up at her, as if she'd won a prize.

'Please follow me.' Again that slight bow with the incline of the head.

He paused at a table that was sat in front of the bar – almost a thoroughfare, and not where she wanted to sit. Not at all.

'No, thank you. Erm . . . we'll take that one.' She pointed to a table set perfectly for two by the window.

'Of course, madam.' He did his best but failed to control the twitch of irritation under his left eye. 'May we get you some water for the table?' He clasped his hands at his chest, as if in prayer.

'Yes. Sparkling, thank you.'

She glanced at him briefly before he walked away, keeping her smile small and her attitude professional, just like her ex-boss and mentor, Rebecca Swinton, would have done. Madeleine, having watched her every move in social situations, now understood that to allow people to flourish and perform it was best not to be over-friendly, to not break the boundary that kept everyone feeling secure. To do differently only smudged the lines of operation and muddled your responses. She took her seat and placed her bag on the windowsill, moving the cutlery to her right, to give her and her guest more space. She studied the small, printed menu in front of her, already knowing what she was going to choose, having looked up the options online this morning.

'Madeleine!'

Nico called her name, unabashed and confident as he walked towards the table, two steps behind the maître d'. There was the unmistakable flare of attraction in her gut that she'd felt the first time they'd seen each other across the boardroom table at Field and Gray – the lawyers who advised the agency on all manner of property law, both here and abroad. Nico's mother, Belinda Yannis, was a partner; his maternal grandfather, Horatio Gray, one of the founders; and Nico was, according to the gossip flying around the bar of The Ned for their post-meeting analysis, being prepped to take over the reins when his mother retired – if she ever retired. From what Madeleine could tell, the immaculately groomed, wrinkle-free Belinda was more likely to collapse while poring over contracts in her office than bow out gracefully to tend to her garden or join the bowls club. Madeleine had been in awe and petrified of her in equal measure, noting the way she delicately and loosely rested her hands in front of her – Cartier tank catching the light, palms steady, wrists relaxed, no hint of tension – as if to sit at the head of the highly polished table was her absolute right, which of course, as Horatio Gray's daughter, it was. Madeleine had taken a deep, slow breath, knowing that if this was the way the woman conducted herself, she would find any overt nerves in others less than attractive.

Nico didn't have his mother's stern presence. He was as handsome as she'd remembered, with short dark hair and brown eyes that crinkled at the sides as he smiled. His easy-going expression and manner were most alluring. His presence and initial interaction confirmed the connection between them that had been immediate and thrilling. It would also be a lie if she were to say that the stature and status of a man like this didn't hold its very own attraction.

'Lunch!' He sat opposite her and leaned back in the chair, clearly comfortable in these surroundings, and picked up the menu, giving it only the briefest of considerations.

'Yep, lunch!'

'I must admit, my invitations to dinner don't usually get demoted to lunch.' He shook his head.

'Is that right? Interesting you see it as a demotion. I much prefer lunch.'

'How come?' He sat forward, interested, as he placed the menu flat on the table.

'Because if I'd said yes to dinner, and you were dull company or we didn't get on, or you had some truly terrible habits that turned my stomach, then not only would I be trapped with you for hours, but it'd be a waste of a precious free evening. Whereas lunch . . . What do you reckon, hour and a half, tops?'

'Absolute tops,' he agreed.

'I can put up with just about anything for that short window. So if this turns out to be a disaster, the day is not entirely lost. And if we *do* get on – and you don't reveal your horrid habits and you're not a complete bore – we can progress to dinner. Whereas if we start there, we have nowhere to go.'

'It feels like a test.' He pulled a face.

'I guess it is, for us both.' She liked their level of eye contact, the ease of conversation, the shared humour, the way she set the rules and he went along with it, falling into step as she played hard to get. A ploy that she felt only enhanced her attractiveness.

'Here's the thing: based on our very flirty texts, I already like you. It's been fun.' He sounded sincere and she took the compliment, unwilling to admit that she'd read and re-read their exchanges before falling asleep for the last couple of nights.

'Well, you should have said! We could have carried on texting and saved ourselves the price of lunch! This is probably a good time to point out that we're going Dutch, just to make sure there's no sense of obligation on either of our parts.'

'Dutch it is, perfect.' He laughed. 'And you raise a good point, but, just so you know, I do think there's somewhere to go if dinner goes well. I usually like to progress to a weekend at my cottage.'

'Usually? So you do this a lot?' she half-teased.

'Actually, I really don't.' He dropped the humour and his expression became intense. She felt a shiver of longing ripple through her bones.

'Hmmm, interesting. You see, I think a weekend away after one dinner is too big a leap for me, but a weekend away after one lunch and two dinners is just about acceptable.'

'I can see you've given it some thought.'

'I have,' she admitted, 'and this is also probably as good a time as any to tell you that I'm leaving for LA in two weeks. So don't get too attached, as I'll be jetting off into the sunset for the foreseeable future. I'm sure it's going to be just like *La La Land* and I'll probably get whisked off my feet by a budding actor, who ultimately will make it big and buy me diamonds.'

'I can buy you diamonds right now.'

'I don't even like diamonds! Plus, I could buy my own,' she emphasised.

'Touché.' He beamed. 'I like LA. Maybe I'll come visit you.'

'Too soon! We haven't finished lunch number one yet. We absolutely cannot be making those kinds of plans!' She widened her eyes in mock horror, although her stomach flipped in excitement at the prospect, more than a little enamoured by the fact he could indeed come visit and buy diamonds – one of these a significantly more exciting prospect than the other. Diamonds – in fact baubles of any kind – had never impressed her.

'Shall we order? I'm starving.' He clapped his hands together.

She liked his honesty and his humour. She raised her hand and the waiter came over.

'Madam?' The moustachioed man stared at her.

'The gnocchi for me, please.' She ordered with confidence.

'Oh, good shout. Yes, for me too, please.'

'Certainly. And to drink?'

'Just the water. Sparkling.' She reminded the man of her drinks order, which was yet to materialise.

'For me too.' Nico smiled. 'Copycat.'

The waiter walked away.

'Oh God, have I failed already?' Nico laughed.

'No, you won't know if you've failed or progressed to the next round until we leave. If it's been great, I'll text you a thumbs-up, and if it's been rubbish then I won't text you at all.'

'Harsh!' he fired back.

'Yet clear, and I think clarity is important, don't you?'

'I do. And I shall adopt the same. A thumbs-up means you did well and no text . . . well, means you'll be back to swiping right.'

She laughed at his cheek, and they shared a moment – a lingering look, both aware of how they were using humour to further break the ice, relax, get over any nerves, and to see if the instant attraction might have anything more substantial behind it.

It was typical of her luck. She had been on numerous dates over the last year with people who had all held promise until she actually spent time with them. It had helped her realise that she often preferred the idea of spending time with someone to the reality of it. Not that she considered herself to be overly picky or demanding, just that her standards were high and her list of traits in a potential partner non-negotiable. The fact that it was a long and complicated list was neither here nor there.

An image of Richard entered her mind – gorgeous, funny Richard, who had shown much potential until he'd flashed her his tattoo of Dolly Parton, smack bang in the middle of his chest. Madeleine loved a blast of 'Jolene' as much as the next person, but a tattoo on his chest? The thought of being in a semi-naked state, staring down at the perfect curves of Dolly, against whom no woman could compare . . . She'd blocked his number shortly after. Then there was Quentin, who was fabulous and flirty. A silver fox dentist with a classic Porsche who smelled as if his pores actually secreted Tom Ford's Tobacco Vanille. She could have happily sat and sniffed him for hours. That was until she realised he started most sentences with, 'I am not lying when I say . . .' or 'To tell you the truth . . .' and 'I swear to God . . .' which gave her the distinct impression that he was indeed lying, not telling her the truth and about to let God down badly. It put her right off. She had been with him in Covent Garden when she had bumped into her old best friend Trina, who she hadn't seen for a while. It was a little awkward, yet still Trina knew her well enough to text her immediately with a thumbs-down symbol. It told her all she needed to know. So yes, typical of her luck to feel this attracted to Nico when she was about to fly across the pond for good. Not that it was going to stop her enjoying her time with him until she left. She would, she figured, be mad not to.

It was easy to make light of her dating disasters, simpler to concentrate on the frivolous. The truth, she suspected, when it came to her lack of success, was far more about not being able to be herself, not fully. Having to play a part and be wary – always wary – of when she would have to pull off her mask and tell all.

'Have you been here before?' She let her eyes rove the ornate dining hall with the frescoed walls and busy tables where men in tailored, starched, button-down shirts sipped wine, and the laughter was loud, bullish.

'Yes. But only ever for working lunches.' 'Me too.'

'My parents are big foodies. My dad's Greek, so food and wine are in our blood – big feasts for every celebration, and nearly everything warrants a celebration. My mother, who you have met *of course* . . .'

'I have indeed.'

She noticed how he paused for a second, as if inviting or expecting her to offer an opinion on Belinda Yannis, which *of course* she did not.

'Yes, so my mother comes from a farming family.'

Madeleine was aware of the farm. Rumour had it that it covered most of the South Downs, and also that it was no ramshackle cottage in which they brewed tea and discussed their day, but rather a vast country house plonked in the middle of the estate. A house that came with a title, as far as she recalled.

'She grew up hunting, fishing and foraging – eating what they caught, what they found, growing fruit and vegetables and baking for great parties.'

'It sounds idyllic. So you grew up on the farm?'

'Not really. I visited it.' He raised his hand and smiled in acknowledgement of the bottle of sparkling water deposited on their table and the two tall glasses with ice, mouthing, 'Thank you.' She liked his respect for the waiter. Things like that were important to her. 'But I spent most of my time away at school. During the holidays, which, thank goodness, felt endless, we went to Skiathos, where my father's family has a home. It's on a cliff with the most incredible view of the sea and sky I've ever seen. If you took me there blindfolded, I'd know it by the scent alone.' He closed his eyes and took a deep breath. 'The pine forests, the rosemary and thyme that's abundant, ripe mandarins, the woody-scented bark of the olive trees, eucalyptus leaves – all underpinned with the fragrant incense and oils from the church. It's like nothing else.' He breathed in through his nose and she envied him the memory.

'It sounds glorious.'

'It really is.' He nodded and sipped his water. 'A special place.'

'My upbringing was a little different. Not quite so privileged.'

The waft of dog shit on the breeze, the diesel fumes, the ripe fruit chucked off the roof by bored kids just to watch the splat, the scent of the overflowing communal bins, the weed being smoked on the balconies . . . and the heady scent of piss wafting from the lift and stairwells.

She swallowed. Here it was. The thought that was always waiting in the wings. The awareness that if this attraction developed, she would need to tell him about her past. It was all a question of timing, and something she relished – it felt good to detail just how far she had come – yet dreaded in equal measure, knowing she had never once shared her story and not felt the sharp lance of judgement at her breast. It was, however, going to be hard to avoid if he stuck around; she felt the need to speak the truth, which she was certain would either see him scurrying for the hills or applauding her achievements, as if she were a shining example of rags to riches . . . not that she was by Nico's standards rich, but she was certainly comfortable. And not that she'd be telling him anything today – far, far too early in developments to be shedding skin.

'But happy? A happy upbringing?' he asked, with such a look of concern it was almost as if anything other than this would be hard for him to imagine, and even harder for him to bear.

'Yes, happy.' She quickly buried the pang of sadness that sprang up when she considered how things had changed.

'And that's all we can ask for, right?' he asked softly.

She smiled and sipped her water, as the *nyor-keeee / nyo-kee* arrived.

'God, I'm famished.' She lifted her fork.

He smiled at her as she went in.

'What?' she asked, the delicious, soft gnocchi nestling on her tongue beneath the salty tang of parmesan.

'I like a girl who eats.' He nodded, as if in approval, and reached for his fork.

'Oh, you'll like me, then. A lot.'

'I think you might be right . . .' He let this trail and her heart jumped with joy in her chest.

Eleven hours and twenty-five minutes.

That was the length of the flight from London Heathrow to LAX.

Not so long really. Not even a day.

◆ ◆ ◆

After waving to Nico as he jumped in a cab, she texted him a thumbs-up.

It felt good, exciting, as it always did at this stage, when everything was flimsy, insubstantial, and therefore mattered little if it solidified into something more or not. It was a frivolous time in any courtship, and possibly her favourite part – without weighted conversations about the future or their wants, without deep analysis of where they were heading or whether they wanted to jump ship; without having to open up about the past, how they'd lived, how they'd got to this point and the experiences, good and bad, that had shaped them. It was enough that they wanted each other physically and that they made each other laugh. She was determined to live in the now and enjoy the moment, doing her level best not to think too far ahead – trying not to picture cosy winter walks wrapped in wide scarves as they strolled hand in hand, lazy summer days spent with the sun on their skin and cold, cold wine drunk al fresco. Of a more practical – some might say cynical – nature, she had never been a romantic and saw no reason to let her guard down now.

Dr Schoenfeld would be proud of how she remained present. Heading there now, she saw her therapist at least a couple of times a week – it was her me time, provided clarity to her jumbled thoughts, and was entirely necessary to keep her worries and anxieties in check.

Her phone beeped as Nico responded to her text in kind. She laughed loudly at the thumbs-up and swallowed the bubble of happiness that rose in her throat, feeling a lot like a giddy teen who has just heard third hand from a friend of a friend that the boy she liked might actually like her in return. The kind of moment she would have shared with Trina, if things were different. Quickly she suppressed the image of the girl who had been her best friend, her confidante, her sounding board. It happened like this sometimes – fleeting, crushing moments that reminded her of what she had lost. Not that this was a time for lament, not with things having gone so well with Nico and her so looking forward to her move to LA.

If the pavement had been empty and the street not nose-to-tail with cars, cabs, buses, and bikes, she might have skipped a little, not that she was the skipping kind, especially not in these heels. Well, that and the fact that she hadn't skipped since she was a child. But that was one helluva good lunch. And she wasn't referring to the overpriced gnocchi that had barely touched the sides.

Nico was smart, funny, and extremely attractive, and his aftershave was utterly divine! She loved it! He was the full package and the kind of man she would be foolish not to invest in for a while at least. She'd suggest dinner. Dinner and whatever followed . . . knowing she wouldn't mind seeing what lurked beneath his crisp white shirt and sharp navy suit.

Her phone rang.

'Tan, what's up?'

She and Tan Shi had blurred the lines between colleague and friend. She had even witnessed his marriage to Ramon last Christmas – the only one present who had not sobbed and smudged her mascara on the steps of the Marylebone registry office. She'd done her best to mask her cynicism, knowing that marriage was not for her. It was to her mind a bizarre and outdated contract that made little sense. Her mum and dad, Marnie and Doug, were the one exception to the rule – deeply in love, bound by constraints that were not applicable to her – the grind of a hard life and a horizon that was always within reach. As if they didn't have time or energy to question their commitment, far too busy earning enough to put bread on the table and never having to contend with the bigger life questions of promotion, exploration, and risk. Like goldfish. Happy, contented goldfish who never looked up and just kept on swimming. As a teenager, she didn't know whether to pity or admire them, and that was the truth. As an adult, she only hoped that she might find a love so steadfast and unrelenting, knowing the kind of stability that could bring to a life, but she'd do so without putting on a big frock and organising a buffet. Theirs was indeed a steadfast and unrelenting love that they were happy to share with the little girl who sat at the centre of their world. Her wonderful, wonderful mum and dad . . .

'Couple of things.' Tan broke her thoughts. 'First, Stern has come back and he likes the chandelier!'

'That's great news!'

She felt a familiar flush of joy that their client had approved the expensive option, knowing it would make all the difference to the final appearance, and their bottom line. The mark-up was hefty. The ornate, coloured glass had a slight dapple and was almost iridescent – the perfect centrepiece for the open-plan foyer of the high-end apartments that would sit on top of the retail space of the renovated factory complex, only a stone's throw from central Manchester. It was also vital she leave the agency, which specialised in the redevelopment and regeneration of commercial premises, on a high. This was her last commission before she took up the new position offered by her old boss, Rebecca Swinton, who was now based in LA. Madeleine couldn't wait to fix up her new apartment, let the heat of the Californian sun warm her muscles, and wander the coast or hike the mountains of a weekend. A whole new life in a different environment. She was beyond excited.

'I'm glad he likes it. We can talk about it when I get back – shan't be much longer, an hour or so. What was the other thing?' She came to a halt outside the narrow white stucco building with its grand Palladian-inspired porch and waited to end the call.

'How did it go with Nico?'

'Again, we can talk about it when I get back, but . . . good.' She smiled; their time together might be short, her flights already booked, but that didn't mean she and Nico couldn't have an amazing couple of weeks. Not to mention the fact her mind kept returning to the idea that it wasn't beyond the realms of possibility that a man like Nico Yannis would pop up in LA now and then, although she tried not to get ahead of herself. It was, after all, only one lunch.

'So when you say it was good, do you mean good or *good* good?' he pushed.

'Bye, Tan!' She ended the call, and shook her head. He was such a gossip, a nosy gossip, but she loved him regardless.

ABOUT THE AUTHOR

Amanda Prowse is a multi-million-copy bestselling author who has published more than thirty novels and is one of the most prolific writers of contemporary fiction in the UK today.

Crowned 'the queen of family drama' by the *Daily Mail*, she writes about life's challenges – from heartbreak and loss to dysfunctional family dynamics – but also about the pockets of delight that can be found in our relationships with others, often when we need them most.

Amanda is known for her relatable characters, emotionally compelling plots, and the sense of connection that readers feel with her stories.

She is an ambassador for The Reading Agency and feels passionately about supporting other women, spending as much time as possible outdoors (preferably by the sea!), and her family.

Follow the Author on Amazon

If you enjoyed this book, follow Amanda Prowse on Amazon to be notified when the author releases a new book!
To do this, please follow these instructions:

Desktop:

1) Search for the author's name on Amazon or in the Amazon App.
2) Click on the author's name to arrive on their Amazon page.
3) Click the 'Follow' button.

Mobile and Tablet:

1) Search for the author's name on Amazon or in the Amazon App.
2) Click on one of the author's books.
3) Click on the author's name to arrive on their Amazon page.
4) Click the 'Follow' button.

Kindle eReader and Kindle App:

If you enjoyed this book on a Kindle eReader or in the Kindle App, you will find the author 'Follow' button after the last page.